The Gunny
A Vietnam Story

A Novel by

Raymond Hunter Pyle

This story is a work of fiction. Names, characters, places, and incidents either are the product of the author's imagination or are used fictitiously, and any resemblance to actual persons, living or dead, business establishments, events, or locations is unintended and entirely coincidental.

Copyright © 2011 Raymond Hunter Pyle

All rights reserved.

ISBN:
ISBN-13: 9781520878812

For Connie

For my wife who had to face her own battles at home alone with the children through two deployments to Danang just seven months apart.

Vietnam Series
Marines in Vietnam
The Gunny
Bullets and Bandages
Master Guns
The Beast
Army in Vietnam
Jump Wings and Secrets
Navy in Vietnam
Walking on Water

Chapter 1

Frank Evans arrived at the Naval Amphibious Base on Coronado Island in California on the second of August, 1966. The Island with its long beaches and Hotel Del Coronado was a great vacation destination for civilians, but not for sailors on their way to Vietnam. The few weeks the sailors would spend on the island were designed to prepare them for a different kind of excitement than civilians were looking for. After a three-day bus trip across country Frank wasn't interested in beaches. He just wanted a hot shower, a good meal, and a rack to crash in.

Check-in and processing went about as expected. A lot of hurrying up to the next check-in station only to wait some more. But the Navy has its own ways and he was comfortable with them. No sense bitching; the Navy wasn't going to change for him. He had been in for six years at that point and he was a Petty Officer First Class (PO1), equal in rank to a staff sergeant in the Army or Marine Corps, pay grade E6. His rating was Gunners Mate, a specialist in weapons repair. He was on his way to Naval Security/Intelligence in Danang, Vietnam with a stop for security training in Coronado.

After a Chief at the personnel office formed up the group of new arrivals, Frank was assigned responsibility for the new men reporting for Security/Intelligence school and promptly, like any good PO1, appointed a PO2 to stay with them and make sure they arrived as a group at their assigned stations. He went ahead at his own pace and jumped the line at each station. He would check back on the section to make sure the PO2 was taking care of business, and later he would find his charges and make sure they had berths for the night and chow passes before he quit for the day. After chow, they were all on their own until 0600 the next day.

A lot of the troops would be making the long hike up Coronado Island to catch the short ferry ride over to San Diego. They wouldn't have the money for a cab. Why San Diego didn't just build a bridge there was a mystery. The ferry trip was only two or three hundred yards. There was a pancake house near the ferry and they'd do a booming business with sailors on the way up and again on the way back. All you can eat silver dollar pancakes. When the boots matured a little they'd time their return for mid-rats (midnight rations) at the base and save their beer money for beer.

Many of the troops were freshly minted boots on their first night of liberty in a Navy town. The go-go joints and peep shows in San Diego were beckoning, and he knew a couple of the troops would be missing in the morning. A couple of them wouldn't make it back in time for muster. A few more wouldn't be able to eat breakfast and would wish they were dead for the rest of the day. Part of their education, he thought. If the Master-At-Arms wasn't too much of a prick, and the troops weren't too late, he'd send them to Frank and he would give them two days of extra duty. The first night of cleaning heads while they were so hung over they had to puke their guts out in every other toilet would teach them a valuable lesson: no matter how hung over you are, you *will* be at the appointed place, at the appointed time, in the specified uniform.

With the duty day behind him, Frank decided to get some chow and then let his body recover from the three-day trip across country. He had been hearing rumors about what was in store for the troops when Security School started. It was probably a good idea to stay on base and rest up.

The chow line was short with most of the troops heading for San Diego as soon as they could put a fresh liberty uniform on. He filled his tray and made his way through the tables to the E6 mess. As he passed a table occupied by a Marine Staff Sergeant sitting alone, the Marine caught Frank's eye when he spotted the crossed cannons on Frank's stripes.

"Join me, Gunner?"

"Yeah, sure. How's it going, Sarge?"

"Not so good. You qualified on small arms?"

"Yeah," Frank said.

"How about Fifties and Sixties?"

"Sure."

"BARs?"

"Of course."

"Damn if this isn't a stroke of luck," the staff sergeant said. "Name's Stoner."

Frank took the hand reluctantly. Marines asking questions like that were not good news. Marines with a desperate look and being polite and asking questions like that were especially bad news.

"Frank Evans," he said.

"Evans, I lost my armorer today. He'll be in the hospital at Pendleton for a week and I'm in a spot."

Here it comes, he thought.

"I've got to clean and inspect all the weapons the security school used for their final exercise and I can't get any help from Pendleton till Thursday. Can you lend a hand?"

"I'm still checking in for security school," he said. "Not sure I can get out of that."

"I can take care of it. The school commander can get you assigned to the armory for a couple of days and have someone walk your stuff through the rest of the check-in. What do you say? It's only for two days."

Frank thought about it. He was a Gunners Mate after all, and if he turned this down, he'd be babysitting a bunch of boots until school started. The choice wasn't hard to make.

"I can see how I can help you with your problem," he said. "What do I get out of it?"

"You say you're doing security school?"

"Yeah."

"Then you have to do two weeks of weapons training at Pendleton. I could put a word in with the trainers over there that you're a good guy and to take care of you. They normally love to bust squid's asses."

"That's worth something," Frank said. "Can you clue me in on Vietnam while we clean the weapons?"

"I can do that. I've done two tours. So, we got a deal?"

"Yeah, sure. Where's the armory?"

"Eat up," Stoner said. "I'll take you over there and show you around after chow. Buy you a couple of beers at the NCO club too."

Stoner wasn't a bad sort—for a Marine. Of course, they're all brainwashed in boot camp and think that intelligent life doesn't exist outside of the Corps. That's assuming a Marine knows what intelligent life is. Frank's thoughts followed the Navy way of thinking, but he wasn't really down on the Marine Corps. He had considered the Corp when he was trying to figure out which service to join—his dad had been a Marine in WWII—and over the years he had wondered several times if he had made a mistake in not picking the Corps. The Corps had an identity, an identity that stayed with you for the rest of your life. If you were a Marine, you were a Marine first and last, no matter what else you did or where you were stationed. The Navy had an identity problem. You were an Atlantic fleet sailor or a Pacific fleet sailor or Naval Air or a tin can sailor or a carrier sailor, etc., etc. But the Corps was a big commitment and at the time he enlisted, he hadn't been ready for big commitments. Stoner bought Frank the promised beers and told him that 0800 would be fine for starting time.

Over the next two days Stoner and Frank stripped all of the weapons except those Stoner's armorer had already cleaned and locked in the racks. The Fifty caliber machine guns and M-sixties had been well maintained, so there weren't many problems, but they were especially dirty from the blank ammo used in the security school exercise. He went through the BARs, M1s, and carbines fast. The weapons were obsolete and not used in active service, but they served well for exercises. The barrels, breaches, and trigger mechanisms were all worn and barely serviceable, but they were only used for blanks, so he cleaned them, made sure they would function, and stacked them for the next exercise. He and Stoner finished up at 1600 on the second day.

"Want to get a beer?" Stoner asked.

"Sure. Let's get some chow first."

"The club has steaks and fries tonight. Let's get a steak. I'm buying. You saved my ass."

"Hell, Sarge, it wasn't that big a thing," Frank said. "A boot could have done that work."

"Maybe so, but I didn't have a boot available and I couldn't have taken the chance anyway. My Lieutenant is coming over to inspect the armory in the morning and the prick doesn't give a shit about my armorer being in the hospital. This is good duty and I don't want to lose it, so I owe you. Come on. Let's suck on a beer and chow down on a couple of steaks."

The steaks were good, but probably no better than the ones the mess hall fixed. But the mess hall didn't serve beer. Frank and Stoner finished their steaks and ordered another beer.

"Frank, you don't seem like a run of the mill squid."

He looked at Stoner and grinned.

"I guess I should say thanks—I think."

"No, what I mean is you don't talk like a squid. Did you get any college before you joined?"

"I have a degree in math," he said.

"You finished college? How come you didn't go for a commission?"

"At the time they wanted more commitment than I was willing to make, six years. As it turned out I guess I should have went for it. I stayed in anyway."

"You still could."

"No. I like what I'm doing," he said. "I'm not cut out to be an officer."

Stoner and Frank drank their beer quietly for a few minutes. Eddie Arnold was singing *What's he doing in my World* on the jukebox. Frank mouthed the words along with the song.

"Where are you going to be when you get in-country?" Stoner said.

"Orders say Danang. Naval Security Intelligence."

"You'll be out by Third MAF (Marine Amphibious Force) headquarters then. Near Marble Mountain. If your outfit is the one I think it is, you'll be seeing some action. I believe they have security for all the Navy facilities and compounds in Danang. They have a site out beyond Marble Mountain in Indian country too. So listen up. Learn everything you can learn from the training corporals at Pendleton. They all have at least one tour in-country and they all have been in the shit. You know the weapons as well as I do. How are you at using them?"

"Hell, I've fired all of them," he said. "Have to shoot them in school. But I can't say I'm a marksman. We fix them and maintain them, but we don't use them much. That's the Marine's department."

"Have you had any training on tactics or setting up a defensive position?"

"I guess that's what they'll teach me here," Frank said.

"Well, pay attention and learn what you can. I'll talk to the troops at Pendleton and tell them to give you everything they can in the two weeks you'll be there. You might hate me before that two weeks is up, but believe me, you'll thank me some day."

"Okay. I appreciate it. But look, I was told that

not much happened around Danang. Do you really think I need the extra effort?"

"Listen to me," Stoner said. "There isn't any place in Vietnam that's safe. You never know who the freaking enemy is. Everything can go along real quiet, and then one day a little girl walks up to you begging an apple and while she's smiling at you she pulls the pin out of a grenade under her blouse. It's a major clusterfuck over there and the American officers running the thing are the biggest cluster around. Listen to the Marines at Pendleton and cover your own ass at all times."

"She-it, Sarge, I was feeling pretty good until just now,"

Stoner grimaced at Frank's use of "Sarge", but he let it go. Frank was a squid.

"Good. Maybe you're starting to get in the proper frame of mind. Drink up."

CHAPTER 2

Security school was mostly classroom training on Vietnamese customs and culture, internal security methods, defensive positions, security tactics, Viet Cong and North Vietnamese army organization, weapons and tactics, and the role and responsibilities of the Security/Intelligence division of Naval Support Activity, Danang. But there were four notable exceptions to the classroom model. Weapons training was provided by the Marines at Camp Pendleton, SERE (Survival, Evasion, Resistance, Escape) training was provided by a cadre of Navy and Marine Corps instructors in the mountains, and explosive booby-traps was taught by UDT and EOD instructors out in the sand dunes at the end of Coronado Island. And then the final challenge: the big class exercise at a mock village outpost near the harbor where the students put together all they had learned and defended the village for twenty-four hours against cadre attackers. "Number one John Wayne bullshit for sure," Stoner assured Frank at the club.

As promised, his two weeks at Pendleton were a strain. Mentally and physically. The strain started with the first morning formation when the Marine instructors introduced themselves. A Gunnery Sergeant (E7) in starched utilities and starched eight-point cover stood in front of four corporals and addressed the Navy formation. He was ramrod straight, his hair was trimmed high and tight, and he looked like he could take a gorilla apart.

"Have a seat, gentlemen. I know this is not a normal squid environment, but don't worry about the dust and sand. Just think of it as water that feels different. If you sit on a scorpion just brush him away. Rattle snakes take a little more care. Get used to them; they're everywhere out here. I am Gunnery Sergeant Hawkins, your chief instructor. You will *not* address me as Hawk, the hawk, or by any other endearing term. Nor will you call me Sarge. I am not in the Army. I am a Gunnery Sergeant in the United States Marine Corps. Gunnery Sergeant Hawkins or Chief Instructor Hawkins are both acceptable. My corporals may call me Gunny Hawkins. You may not. Are we clear on that?"

Silence.

"Now I realize that you all are sailors," Hawkins said in a gentle sing-song. He relaxed slightly and the muscles in his neck bulged when he lifted his chin. "Why, just last night when you all got off the bus, I was saying to my corporals, They're wearing their sailor suits. Isn't that cute. Wasn't I saying that just last night, Corporal Hanson?"

"You did, Gunny. I was right there and that's just what you said. Sailor suits."

Frank felt a little chill in the desert air and thought, Oh shit.

"So you see, I understand you might be a little slow on the uptake. I am an understanding NCO, am I not, Corporal Hanson?"

"Yes, you are, Gunny. Understanding. That's what everybody says about you. Gunny Hawkins is an understanding NCO."

"So let me spell this out," Hawkins said. "On a Marine base, when a Gunnery Sergeant or any NCO or officer asks you a question, you are not only allowed to answer, we rather expect one. Again, are we clear on that?"

"Yes, Sergeant," came the reply from a few of the men seated on the ground.

"This is hard for you, isn't it?" Hawkins asked in a sympathetic voice. His neck muscles bulged again and his face got a little red. "Let's try this again, ladies. Now listen closely. When the formation is asked a question, the entire formation will answer in a loud and confident voice. You will not address me as Sarge or Sergeant. My rank is Gunnery Sergeant. Again, are we clear on that?"

This time the Gunny got a loud and forceful response, "Yes, Gunnery Sergeant."

"There," the Gunny said. "You all almost

sounded like Marines. Before I turn you over to the Corporals, let me do a little survey. Are there any Boatswains Mates in the class?"

Three members of the class raised their hands.

"Oh goody," Hawkins said, and Frank felt another chill. "Anybody in the class ever serve on Amphibs?"

No one raised a hand. There was something in Hawkins voice, something in the way he stood, like he was ready to pounce.

"Come on," Hawkins said. "Don't be bashful. Us Marines appreciate the sailors that support us when we put to sea. Any Gator Navy sailors in the class?"

A few hands raised, but not very high.

"Yes, very good," Hawkins said slowly, drawing out the "yes" into a hiss. "Let's share a little memory. Remember those times when the Marines were conducting a landing exercise and climbing down the nets to the landing boats?" Hawkins let his eyes fall on each of the Boatswain Mates and moved his eyes to each of the men that had raised their hands. "And remember when you walked to the side of the ship and watched us on the nets below you and you with a cup of coffee in your hands. And how you tilted your cups and shared your coffee with the Marines hanging from the nets below you? Ha-ha. It was all in good fun, wasn't it? Well, we remember too. Payback is hell."

Christ, Frank thought, I hope he knows the difference between a Gunners Mate and a Boatswains Mate.

"Corporal Hanson! Take charge of the class."

Frank was lucky in one way. Stoner's word had been good and he was pulled out of the formation on the first day and taken to the armory. But then he found out that favors can have their own downsides. Fourteen straight twelve hour days of intensive training—and weapons maintenance. A few days ran to sixteen hours when the corporals thought he needed more night firing practice—and when they wanted to get a few rounds in on the Navy's dime. The class trained on a makeshift range out in the boonies that consisted of a hillside with fifty gallon drums set up as targets. He trained there too, but his corporals also trained him in marksmanship on the known distance range so he could qualify for the Navy marksmanship ribbon.

Stoner's corporals got him out of his rack an hour before the rest of the class, briefed him on the day's training, and let him draw his weapons and ammunition. But Marines never do anything for free, not even as a favor to Stoner. One Corporal was assigned to Frank each day to give him one-on-one instruction on the weapon of the day. But in return for this extra effort, he had to do the corporal's armory job at the end of the day while the Corporal was released to drink beer. He didn't mind, and as it turned out, a couple of the corporals would end up back in the armory helping him clean the weapons, or, more likely, checking to make sure he did a good job, and talking about their experiences in the Marine Corps and their hopes for the future. Frank found their stories fascinating. They found him easy to talk to.

While the Navy class was chilling out for the evening, Frank was humping the mounting-base of a Ma-deuce fifty-caliber or the inner ring of a base-plate for an 81mm mortar with Marines and setting up and tearing down until he could function on the team as well as a Marine. Of course, being the fifth man on the mortar team, or second humper, all he did was carry the base plate and hump ammo. But that was training the other sailors didn't get. Frank was six-one and one-ninety, qualified for maintenance on crew served weapons, and Stoner had told the corporals he was sending them a live one. They had to do maintenance on the fifty and the eighty-one due to other training earlier anyway, so they used the same weapons to give Frank some experience and then had him available to help clean them. After cleaning the heavy weapons, the small arms firing started again and went on well into the night and then the cleaning started again. The class got one night of night-fire training. He received several nights of night-fire training.

The corporals took special delight in making him an expert on the M-14, M-16 and the 1911 Colt forty-five. Well, they took delight in showing him how un-expert he was. The Marines didn't like the M-16, and the 16s were only issued to front-line troops in Vietnam at that time, and not all of them, so the corporals only did a familiarization on it and concentrated on the M-14.

Off-hand, prone, sitting, kneeling, snapping-in, hour after hour with the M-14, and a Marine corporal marksman next to him, giving advice, correcting stance, trigger control, sight picture, making him a marksman out to five hundred yards. The Marines were the only service that had to qualify on their rifles at that distance and they made sure he could shoot like a Marine. Praise when it went well, ridicule when he didn't listen or listened and didn't do what he was told. The corporals didn't give a shit about Frank's rank. He was a student and they were the instructors. On the range, he was a boot.

In time, Frank learned the highest praise in a Marine corporal's vocabulary. "Now you're shooting like a Marine." It was demanding and his shoulder was bruised from the hard recoil of the M-14, but the intensive training from experts paid off, and by the end of his two weeks he had received more hours of one-on-one rifle and pistol live fire training than most Marines get in their entire recruit and infantry training. The Corporal's didn't mind. Hell, it was easy duty, and apparently, the Gunny owed Stoner a favor. Frank had also cleaned and pulled maintenance on more dirty weapons for the Marines than he had ever cleaned in a year. They also had him do "training maintenance" on various weapons in the armory while they "observed" his proficiency and happily watched their maintenance backlog disappear. A Navy Gunners Mate First Class is qualified to maintain everything a Marine MOS 2111 weapons repairman is qualified to maintain.

Frank could disassemble, reassemble, clean, repair, and maintain everything in the Marine's armory before he got to Pendleton, and now he had qualified for the expert badge for rifle and pistol. He could also operate and deploy every type of hand grenade in the Marine arsenal. He was especially proud of his new skills as a crew member for the M29 eighty-one-millimeter mortar and the ma-deuce (M2) Fifty Caliber Machine Gun. Staff Sergeant Stoner's friends had been thorough. Marines don't have a lot of respect for sailors, squids in their parlance, but they do respect a gunner who is willing to hump a mortar base plate and can shoot like a Marine. The Gunny at the Armory made sure Frank's expert qualifications were noted in his record so he could apply for the Navy marksmanship ribbon.

When the class returned to Coronado, Frank was a little thinner, a little harder, slightly gaunt from fatigue, and more than a little dehydrated. And he was starting to talk with the strange huffing cadence the corporals all seemed to emulate.

The class began explosive booby-trap training. Explosives training was two days of classroom and one day out in the sand dunes. EOD (Explosive Ordnance Disposal) instructors and UDT (Underwater Demolitions Team) experts spent two days in the classroom explaining different types of explosives and demonstrating the construction of common explosive booby-traps. All kinds of detonators—pressure sensitive, pressure release, time delay, cord, and electrical—were explained and the students were taught how to detect them and neutralize them. Then the fun part started.

The instructors went to the practical exercise site first and used different detonator devices connected to small, harmless charges to booby-trap an area that was roped off in the dunes. The students were brought to the site and turned loose to find and disarm the devices. Mostly they were blown up, figuratively, of course. The instructors offered encouraging comments such as, "Oops, there goes an arm," and "Lost a leg on that one," and "You'll be going home in a bag." They took special delight in describing the scattered body parts of booby-trap victims they had seen. All in all, the students learned a healthy caution for entering an area that had been occupied by the enemy.

One of the instructors, a Chief Petty Officer, pulled Frank aside on the last day to give him a little advice.

"Evans, you need to square away and show a little leadership. You're the class NCOIC (NCO in charge) and you're just laying back and letting the class float."

"They have different speeds, Chief. They're all getting through."

"I don't give a shit about their speed. They need what we're teaching here to stay alive. It's your job to see that they get it. Now get your ass squared away and lead your class or I'll find someone who can."

The Chief spun and walked away.

Come on, Chief, Frank thought. *We're not frigging Marines, for crying out loud.*

Frank didn't say much about SERE training when he returned to Coronado from the mountains. It was grueling, hungry, unfair, humiliating, and scary. But it did help him to develop a healthy fear of being captured and gave him plenty to think about while alone in his bunk at night. He didn't figure he'd last long under torture and wasn't sure he'd last long in an escape and evasion situation. *Well,* he thought, *the thing to do is not get captured. Keep fighting until they put you down. One thing though, if the enemy is as scary as the instructors at SERE training, they'll probably have to knock me out to get me to stop talking.*

The class was given a day off to recover from SERE training, and then two days of review classes were conducted by the instructors. No written test in this school. The test would come the following day and night when the class was expected to perform effectively as a security detachment in the final exercise. The last class was shipped out the day after their final exercise, so there wasn't any way to find out what the exercise was going to be like. The instructors just grinned when asked.

CHAPTER 3

The final exercise lived up to the rumors. Frank had been appointed security officer for the exercise. The students were briefed in the afternoon. The chief instructor warned the class to treat all incoming weapons fire as though it was real. He explained that sometimes mistakes were made on assembly lines and belts of ammo sometimes ended up with actual live rounds mixed in with the blanks. Probably a bullshit story, but it did get the troop's attention.

The class was turned loose to secure the mock village they had to defend for the night. That meant they had to enter the village as though the enemy had occupied it before them and clear it of mines and booby-traps. The instructors made sure the class would have some surprises waiting for them. If the team found a booby-trap or a suspected mine, they called for EOD. One of the instructors would then check it out and declare it disarmed. If a team member blew one of the small charges by mistake, Frank lost a man. Frank lost two men before the ville was secure. The losers didn't get out of the fun to come that night though. They had to put on red shirts and sit in one of the bunkers without a weapon.

By dark the ville was secure and Frank had deployed his team into defensive positions. Within minutes the sense of fun ended and the feeling of combat started. Mortar simulators, grenade simulators, constant fifty-caliber and M-60 machine gun fire, Cadre coming through the wire and capturing Frank's troops and letting him know they were coming after him and it wouldn't be fun if they captured him. To add some realism and spice to the class's experience, the Cadre fired fifty live rounds from an M-60 across the ville into a dirt bank. Tracers in that belt were stacked one in two and made an impressive arc of fire ten feet off the ground. The class discovered how deep they could press their bodies into the sand in their bunkers.

The exercise was an all-night simulation of actual combat stress that left dilated pupils, shaking hands, and a thankfulness it was over. Frank's ears were still ringing from the constant bombardment and stress of that one night. The instructors took the students as close to actual combat shock, noise, and stress as they could without blowing them up. And in two instances they almost did that. Mortar simulators are only simulated in that they have no shrapnel. The explosion is real. And it hurts like hell when it's close. They were all close.

The exercise was scary as hell and left the men shaken and wondering what the hell they were getting into, but it did what it was intended to do: teach men they could keep fighting, functioning, and thinking, even when the world was blowing up around them. The day after the exercise, the class was taken by bus to the Air Force Base at San Bernardino to catch a flight to Danang.

After a stop at Anchorage Alaska (there was a stuffed Kodiak bear about twelve feet tall in the terminal) and another stop in Guam (hot and so damn humid you couldn't breathe), the World Airways flight carrying a cargo of fresh troops for Vietnam started on the final leg into Danang. But the landing at Danang was not to be. An hour out of Danang the pilot made an announcement over the intercom.

"The weather at Danang has closed the runway and we've been diverted to Tan Son Nhut airbase in Saigon. Air Force dispatchers will meet the plane and direct passengers to transient facilities and arrange alternate flights to Danang when the weather clears. Sorry for the delay, gentlemen."

"Bullshit!" the Marine Gunny sitting next to Frank said. "I'm in no mood to ride a slick all the way to Danang."

The Gunnery Sergeant looked every inch a Marine. He was taller than Frank and his shoulders encroached into Frank's seat space. His nose was crooked with a displaced septum and his posture said, "I am taking no shit today." Christ, Frank thought, do they pop them out of molds? There was no mistaking the authority and no-nonsense attitude in his presence.

"What's a slick?" Frank asked.

"A Huey. Helicopter. This your first tour?"

"Yeah. Don't they have planes flying between Saigon and Danang?"

"Sure, if you're lucky. You're Navy, so they might put you on a C-130. Too many grunts going north, though. They'll put us on anything heading that way. Probably a slick going somewhere north of Saigon, then I'll have to beg another ride somewhere further north, then maybe a mike-boat. Eventually, I'll get there."

"Hell of a way to run a war," he said.

The Gunny harrumphed. "You ain't seen nothing yet. Well, it is what it is. Might as well get some titty-bar time in while I'm in Saigon."

"Are you reporting to a unit up north?"

"I'm attached to the Ninth Marines way up north. I've been on TAD to Pendleton (temporary additional duty) for the last month. I'll be hitching rides all the way to Dong Ha. Good luck getting a flight."

The Gunny leaned against the window and pulled his cover down over his eyes.

"Ladies and Gentlemen, please fasten your seat belts. We are starting our approach to Tan Son Nhut airbase and should be on the ground in thirty minutes. The temperature in Saigon is one hundred and one and the humidity is ninety-two percent. The skies are overcast and ground fire is light to medium."

"Ground fire?" Frank said to no one in particular.

"He's kidding," the Gunny said. "Pilot humor, I guess. If they're fighting at Tan Son Nhut, this whole country is in the shitter. And he wouldn't be landing. Relax."

The pilot brought the plane in without incident. The wheels kissed the runway and the roll out was uneventful. Frank began to relax. Without much knowledge of what the war in Vietnam was like, he kept thinking about missiles and halfway expected to feel the plane bank sharply in some avoidance maneuver. Hell, why not? It was Vietnam. There were people shooting at each other down there.

"You did a good job keeping the plane up with those armrests," the Gunny said.

"Yeah, I held on to the seat with the pucker in my ass too."

The Gunny laughed. "Well, enjoy your stay in Saigon. If you're going to I-Corps you probably won't see Saigon again."

"I-Corps?"

"Danang is in I-Corps. Vietnam is divided into four corps or commands. I-Corps is the most northern and includes Danang. You'll get used to all the jargon."

"Thanks. Are you stopping at Third MAF?"

"Yeah. They might be able to get me on a slick

going up to Dong Ha. How'd you know about Third MAF?"

"My camp is supposed to be located between Third MAF headquarters and Marble Mountain in east Danang. The Marines that gave me weapons training at Pendleton clued me in to some things."

"Remember any names?"

"Sure. Staff Sergeant Stoner helped me a lot."

"Stoney? What'd you have to do for him?"

Frank grinned. The Gunny obviously knew Stoner. He told him about helping Stoner get ready for his inspection and what Stoner did for him.

"And he trusted you with his weapons? What do you do in the Navy?"

"Gunners mate. I'm qualified in small arms up to and including crew served weapons."

"Damn! Stoney did luck out. Do you just work on them or can you shoot too?"

"I've got Marine Corps rifle and pistol expert badges. I'm a qualified second loader on the eighty-one mike-mike and I can crew the fifty. I've humped a few baseplates in my time."

"She-it, boy, why aren't you in the Corps?"

"My parents were married," Frank said.

The Gunny grinned a crooked grin.

"Give me a break. That's so damn old, I'll bet my daddy said that to some WW1 Marine. No, I'm serious. Those kinds of skills are appreciated in the Corps. Can't imagine the Navy cares much."

"I do okay. I made E6 in six years."

"That's pretty good. But you could have done the same in the Corps. And the next step would be Gunny."

"Next step in the Navy is Chief. New hat, new uniform. But I know what you mean. The Marines treated me pretty good at Pendleton after they found out I knew my way around an armory. But life is what it is. Too late now."

"Not necessarily. The Corps is growing and we're losing a lot of talent over here. You could probably do an inter-service transfer. You'd probably have to redo recruit training, but then you'd be a Marine."

When the Gunny said, "you'd be a Marine," it sounded like he was saying, "you'd be human."

"Nice thought," Frank said. "But like I said, life is what it is. Here comes the ladder. Better get our gear together."

The Air Force did a good job of checking the flight in. Each of the passengers had some time with a router (ticket agent) and several of the troops were told to stay in the terminal for a C-130 leaving at 1800 if the weather cleared in Danang. Frank wasn't so lucky. He gave up his seat so a young sailor could get on the flight. The kid looked nervous and confused. Danang was his first duty station. He talked to the Air Force router and the kid got on the flight. The router sent him to see the transient quarters manager and to report back at 0800 the next day.

On the way across the terminal to find the quarters manager, he was spotted by the Marine Gunny from the plane.

"Hey, Evans. Did you get a flight?"

"Hi, Gunny. No. They're going to try again tomorrow."

"Want to see some of Vietnam?"

"How?"

"I got a seat on a helicopter taking a General north. He'll make a couple inspection stops on the way, but he's stopping at Danang eventually. Want me to see if I can get you a seat?"

"Generals get their own helicopters?"

"Yeah, but it's a Huey mostly. This is a big one. Probably a MAG bird attached to his command. Do you want on?"

"Hell, I guess so. I don't feel like hanging around here. What do I have to do?"

"Follow me."

Gunny Garzinski—Frank found out his name on the way to the Marine Liaison—pulled a Marine Master Sergeant aside at the counter, talked quietly, and then pointed at Frank. The Master Sergeant flipped some pages up on a clip board and nodded. Garzinski waved him over.

"Give him a copy of your orders. Do you have a weapon with you? You have to let the crew chief know."

"No," he said. "The Navy doesn't issue weapons

unless you are expected to be in direct combat."

"Damn. You mean even after you get to your unit?"

"That's what they told me. Heck, Gunny, would you want to see a bunch of squids running around with locked and cocked weapons?"

Gunny Garzinski thought about that, but not for long.

"No, I guess not," he said. "We're going to be landing in some hostile places. Shouldn't be anything close in, but you never know. You okay with that without a weapon?"

"If it will get me to Danang, sure."

"Well. . .shit. . .I guess it'll be okay. Most of the troops on-board are replacements and have their weapons. Let's load up."

CHAPTER 4

The skies had cleared over Saigon and the big CH-53 Sea Stallion heavy lift helicopter's engines were warming up as Frank and the Gunny crossed the tarmac. The crew chief loaded their sea bags, led them up the ramp and showed them where to sit in the net seats that lined the sides of the chopper cargo hold. The inside of the giant chopper looked as big as the inside of a C-130. More than twenty Marines were already on board.

The front of the cargo space was partitioned off, blocking a view of the flight deck. The partition wasn't a normal thing. It was a modification for the General. Two M-60 machine gun stations, one left and one right, were mounted at doors in front of the net seating and two Marines manned the guns.

The engine pitch increased and leveled off. The huge rotors began to revolve slowly as a green staff car crossed the tarmac and stopped next to the chopper.

The staff car had a flag on the front fender with two stars. A second staff car without a flag stopped behind the General's car. The General's driver opened the backdoor and Major General Patrick Muldavy USMC got out and tugged at his flak jacket. He wore jungle boots with his utility trouser legs bloused and the black leather toes and heels gleamed in the sun. He wasn't covered, his Marine Corps eight-point cover in his hand, but no one would mention that. The General was built like a bulldog, all shoulders and chest, and what hair he had was gray and short. They must have popped him out of the same mold they make Gunny Sergeants from, Frank thought. Colonel Logan Harris exited the other rear door. The doors opened on the second staff car and four officers got out. Two light colonels, a Major with heavy satchels in each hand, and a Captain with a brown, two-rope aiguillette on his left shoulder and satchels in both hands hurried onto the helicopter. General Muldavy and Colonel Harris followed but didn't hurry.

When the general started up the ramp, Frank started to stand, but Gunny Garzinski grabbed his arm and pulled him down.

"Not necessary on an aircraft getting underway," he said.

The crew chief snapped a salute and spoke into his boom-mike. The general and the colonel went forward and through the door in the bulkhead at the front of the aircraft. The general's staff took the most forward seats and the noise from the huge rotors above them increased. The tail ramp closed and the big chopper started rolling toward the runway.

"Here, put these on," the crew chief said to Frank. He held out a flak jacket and a green steel helmet. Frank was dressed in Navy dungaree utilities and wearing low cut utility shoes called boondockers. He took off his white hat and put the helmet on his head. The Gunny showed him how to put the flak jacket on.

"Roll that Popeye hat up and put it in your back pocket. The damn thing makes you stand out like a pig at the Marine Corps ball."

"Put a globe and anchor on him and no one would notice." Frank said.

"Smart ass. Look, we have a stop in Dak to in the highlands. It ain't a friendly place. Stay close and do what I say and you'll be all right. Bad ass battle there a few weeks back."

"Viet Cong"

"The battle? Yeah. But now the Army is in the area. I wouldn't put it passed those idiots to shoot us down. . .I'm kidding. Relax."

Garzinski told Frank some of his story while Frank questioned him quietly. Normally Garzinski's answers to personal questions would have been grunts or single syllables, but Frank was so damn interested Garzinski couldn't resist.

Later he decided to stretch his legs. The flight was smooth and the crew chief said it was okay to go forward, so he wandered up the isle to stand behind one of the machine gunners. He had a good view through the gun port. The machine gunner looked over his shoulder, spotted him, and motioned him closer.

"Check that out," the gunner shouted over the engine noise.

Everything below was hills, valleys, and steamy greens. The humidity was so thick the view had a rounded look, no sharp edges, just blurred green shapes outlined with darker green shapes and mist. He looked where the gunner was pointing and saw a lot of smoke billowing out of the jungle on the side of a hill.

"A Marine Company found Charlie (Viet Cong). The General wants to see if we can help."

"Is he going to land?" Frank yelled back.

"Hell, no. But from up here these sixties can make life interesting for Charlie. Better get back to your seat. The old man might have to do some maneuvering."

"Is the General flying this thing?"

"Ha! That's a good one. The old man is the pilot. The General has a private space on the other side of this bulkhead. He has a ringside seat."

Frank waved and returned to his seat. He leaned close to the Gunny and told him what the gunner said. The Gunny frowned and shook his head back and forth slowly.

"God save us from John Wayne Generals," Garzinski said.

The helicopter banked and then righted, the tail lifted, and the noise from the rotors increased. Frank could sense the increased speed. Then the chopper seemed to slow and the tail leveled again, but the sense of forward motion disappeared and the noise of the rotors increased again. The whole fuselage started vibrating and suddenly the sixty on the left started firing short bursts. The chopper felt like it was turning in place and suddenly the sixty on the right opened-up as the one on the left fell silent. The pilot was allowing the bird to rotate in a hover so that both guns were being brought into play for a few minutes each.

"I wish he'd keep this thing moving," Garzinski said. "I doubt Charlie has any missiles or AA, but damn it, it's still stupid to screw around like this."

"We're safe up here, aren't we?" Frank said.

"Yeah, sure. Sorry. . . Come on, come on, get this big frigging target out of here. The gooks got fifties, damn it."

The helicopter tilted, flew in a circle, and then dropped lower. Both machine guns opened-up. Frank noticed Garzinski tensing up. "Come on, get out of here," Garzinski said quietly, like a mantra.

As Garzinski finished talking Frank felt four sledge hammer blows hit the side of the helicopter. The first round hit low near the floor and the next three walked up the fuselage toward the top of the machine. The third blow smashed the port window three seats forward of Frank and the round tore a hole in the roof of the cargo compartment. The bird slewed sideways and went into a steep bank to the left and then banked to the right. Two more hammer blows slammed the tail ramp and the whole helicopter shuddered. A loud squealing noise started near the front and top of the ship.

"Lock and load while you can," Garzinski yelled. "And safe those damn weapons."

Frank looked at his empty hands and said, "Shit!"

Smoke began seeping into the passenger space and the crew chief staggered up the center aisle.

"Strap in! Strap in!"

He pulled the belt across his lap and cinched it tight. The whole aircraft was shaking now and the squeal of metal on metal had turned into a scream. All of the Marines in the cargo hold were strapped in and pushing their backs hard against the back cushions mounted on the bulkhead behind them, M-14s and a few of the newer M-16s held muzzle up between their knees. The big bird slewed right and left and then began to spiral, the whole fuselage rotating beneath the massive rotors slowly. His ears popped and popped again.

The door in the front bulkhead opened and an officer poked his head through.

"We're setting down," he shouted. "Pilot's putting us as close to Echo Company as he can get us. We should be okay, but brace for it."

The officer's eyes traced up and down the seated Marines and stopped on Gunny Garzinski.

"Gunny! As soon as the ramp is down, set up a defensive perimeter."

"Aye, aye, sir."

The door closed and the descent quickened. Smoke poured in through the left machine gun port. The vibrations increased until it felt like the tail of the helicopter was going to separate from the fuselage. Unknown to the Marines inside, the CH-53 had lost its port engine and had also sustained damage to the tail rotor. Only one blade was damaged, but the vibration threatened to destroy the tail rotor assembly.

The pilot nursed the damaged tail rotor with his anti-torque pedals, allowing the body of the ship to rotate slowly under the main rotor. He was able to maintain a minimum of control by keeping the aircraft in a tight spiral as he chose his landing site. But he had another problem and had to get the helicopter on the ground quickly. The main rotor assembly had been damaged by the first hits and was slowly grinding metal on metal and lighting red lights on the instrument panel.

Keeping the nose down and using the reduced effectiveness of the tail rotor to descend in a tight spiral, the pilot saw the LZ (landing zone) he wanted. The top of a small mountain had been cleared by artillery and bombardment and appeared to be relatively flat. He could see craters, but one end was covered with brush and looked pretty good. It wasn't ideal, but it would do if he could flare at the last moment without the main rotor freezing or the tail assembly failing—and if he could get enough power out of the remaining engine to bring up the flair and hold it long enough to set the machine down without further damage—and if the tail rotor assembly would hold for a few more seconds and take the sudden increased torque to stop the spiral while he set the bird down. It didn't matter though. He didn't have any other options. The hill, although steep on the sides, was the closest clearing to Echo Company's location. The heat build-up in the main rotor assembly had already passed the emergency threshold and the minimal LZ was the only one the bird could reach—hopefully. He clicked the intercom button on the Cyclic handle.

"Chief, prepare the hold and passengers for a hard landing."

"Aye, aye, sir."

Inside the cargo hold Frank tried to keep his head from slewing sideways as the helicopter spiraled toward the ground. His gut twisted until he hurt all the way into his throat. No panicked screams, no wild, wide open eyes, just hands clutching anything they could hold on to, muscles tightened and stressed in anticipation of the coming shock, eyes focused on the deck, and gritted teeth. The men around him were Marines. When control was taken from them, they still had discipline. The influence of their discipline kept him from screaming as the noise of increasing wind through the machine gun ports, the stench of smoke from burning wires and insulation, the sounds of metal grinding on metal, and the vibration increased.

"When we get down, see if you can help the machine gunners," Garzinski said.

"Got it. Are there any extra weapons on board?"

"We'll work something out. Focus on the sixties. If one fails, see if you can get it back in service. When we have the perimeter set up, see if you can dismount the sixties."

"What if I have to leave the chopper?"

"Find me."

"Got it."

As you would expect of a general's pilot, this one was very good. He was also very worried along with the fear. He was flying a multimillion-dollar machine that wasn't supposed to be flown into hot zones. The Corps had cheaper machines for this kind of work. But he was here at the General's request and his machine was in big time danger. So was the pilot's career. Strange how you can consider those kind of things even when your life is on the line.

The pilot played the cyclic, collective, and anti-torque pedals minimizing the strain on the tail rotor while still maintaining minimum control of direction and altitude. He had to keep the movements of the CH-53 inside of a tight envelope of altitude, pitch, spiral, lift, and airspeed to arrive at the LZ at exactly the right altitude and forward speed to minimize strain on the rotors and engine when he flared and set the big bird down. And he had to do it before things started freezing up and coming apart.

Having lost one engine, the pilot overrode the governor, and the co-pilot controlled the throttle manually to keep the rotor tack and engine power in the green. The pilot held the anti-torque pedals at exactly the right opposition to minimize the pitch of the tail rotor blades while still controlling the speed of the spiral to minimize the strain on the tail rotor assembly. That was a very delicate operation. An under or over correction would require more pitch to correct the torque and therefore more strain on the tail rotor assembly. He found the spiral he could live with and held it with tiny, instinctive adjustments. His care still might not be enough to save the tail rotor, but it was all he could do. That and pray.

The big CH-53, twin turbo engine, heavy lift helicopter was not designed for precision seat-of-the-pants flying, but with the damage the ship had taken, Major Harkness didn't have much choice. The AFCS (Automatic Flight Control System that could control pitch and roll) was off and Harkness was flying by feel to minimize stress on the rotors. He had practiced most of what he was doing a thousand times, but this was his first real emergency. Harkness blocked out everything but his co-pilot's voice and focused on getting the helicopter on the ground in one piece.

"One minute," the Crew Chief yelled and took the last

seat automatically strapping himself in.

The centrifugal force of the spiral had lessened so Frank figured the helicopter was flying a straighter line. He leaned toward the Gunny.

"Good luck," he said.

"Knock that shit off and hold on."

The bird righted, leveled for a moment, slowed, and then the engine noise increased to a scream.

"LZ three hundred meters," the co-pilot said. "Wind from the left. Looks like about ten to twelve knots. Boulders on the left side. Slight downward slope from the center toward the trees. Far end of the clearing has the least obstructions. Brush maybe five feet high."

"Roger. I'll set it down on the far end. Landing gear down."

"Roger. Gear coming down. . . Gear down. . . Gear locked."

"Rotor tack holding?"

"Roger. We've got enough power so far. The shaft worries me though. I'm already having to increase power to keep the rotor in the green."

"Hold it for just a few more seconds."

"Roger. You're looking good. Radar altitude three hundred feet."

"Altitude two hundred feet. Airspeed forty knots."

"Here we go," the pilot said.

Harkness eased the collective decreasing the lift of the rotors and pulled back on the cyclic lifting the nose, bleeding off altitude and forward speed at the same time.

"One hundred feet. . .seventy feet. . .fifty feet. . .airspeed twenty knots."

"Roger. More power, it's feeling sloppy."

"Roger. Heat is critical."

As the clearing slid under him, Harkness increased the flare and called for more throttle, playing the collective to slow the helicopter to a crawl in the forward direction. The co-pilot was quiet now. Harkness saw the spot where he wanted to put the bird down and began lowering the nose and transitioning to hover, inching forward with the cyclic.

"Five feet," the co-pilot said.

Harkness eased the collective and allowed the bird to settle the last five feet. The main and tail rotors had held. He began to breathe a sigh of relief as the helicopter squatted on the landing gear, but. . . his head snapped to the side as the tail of the chopper was jerked sideways and three loud thumps slammed into the fuselage. The helicopter jerked around another twenty degrees throwing everyone sideways in their seats. Harkness and the co-pilot were already lowering the ramp and shutting the engine and systems down.

"Tail rotor went," the co-pilot said. "Glad the RPM was down and the wheels were on the ground."
"Roger that," Harkness said. "Hope we get some help quick. We're going to be here for a while."

CHAPTER 5

Gunny Garzinski and the General's Aide were standing next to the crew chief waiting for the ramp to touch the ground. Frank unstrapped and ran forward to stand behind the machine gunners. When the ramp was secured, Garzinski started yelling quick short orders sending Marines down the ramp to set up a defensive perimeter. The first man to reach the bottom of the ramp suddenly fell face forward into the brush. Two final incoming rounds of the small arms burst of fire that hit the first man struck the ramp behind him and sent a screaming ricochet into the overhead of the cargo hold. A cloud of dust whipped across the ramp and into the chopper.

"Get those damned sixties working," Garzinski yelled. "Give me some cover here."

Garzinski ran down the ramp when the sixties opened-up. The Captain joined him and they grabbed the fallen Marine and dragged him off to the right of the helicopter. The rest of the Marines filed down the ramp in quick sprints and followed the Gunny. The level of small arms firing increased as the Marines added their weapons to the defense.

The door to the flight deck opened and the General and his staff filed out with the flight crew behind them. They moved to the ramp area and stopped there. The officers only had side arms with them and waited for a lull in the incoming fire to give them an opportunity to get to cover. The helicopter would not be a safe place to be if the enemy had mortars. They probably did.

"Open that hatch and pull out some ammo," the machine gunner closest to Frank said. "Stack the cans close to each of us."

"Shit," the gunner on the other side said. "I haven't got any targets this side."

"Just watch then," the first gunner said. "They might try to flank the troops before the gunny can get set up."

The first mortar hit about fifty feet from the helicopter on the side that didn't have any targets. The CH-53 was armored, so shrapnel and small arms weren't a big problem. But then a second mortar hit 25 feet away and rocked the fuselage.

"Okay," the lead gunner said. "It's time to get out of here. Grab all the ammo you can carry, Navy."

The ammo locker was a four by eight compartment under the floor hatch. It was about three feet deep and contained more than M-60 ammo. Besides the ammo cans of 7.62 for M-14s, several cans of 5.56 for M-16s, and Bandoliers of belted 7.62 for the M-60s, Frank also saw cans of fifty cal. He started pulling cans of linked M-60 up to the cargo deck while the gunners dismounted the M-60s. The intensity of the firing outside of the chopper had increased significantly by the time he had all the M-60 out of the locker.

"Where's the Fifty?" he yelled to the lead gunner."

"Rear cargo hold. There's a crate of M-sixteens in there too. Don't stop for that shit now. We have to get these sixties back in service outside."

"Got it," He yelled over the increasing sound of small arms fire. His ears picked up a new sound. Crew served weapon, he thought. Probably a fifty and it's not ours. Suddenly, sledge hammer blows rang down the side of the fuselage. Then he heard things shattering in the cockpit behind the bulkhead that separated them from the flight deck. The bulkhead shattered near the roof of the cargo compartment.

The two machine gunners humped their sixties to the ramp with belts of ammo hanging out of the breeches and two more belts each crisscrossed on their chests. Locked and loaded, they were ready to get into the fight, but they also carried an extra barrel and bipod mounts for the machine guns. They wouldn't be moving quickly for long, and they wouldn't be providing any effective fire until they set up in a fighting position. Frank followed right behind them with a can of M-60 ammo resting under each arm on top of the cans he was carrying in his hands by the handles. It felt like his arms were stretching, and the handles on the cans were cutting into his hands. He had to hold on to them though, the next mortar might land on the helicopter and that would be the end of their ammo supply.

The gunners went into the brush fast and low. He followed them and tried to copy their moves. Branches on the scrub brush scraped his face and tried to poke his eyes out as he pushed through and tried to stay bent over below the tops of the brush. They were all weighed down and had to move slowly, stopping frequently. The lead gunner found a small rise in the earth away from the chopper to cover them and waved him and the other gunner down beside him. The day was overcast, hot, and humid. Frank was already soaked with sweat.

"Looks like we're taking incoming from the far end of the flat. We've got to find the command and find out where he wants us. What's your name, Navy?"

"Frank Evans," he said.

"Know anything about these weapons?"

"Yeah. I'm a Gunners Mate."

"Damn. You stick with me. I'm Turbo and that's Mike."

Mike slapped Frank on the back. "Stay close with that ammo. We only have three hundred rounds each with us."

He started to answer but a water splatter on his face made him look up. Clouds were moving fast across the sky and getting thick. He just nodded.

"Shit," Turbo said. "That's trouble. We're not going to get air cover anytime soon. Soon as we get a break in the fire, move for the edge of the brush. I saw lots of craters when we came in and there's a small rise up there. From the sound of it, that's where command is dug in."

Frank didn't notice any let up in the incoming, but Turbo moved out anyway. He tried to ignore the terrifying *phiitt, phiitt, phiitt* sound of rounds zipping by close to his head. He was able to put the small stuff out of his mind and concentrate on following the Marines, but the bigger stuff couldn't be ignored. The fifty or whatever it was went by with a loud flutter sound and then clanked on the side of the helicopter fuselage. The sound of the impact as the big rounds struck the armor on the chopper was so loud he thought he could feel it. Looking over his shoulder, he watched rips and sparks stitch up the side of the big bird. Looking back was a mistake and he bumped into Mike who had stopped at the edge of the brush.

"Keep your head in the game, Navy. We can hide in this brush, but it won't stop a round if they see us."

"Mike, I'm going to lay down some cover for you," Turbo said. "Make a break for that crater dead ahead. You can see some of the platoon up ahead. When you get there, get their attention and give me and Navy some cover."

"Got it. Whenever you're ready."

Turbo dropped his extra barrel and tripod and stood in a crouch. When he started squeezing off bursts, Mike took off. Turbo stood higher and fired bursts at the far end of the flat hoping to keep the enemy's' heads down. Two friendly heads popped up in a crater further out on the flat and looked back at Frank and Turbo. Frank heard shouting and then saw heads pop up in several holes and the whole line began firing, giving Mike more cover.

"Come on," Turbo yelled. "We won't get better cover than that."

Turbo picked up his extra barrel and bipod and he and Frank sprinted to the crater hole where Mike had disappeared moments ago. It was a slow sprint with all the weight they were carrying. Mike was attaching the bipod to his M-60 when they dropped into the hole. The bottom of the hole was covered with three or four inches of red muddy water. Frank dropped the ammo cans and tried to flex his numb hands. Even numb, his hands were shaking. When he rose up a bit to look over the rim of the crater, he saw a figure running and weaving towards them.

"Looks like the Gunny is coming," he said.

"Good. Maybe we can find out what's going on."

The Gunny jumped into the hole feet first and let his body collapse to the bottom soaking his utilities and splashing Frank and the machine gunners. Several *phiitt* followed the sound of his boots hitting the slop.

"Who we got here?" he said.

"Turbo here. Mike there. And that's Navy."

"Yeah, I know Navy. Good Job, Evans. Turbo, I want you on the right flank all the way over on the edge of the hill. They're going to work their way around that way to get behind us. Mess them up if you can. Mike, get on the left flank. For now, keep an eye behind us. They are going to get behind us at some point. Evans, stay with me. I'll put you with the General's staff."

"I haven't got a weapon, Gunny. But there's plenty on the helicopter. Give me a couple troops and I'll get what I can."

Garzinski lifted his head carefully and checked out the chopper. Charlie's mortars hadn't nailed it yet. But they had it bracketed and should be able to put one right on top of it anytime they wanted to. Why were they waiting? They wanted it just like it was, that's why.

"You sure you want to try?" he said. "They can drop one on it anytime they get ready."

"Yeah, I'll do it. I need a weapon. Give me three guys and we'll get the ammo off first. Then I'll get the M-sixteens and the fifty."

"There's a fifty on that thing? You sure?"

"Turbo says there is."

"Sure," Turbo said. "Rear cargo hold. We're taking it and a crate of M-sixteens to Danang."

"Ammo?"

"Yep. Not sure how much, though. Several cans anyway."

"All right, cover me. I'll send back three men. Turbo, Mike, don't wait. Get over on the flanks."

CHAPTER 6

Gunny Garzinski sent the grunts back and Frank led them back to the chopper. They had plenty of concealment in the brush, but like Mike said, brush won't stop bullets. Frank went up the ramp first. When he was under cover, he signaled for the next man. They took a few incoming, but no one got hit. That was the easy part since Frank was empty handed and the grunts only had their personal weapons. Going back with four cans of ammo each wasn't going to be as easy.

They emptied the ammo locker and stacked the cans by the ramp. There were a lot of cans and that left Frank and the grunts elated and daunted at the same time. Elated at discovering their personal and limited issue of ammo wasn't all they had to defend the hill with, but daunted by the thought of having to carry it all to the defensive positions while under fire.

The Gunny had picked his strongest men for the

job and that lifted Frank's spirits. They could hump a lot of ammo in a short time.

"Let's get it all off the ramp and into to brush so we don't have to go up and down that damn ramp each time we come back. Four cans to a man."

He showed them how he had carried the M-60 ammo.

"She-it," one of the grunts said. "Give me six. It's just ammo cans. I been humping that shit since I left the Island."

The grunt was as good as his word and the other two loaded up the same way. Frank took four. It only took three trips up and down the ramp to get it all off the bird. Sixty-six cans of ammo and grenades. They took incoming each time, but moving in quick sprints, they didn't give Charlie any time to sight in.

Next, he opened the rear hold and had the grunts lift the crate of M-16's out and place it on the deck. He wished they were M-14s, but he was glad to have any weapon right then. The crate had already been opened by someone and was easy to get into. He opened the lid and lifted a rifle out. Not new, but in good shape. He smiled. No Cosmoline to worry about. The rifles had been cleaned and it looked like they had been boiled and given a light coat of lube. Cosmoline is a rust preventive weapons such as rifles are covered with when they are packed for shipment or stored for extended periods of time. It is thick, nasty, waxy, and hard as hell to get off. If those rifles had been stored with Cosmoline, the Marines would be out of luck.

Three stars for the Marine Armorer that had prepared these rifles for their final destination. He would need to field strip his and make sure it was ready for service, but at least he wouldn't have to spend a week he didn't have, or a boiling drum of water he didn't have either, to get the rifle in serviceable condition.

Next, he had the crate holding the fifty-cal. lifted out of the hold. The firing outside had subsided somewhat raising his hopes they could get the weapons off the bird without too much incoming hindering their efforts.

"Break it open and lay the components on the deck. We'll leave the rifles in the crate and push them to the bottom of the ramp and into the brush, and then we'll take the fifty down in components."

They moved quickly. The incoming picked up again and was getting more accurate and the shooters were getting quicker. The grunts began bellying down the ramp and pushing their cargo in front of them. When they had it all in the brush, the four men started to hump the ammo to the fighting positions. This time even the Marines only took four cans. Carrying the weight bent over was a lot harder than it was with a straight back.

It took several trips to get it all, and Frank wasn't sure he was going to have any help left by the time they were ready to bring the Fifty up. Forcing himself out of the hole got harder each trip. Charlie was shooting randomly into the brush now and he had one earlobe clipped by a round. It stung like crazy. One of the Marines wasn't as lucky. He took one through the hip right next to Frank. He didn't know where the will to keep going back was coming from. He wasn't brave. Hell, he was scared to death. But right then it wasn't about being brave; it was just something that had to be done and he was too damn scared to do anything else. The Marines kept doing what had to be done so Frank kept doing what he had to do.

When they got the wounded Marine back to the firing positions, Frank had trouble getting more help. The Gunny took over and he had three new helpers. But Garzinski was reluctant to give up any men again; they were cutting trenches between the craters and improving their defensive positions. Dirt was flying and a mound was building up on both sides of the fighting positions. The Gunny needed all the muscle he could get. For some reason the VC weren't pressing the Marines, probably because they didn't know what they were facing, so Garzinski was using the respite to dig in. Even the officers were digging. But the Fifty was important. The platoon had M-16s and M-14s, both with full automatic capability, and a couple of M-79 grenade launchers, but the Fifty could drill through concrete block and cut down trees. Garzinski couldn't see any concrete out there, but the Fifty gave him power and range and machine guns at three points on his line. Frank and three new helpers started back toward the chopper.

He lost another man by the time they had reached the chopper. He heard the smack of the round into bone and flesh behind him and he dropped prone on the ground. The Marine behind him didn't make a sound. He was face down spread eagle on the ground and the back of his head was missing. A young story ended. A kid who would never make a baby. He swallowed hard to keep the gorge from rising in his throat and he froze. He knew he had to keep moving, but he couldn't figure out what to do. The fear had been building into terror and the confusion of the moment just overwhelmed him and left him shaking and staring.

"Come on, Navy," the Marine in front of him said. "We'll come back for him. Let's get the Fifty so we can get the hell out of here."

At that point he was ready to be led by anyone that sounded like they knew what to do. He felt like a child again, waiting for an adult to tell him what to do. It wasn't a conscious thing. The sight of the Marine lying face down with the back of his head blown away had stripped him of his breath and his will as if he had been hit himself. The guy didn't move. He was gone. He had been pushing Frank's back and yelling, "go, go, go," just a few moments before and now he was dead.

They rose to a crouch and ran bent over toward the chopper. The incoming was hitting randomly in the brush so it didn't make any sense to dodge and weave. When they got to the brush at the bottom of the ramp, two men lifted the main body of the fifty. Frank had already assembled the receiver, barrel support, and barrel group into a single unit. The other men took the tripod mount, pintle, and traversing mechanism. He grabbed the tool kit and they all started back toward the fighting positions.

By the time they had reached the half-way point, Frank was running on auto. He hadn't said a word since the Marine took the hit in the back of the head. His eyes were glassy and his breath was coming in short gasps. And the gasps weren't from exertion. He had never been in combat, had never seen anyone killed before, and his training wasn't helping. He was so scared he couldn't even think about stopping. He just watched the Marine in front of him and kept putting one foot in front of the other, and silently, in his head, he screamed for all the noise to stop. Losing the tip of his earlobe should have been enough for a combat rookie, but Frank took his second hit when they broke from the brush and started running for the first firing position.

He rose to a crouch and waited for the Marines to move. They knew what they were doing and he was just a squid in the wrong place. He knew the Marines were firing from the position he was trying to get to, but he couldn't tell incoming from outgoing. It was all noise and too damn much of it. The two men carrying the main body of the Fifty suddenly stood and sprinted toward the American positions and he followed without thinking about it. They moved, he moved.

Several *Phiitts* sounded close his ears. Both sides. Close. He slapped at his ear as he moved. But then he stopped and stared at the blood on his fingers.

Old news, he thought. My ear was already messed up. A funny kind of happiness filled him and he wanted to call out to the Marines that he hadn't really been hit again, but they were way ahead of him now. A little bit of sanity returned and he realized he was standing still with incoming hitting all around him. He started running again. On his third stride, his right leg kicked out to the side and spun him so that he fell on his back. He stared at the dark, swirling clouds above him and wondered what happened. Then a Marine was next to him on the ground.

"You okay, Navy? What the hell are you doing?"

"Yeah. I'm good. I must have tripped."

The Marine watched Frank carefully for a few moments and then shook his head.

"Fucking Squids," he said. "Okay. Get on your gut and keep your head down. We belly it from here."

Frank rolled over on his belly and pulled his leg up to push forward with, but when he pushed nothing happened. He couldn't feel his leg.

"Hey, wait, something's wrong. My leg's numb."

He looked back over his shoulder and saw a dark spot spreading on his lower pant leg.

"Shit, I think I got hit."

"Can't stop here," the Marine said. "Come on, I'll help you."

He was able to move forward with the Marine's help, but the pain started soon after he moved. He bit his lip and kept pushing forward.

"I've got to rest," he said.

"You okay? You're not going to pass out, are you?"

"No. I'm not dizzy or anything like that. But the leg hurts now."

"Can't be too bad. Suck it up. We've got to keep moving. Just a few more feet and we've got some cover."

Stay with me, Frank thought. We're out here in the open, nothing wrong with him, but he isn't leaving me. Good guy. Stay with me, man. He looked up to see how far away the first hole was and that's when the mortar exploded. It wasn't close, more to the front near the fighting positions, but this wasn't Frank's day. A piece of shrapnel, very small and sharp, glanced off something in the dirt and hit him in the eyebrow over his left eye on an upward trajectory, sliced the flesh on his forehead as neat as a surgical incision, and continued toward his steel helmet. The shrapnel would have continued on its upward trajectory and ended its damage, but being subject to the laws of physics, when it reached the curve in Frank's skull and the liner in his helmet at the same time, it sought the path of least resistance and was channeled by the helmet and skull and sliced his scalp back to the middle of his head before losing enough energy to be stopped. Scalp wounds are messy. The flood of blood was immediate and impressive. Blood poured down his forehead, into his eye, and covered one side of his face.

The Marine with him had buried his face in the dirt when the mortar hit and now he looked up to make sure Frank was okay. As soon as he saw Frank's face he started screaming for a corpsman. Frank saw the terror in the Marine's face and passed out. Probably more from fear than anything else.

When he came to, he was in a hole, his head and leg were bandaged, and the General was kneeling over him.

"It looks a lot worse than it is," General Muldavy said. "How are you feeling?"

"A little shaky, sir," he said. "I got hit in the head, didn't I?"

"Yes, but it's just a flesh wound. You'll have a scar, but nothing important was damaged. Your eyes are okay."

"I thought I was blinded when I got hit."

Frank noticed the sounds of the battle again. His ears were working okay.

"Three separate wounds in one day," the General said. "You did a good job with the ammo and weapons. Kept going back out there. I'd be proud to have you in my Corps."

Frank looked away from the General's eyes. If he only knew how screwed up I was, he thought, he wouldn't be. . .screw it, he doesn't know. *But I do.*

"The corpsman will be back around in few minutes to check on you," Muldavy said. "He's a bit busy right now. We've taken casualties and we'll take some more before it's over. Hang in there. You're going to be fine."

The General stood in a crouch and made his

way along the trench line to the other officers. The trenches between the holes were only about waist deep so far, but the Marines were still digging. Every chance they got to set their rifles down they grabbed an entrenching tool and extended, widened, and deepened the trench.

Frank watched the general go and then tried to lift his leg. He could make it move and the numbness was gone, but that wasn't all good. It hurt like hell. He touched the bandage over his eyebrow but couldn't feel anything but bandage. What surprised him was how good he felt. The leg hurt and his head was starting to hurt, but he wasn't dizzy or weak. He tried to sit up and didn't discover any new pains. His body seemed willing, but he wasn't sure his spirit was.

He listened for the fifty hoping the Marines had put it in service, but he only heard small arms and not a lot of that. The Marines not on the firing line were filling empty green sandbags and stacking them along the top edge of the trench. They each seemed to have a few. Where they got them, he didn't know. Other Marines were deepening and extending the trenches with their entrenching tools. Gunny Garzinski walked in a crouch toward Frank.

"How are you doing, Evans?"

"I'm good, Gunny."

"You don't look good. The whole side of your face is swollen and turning blue. The Doc said for you to take these."

Corpsman in the FMF were almost always called

Doc. Garzinski handed him two big pills and his canteen.

"Darvon," he said. "He was worried about shock and wouldn't give you any morphine. He didn't think you'd need it anyway. It'll hurt, but you only have flesh wounds."

Frank took the pills and handed back the canteen.

"Why isn't the Fifty firing?" he asked.

"The breech is messed up. Maybe cosmoline. Should have stripped that thing before they tried to set it up."

"Did somebody bring the tool bag I was carrying?"

"Yeah, we got it."

"Help me up. I'll take a look at it."

"You sure you're up to it?"

"I don't know, but I can't just sit here. I can rest just as easy sitting next to the Fifty as I can here. I think I'd feel a little safer there, too."

"Well, I won't argue. These guys are replacements heading north for rifle platoons, but not one of them is from a weapons platoon. When I get you up stay leaned over and put your arm across my back.

Garzinski helped him through the trenches to the Fifty pit. Frank was shaky, but he could move without falling. And now that he had been hit and survived, a funny thing happened. A lot of the fear, at least the paralyzing kind, went away. He was able to think about what needed to be done.

By the time he got to the pit, Frank was

sweating and hurting and wondering if the move had been a smart one after all. He was getting dizzy and seeing spots in his vision. Garzinski helped him sit next to the machine gun and pulled the tool pouch over to him. Frank wasn't too worried about the gun. Gunny was probably right. Cosmoline. He hoped so anyway. The grunts knew their weapons, but no grunt in his right mind would dare disassemble the trigger and cyclic mechanisms in the receiver without the right tools and a qualified armorer right there to guide him. He opened the tool pouch and picked his tools.

Fifteen minutes later he started the reassembly process. Ten minutes after that he called the Gunny and told him to have the crew set the gun up and put a belt in it. The gun crew was makeshift, and not having worked together on a Fifty before, the process took some time and a lot of advice from Frank. But they got it done and he reached his hand up for a Marine to help him behind the gun. He worked the charging handle and looked at Garzinski. Garzinski gave him a thumbs-up.

The firing along the line had stopped and it seemed like both sides were catching their breath. A lot of firing could still be heard way off, further down the mountain, but it was too far away to bother them. It was probably coming from the Marine company the General had originally tried to help. Frank eased his head up to look through the sights on the Fifty. He worked the traverse and elevation to set the sights on a boulder sticking out of the earth at the edge of the flat on the far end. He locked the settings down, grabbed the handles, and fired one round. He watched the round strike the boulder. Good. He squeezed the trigger and said the old gunner's timing chant in his head, *fire a burst of four*, and let up on the trigger. The boulder cracked and one side slid to the right and out of sight.

"All yours," he said as he slid out from behind the gun and turned it over to the crew. Where's my rifle, Gunny?"

"Take your pick," Garzinski said.

He looked where Garzinski was pointing and spotted a row of M-16s leaning against the side of the trench. They all had their dust covers closed, a magazine in, and a cleaning rod taped to their barrels. A condom was pulled over the end of their barrels to keep dust and rain out. Leave it to the Marines to improvise. He hobbled bent over to the weapons and picked one for himself. He grabbed a half dozen loaded magazines and stuffed them in one of the cloth bandoliers lying next to the magazines and put it across his shoulders. He thought about it for a moment and took two white boxes and one brown box of loose ammo and shoved them in his pockets. He felt a little better. Garzinski's work detail had loaded all the magazines that came in the crate, about three to a rifle, but they might not have time to load any more if the action got hotter. Frank reminded himself to top off his magazines whenever he got the chance.

He leaned back against the dirt side of the trench and cradled his rifle in his lap. One of the Marines lent him some lube. He had already field stripped the M-16 and made sure everything was clean and ready for firing. He also ran a rod with a wire brush through the barrel and then used a swab cut from his undershirt and soaked with LSA oil to make sure it was clean and all the Cosmoline was gone. He followed up with clean patches and ran them through until they passed along the barrel without picking up any color. His rifle was good to go. He kept the dust cover closed and also kept the condom over the end of the barrel. He liked that idea with all the rain that had started shortly after he fired the Fifty.

Frank had read a lot of reports of problems the Army was having with the M-16 in Vietnam and suspected they all came back to maintenance issues. It was a good weapon if you kept it clean. That, at least, was the official line. Clean was difficult in Vietnam, but there it is.

His head and leg were hurting and he was running a fever. His ear burned too, but that was minor, just a little chunk out of the lobe. The corpsman had changed the bandage on his head and checked the butterfly stiches. He said it would heal well if Frank kept it clean. Right. Keep it clean in a dirt hole. Every freaking thing in that place was dirt or mud. The leg was another flesh wound. The bullet had put a groove across the calf muscle but hadn't touched the tendon. It also would heal if he kept it clean. Could have been worse. That was not a comforting thought.

CHAPTER 7

"How are you feeling, Navy?"

"I could use a cold beer, sir."

"Couldn't we all," the Captain said. "Where are you stationed?"

"I'm reporting in to Naval Security Intelligence at Danang."

The Captain winced and ducked his head as a round screamed off a rock near them

"How'd you come to be on the General's bird?" he asked.

He was a cool one. Frank noticed the shine on the toes of the captain's boots where the mud hadn't completely covered them.

"Got diverted into Saigon because of weather," he said. "Gunny Garzinski got me on the helicopter. Maybe I should have waited for the flight they wanted to put me on tomorrow."

The Captain grinned. "Well, I for one am glad you picked us. You've done a hell of a job today."

The Captain took a little note book out of his breast pocket and flipped it open.

"Can I get your name, rank, and serial number?"

"Yes, sir. If I can give it to the enemy, I guess I can give it to you. Frank Evans, Gunners Mate First Class." He gave the Captain his Serial number/Social Security number.

"Thanks," the Captain said. "I'm Captain Brooks, the General's Aide. I'm sure he'll want to let your command know how much he appreciates the job you've done."

"Think there's a chance of that, sir? I mean, you know, that we'll be around long enough for the General to. . ."

"Yeah, I do," Brooks said. "We're in a bad spot right now, but that's what Marines do. Hang in there, I've got to get back."

Pretty decent officers, Frank thought.

As the shadows stretched across the flat on top of the mountain and the slanted rays of the sun made the dark circles of shell craters stand out in contrast to the dusk lighted surface around them, not unlike a construction site, the Marines prepared for a new assault. Charlie liked the night. Garzinski showed Frank how to dig a grenade sump into the side of the trench to kick grenades into if they landed close to him. He appreciated the advice from the veteran, but wasn't happy about the new fear the advice started. They'd have to get pretty close to lob a grenade into the trench. Was Garzinski expecting that?

Two Marines darkened their faces and hands with clay and waited against the trench wall for dark. Garzinski was sending them out to man listening posts on both sides of the line. Captain Brooks had taken command of the Marines, nominally at least. But Garzinski knew what he was doing and the Captain let him do it. When it was dark enough the Marines went over the edge of the trench on their bellies and disappeared into the dark. Damn, these guys are good, he thought. This morning we were a bunch of strangers and now they act like they've been fighting together forever. Garzinski stopped next to Frank to talk.

"Evans, are you up to helping out with the Fifty? You don't have to do much. Just be there in case they need help and provide some security for the crew."

"Sure. I was going to ask anyway. How about the sixties? You going to leave them out there tonight?"

"Yeah. I need them on the flanks. We left a few surprises behind us if the VC come in that way. They ain't the only ones who know how to rig a booby trap. Amazing what you can do with a piece of wire, a C-rats can, and a frag grenade. We've fortified two pits on the flanks and we have the sixties there with interlocking fields of fire. The gooks are going to get around us further down the hill in the dark anyway, but we've got a fair position here. It's not the one I would have picked, but it is what it is. At least we can fight both ways. Look, it's probably going to get bad tonight. We haven't got coms and Echo Company hasn't been able to link up with us. I'm not sure why they haven't made it, but I suspect there are a lot more VC out there than we knew about. A lot of fighting has been going on down below us all day. And the damn weather is getting worse. If this damn rain keeps up we're going to be fighting in mud and water up to our asses. So . . . hell, hang in there and do what you can."

Frank made his way to the Fifty pit and found a good spot on the trench wall that allowed him to lie against the dirt and sight his rifle down range. The area in front of them was close to the size of a football field and barren except for a few blasted and twisted trees. Artillery and bomb craters pockmarked the entire surface. Behind them they had about a thirty-yard clear field of fire and then the brush started. But as he had found out, brush doesn't stop bullets. So, if Charlie came that way, he wouldn't find much cover. He was facing down the long axis of the flat towards the area the enemy had occupied all day. Later he might have to shift to the other side of the trench if the VC got around them and came up from the other side of the mountain. But right then he concentrated on the dark flat in front of him. The dark was enormous. No moon. Not even any starlight. They were left with only the listening posts to warn them if the VC slipped in close in the dark.

    The Marines had taken several casualties during the day, but not all of them were KIA. Besides Frank, three Marines were wounded, but could still fight. The platoon, just two squads in reality, had five KIA. So far. They had started with twenty-six Marine enlisted, Frank, the flight crew, and the General's staff. All of them, except Frank and a Navy Corpsman, were Marines, so all of them were riflemen, even the officers. Thank God for whatever need had put the Corpsman on that flight. Gunny Garzinski had sorted out his NCOs quickly and organized the platoon into squads and rifle teams. The M-60 machine guns were set up with the big circular aerial sights, but the Marines had figured out how to use them on the ground. Frank was amazed at how quickly an unrelated group of replacements catching a ride on a helicopter had become a functioning infantry platoon. The Marines impressed him.

Of the thirty-six enlisted and officers they had started with, thirty-one remained and could fight. But that was just a little over two squads, not a platoon. The extra M-16's and ammo had been more important than he knew when he agreed to go back and get them. The officers including the flight crew carried only side arms and were glad to get a rifle. With it, they became effective fighting troops. But even with the additional ammo, the platoon would have to be very careful with their firing. No one knew when they would get any help. Gunny Garzinski stopped to check on Frank while checking on the men.

"Good spot, Evans. Let me show you something though."

The Gunny

The Gunny pulled two sandbags from the left and two more from the right and formed kind of a V shaped rampart for Frank to shoot through.

"Where did you all get sandbags?" Frank asked.

"Marines carry a few in their ruck. Empty of course. They can give you a little extra cover in the grass. Keep your head down below the tops of the sandbags," he said. "You can see all you'll need to see between the bags. Make a rest for the rifle and keep it on semi. Don't shoot unless you have a definite target. Don't screw around with full auto. We haven't got enough reserve ammo for that."

"Aye, Aye." he said.

Garzinski grinned. "You'd make a decent Marine, Evans. A little training, a lot of attitude, some motivation, yeah, I'd let you in my Corps."

That was high praise for a squid from a Marine Gunny Sergeant.

"Any idea what's out there?" Frank asked.

"The Captain figures platoon strength. From what I've seen, I agree. But that don't mean it will stay that way. That's a big fight down below us, maybe company size, and could be a battalion. They must be between us and Echo Company and they have the high ground above Echo, so they can reinforce the platoon up here, but Echo can't get to us to help."

One of the Marines manning the Fifty was listening and said, "Shit, Gunny. Bring it on. Miss Misery here wants a little taste of the fight." They had already named the machine gun.

"Keep your eyes out there," Garzinski said, pointing into the dark. "The posts have pop flares and they know to stay down deep in their holes if they pop one. But, damn it, listen to me. Make damn sure you have a target before you start emptying those cans. That ammo right there is all you have and all you're going to get. Got it?"

"Got it. But I say again, bring it on."

It was bravado. Frank had seen and felt the fear in them before the Gunny got there, but the bravado made him feel better. They were probably scared, maybe as much as he was, but they were Marines and they would fight. He wondered what the Marine Corps did to them to make men like that. Navy boot camp hadn't been any fun, but nothing in his training had prepared him for this. Not even Coronado. But the Marines shrugged it off, maybe with a platitude or two about this being what they did. Or maybe it wasn't a platitude.

"I think you'll get all the bring it on you want tonight," Gunny said and moved on to the next firing position

When Garzinski moved on down the trench, Frank asked one of the Marines where he was from then what he did for a living before he enlisted in the Corps. Before long the Marines were telling him their stories. Fascinating people, he thought.

CHAPTER 8

It started with an illumination-round from a mortar. He heard the hollow sound of the launch and then a few moments later, the pop high over their heads. At first there was just a point of light high in the clouds, then the flare burst into full illumination, and then the whole flat appeared under a strange dim twilight that shouldn't be there. Light reflected off the low clouds and made a very eerie scene. As the flare descended under its parachute, the light got brighter and shadows elongated and slowly moved in an arc around whatever was at their base. No commands were shouted to get ready. The Marines were ready and knew what the flare meant. And they knew their jobs.

Out on the flat near the edge of the cleared space, Frank spotted shadows moving over the rise that marked the spot where the flat ended and the downslope of the mountain began. Small shadows about a football field's distance away. He heard a soft voice.

"Hold your fire. Let them get close. Pick a target. Don't waste ammo."

Gunny Garzinski came by bent over and moving fast, talking quietly while he went. About every fifth man, he tapped someone on the back and pointed at the trench wall behind them. Rear guard. Another pop sounded overhead and a new flare joined the one that was burning out. Fifteen or twenty shadows moved forward toward the Marines, occasionally disappearing into a bomb crater. None had fired yet. Then more came over the rise and moved forward behind the first wave. What was coming was bigger than a squad. Frank was sighting in on one shadow when the first mortar hit.

The first mortar-round hit ten or fifteen meters in front of the Marines and threw a geyser of dirt and rock into the air. With rock and dirt showering down around him, Frank dropped down to the bottom of the trench. The second mortar hit several yards behind the trenches. They had the range now. A new flare popped into light above the Marines and a mortar-round hit the trench down near the right flank. Then it was fire for effect for the VC. As soon as the real attack started he was thankful for the pounding the cadre had given him on the final exercise at Coronado. But his thankfulness didn't last. What happened next took his senses away and turned him into a shaking, crying, snot nosed, blubbering, screaming, ear covering idiot.

The VC knew about time-on-target attacks. They put three mortar rounds in the air before the first one hit the ground. But they added a nice little feature to spice up the terror. They had a Fifty caliber machinegun mounted at the end of the flat. The VC machinegun crew worked with the mortar crew and timed the impact of the first mortar. They timed it so they could open up with the Fifty exactly when the first mortar exploded to create a perfect hell on earth for the Marines.

When the first round hit the trench, green fifty caliber tracers began screaming off rocks and boulders, some slamming down in the trench and through the firing positions. Since the tracers were stacked one in five, each tracer meant that four other non-tracer rounds were hitting without being seen, but they were heard and felt. The mortars hit at about ten second intervals, and the noise and screaming shrapnel was deafening and overwhelming to the senses. Add in the concussions from the exploding rounds, blinding flashes, blasting shrapnel-like shards of rock and dirt, and the scream of incoming fifty caliber rounds, and men should not have been able to function. The world was blowing up. They were in a hell of flying metal, heart stopping concussion, deafening noise, and blinding light.

That was the VC commander's plan, overwhelm the Marines with mortars and automatic weapons fire and attack behind the mortars. But the plan must not have considered the target. They were Marines. The

Fifty next to Frank opened-up on the flashes from the VC Fifty at the end of the flat. Tracers work both ways. The shooter can see where his rounds are going, but the target can also see where they are coming from. Some tracer ammo is designed to ignite the tracer after about a hundred yards of flight to keep the target gunners from seeing exactly where they were coming from, but these were the green Chi-com or Russian variety and left the barrel already ignited. Men stayed at their positions and opened-up on the shadows now moving and firing at the trenches. They had gotten close behind the mortars.

Frank took his hands away from his ears and wiped his nose. He looked around wildly and wanted to run. But there wasn't anywhere to run to. The trench had collapsed twenty or so feet to his left and he could hear screaming on his right. The trench was filled with smoke in that direction. The smell of explosives burnt his nose and the smoke made his eyes water. The Marines on the Fifty were working as a team and the gun kept pumping out short bursts.

He slid back up the side of the trench and pushed his rifle between the sandbags. Find a target. Don't waste ammo. It was something to keep his mind focused on. A mantra. He couldn't stop the shaking, but he could function. The shadows were close now and he could see the flashes from their weapons. Sound was meaningless, just a big jumble of loud noise and confusion. He saw a shadow get bigger, tried for a sight picture, couldn't really see the front sights, squeezed the trigger. Found another shadow, sights invisible, pointed the rifle as well as he could, and squeezed off another round. No way to tell if he was hitting anything, but it didn't matter. Found another target, squeezed off another round. Soon the movement became a routine and he steadied down. Fear is like intoxication. Your brain can only handle so much and then it starts shutting down receptors. The sudden cut off the mortars helped, but the steadiness of the Marines around him helped even more.

As he fired and continued to function a new feeling came over him. He watched a target drop, and the feeling came again. Something ferocious and liberating. Fear changed to rage. They wanted to kill him. He didn't want to be there. Just go away, damn it. But they wouldn't, so he hit back. Pick a target. Fire. Never in his life had he even allowed himself to think about hitting back like this, yet the desire was there. While his brain cringed at the situation he was in and at what he was doing, something deep inside was rising to the surface, closer with each kill, and it was screaming and laughing.

He lost track of time; find a target, squeeze, find another target. As the fight continued, the fear grew and continued to change. The VC got closer and his fear turned into manic, terror-driven hate and then the hate spawned rage. But it was controlled rage. The dark thing in him was enjoying itself. His mouth and throat were dry. His top lip stuck to his teeth forming his lips into an unplanned sneer. His nose was filled with the smell of burnt gun power flaring his nostrils. His eyes stung and watered. He tried to swallow and couldn't. Even though the recoil from the M-16 was light, each time he fired, his head throbbed along his wound. But the pain just made him super aware. He needed a drink, just a sip to make his throat work so he could swallow. But he didn't have time to ask for some water. Targets were still trying to move across the flat.

The battle was only minutes old, but time itself was stretching, and Frank lost all sense of duration. Then later, perhaps only minutes, he squeezed the trigger and nothing happened. He was dazed and confused, elated and hyper, fine muscle control almost gone, but training took over. He pulled his rifle back and looked at the breech. The bolt was stuck half way back. What the hell? he thought. Some sense returned. He looked inside the chamber and found a round cocked at an angle jamming the bolt back. He ejected the magazine, locked the bolt back, tilted the rifle over and shook the jammed round out of the chamber. But a round was stuck in the breech also. He ripped the cleaning rod off the barrel and jammed it down the barrel from the muzzle. The stuck round popped out. Okay, load a new mag, release the bolt, seat the round. Good to go.

Frank pushed the rifle back between the sandbags, but the dark was total again. He couldn't see anything. A few Marines were still popping off an occasional round, but he couldn't see what they were shooting at. The Fifty was quiet. He heard the command to cease fire.

He slid down the dirt wall and sat at the bottom of the trench with his rifle between his knees. He breathed hard and stared at the dirt on the other side of the trench.

"Hey, Navy. Help me check this thing out. Better make sure we're good to go while we have a lull."

"Yeah, okay, I'm here," he said, but it came out as a croak.

"You okay, man? It ain't done yet."

"Yeah, sure, I'm good. Have you got some water?"

The Marine handed Frank his canteen and he let the water slide down his throat. He wanted to wash the crud out of his mouth first but couldn't wait to get the water in his throat. Gunny Garzinski climbed over the rubble that had collapsed on the left and ran toward the Fifty in a crouch.

"Break it down," he said. "Move it down on the left flank. One of the mortars took out the Sixty. Set up on this side of the old pit. They have this spot marked anyway. The next mortar is going to come down right here."

"On our way," the gunner said.

The crew broke the big gun down and wrapped the barrel in a utility blouse. The barrel was still too hot to handle.

"Evans, I want you with the General. The officers are down there on the other side of the smoke. Do what you can to support them."

"How'd we do?" Frank asked.

"Could have been worse. If they had kept the mortar going, it'd be all over. But their troops got too close. We lost ten men. One of the Colonels and a Major among them. I'm calling the listening posts back. No sense leaving them out there now. Why the Captain decided to set up here, I'll never know. We ought to be back on the edge of the hill. They have to come at us from there at some point."

"So, we're down to twenty-one men now?"

"Yeah. And that includes the officers. They're doing okay, though. The Captain's turning out to be a pretty good platoon leader. We got three wounded too, but they can still shoot. How about you? You doing okay?"

The lead gunner behind Garzinski said, "Navy's good to go. He'll do."

Frank felt a little better about himself after that endorsement, but he couldn't forget what happened when the crap started.

"Yeah, I'm good," he said. "If you need me on the Fifty, let me know."

"I will. Go on. Take care of the officers. I can't spare anyone else."

The "anyone else" rang in Frank's ears as he made his way down the trench to find the officers. What the Corps giveth, the Corps taketh away. He grinned to himself and stopped in the middle of the trench. He grinned again. He could still grin after what had happened. Maybe I'm doing okay after all, he thought.

CHAPTER 9

"Evans, isn't it?" Colonel Harris said.

Harris was tall and lean, almost skinny. His utilities were covered with mud and his face was black from smoke and powder residue. Frank noticed that Harris's hands had a slight tremor.

"Yes, sir," he said.

Frank had picked a piece of real estate on the side of the trench that looked like a good fighting position and had a good field of fire. He found some sandbags to make his V shaped rampart. He added an additional one this time to use as a rest for his rifle. He wasn't sure the bags would do any good, none of the Marines had them, but hell, the Gunny ought to know what was what. And he did feel better with the little bit of extra cover the bags provided when he was firing.

"The Gunny speaks well of you," the Colonel said. "I just wanted to add my recognition for your work today. The General is impressed and I think that speaks to a lot. Keep up the good work, Sailor."

"Thank you, sir," he said. "Your confidence means a lot."

Sometimes you said dumb shit when talking to officers. The only thing that would mean a lot right then was a battalion of infantry coming to the rescue. And maybe a couple of beers.

"Quite all right," Harris said.

The Colonel returned to the knot of officers, a knot that was smaller by two now, and said something that made them laugh. Well, hell, Frank thought, they're probably scared too. Glad I could provide a little entertainment. As he finished that thought, the first mortar of the new attack hit the lip of the trench at the old Fifty position.

The officers dove for the floor of the trench, but Frank surprised himself and pushed up the side of the trench and put his rifle on the rest. He closed his eyes for a moment until the shower of dirt ended. He was ready. Two more mortars hit nearby, but away from the trench. Then it got quiet again. Playing with us, he thought. No flares this time. He waited but no troops came over the rise and the incoming ceased.

The rest of the night went along in that vein. Out of the quiet a sound of tubing would come and a mortar would explode, a couple more would follow, and then it would get quiet. Charlie took casualties on the first attack and decided to just harass for a while. But they had to do something soon. There was an edge of murky light on the horizon. During the night, fog had set in or the clouds had dropped lower. In any case the night became not only dark, but swirling fog began to play with everyone's senses. Staring into the dark will produce phantoms anyway, and when you add fog that moves with the breeze, the phantoms become real. Frank would get tired, his eyes would almost close, and then someone along the line would fire into the dark. Probably a good thing too. Without the occasional incoming, half the platoon would be asleep. Well, probably not, but he would.

The final attack came as soon as there was enough light to see. A little light was getting through the clouds raising hopes the cloud cover was breaking up and air power would come to the rescue. Charlie had been hurt on his first attempt to over-run the Marines. The VC commander had been surprised at the level of resistance his troops were finding and was reluctant to press the attack during the night without knowing what he was dealing with. But now, with a clearing sky, he had to attack or withdraw; the VC knew what air support from gunships could do. With air support, Garzinski would probably attack. Frank could hear talking down the line, and Marines were moving around. The General, the Colonel, the Captain, and the pilots were huddled together over a map and discussing something. They had a flashlight on the map. The first mortar hit as one of the pilots folded the map.

    He pushed tiredly up to his rampart again and

sighted down the rifle. Everything hurt, especially his head. His legs shook and he shivered with chill. He had to lock his knees and brace his arms on the dirt to get steady. The wet in the dirt seeped into his damp utilities and caused his shivering to increase. If they were coming, it had to be soon. The clouds were breaking up for sure.

The mortars continued, one, two, three, then two almost at once. The big machine gun they used in the first attack opened-up but it was focused on the Fifty on the left flank. And then he saw the VC come over the rise at the far end of the flat. He had a little light now and that allowed him to get a sight picture. He picked a target, had a good sight picture, didn't want to do it, squeezed the trigger. The target dropped. He didn't have time to think about it though because the flat was becoming what they call a target rich environment. VC kept coming over the rise and moving in waves toward the Marines.

The officers were all lying against the wall of the trench and firing at the oncoming VC. Frank chose another target and watched it drop. Find a target, squeeze off the round, watch the target drop. Not every time, but enough. The Marines were firing with unbelievable discipline. He didn't hear a single burst of auto except for the big Fifty on one flank and the Sixty on the other, and they were firing only three or four-round bursts. Men were picking targets and putting them down one at a time. But something had to give. The VC just kept coming over the rise.

He put a fresh magazine in his rifle and seated the first round. He'd lost touch with time again. Pick a target, shoot, pick another target. One of the officer's M-16 jammed and he just threw it down and ran to where the extra M-16s were leaning against the wall and grabbed a new rifle. He grabbed two magazines with it. Mortars continued to pound the trench and a couple were effective. The firing from the Marines was noticeably thinner now. But the work was hot and Frank continued the routine almost in a daze. His fear turned to terror as the VC got closer, but he continued to fight. There wasn't any glory in this shit and there wasn't any choice.

The VC were getting closer and more cautious; the fire from the Marines was precise and deadly. A mortar hit near the left flank and then Frank notice something missing. The Fifty was silent. The pace of the battle seemed to pick up then. A grenade landed near his feet. He swept his foot at it and knocked it into his grenade sump and rolled away from the opening. The explosion took his hearing away and splattered him with mud. Terrified, he was breathing hard in fast gulps; they were too close; he had to keep shooting. The terror threatened to overwhelm him, but then the manic mixture of fear and rage returned as the VC approached and threatened to overwhelm the trenches.

His knees felt weak. An old cliché, sure. But say you step out in a crosswalk and out of the corner of your eye you see a truck coming and it isn't slowing down. You look. The driver is looking to the side not seeing you in the crosswalk. You freeze, you can't think, you just stare. The truck is getting impossibly big—and then someone grabs the back of your shirt and jerks you back out of the way just in time—that kind of weak knees. And then you get mad, insanely angry.

As the VC got closer the terror disappeared and left only the rage. He screamed at the enemy and a fierce exhilaration took hold. Not courage. Not bravery. Just terror driven rage. He stood his ground and fired into the enemy at near point blank range. The dark thing inside of him rose up and Frank wanted to smash them, gut them, rip their limbs, destroy the thing that was trying to destroy him. They kept coming. He hated them, killed them, and hated them more. He saw his rounds hit, saw gore fly, saw the things crumble and die, and he gave in to the insanity of the moment. Kill, scream, cry, kill some more. They went down in boneless, sloppy tumbles. No dramatics, no half-steps, no arms flung out to break the fall, just collapsing, lifeless, deflated caricatures of once living things. But the bastards kept coming.

A grenade landed close to the officers. One of the pilots spotted it and yelled, but it was too late. Frank just let his legs fold and collapsed into the mud. The concussion knocked him sideways, but he was below the shrapnel, and when the smoke cleared, the General, Colonel, and one of the pilots were down. No time to help them. Six VC loomed large ten feet from the trench.

He flipped the selector to full automatic and squeezed the trigger while fanning across the group. He held the trigger down until the bolt locked back. Twenty rounds at six hundred rounds a minute only takes a few seconds, but it seemed longer to him. He saw tracers hit VC, saw tracers go between them, saw them fall one by one.

He loaded a new magazine and put the rifle back on semi-auto. But when he sighted down the barrel again he didn't have any targets in front of him. One pilot was still standing and firing. Frank looked his way. Three VC were approaching the pilot. Christ, the pilot had stopped firing at them. He was pulling at the cocking arm on his rifle. Frank sighted and dropped one of the VC and then ran toward the pilot.

The pilot heard Frank shoot and began jerking at the charging arm on his M-16 frantically. Frank planted his feet, flipped his weapon to full auto and squeezed the trigger—and nothing happened, it was jammed again.

The pilot looked up at the rim of the trench just in time to catch a round in the center of his head. As the pilot collapsed like a rag doll, Frank threw his M-16 down, turned, and limped back to grab a new weapon. The VC appeared at the top of the trench with rifles at their shoulders. But they were looking at the pilot and not at Frank. He grabbed the last M-16, flipped the selector to automatic fire and hosed the VC from his hip. The first few rounds hit the dirt at their feet, but he adjusted his aim upwards and took both of them. He watched the rounds hit and the men fall. His lips were pulled back in a manic grimace and all his teeth were showing. Black and muddy face, wild eyes, and teeth clamped together to hold the scream in. He was breathing in gasps. Something trickled into his left eye.

His head bandage was gone and the wound had pulled apart and was bleeding again. He had to wipe blood out of his eyes to see. His calf hurt, but the bandage was still on his leg. He hobbled to the officers and checked to see if any of them were alive. One by one, he touched dead men. When he put his finger on the General's neck to feel for a pulse, the General's eyes opened.

"Set me up," General Muldavy said.

"You have a lot of wounds, General. Maybe you better stay where you are."

"Set me up and give me my rifle," he whispered.

Frank got him by the shoulders and dragged him to a sitting position against the trench wall. The General was bleeding from multiple shrapnel wounds. But he was lucky; the colonel took most of the blast. Frank grabbed the first rifle he found and checked the magazine. Half empty. He put a full magazine in, charged the rifle, and put it in the General's lap. That would have to do. He had to get back to the wall.

When he looked over the lip he couldn't find any targets close, so he waited. He didn't want to draw any attention to his position.

"Navy," a voice said from a distance.

Frank looked to the right and saw the Sixty

gunner humping his Sixty with a belt in it and the bipod attached.

"Coming in," Turbo said. "Anybody left here?"

"The General is still alive, but he's hurt bad. Why aren't you on the flank?"

"The gooks are all over us. I saw some of them go into the trench down where the Fifty was. I saw some coming up behind us too. I think we fucked the duck this time. Watch the gun. I've got to go back and get the last can of ammo."

He didn't wait for an acknowledgement. Turbo took off towards the flank.

"I can't be taken," General Muldavy said.

"What did you say, sir?"

"I can't be taken alive," he said. "Understand? If I can't do it myself, you have to. That's an order."

"We aren't dead yet, General. Turbo brought the Sixty and he's bringing ammo. We're okay."

"I asked you a question, Evans. Do you understand?"

Frank didn't want to answer, but he had to. "Yes, sir. I understand."

The quiet remained except for a few scattered shots on the left. Frank wondered what the hell was happening. Why hadn't the VC taken him and the General yet? He drummed his fingers on the stock of his rifle. Then the firing picked up again. Somebody was still fighting on the left, a lot of somebodies. Turbo returned with the Sixty ammo.

As Turbo passed the General and reached for the Sixty, his head exploded.

The surprise caused Frank to freeze and set him up for his fourth wound of the battle.

The next shot from the VC behind them hit him in the side and spun him around. By some freak of nature, he held on to his rifle. As he hit the ground on his back he raised the rifle and pressed the trigger. He hosed the VC.

The firing increased on the left and Frank heard shouting in what he assumed was Vietnamese on both sides of the trench. It wasn't English. Well, this is it, he thought as a deep, irresistible sadness filled his mind. Shit! I never figured. . .

The firing on the left stopped and the voices got closer. He slid across the dirt and sat next to the General facing the back wall. Frank's head was bleeding again and now the gash on his side was soaking his shirt. The General had the muzzle of the rifle under his chin and his arm stretched to pull the trigger. The sight felt obscene, like catching someone masturbating.

"Figure that's better than them?" he asked the General.

"For me, yes."

"Wait until you're sure, okay?"

"I will."

Frank loaded his last full magazine and jacked a round into the chamber. He seated the round and made sure the rifle was on full automatic. He held it to his shoulder with one hand holding the rifle's pistol grip and sighted down the barrel at the lip of the trench. The General probably knows what he's talking about, he thought.

It was then he heard the flutter of helicopter rotors. It was also then six VC appeared on the lip of the trench. He pulled the trigger and swept his sights across them. When the rifle was empty, he knocked the General's rifle from under his chin and rolled on top of him. It wasn't a conscious act, he just did it without thinking. And it wasn't pretty. Frank on top of the General, his chest and arms shielding the General's head and chest, and Frank's butt in the air. And that's when he got his fifth and worst wound of the battle. The round entered his left buttock, passed through the opening next to his sacrum missing his hip and pelvis bones, pierced his colon in two places, and exited from his right side. Frank didn't get to hear the miniguns as the American gunships opened fire and cleared the mountain top of VC.

CHAPTER 10

"Christ, what a mess," Lieutenant Jenkins said.

"Lieutenant, this one's still alive and so is the one under him," the corpsman said. "Hey, this guy's a sailor. Oh shit, it's the General under there. Give me a hand here."

Jenkins and the corpsman rolled Frank off the General and Frank moaned when his hip hit the ground.

"Get me another corpsman over here. Christ, the General must have a dozen wounds. Come on Lieutenant, get on the fucking radio."

Lieutenant Jenkins and his platoon were the first troops on the scene. They assumed all the Americans on the flat had been overrun and were dead. They were almost right. Four men had been found just barely holding on to life at the left end of the trench and now they had two more. And one of them was the General.

Echo Company had been battling a Battalion sized force of mixed North Vietnamese Army (NVA) and Viet Cong (VC) for three days. It was a remnant of the regiment that had fought the Dak To battle a few weeks before. The tide had turned in Echo Company's favor when the VC commander split his force to capture the helicopter. The VC commander probably didn't know that Major General Muldavy and his staff were aboard the helicopter or that the helicopter carried thirty-six shooters, but the helicopter was important itself. The Marines of Echo Company had fought their way up the mountain and made their final push when the gunships arrived.

The gunships had come in low and then up the side of the mountain and caught the VC in the open. There wasn't much left alive on the mountain top when the gunships were done. A few VC had managed to get off the other side of the flat and into the jungle on the side of the mountain, but not many. A medevac slick was waiting to load the General in case they found him alive—or found him at all.

"Corpsman on the way," the Lieutenant said. "He's bringing a stretcher for the General."

"Make that two stretchers," the corpsman said. "This guy has to be evacuated with the General. He's not going to make it much longer without surgery."

"Let's get the General out of here," Jenkins said. "We'll bring in another slick for this guy."

General Muldavy opened his eyes.

"Lieutenant," the General whispered. "Lean

down here."

Jenkins leaned down to hear what the General wanted. He listened as the General spoke in a whisper. Jenkins's face blanched. He keyed his radio.

"Get another stretcher over here, we have two going on the General's slick."

Frank came-to when they slid his stretcher into the Huey. He looked around with his eyes, the image faded, and he let his eyes close slowly.

He regained consciousness again when they pulled his stretcher out of the helicopter. He looked into the beautiful blue eyes of an Air Force nurse. She looked like an OD green angel. She pulled his eyelid back and he moved his eyeball up and down. She smiled. He closed his eyes.

The doctors with typical military efficiency worked on all of Frank's wounds at once while he was in the operating room. After major surgery on his abdominal wound, the calf was cleaned and sutured properly. Miraculously, the bullet that entered his buttock had missed the bone in his pelvis and hip and passed through his midsection without any bone damage or fragments complicating the mess. His insides were cleaned out, his side wound was cleaned and sutured, and a plastic-surgeon dressed his head wound and put cosmetic sutures in. The next time Frank woke up he had tubes attached to various parts of his body and wires running from his chest to various machines. He was in a bed and the angel was watching him. He smiled and closed his eyes.

"Come on, Sailor, it's time for you to wake up."

Frank heard the voice but didn't want to disturb the dream he was having.

"Petty Officer Evans, time to wake up."

He was getting pissed. He scrunched his eyes closed.

"That won't do you any good," the voice said. "I can see your eyes scrunching up. Come on, open the eyes."

He opened his eyes. The fogginess lifted from his vision slowly the way a steamed windshield clears when you turn on the heat. The light hurt at first, but it wasn't bright. He closed his eyes again for a moment and then tried again. Better this time. He moved his eyes around to see where he was. A room. Not a barracks room, a white room. Lots of stuff with green lines moving across dark circles. A hospital room. Hospitals are places where they hurt you. He moved his eyes to the other side and saw the angel looking at him.

"Welcome back," she said. "How are you feeling? Can you talk?"

"Think so," he said, but his voice was just a croak.

"Don't worry, it will get better. Any pain?"

"No."

"Good. The pain will come later as we wean you

off your meds, but for now we'll let you heal."

"My throat is sore. Can I have a drink?"

"Maybe an ice chip. Here, let me put this on your tongue."

He felt the ice on his tongue melt and it was a delicious feeling.

"Another?" he asked.

"Okay. Then we better wait a bit before the next one."

The second chip was just as good as the first. He let his eyes close and drifted off.

Frank didn't know it, but that night his vitals took a nose dive and he was taken back into surgery. He lost a small portion of his colon and the surgeon installed a colostomy bag, but he saved the rest of Frank's colon. The bag would allow his colon to heal. He was out for another twenty-four hours.

"Petty Officer Evans. Come on, time to wake up again."

He opened his eyes and saw his angel watching him. But a leprechaun was sitting on her head. He closed his eyes and opened them again. The Leprechaun was still there and it was smiling at him.

"There's a Leprechaun sitting on your head," he said.

"A what?' the nurse asked.

"A Leprechaun. He's smiling at me."

"Really?"

"Yes."

"Oh my," she said. "I think someone has been under anesthetics too many times. Don't worry, it will pass."

"The Leprechaun?"

"Yes, and anything else you see that's strange."

"There's a blue horse coming through the door. Will you let him pass?"

The nurse frowned and looked at the monitors above him.

"I'm kidding," he said. "You only have a leprechaun."

Angel smiled.

"Kidding is a good sign. Do you really see a Leprechaun?"

"Yes. Do you think he'll go away if I go back to sleep?"

"Why don't you try."

"Okay."

When he woke up again the Leprechaun was gone, but so was his angel. And he felt a new presence. Pain. Pain everywhere. Not crushing pain, just a general ache throughout his whole body, but especially in his stomach. He looked around but everything was still the same. He wondered where his angel was.

He tried to sit up and that was a big mistake. As soon as he contracted his stomach muscles pain hit his midsection with a vengeance. His abs cramped and froze him in position with his shoulders off the bed unable to rise or lay back down. He moaned as beeps started sounding from the machines over his head.

The door to his room flew open and a new green angel rushed in. This one was big and heavy.

"Oh no you don't. Back. Lay back down right now."

"Can't," he said and groaned.

"All right. Let me get my arm behind you. Now relax against my arm. There, that's good. Just relax and let me lower you back."

He relaxed and let her ease him back to the bed.

"What in the world were you trying to do?" she said.

He took a big breath and sank into the mattress. The nurse started pushing buttons on the machines he was connected to. The beeping stopped.

"I was hurting and thought sitting up would help." he said.

"Well don't do that again. Let me check your sutures."

As the nurse lifted the dressings on his abdomen, Frank watched quietly.

"You're a captain," he said.

"Yes, in the nurses corps."

"Do I have to call you Captain or can I just call you nurse?"

"Either will do."

"Nurse what?"

"My, aren't we full of questions. Try Nurse Wiley."

"Thank you, Nurse Wiley. Who is my other nurse?"

"Your day-time nurse is Major Dean. She's your case nurse."

"Thanks. How am I doing?"

"From the sound of all your questions, I'd say you're doing very well."

"No, you know what I mean. I didn't mess up anything. . .you know, anything important?"

"No, I think the doctors put you back together nicely. Nothing is missing."

"Well, that's a relief," he said. "Where am I?"

"Medical command, Saigon. And you will be here probably for two more weeks until they can get you on a medevac flight back to the states."

"The states? I haven't even reported in yet. I was on my way to my new duty station in Danang when all this happened."

"Why don't you rest now. I'm sure someone will answer all your questions now that you seem lucid again. Is your Leprechaun still in the room?"

"No, I'm fine now. One more question. How's the General? He didn't look too good the last time I saw him."

"Which General is that?"

"How many Generals have you got in the hospital? General Muldavy. How is he?"

"General Muldavy is recovering from his wounds nicely. Are you feeling well enough for a visit? I've got a feeling you'll be having some visitors tomorrow."

"Sure. I guess. Who?"

"Wait and see."

He watched Nurse Wiley tape up his bandages.

"How do you become an Air Force Nurse?" he asked.

"Are you sure you want to talk?"

"Yes. I've been asleep too much. I could use some company. Did you go to regular nurses' school or did the Air Force send you?"

Nurse Wiley told Frank about her nursing school and all the things she planned to do. She wanted to become a nurse anesthetist. Frank thought that would be a fascinating job. She had a husband who was also an Air Force nurse and a child she missed very much. He admitted it took a lot of dedication to sacrifice that much. After thirty minutes of talking, Nurse Wiley realized Frank hadn't said one word about his own life or his wounds. She decided he needed some rest. She looked at his chart, made a note, smiled, and left the room. She returned a few moments later with a syringe.

"Relax," she said. "The doctor left orders for this to help you sleep.

Chapter 11

When Frank woke up in the morning Nurse Dean was running her fingers along one of the tubes that connected to a needle in the top of his hand. He didn't say anything and watched instead. She finished her inspection and saw his open eyes watching her.

"How's the pain today?" she asked.

"Not bad right now. My stomach itches though. My head too."

"That's the sutures. Don't worry, I just hooked up a new drip. You shouldn't be having much pain. I just hooked up your breakfast too. Steak and eggs. How's it taste?"

"I wondered what that was. When can I have some coffee?"

"That will be a while I'm afraid. How's your stamina? Are you up for a visitor?"

"I am now. But I don't know how long I'll last."

"Well, I'll see if I can hurry them up. Why don't you rest now? I'll wake you before they get here."

Nurse Dean woke him an hour later and had an orderly come in to shave him. The orderly was tall and thin. He looked like the character called String Bean on the new television show in the states called Hee-Haw. It was a silly program, but he liked it better than Laugh-In. Hee-Haw just tried to be funny and had some good country music. Laugh-in was typical network, too political and too hippie for Frank. The shave felt weird, but for the time being the pain was just a dull ache and he figured he ought to get the visit over. The pain only seemed to take a break a few minutes at a time.

The door opened a few moments after the orderly left and another orderly wheeled General Muldavy in. A major followed him in and a photographer followed the Major. The General looked like hell. He looked shrunken and wrinkled and his eyes had dark rings around them. He was obviously in pain.

"Evans, I can only stay a moment, but I wanted to come and thank you. Major, pin his medal on his pillow."

The General didn't say anymore until the Major had the Purple Heart pinned next to Frank's head.

"You rate four clusters on that," the General said. "And my personal gratitude. If you hadn't rolled on top of me, I wouldn't be here to thank you. That was one of the gutsiest things I have ever witnessed. If it were possible, I would pin more than a purple heart on your pillow, but for now I hope my heartfelt thanks will be enough."

Frank blushed. He found that accepting this gruff man's gratitude was harder than a chewing out.

"I . . . well, it wasn't really. . ." he began to say.

"That's enough of that," Muldavy said, but he smiled. "The proper response to a General Officer of the Naval Service is, Aye, aye, sir."

He smiled and said, "Aye, aye, sir."

"Wheel me over there, Major, and let's get the picture."

With the General sitting next to Frank's bed, the photographer snapped several shots with the General shaking Frank's hand. Actually, the General's hand was just lying on top of Frank's but no one mentioned it. When the pictures were taken and the Major had stepped behind the General's chair to push him out, Muldavy stopped him.

"Evans, why aren't you in the Marine Corps?"

Frank remembered his stock reply about the marital status of his parents, but thought better of voicing it.

"I don't know, sir. The Navy seemed the way to go when I joined. But I'll tell you something. I admired the hell out of those men back on the mountain. And I felt like I belonged."

"If you want to come over, it can be arranged. You'd make a good Marine. Think about it. My aide—my *new* aide—will have your name. Give my office a call."

Later that day Frank had a visit from the Navy. A lieutenant in tropical whites along with a petty officer second class in green utilities visited to let Frank know his sea bag and personnel records had been recovered from the downed helicopter. The petty officer was there to update Frank's records before he was shipped back to the states. The lieutenant interviewed him to give the Navy an explanation for why he hadn't reported in and to get background on Frank's actions while on the mountain. Apparently, Frank had been recommended for a medal by someone in the Marine Corps and the Navy wanted details from the horse's mouth.

While the Lieutenant asked questions and the petty officer took notes, Frank surveyed the Lieutenant's ribbons on his uniform shirt. He had a pretty impressive spread of fruit salad, and above the ribbons he wore an emblem that looked like the eagle on a Budweiser beer bottle except it had a trident and pistol. Navy SEAL, Frank thought. Well, at least he'll know what I'm talking about. Probably why they sent him. The SEAL officer wore four rows of ribbons. He scanned them to see where the officer had been and what he'd done. Ribbons and badges serve a larger purpose than just ego between military men. The insignia and awards serve as a quick summary of the man's career and sometimes, for those who know what to look for, an indication of what kind of man is behind the ribbons. The insignia tells what he does, the branch of specialty he is qualified in, and often any special skills. The ribbons provide a history of significant events in his career, special recognitions, and even where he's served. Ribbons represent medals and are ranked from the top left (the viewer's left) to the bottom right by importance of the medal they represent.

The SEAL officer had the ribbon for a Silver Star in the senior first left position of the top row. The ribbon had a cluster (small oak leaves, stars, or other shapes) indicating he had received the award two times. Next to the Silver star was the Bronze Star with a cluster and next to it was a Navy Commendation Medal with a gold V indicating it was awarded for valor. The rest of the ribbons were campaign ribbons and service medals such as the national defense medal. Frank figured this guy would know the score.

"Tell me about your wounds," the Lieutenant said. "What were you doing when each of them occurred? Start with the first and take them one at a time."

Frank was getting tired and his stomach and head were hurting so he didn't spend a lot of time on detail. And he'd rather talk about the SEAL officer anyway. The officer made him slow down and describe the action and drew the story out of him one wound at a time. By the time Frank got to the General, the SEAL's expression had changed and the petty officer had quit taking notes so he could listen.

"I think I'm beginning to understand the General's recommendation, the officer said. "Tell me,

Evans. It's not important, but I'd like to know for my own reasons. Why did you cover the General with your own body?"

He tried to think back and he tried to understand his own motives. He didn't have a nice pat answer. The sound of explosions and screams from dying men came back and he remembered the hopelessness he felt on the mountain, the feeling of it all being over. He wasn't brave and that wasn't what it was about. He tried to remember some feeling or thought that made him do what he did, but nothing came.

"I'm not sure I can tell you," he said. "The General was hurt and bleeding. He couldn't defend himself, Lieutenant. You know, I wasn't even thinking of him as a General right then. He was just a guy who couldn't do anything for himself and he needed help. I don't remember even thinking about it. I figured I was dead anyway and I just did the only thing left to do. . .Look, sir, I'm starting to hurt pretty bad. Could you call the nurse in here?"

The officer jerked his head at the door and the petty officer left the room. The Seal officer stood and looked at Frank.

"Evans, the letter we got from the General's staff backs up everything you told me. In fact, I was skeptical about their story. You did a hell of a fine job on that mountain. For what it's worth, I can say that because I've been there too. I think the Navy will have a recommendation of their own when your command gets my report."

"Thanks, sir, but can you get the nurse in here?"

The following two weeks were a time of improvements and setbacks for Frank. He felt good, relatively speaking, one day, and the next he begged for pain medicine. His colostomy bag stank, and all his incisions alternately hurt and itched. The wound on his buttock was healing well, but it hurt more than the others and left him without a position of comfort. Sleep only came with the aid of medicine. But the body has its own ways and the day finally came when the doctors felt he was strong enough for medevac to San Diego.

Chapter 12

The flight hadn't been bad and the nurses and medics had taken good care of him. He helped them to pass the seventeen hours by asking them about the medevac job and about their careers. They were busy with other patients, but most of them found time to talk with Frank. He just seemed so darn interested. He was tired when he got to his ward but he was surprised at how good he felt after the long flight. It would have been nice to have had a window to see the coast line as they entered the U.S., but there weren't many windows on the plane. He knew he was home when the pitch of the engines dropped and the big bird banked and the flaps came down. Home. He began to relax.

When he was put in his bed on the ward, a surprise was waiting for him.

"You look like shit," Gunny Garzinski said from the bed next to Frank.

Frank didn't recognize the voice and when he looked he didn't recognize Garzinski at first. Then, slowly, the bruised and stitched face decoded itself for his eyes.

"Damn, Gunny. You don't look so hot yourself. The nurse in Saigon told me they got you out, but they wouldn't tell me anything about your condition. How are you making it?"

"I'll get there. No fun right now, but soon it will be time for some I&I. At least I'm not over there."

"You mean R&R, Rest and Recreation, don't you?"

"No, I mean I&I time."

"What's that?" Frank asked.

"Intercourse and intoxication."

That was pretty good, but Frank didn't feel like laughing.

"Yeah. me too," he said, "but I doubt I could handle either one right now."

"You'll get there. At least you have some nice shiny campaign ribbons."

"Hell, I didn't even get to report in to my unit," Frank said. "Probably won't even get the campaign ribbons."

"You were there. You got a Purple Heart, too. You'll get the ribbons. I hear you saved the General's life."

"Oh hell, not you too. I probably just slipped and fell on top of him. And I got shot in the ass for my clumsiness."

"Ain't what I heard. But whether that was true or not, you did good on that mountain. I wanted to thank you for that. I didn't figure a squid could fight like a Marine. And getting those weapons and ammo off the bird was smart. I didn't even know they were there."

"It was my ass too," Frank said.

"Yeah, I know, that's part of it. But a lot of guys, not knowing what to do and not having any combat experience would have curled up in a hole and hid. You have to learn how to take a compliment, Evans. There's no shame in just saying thank you and shutting up."

"Thank you," he said.

"That's a start. I hear you're coming over to the Marines."

"Where'd you hear that crap?"

"Is it crap?"

"I've never told anyone I was considering a service transfer. One damn fight doesn't make a Marine, Gunny. But one fight like that one will make you think long and hard about ever being a Marine."

"Somebody thinks you're considering it. Well it's early yet. You're still healing and all."

"Not that I'm even thinking about it, but could I keep my rank if I did?"

"I guess so," Garzinski said. "We're Navy Department too. And besides, a General can do anything he wants to do."

"What's the General got to do with it?"

"He didn't talk to you about it?"

"Well, yeah, he mentioned it. But we didn't

really talk about it. He just said to call his office if I was interested."

"There it is."

"What?"

"A General can do anything he wants to do. I'll tell you something I never thought I would say to a sailor. You'd make a good Marine, Evans. Want some advice?"

"Sure."

"If the General wants you, it could be a good life. I figure he wants to do some pay-back. He probably figures he owes you and he'll probably take care of you."

"He doesn't owe me anything. Hell, Gunny, he doesn't have to do that."

"You didn't have to take a bullet for him either. I told you, you have to learn how to take a compliment. Do you want to be a Marine?"

"I don't know, damn it. I liked being part of that platoon on the mountain. Man, it felt right. You know what I mean?"

"Yeah. I saw it. The Marines accepted you and accepted your leadership too. You're staying in, aren't you?"

"Yeah, I'll put my twenty in. Hard not to now."

"As I said, you'd make a good Marine. If you're going to make it a career you ought to be where you belong. I think you'd be making a mistake if you didn't take the General up on his offer. I told you on the plane when we came into Vietnam, your skills would be appreciated in the Corps. I watched you tear down that Fifty in the middle of a battle."

"Hell, that wasn't anything special," he said. "It's what I do."

"There it is."

"Do you know what I'd have to do? What kind of training I'd have to take?"

"Recruit Training for sure. You aren't a Marine until your drill instructor pins the globe on you no matter what the General does for you. But hell, Evans, you can handle that. It's a bitch, sure, but after what you've been through, a piece of cake."

The Gunny looked away and grinned an evil grin.

"And besides," he said. "You got time in service. You're an E6 in the Navy. Maybe you'll have to train as a corporal and do some time as a squad leader, but I'll bet the General will get you in the right MOS and see that you get your stripes back inside of a year. That, the General *can* take care of."

"I wish you hadn't even mentioned it," Frank said. "I was feeling pretty good till now. Now you have me thinking about it."

"All right. Let me help you. What do you like most about the Corps?"

"Well," he said. "I like a uniform that has pockets and a zipper in the trousers."

The Gunny grinned and shook his head. "That's a start, I guess. Okay, no more thirteen button, bell bottoms and you get pockets in the front. But you probably ought to have more reason than that for joining the Corps."

"Just kidding," Frank said. "My dad was a Marine in World War Two, and I almost joined the Corps instead of the Navy to start with. But that's not all of it. Gunny, what got me thinking about it was the way you put that platoon together on the mountain. You started with a bunch of guys from different units that didn't know each other and ended up with a functioning platoon in just a few minutes. And every one of them did their job even when it got bad. I don't know. Not one bitch the whole time. That's something worth being part of."

"You're right. That's exactly what the Corps is all about. You'll hear all kinds of motivational bullshit on the Island, but all of it boils down to what you just said. Give me forty Marines from anywhere in any specialty and I can make a functioning infantry platoon out of them in thirty minutes."

"What Island?"

"Parris Island, of course. I suspect you'll find out all about the Island not long after you're recovered. Give the General a call."

"What if..."

"Evans! Shut up and let me get some sleep."

He was in Naval Hospital San Diego for two months. At the end of the first month, the surgeons removed the colostomy bag. For three days he waited for his colon to begin functioning. The nurses checked on him every hour. At first, he just had a lot of gas, but finally the cramps started and shortly after that he had his first bowel movement. Over the next week, his bowels began to function normally and regularly. His side healed into a pinkish puckered scar and the gouge in his calf filled in with more pinkish scar tissue by the end of the second month. The hair along the scar on his head began to grow back, but it would never completely cover the scar. The scar itself filled in nicely, and other than the redness, he had only a slightly jagged but very thin line that ran from his left eyebrow into his hair line and stopped in a depression in the middle of his scalp. But a small piece of his eyebrow was missing and wouldn't grow back. Frank didn't mind. It gave him a slightly roguish appearance. Or at least he thought so.

By week six, he was allowed to sit up in a chair for his meals, and physical therapy started. The Abs exercises were the worse. His abdominal muscles had shrunk and had to be stretched. In week seven, Frank was allowed to walk the hallway several times a day and make trips to the hospital PX when he wanted. Before one of his walks, he dug out the General's card and walked to the phone in the communications center.

He sat in front of the phone and stared at it for several minutes. His hand snaked out toward the handset, but was snatched back at the last moment. He stared some more. Did he really want to do this? Could he function as a boot again after being a senior Petty Officer? It would only be for three months. Still. . .could he put up with the crap he was going to get? Three months. Take the crap. Then he'd be a senior NCO again, if Ski knew what he was talking about. He reached for the phone and dialed the number.

"General Muldavy's office. Sergeant Major Cooper speaking, sir."

"Sergeant Major, this is Frank Evans. I'm a Navy Gunners mate and I served with General Muldavy in Vietnam. Is he in?"

"What's the call is in reference to, Evans?"

"Well. . .We talked about something in Saigon and he. . .well, he said to call if I was interested."

The phone was silent for a moment and then he heard the Sergeant Major speak to someone else through the covered mouthpiece.

"Let me transfer you to the General's Aide. Hold one."

The wait wasn't long. In a few seconds Frank heard a click in the phone.

"This is Captain Sharp. Can I help you?"

Frank went through it all again and started to say he would call back at another time, but Sharp interrupted him.

"Wait a minute. Did you say Frank Evans?"

"Yes, sir"

"You were with the General when he was wounded?"

"Yes, sir."

"Sorry, Evans. I shouldn't have missed that. I'm

aware of your conversation with the General. The General is on medical leave right now. But I'll be talking to him in about an hour."

"How is the General, sir? He looked pretty bad when I saw him at the hospital in Saigon."

"He's recovering nicely. They have him taking long walks now and he's getting some of his weight back. If I had missed this call, he would have shown me just how much better he is. How are you doing, Evans? He'll want to know."

"I'm doing good, sir. Please don't trouble the General on my part. I'm up and walking now, and everything seems to be healing well. I don't want to disturb him, but he said to call if I was interested in transferring to the Marine Corps."

"Are you?"

"Yes, sir. I've been talking with Gunny Garzinski. He was with us on the mountain too. He's doing good also. Anyway, I am interested, but I'd like to talk to someone who could tell me what I need to know about what an inter-service transfer would involve, you know, what I have to do and what training I'd have to take. And if I get to keep my stripes. Somebody official that can give me the straight skinny."

"Tell you what," Sharp said. "Let me talk to the General first and then we can see about getting someone out there to see you. You're at San Diego?"

"Yes, sir. The Naval Hospital."

"All right. I already have your official information. Expect a visit from an officer that can answer your questions."

"Thank you, sir. Please give the General my best."

"I will. Good to hear from you, Evans. You must be one hell of a sailor for the General to want you in his Corps."

"Thank you, sir. I've got to get back to the Ward. Thanks for your help."

When he was in his bed on the ward again, he wondered if he was doing the right thing. Maybe he should have waited and thought on it more. Christ this was a big step. Ski had been transferred to the hospital at Camp Pendleton so Frank didn't have anyone he trusted to talk to. But the idea of being a Marine, being part of something that lasts a lifetime, had grown in his mind every day since Ski left. He'd probably already seen the worst a Marine could ever expect to see, so why not? After the mountain the thought of returning to a Navy base or ship and sitting in an armory repairing small arms didn't hold much appeal. The thought of being a Marine wouldn't leave him alone.

With the General involved, things moved quickly. A Major from Camp Pendleton showed up on the ward the next morning. He obtained Frank's service record and made notes before seeking out Frank. Next, he spoke with Frank's doctors and got an estimated date for his return to duty and their best guess at the recovery period before he could participate in anything as demanding as Marine Corps Recruit Training. With that out of the way he sought out Frank.

"Petty Officer Evans?"

"Yes, sir."

"I'm Major Gray. Marine Corps Headquarters asked me to stop by and answer your questions in regard to an inter-service transfer to the Marine Corps."

"That was quick," Frank said. "Thanks for coming."

"I understand that General Muldavy has an interest in this request."

"I wasn't going to mention that, sir. Sorry. I'm not trying to use any special influence."

"Relax. I was just interested. How do you know the General?"

"I don't really know him, Major. I don't want to give that impression. We were only together for a few hours."

"Evans, relax. Am I going to have to pull this out of you one question at a time? Relax, I'm on your side. What was the occasion that brought you to the attention of a General officer?"

Frank still wasn't comfortable with name dropping so he hedged.

"I was on the mountain with him when he was wounded."

"The mountain?"

Then a light went on in the Major's brain and it showed in his eyes.

"You're him! You're the sailor that. . ."

"Major, please. I've been through this too many times. Yes, I'm that sailor."

"The Marine Corps is a small service, Evans. Word gets around pretty fast. Okay, I think I understand some things now. What do you need to know?"

"First of all, is a transfer possible?"

"I don't see why not. Your skill rating is a critical skill in the Corps. You apparently are qualified as a 2111 weapons repairman right now. You have a clean record, an exemplary one, in fact."

"If I transfer, will I keep my rank?"

"Apparently the answer is yes, with a caveat. You'll have to complete Marine Corps Recruit Training and demonstrate proficiency in your skill. During recruit training you will hold the rank of recruit, but you will be paid as an E6. You will be raised to Staff Sergeant at some point after graduating from training. I wasn't aware of this kind of transfer. It's a bit unusual for the Corps. Normally, if there is a normal for this situation, you would have to take a reduction in grade to E3 to get the experience you'll need to function as a staff sergeant. But headquarters informed me, in your case, you will retain your rank."

"If I put in for the transfer, what happens next?"

"Evans, I'm not sure. With General Muldavy behind it, I suspect the paperwork will go through quickly. But I'm not sure where you'll be until your orders come through. A lot depends on when the Doctors release you for that kind of duty. I assume the Navy will control that. Would you like me to assemble the paperwork for you?"

"Yes, sir. I'd appreciate that. But I'm expecting orders. The Docs said I can be released soon."

"Okay. I'll send a personnel sergeant over with the paperwork tomorrow. By the way, have you received the citation for your medal yet?"

"I got my purple heart in Saigon. I haven't seen a citation though."

"The purple heart with clusters is already in your record. The citation for your medal should have arrived by now. I'll check with the Navy. The General was interested."

"Nope, haven't seen it."

"Okay. Any other questions?"

"No, sir. I'm good to go."

"You sound like a Marine already. Hang loose tomorrow so the sergeant can find you."

Chapter 13

December in Washington D.C. is cold, especially for a man who has spent the previous four months in Vietnam and San Diego. Frank Evans was released from the San Diego hospital to limited duty and received orders to report to Naval Detachment, Quantico Marine Corps Base, Virginia. His transfer to the Marine Corps had been approved, but he couldn't be ordered to Parris Island for recruit training until the Navy released him for full duty, and he had to remain in the Navy until he was fully recovered. His medical records were transferred to Bethesda Naval Hospital in Bethesda, Maryland, just outside of Washington D.C. He had to report twice a week for examination and therapy.

General Muldavy couldn't get Frank into the Corps until Frank was physically ready, so he did the next best thing in his opinion. He pulled some strings at the Pentagon and had him assigned to the small Navy

Detachment at Quantico. He also let people at Quantico know he expected the Marines to prepare him for Parris Island while he was recovering. Generals can grease a lot of wheels, especially in the Marine Corps. It's a small service and it doesn't have a lot of Generals.

Muldavy had fully recovered from his wounds, but he still had nerve pain to remind him of that night on the mountain. He wouldn't forget that night, the night he had come so close to death, and he wouldn't forget Frank Evans. Frank's career was now in General Muldavy's hands. Muldavy wanted him in the Corps and on Muldavy's staff. It wasn't completely rational, but Muldavy owed more than his life to Frank and he meant to repay that debt by seeing that he was taken care of. He remembered the feel of the M-16 muzzle under his chin and how close he came to taking his own life. And actually, taking care of Frank's career was a small task for a General. Sure, he had to follow regulations like anyone else. But Generals often made the regulations and they knew how to make the regulations work for them. For Generals, regulations were a guide, not direction. God help the man who came between General Muldavy and payment of his debt.

When Frank reported in for duty at Quantico, he still had most of six months' pay on the books and he still had most of his previous reenlistment bonus in the bank in addition to the savings he had built up while he was on sea duty. He wasn't a hell raiser or a spend thrift. He had his fun, but he saved his money. The first thing he did when he got to Virginia was buy a car and the second thing he did was sign up for Commuted Rations, money in lieu of eating in the mess hall, and housing allowance to get a pad on the beach. Since the base didn't have berthing for Navy NCOs, E6s and above were allowed to live on the beach and draw housing allowance if they chose. "On the beach" is a term sailors used for anyplace off the ship or off base even if there wasn't a beach within a thousand miles. He bought a used 1965 Impala SS with four on the floor and rented an apartment in a garden apartment complex not far from the base. His housing allowance and Com-Rats covered the cost of the apartment and even left him a little for beer.

The Navy at Quantico had been given the word about Frank. The day he reported and checked in, the Detachment Commander assigned him to the Armory supporting the Marine Corps Officer Basic Course. That was the last contact he had with the Navy except to pick up his pay check.

Frank spent five months at Quantico and he was released for full duty in April. The Marines had been thorough in getting him in shape. By the time his orders came, he was doing full PT with the Marines in the morning and running with the company every day. He passed the Marine Corps PFT in April. The Marines also worked with Frank on Corps history and chain of command. They helped him to memorize the general orders until he could recite which ever order was called for and do it in his sleep if necessary. They drilled him in manual of arms and marching drill. He even learned to understand the strange sounding Marine Corps cadence calls that sounded like a foreign language spoken with a mouth full of cookie dough. At first they sounded like, Har rar harar har, hurar har har hurar. Hua rar! raaaa Har! Hoard har! It made sense when you learned the language. Frank was as ready for Parris Island as the Marines at Quantico could make him.

His orders came in early May and the Marines held a sendoff beer-bust for him. Wives came too. During his time at Quantico, several of the Marine NCOs invited him home for dinner and talk. The wives enjoyed talking with Frank and he, being single, became a project. Also, the invitations might have had something to do with his reputation for bringing steaks when he visited. Frank became fair game for sisters, cousins, neighbors, and any single female known to the wives.

He took a lot of ribbing about what he was facing on the Island. When he asked a Marine for details, the Marine would look at him and laugh. That didn't give him a warm and fuzzy, as they say in the Navy. The day he checked-out from the base his Marine buddies helped him pack and gave him a lot of useless general advice. "Keep your mouth shut." "Listen up at all times." "Do what you are told immediately." "Don't make eye contact." "Get motivated." It was well intended, but useless. No matter what you have been told, nothing can truly prepare you for Parris Island.

He was a little perplexed when he checked-out to leave for Parris Island. The Navy couldn't find his records. Normally when a sailor transfers, he carries his personnel file and his pay records with him. But this time he was given an honorable discharge from the Navy and signed enlistment papers for the Marine Corps at the same time. He was informed that his records would be sent to Marine Corps Headquarters. He finally got all of the paperwork done and was told to report to the Marine Corps recruiting office in Arlington, Virginia in the morning for travel and reporting instructions.

Frank was authorized POV (Privately owned Vehicle) for travel to Parris Island in South Carolina and his orders authorized vehicle storage by the housing office on base. Highly unusual. The recruiters in Arlington couldn't remember ever having seen orders like his. The recruiters provided him a voucher for a hotel where he would hook up with other recruits and ride the infamous night bus to the equally infamous yellow footprints. And thus it began.

Chapter 14

The beginning of recruit training was as shocking to the system and unpleasant for Frank as it was for every other recruit in his training command. He had a slight advantage over the other recruits in that he had already been through Navy boot camp and knew when to sound off and when to keep his mouth shut. He already knew much of what the recruits would have to memorize and he was in shape. He was also already familiar with Naval terminology such as head for bathroom, deck for floor, overhead for ceiling, and ladder for stairs, so the recruit environment wasn't completely strange, as it was for the eighteen-year-old boots. And the biggie: he knew weapons and he knew how to shoot, knew how to shoot the way the Marine Corps Corporals taught it at Camp Pendleton. He could field strip and properly maintain his rifle as soon as he received it.

But his prior service was more disadvantage

than advantage. He had been a senior NCO in the Navy with privilege and authority. Now he was a recruit again without authority or privilege, a form of sub-human without even the right to refer to himself in first person. But he toughed it out.

Through the first two and half months he managed to keep his military past to himself. His drill instructors weren't completely fooled though, just mystified. He handled weapons too well, he had too much military bearing, and he had scars. Combat Marines knew what scars from bullets and shrapnel looked like.

When it came to maneuvers, combat gear, uniforms, and daily Marine Corps life, Frank was on a level with his fellow recruits. He made the same dumb mistakes and got chewed out just as much as the rawest recruit. He did his share of extra duty on the quarter deck and spent his time in the sandpits getting motivated. And he fit in well with the other recruits. They enjoyed having someone to talk to about home. His maturity, obvious interest in their stories, and in them as people made him the de facto recruit leader in his platoon even when the DIs wished it to be otherwise. The recruits began calling him the old man. So while Frank's maturity and weapon skills were a mystery that itched at the Drill Instructor's curiosity, he managed to stay under their radar for most of his training.

But Generals have influence, and even if used only to check up on progress, it is felt. Marine Corps

NCOs are finely attuned to influence. And in Marine recruit training the DIs curiosity is always satisfied.

"Recruit Evans, report to the Senior Drill Instructor immediately."

"Sir, aye, aye, sir!"

He made a quick motion to smooth his bunk and looked around quickly to make sure his area was squared away before he double-timed to the Senior DIs office.

Drill Instructor Asshole, the second hat, had been on Frank's ass since he started training. For some reason DI Asshole was personally offended that Frank at twenty-six years old wanted to be a Marine and furthermore had the audacity to try. And, perhaps, he was a little irritated with the respect Frank's platoon gave him. His name wasn't really Asshole. It was actually Ashow pronounced ass-how. It was just too good for the recruits to pass up. When he got to Senior Drill Instructor Wallace's office, Asshole was already there waiting. Crap!

"Sir, Recruit Evans reporting as ordered, sir!

"Stand at ease, Evans."

That was unusual and put him on his guard. He shifted from attention to a rigid parade rest. Drill Instructors being nice meant trouble.

"Evans it's time to level with me. What the hell is going on with you?"

"Sir, this recruit doesn't know what the Senior Drill Instructor means, sir."

"Evans, answer the question or you will be eating sand for a week," DI Asshole said.

"Staff Sergeant Ashow, wait outside please," Wallace said. "Hang around. I want to talk to you when I'm done here."

"As the Senior Drill Instructor wishes," Ashow said and left, closing the door.

"I said at ease, Evans, not parade rest. And just for the next few minutes you don't have to shout. Talk to me like a normal human being."

Uh oh, Frank thought. He relaxed marginally.

"Now let me explain what I mean," Wallace said. "Something isn't right with you. First, you are not our normal recruit. You are twenty-six for one thing and while most twenty-somethings are seeking out any deferment they can get, you enlisted in the Marine Corps. You qualified expert on your weapon on the first range. You handle it like an expert. Throughout the snapping-in you knew exactly what to do. I'd say you probably did something with firearms before you entered the Marine Corps. Am I right?"

"Sir, this recruit is a qualified gunsmith, sir."

"Thought so. Strange that nothing to that effect is in your file. In fact, it's strange that I only have excerpts from your file and none of what I have tells me anything about you prior to entering recruit training. Do you know why that is, Recruit Evans?"

"Sir, this recruit hasn't seen his file, sir."

"Um hum. Strip to the waist, Evans."

"What?"

"Lost your military bearing, Evans. I said strip to the waste."

Frank complied immediately.

Wallace looked him over and made angles with his hands, considering what he was seeing.

"Looks like you took one across the ribs. Probably just a glancing hit and didn't break any ribs. That pucker is an exit wound. The scar over your eye was probably shrapnel and the tip of your earlobe probably was the victim of a stray round. From the shape of the pucker scar, I'd say you probably have a similar entry scar on your ass. Prior service?"

Frank hesitated.

"Answer me, Evans. I am getting very pissed at this point. These are things I should have known. And I shouldn't have been left to figure it out myself. It makes me feel like my own command doesn't trust me. Now, what the hell is up with you?"

"Sir, this recruit..."

"I said you can knock off the recruit bullshit for now. Just tell me what the hell is going on."

"Sir, this recruit is prior service, sir" Frank said while tucking his utilities in. Even when told to, knocking off the recruit "bullshit" wasn't easy.

"What branch? Army?"

"Navy."

"Navy? What was your rate?"

"Gunners mate."

"Small arms or artillery?" Wallace asked.

"Small arms up to and including crew served."

"Where did you learn to shoot like you did on qualifications?"

"At Pendleton. I had two weeks intensive training before I went to Vietnam. If you ever find my service jacket, you'll find I qualified for Marine Corps expert badges for rifle and pistol."

"How in the hell did you. . .no, not now. I'll need it all eventually, but we don't have time now. What happened to your service jacket?"

"Senior Drill Instructor, I don't know. When I did the discharge from the Navy to enlist in the Corps, they told me my records would be forwarded to Marine Headquarters. I haven't seen them since."

Wallace tapped his fingers on the desk and watched Frank for a few moments.

"Well, that explains some things," he said finally. "I was going to ask you why I get inquiries about your progress every two weeks. I asked the Captain, but he just shrugs off the question. So, why am I getting the inquiries? Who's watching over you?"

"Sergeant Wallace, I told Captain Sharp that I didn't want any special treatment."

"Who the hell is Captain Sharp?"

"He's General Muldavy's Aide."

"Major General Muldavy?"

"Yes, sir."

"Christ this is getting more and more confusing. How'd we get from your service jacket to General Muldavy?"

"Senior Drill Instructor, I'd rather not say. I'll be

glad to tell you after I graduate."

Wallace spoke quietly, but the sound was not comforting. "Evans, if you think you can drop names like that and then tell me to butt out, you are out of your fucking mind. Now, you better have one hell of a story if you want to graduate at all."

He took a deep breath and let it out slowly. He figured this day would come, but he had hoped it wouldn't come until after boot camp. Well, graduation was two weeks away. The DIs had already let up on the Mickey Mouse bullshit and were teaching instead of harassing. And he had come this far on his own merits. He was sure of that. He looked Sergeant Wallace in the eye and told his story. It took a while and DI asshole interrupted once, but Wallace told him to wait and listened to the whole story.

"So," Frank said in conclusion, "There it is."

Wallace just stared at him for a few moments. Frank couldn't read his face. Wallace just stared with a blank look, then he blinked.

"I heard part of that story recently when I talked to an old buddy of mine. He's been out of action for a while. He recently transferred in here on temporary duty. He's over on Main Side working in security. Ever heard of Gunnery Sergeant Garzinski?"

"I know the Gunny," Frank said. "He was with us on the mountain. We were in the hospital in San Diego together too. The Gunny is one of the reasons I wanted to join the Corps."

Wallace stared some more. He took a deep

breath and seemed to reach a decision. He let his breath out slowly.

"Evans, I should have known about all this when you got here, but maybe I can see why this information was held back. I'm not sure, but maybe. And I'll give you this, you never tried to use it for your own benefit. What was your rank in the Navy?"

"Petty Officer First Class."

"E-six," Wallace said. "How much of a bust did you have to take to join the Corps?

"I'm supposed to be able to sew on staff stripes sometime after graduation. Not sure how or when. I'm qualified in MOS 2111, weapons repair."

"Christ, this is the screwiest thing I've ever heard of. Look, I've got to think about this. You are still a recruit and you will be one until I pin the globe and anchor on you. Nothing has changed. Stand up. Attention. Recruit Evans, return to your squad."

"Sir, aye, aye, sir."

Frank did an about face, opened the door and marched out.

"Staff Sergeant Ashow, you can come in now."

Ashow sat in the chair in front of Wallace's desk and waited to be told what was going on.

"Ed, you've been riding Evan's ass pretty hard. Want some advice?"

"Did that little prick complain? I'll put his ass in the pit until sand comes out his ears. That little bastard. . ."

"Ed, I asked you if you wanted some advice."

"What?"

"Lay off Evans. I'm not telling you to make it easy for him. Treat him like any other recruit, but lay off the crap you've been dishing out since he got here. Everybody in the Platoon knows you have it in for him. Okay, you've made your point, and he toughed it out. He deserves some respect."

"What's going on?"

"Just take my advice, okay? It's way, way, way above your pay grade."

"He's got a Rabbi?"

"You don't even want to know."

Ashow did lay off with the extra grief he had been giving Frank, but that just made him take special delight in the tongue lashings he gave Frank when it was justified. He had to be careful though. Wallace implied Evans had a Rabbi, a term he and Wallace had borrowed from cop novels meaning a high level protector and mentor. On top of that, Evans's shooting had helped win two trophies in marksmanship for the platoon, a fact that was enjoyed by and benefited the drill instructors also. Ashow was an asshole at heart, but he was also adept at looking out for Ashow.

Chapter 15

The final field problem lived up to everything the rumors had made it out to be. Long marches, little sleep, lousy food, and plenty of harassment. But putting together everything he had learned to solve field problems made the challenge interesting, gave Frank confidence, and made him feel like a Marine. He could understand the Marines back on the mountain in Vietnam better now and his respect for the Corps had grown almost into a religion. In its slow grinding way, the Marine Corps reformed Frank into a Marine. No surprise there. In Marine Recruit Training, you are either motivated, or you get motivated. There isn't any other choice.

DI Asshole had let up on the mickey mouse crap and Frank rechristened him with his proper name. Maybe he wasn't such an asshole after all. Frank sang cadence as loud and emotional as any of the younger recruits on the final march back to the barracks. Marine Day tomorrow. That's when the DIs would pin the globe and anchor on the recruits giving them the right to call themselves Marines. They would get their orders later that day and graduation would be on the following day. Then, ten days leave.

He didn't have any idea where he would be stationed. Infantry school wasn't in the picture if Staff Sergeant stripes were in his near future. But they might keep him a private until he finished training. He doubted he would get ITR even though most of the platoon would be sent there next prior to getting orders to Vietnam. He also doubted he would be assigned as a platoon sergeant without infantry training. But a special skill MOS seemed to make sense. Probably as an infantry weapons repairman, and then a weapons platoon. He wouldn't know if he had been given a MOS school until the orders came in. Staff stripes wouldn't make him stand out in a specialty school, so he hoped for that—and hoped the stripes would come soon. Being a private in the Corps really sucked.

Frank hadn't thought much about the General since his talk with Senior Drill Instructor Wallace. When he put his feet on those yellow footprints that first night on the Island, he had assumed he was on his own. His treatment as a recruit convinced him that no one was doing him any favors. Wallace's talk had bothered Frank, but nothing came of it. He hoped they would find his records before he was transferred.

When the platoon was dismissed at the barracks to police the area and prepare for chow, Senior Drill Instructor Wallace called to Frank and told him to meet with the Drill Instructors in the Senior DI's office. He double timed to the office and stood at Parade rest at the door.

Wallace and his DI's filed in and then Wallace called Frank in.

"Recruit Evans, you have been designated an honor graduate. Your academic scores and marksmanship are outstanding. Congratulations."

"Sir, this recruit thanks the Senior Drill Instructor, sir."

"I'm glad to be the one to inform you. What this means for the short term is you will be allowed to wear the dress blue bravo uniform for graduation. Describe that uniform, Recruit."

"Sir, the dress blue bravo uniform is the same as the dress blue alphas, but with ribbons and marksmanship awards instead of full dress medals, sir."

"Have you ordered dress blues, Evans."

"Sir, dress blues are an optional uniform and this recruit has not purchased the uniform, sir"

"Can you afford to purchase dress blues and would you like to do so?"

"Sir, this recruit can afford the uniform and this recruit would like to purchase one, sir."

"Sergeant Collins, you will escort honor

graduate Evans to the tailor at the PX on Main Side and assist him in purchasing his uniform and assure that the tailor can have it delivered in time for the ceremony."

"Aye, aye, Senior Drill Instructor."

"And just so Honor Graduate Evans will not be out of uniform on graduation day, you will also help him purchase the ribbons for the National Defense Medal, the Vietnam Service Medal, the Vietnam Campaign ribbon, and the Purple Heart medal with four clusters and a rack to mount four ribbons on. You will also purchase expert badges for the rifle and pistol."

"Sir, this recruit rates the Navy good conduct medal also, sir."

"Make that a rack to mount five ribbons, and find the GCM ribbon." Wallace said.

"What the hell is going on?" Ashow said.

"Ditto," Collins said. "What the hell, Gunny?"

"You are addressing the Senior Drill Instructor," Wallace said.

"Then what the hell is this all about, Senior Drill Instructor?"

"Gentlemen, I have a bit of information I'd like to share. It is information that only recently came to my attention. Recruit Evans is prior service and was wounded in combat near Dak To in the Central Highlands with a Marine unit. When he was fully recovered, he had the good sense to realize he belonged in the U. S. Marine Corps. Part of the reason we didn't know these things is that Recruit Evans wanted to complete recruit training on his own merit without his medals influencing the staff. The other part is that his records were lost by the Navy. Personally, I think Evans's reason deserves respect. Sergeant Collins, take charge of your detail."

Once away from the recruit environment, Collins actually treated Frank like a human being. He seemed like a pretty decent guy. Collins guided him through the purchase and made sure he had all parts of the uniform. Frank was easy to fit. His measurements were already on file from his fitting for his service uniforms. The tailor promised Frank's dress blues would be delivered to the barracks in time for the graduation. What he didn't know was an order for his dress blues had already been placed and the tailor had only been waiting to verify Frank's measurements. The uniform was already available and most of the work was already done. Next, Collins helped him pick out his ribbons and marksmanship badges. They took them back to the tailor and asked him to pin them on in the proper places before he delivered the uniform.

The following day the Platoon received their globe and anchors. Most of the recruits had trouble holding back the tears, including Frank. Many failed to hold them back. What they had been through to earn the right to be called Marines was harder than anything any of them had ever imagined, harder than anything most of them would ever go through again. The platoon was given the afternoon to prepare their uniforms for the graduation ceremony, and of course, to clean the barracks, stand fire watches, clean weapons, complete extra duty, form up for chow, and all of the other daily tasks that made a Marine recruit's day interesting including one final drill to make sure the platoon was prepared for the parade deck. Ashow assigned Frank to fire watch for four hours to allow the others some extra time. He didn't mind. His uniform was being prepared for him.

He took a lot of ribbing from the rest of the platoon, but it was good natured. At that point, the new Marines had nothing but good nature. It was over. They were U.S. Marines. Home the next day. Frank had made a lot of friends during recruit training. He was older, but Marine recruit training grinds equally on all recruits. He hoped those friendships would survive his Staff Sergeant stripes. But most of the platoon would never know. They would be gone as soon as the ceremony was over. But right then everyone was waiting for Senior DI Wallace to show up and tell them where they were going.

Wallace arrived at 1800 and gathered the platoon into a circle and told them to sit and relax. He pulled a chair to the center of the circle and put his clip board on his lap. He began reading names with newly assigned specialties. Most got Infantry and would be heading to ITR after their leave. Wallace started out alphabetically, but when he got to the E's he skipped over Evans. Frank waited, not wanting to interrupt and thereby delaying someone else from finding out what their assignment was. He waited, but the question burned in his mind.

"And that finishes it," Wallace said. "Except for Evans. Evans, your orders are on hold. I don't know what the problem is, but I'm sure you'll find out tomorrow."

"Sir, this recruit. . ."

"You're a Marine now, Private Evans. You may talk like a human being."

"Gunny Wallace, didn't they tell you anything at all?"

"Just that there were some last minute changes. That's all I have. Be patient, Marine. The Corps moves at its own pace."

"Thank you, Senior Drill Instructor."

The tailor did better than he promised and Frank's dress blues were delivered that evening and as promised his ribbons and badges were all in place. The rest of the platoon not on watch gathered around as he lifted the plastic to see how good the blues looked. Frank got confused when he lifted the plastic. The uniform didn't look right. For one thing the trousers had a red strip down each leg. NCO stripes. For another, the sleeves of the jacket had staff sergeant stripes on them and one hash mark. And there was a sword and scabbard hanging from the hanger hook. The squad bay had suddenly become very quiet.

"Whose uniform is that?" one of the recruits behind him asked.

"Mine, I guess," he said.

"You're a staff sergeant? Bullshit."

"Hey, there's an envelope inside of the blouse."

"Crap!" he said. "Can you all back off for a minute? Let me figure this out."

Frank took the envelope out and opened it. He took out a card. The card had a USMC command seal embossed at the top and a note in handwriting below.

"With my complements, Major General Patrick Muldavy USMC."

The ribbons were right and the badges were right also. What was with the sword? He looked at the card again and tried to figure out what it meant. Then the voice of Gunnery Sergeant Wallace sounded behind Frank and the platoon.

"Private Evans. If you were to put that uniform on tonight I would have to write you up for being out of uniform and impersonating an NCO. But if you were to put it on at 0001 of the coming day I would address you as Staff Sergeant Frank Evans. Your orders came in, Evans. This was the hold up.

Another voice chimed in. "And I expect to be here at 0001 to show you how it all goes together and to instruct you in how to mount and wear the USMC NCO Sabre." The voice belonged to Gunnery Sergeant Garzinski.

He just stared at the stripes on his new uniform. He couldn't talk and didn't even reply to Wallace's announcement or acknowledge Garzinski's presence.

"Except for Private Evans—Platoon, fall in at the

quarter deck," Wallace said. "You deserve an explanation."

When it was quiet again and the platoon was at the other end of the squad bay, Garzinski moved up to stand next to Frank.

"Pretty things, ain't they?"

"I feel like a phony," he said. "Christ, I'm just a boot."

"Don't. You've seen more actual combat in one day and night than many of these young men will see in their entire enlistment. And, hopefully, you took more wounds than any of them will have to suffer. And don't forget. You led Marines in combat."

"There wasn't much leading involved," he said.

"Yes there was. They relied on your knowledge and followed you to that chopper many times. Frank, the General came through for you. This is a big deal. Don't cheapen it."

He stared at the stripes on his new uniform and then he smiled.

"Yeah, he did, didn't he? And I'm a Marine now. And I got it the right way. Shit, Gunny, I wouldn't want to go through that again."

"The mountain?"

"Hell, no. Boot camp."

Garzinski slapped Frank on the back and laughed.

"I know the feeling," he said. "Well, come on. Let's take this thing down to the Senior's office and get you suited up."

"It's not midnight yet."

"Formalities. I won't tell if you won't. Don't worry, Wallace is onboard."

Garzinski helped him with the uniform and then showed him how to mount the Sabre.

"You won't be required to draw the sabre. That's only for NCOs leading troops. The General wanted you to wear it, though, in recognition of your work on the mountain."

"Where did the sabre come from?"

"His gift. He wanted too. The blues too."

"You talked to him?"

"Hell yes. You haven't figured it out? I work for him now. He's had me down here doing some mickey mouse shit over on Main Side, but I was really here to make sure nobody screwed with you."

"Oh shit, Gunny, he didn't interfere with my training, did he?"

"No. And neither did I. It was just in case."

"Okay. So what happens tomorrow? I mean, you know, a staff sergeant graduating from boot camp. That's got to raise some eyebrows."

"You don't know? Crap. I guess Wallace didn't get around to it yet. Look, the General is attending the graduation. He's the guest speaker. He's got some kind of recognition for you."

"Recognition?"

"Yeah. I can't talk about it, but he's going to call

you up to the podium."

"Oh crap! Shouldn't someone have told me about this?"

"Well, yeah, but Muldavy is keeping it pretty quiet. Look, it's no big deal. He'll call for you to post front and center. You go up to the podium, he says a few words, you go back to your formation. Easy."

"That's all? You're sure?"

"Yeah, yeah. Nothing to it."

Chapter 16

Graduation day. The platoon didn't have to be wakened. Few managed any sleep the previous night. Everywhere Frank looked, men were making final adjustments to their green service uniforms and preparing to form up and march to the parade deck. In the middle of a sea of green, his midnight blue jacket with red trimmed stripes and hash marks, white web belt with gold waist plate, sky blue trousers with red stripe, white gloves, and white barracks cover stood out like the stars and stripes over a cornfield. In his utilities he looked like the Marine he had become. In his dress blues he was a recruiter's dream image. On graduation day, like the rest of the recruits, Frank was one hundred percent Corps.

The platoon was formed and marched to the parade deck where family, guests, and the senior staff were already seated. Frank was honored by being allowed to march in the left corner position in the front row.

The Battalion, companies, and platoons formed on the parade deck. Introductions were made. A Light Colonel stood before the Marines and addressed the guests, then he addressed the Marines. Finally, the special guest speaker, Major General Patrick Muldavy was introduced and invited to the podium on the reviewing stand.

General Muldavy addressed the guests and congratulated the Marines. Then he paused.

"Ladies and Gentlemen, now I have the great privilege to recognize the heroic actions of one of our Marines. Leading Marines is the greatest honor a Marine officer has. Recognizing the outstanding service of our Marines is a privilege conferred by that honor. In this case, I am especially honored to present the following awards because I was present when the heroic actions took place. This is an unusual situation because the Marine in question is graduating from recruit training today with Platoon 2043. He has also been promoted to Staff Sergeant today. I know this must be confusing to guests and Marines alike so let me give you some background. . ."

General Muldavy told the story of the Marines on the mountain top near Dak To. His voice was the only sound heard during his entire recitation. As the General spoke Frank felt the stillness around him as the new Marines near him listened intently. He felt the blush starting up his neck. He stood at rigid parade rest and stared straight ahead. The story the General told was well known to Frank, but it still gave him chills. So many men had died that night, men he didn't know except for a few hours of shared terror. Then. . .

"Training command, atten-hut! Staff Sergeant Frank Evans, Post."

He marched to the podium, up the steps and came to attention facing the General and snapped a salute. General Muldavy returned the salute and then addressed the crowd.

"Ladies and Gentlemen, the following Citation is forwarded by the Secretary of the Navy. Attention to orders."

"Petty Officer First Class Frank Evans is awarded the Bronze Star with V device for extraordinary acts of valor while under direct enemy fire during ground operations against a superior hostile force in the Republic of Vietnam. Petty Officer Evans distinguished himself by his heroic actions while supporting Marine Corps elements after their Marine helicopter was downed by enemy fire. . ." the narrative continued and Frank tried not to move. . . "With total disregard for his own safety and braving intense enemy gunfire, Petty Officer Evans returned to the wrecked helicopter fuselage to recover critically needed ammunition and weapons for the Marines. . ." He was no longer hearing the words. He tried not to sway, the words went on . . . "His bravery and professionalism is in keeping with the highest traditions of military service and reflects great credit upon himself, his unit, and the United States Navy."

The General stepped up to Frank, pinned the medal on his chest, and stepped back to the podium.

"Remain at your post, Staff Sergeant Evans. Attention to orders."

"The President of the United States of America takes pleasure in presenting the Navy Cross to Staff Sergeant Frank Evans, United States Marine Corps, for extraordinary heroism in action against the enemy in the Republic of Vietnam. Staff Sergeant Evans and other members of a hastily organized team of survivors of a helicopter crash near Dak To, in . . ." His knees were getting weak and his back hurt. He flexed his knees inside of his trousers to get the blood flowing to his feet and shifted his weight slightly while the General's voice continued . . . "During the afternoon, the survivors came under intense enemy mortar and automatic weapons fire, sustained several casualties and was temporarily pinned down. . ." His legs were beginning to shake. . . "While returning to his position for re-supply of ammunition, he was wounded in the head, leg and ear in three separate incidents. Undaunted, he obtained the ammunition, again maneuvered to the exposed forward area and steadfastly provided defensive fire for his team . . ." Frank hoped it would be over soon so he could move his legs before the cramps started. He heard the General say something about him shielding a wounded Marine with his own body. . . "By his extraordinary courage, bold initiative, and selfless devotion to duty at great personal risk, Staff Sergeant Evans upheld the highest traditions of the Marine Corps and of the United States Naval Service."

The General stepped up to Frank again and pinned the Navy Cross on his chest. He held out his hand and shook his hand. Applause sounded from the reviewing bleachers.

"Thank you, Staff Sergeant," the General said quietly and smiled. He stepped back and saluted Frank. Frank returned the salute without even realizing the General had saluted him first as a sign of respect.

"Staff Sergeant Evans, Face your fellow Marines."

Frank did a snappy right face and faced the recruit company.

"Company. . ." The General shouted and let it hang.

"Platoon," the reply came from several DIs in the company.

"Present arms."

The Di's snapped their sabers to present arms, the guidon bearers dipped their flags, and the platoons remained at attention.

"Return the salute, Staff Sergeant," the General said quietly."

Frank snapped a salute and held it.

"Recover," the General said into the

microphone.

"Staff Sergeant Evans, post."

He did a left face and snapped a salute. When the General returned the salute, Frank did an about face and marched back to his platoon.

They passed in review, more introductions were made for the Sergeant Majors and First Sergeants, the Marine Corps Hymn was played, and the company was turned over to the First Sergeant for dismissal. The shouts and screams that followed were pure joy. Free, free, free at last. Well, for ten days anyway. Marines slapped Frank on the back and many hugged him. Each of the DIs shook his hand and congratulated him. He didn't realize it right then, but not only was he honored, but he had been used as a motivational tool as well. The Marine Corps doesn't do anything for free.

As the platoon broke up and Marines sought out their families, those that had family there, the events of the day caught up with Frank and he began to shake. He looked around and didn't know what to do or where to go. He had to change into his service-charlie uniform, but for the moment the barracks didn't even cross his mind. Then he felt a hand on his back.

"Staff Sergeant, I think you'll want these."

He turned and saw a Marine Corps Captain in service alphas holding out two blue snap cases. Frank saluted. Captain Sharp returned the salute and then shook Frank's hand.

"I'm Captain Sharp, the General's Aide. It's really good to finally get to meet you, Staff Sergeant. These are the cases for your medals. The ribbons are in there also. Congratulations."

"Thank you, sir. Sorry if I seem spacey. I'm just confused right now."

"That's understandable. I have your orders also. Here you go. You won't need your file or finance records, they're already at your new duty station."

"Where am I going?"

"You don't know?"

"No, sir. I was told my orders were held up for last minute changes."

"They were, but that was just to change them from Private Evans to Staff Sergeant Evans and authorize POV to your new duty station. You should have been told."

"Can you tell me?"

"Yes, sorry. Here's your orders. You have been granted thirty days leave instead of ten. You are now part of the General's staff and you'll be operating out of Quantico."

"Really? What will I be doing? Armory?"

"In a way," Sharp said. "Weapons evaluations. You'll be briefed when you get back from leave."

"I might take a few days to find a pad near the base again, but I don't need any leave right now. I just need some normalcy."

"No family?"

He held out his arms. "All around me."

Sharp grinned. "Are you sure you weren't Marine Corps all along?"

"I'm not sure what I was before, Captain, but the Marine Corps is my home now. Thanks for finding me, sir. I better get out of these blues before I sweat through them. And I've got to go over to Main Side and pick up my car. I hope the damn thing will start."

"Hell, come on. I'll give you a lift."

Chapter 17

Captain Sharp gave Frank his new ID card and took him to the tailor to have Staff Sergeant stripes sewn on all his uniforms that required stripes. The tailor took care of one service uniform blouse quickly so Frank could get out of his dress blues and told Frank to come back in three hours for the rest. Sharp helped him find a ribbon rack for eight ribbons and helped him put the ribbons in order. Frank pinned the ribbons on his blouse and added his marksmanship badges.

Since he had to wait for the uniforms, Captain Sharp dropped him at the NCO Club and told him to relax and celebrate. he was happy to comply. He stood in front of the club and looked at the door. NCO club. God's country. He'd been an NCO once, but that was so long ago, three months, an eternity in recruit training. He hesitated a moment, made himself look at the new stripes on his sleeves, took a deep breath, smiled, and pushed the door open.

Trying to be inconspicuous he took a seat at the very end of the bar. It took a few minutes to get the bartender's attention. Someone slapped Frank on the back and sat next to him.

"I figured you'd be a hundred miles north of here by now," Gunny Wallace said.

"Waiting for some stripes on my uniforms," he said. "How are you, Senior Drill Instructor?"

"Just Gunny now," Wallace said. "It'll take you a while to grow into those stripes. Evans, this has got to be one for the record books."

"I know I'm having trouble making it seem real. Can I buy you a beer?"

"Hell, yes," Wallace said.

Frank finally got the bartender's attention.

"What'll it be?" the red jacketed bartender asked.

"Two beers," Frank said. "Can we get a steak here at the bar?"

"Not at lunch. Best I can do is a bowl of chili. You just reporting in? I haven't seen you before."

"Actually, I'm checking out. But this is the first time I've been here."

"What'll it be, Gunny?"

"He's with me," Frank said. "A bowl of chili and a beer for both of us."

The bartender held out his hand. "Staff Sergeant Shaffer," he said. Most of the staff at military clubs were enlisted men working part time.

"Has Gunny Garzinski been in today?" Frank asked.

"No. Ski said he's was heading back to Quantico last night. You know Ski?"

"Yeah. We were in Nam together."

Shaffer automatically looked at Frank's breast and his eyes got a little wider.

"I'm buying this round," Shaffer said.

Shaffer delivered the drafts and looked over his shoulder.

"Got a call down the end of the bar," he said. "Enjoy your beer. Chili will be up in a minute."

When the bartender left, Wallace grinned at Frank and said, "Get used to it. Not many men have a rack of ribbons like yours." Wallace laughed. "And you're just a boot. There is only one higher than your top ribbon and that's *The* Medal."

"I know. My knees almost buckled when the General said Navy Cross. I'm not sure how I feel about it yet."

"I'll tell you how you should feel," Wallace said. "Enjoy it and be proud of it. The Corps doesn't recommend Marines for the cross lightly. I heard the citation. You earned it."

"Well, I have the scars to show for it. But I got everything in one day and a night. Most of these NCOs have been Marines for years and have multiple combat tours behind them. It feels like grandstanding when I'm around real Marines."

"Evans, I know it's going to take a while. You

just got out of recruit training. Hell, it's hard for me to accept you sitting here. But try to get over it. You earned the medal and you earned the right to be called a Marine. Too much modesty can be as unattractive as too much pride. Keep that in mind."

"Yes, sir. Here comes the chili. Another beer?"

"You can drop the sir, Evans."

He put his civvies on before he left the base. He stopped for a McDonald's burger at an exit off one of the pieces of the new interstate highway, I-95, that was open. The golden arches were beginning to pop up in more places by then. The sign said they had sold over a million hamburgers. Hard to believe. Another fad business that would be gone in five years. The chili was good at the NCO club, but it didn't satisfy the constant hunger that had built up over three months on the island. He ordered three burgers and fries. When he finished off the feast, he felt full for the first time since he had joined the Corps.

By the time he got to the Virginia line after intermittent U.S. 1 and U.S. 301 detours around sections of I-95 still being built, he was grainy eyed and fidgety from too much coffee. Frank decided to stop before Richmond for the night instead of driving straight through. North-south travel on the east coast was going to be great after they got all the I-95 pieces completed. He had another three or four hours if he continued, and he knew he wasn't going to be alert in the heavy I-95 traffic and construction north of

Richmond if he continued. He picked a clean looking motel near Petersburg with a club next door called Smokey's.

The room was small with a double bed and a black and white TV with rabbit ears, a small cupboard like opening in the wall near the door with a rail for hangers, a bathroom so small he couldn't put his foot between the toilet and the tub, and two plastic cups in paper wrappers on the sink. No amenities except for one two-inch piece of Ivory soap and one towel and wash rag. But the price was right and what was there was all he needed.

The check-in was quick and he decided to get a beer before turning in. Maybe he could cancel out the caffeine from the coffee with a beer.

"Evening, sugar. What'll it be?"

She looked pretty good and she sounded friendly, but after three months on the island, a female bulldog would look good, and friendly was optional. The club was almost empty and it looked like they were getting ready to close.

"Draw me a tall beer," he said. "Anything will do as long as it's wet and high-test."

"Coming right up. How about a Bud?"

"That'll work."

She drew the beer in a tall glass. When she set it in front of him she leaned way over and let Frank see plenty of cleavage. He held out his hand and said, "Frank."

"Lisa," she said taking his hand. "Just passing through?"

"Yeah. On my way up to Quantico."

"A Marine," she said. "The high and tight gave you away."

"Get a lot of Marines in here?"

"Not enough, sugar. And usually they're just kids. Nice to see one all grown up."

"You doing anything after you close?"

"I'm open to suggestions."

He grinned. "We could get a bottle and watch some TV."

"Not around here, sugar. No private sales, just ABC stores and they're closed. Tell you what. If you want to wait around, I'll bring a bottle."

"I am your slave."

Lisa grinned and cocked her head.

"You have no idea," she said.

Uh oh, he thought.

Frank slept late in the morning and was alone when he woke up with red grainy eyes. The sheets were on the floor and he was lying on a bare mattress. He was naked and sore. He glanced quickly at the dresser and noted his wallet was still there and he could see the edges of bills sticking out just the way he had left it. He groaned and closed his eyes.

He woke up again at 11 A.M. He reached for the phone and called the desk. They told him he could have another hour to check out and not to worry about it. He walked stiffly into the bathroom and didn't dare look in the mirror until he had soaked under a hot shower for twenty minutes. After that his morning went quickly and almost pleasantly.

He should have been more exhausted than he felt, more depleted. Lisa's persistent enthusiasm had demanded depletion, utter, soul withering depletion as the price of sleep. But now with a little rest the depletion was gentle, with maybe a soft edge of male pride, and spiced with the arrogance of a job well done, well received, and sleepily acknowledged. Three months of deprivation caught up in one night. There is nothing you can get so far behind on, he thought, or caught up on so quickly. After Lisa decided he had given his all, they had lain together talking quietly and laughing about things friends and lovers talk and laugh about. And after three months of nothing but male company, the talk brought as much joy as the sex, just being a man with a woman, enjoying the feminine scents, touches, and gentle sounds.

He dried off with the big hotel towel and took a chance with a quick look in the mirror. Thinner now. Gaunt, and in ways, raw. His cheekbones had angles he hadn't noticed before. Or maybe it was just the light. Certainly, the thin layer of fat that had always given his face a soft look was gone. And the scar. His look was harder now, more determined. Appropriate, he thought. The mountain had been tough, but Parris Island had worked changes in him that would remain for the rest of his life. He was a Marine. There was a look about him, he thought. Competent. Lazily competent. He didn't have to work at it or posture. It was just there. And suddenly he realized he felt very good, much better than he should considering his nocturnal exertions and alcoholic debauchery.

He had a fresh uniform hanging in the closet. The Washington area was hot in August and Frank was thankful for the short sleeves. He transferred his ribbons and badges to the blouse and got dressed. After looking around he put his piss-cutter (garrison cap) on and carried his PX supplied folding suitcase down to the car.

Frank passed the mini Marine Corps Monument near the entrance to Quantico and stopped at the main gate. He was given directions to the personnel office and told to stop at the security office to get a pass for his car. He was amazed at how good it felt to be treated like a human being again. Two days ago, he was a maggot and wasn't allowed to refer to himself in first person. Then, almost before he could come to grips with being a Marine, he was a Staff Sergeant and was treated with deference by Privates, Corporals, and Sergeants. Even officers treated him with respect. It was all very disorienting.

Frank was finding out that being an NCO in the Marine Corps was a very different thing than being an NCO in the Navy. Marine Corps NCOs had clout. It wasn't just a pay-grade, it was a position. A position of trust and responsibility. More authority was given and in turn, more responsibility was expected and more result required. He was feeling good about being an NCO as he checked in. He even began to like the covert double takes when people saw his ribbons. The purple heart with clusters usually caught their attention first. It is a well-known ribbon, especially with the mess in Vietnam going on, and it commanded respect in the Corps. It said he had paid his dues. Then they generally noted the gold V on his Bronze Star. The gold valor V was an eye catcher. Okay, they'd think, he's got balls, or at least had them one time. Then they would wonder what the medal was that outranked the Bronze Star. The Navy Cross is a rare medal and seldom seen so they usually guessed a Silver Star, a reasonably rare medal itself. Some even asked and were duly impressed when he told them, modestly, with just the right amount of off-handedness, that it was the Navy Cross.

So, Frank was feeling rather good about himself when he reported to his new home, the Special Weapons Evaluation Office, with his orders.

"Wait one, Staff Sergeant," the corporal at the desk said as he continued to dig through a file on his desk. He continued flipping pages until he found the one he was looking for, got up, and took the page into the office behind him. Frank heard someone talking quietly and then an exclamation. "I gave you a simple instruction and you screwed it up. Clark, even for an enlisted man you sometimes display levels of stupidity that amaze me. Now do it over and do it right." Frank looked up at the sign over the door. *Lieutenant Robert G. Cummings SWEO, USMC.*

Corporal Clark returned to his desk with a red face and his lips pressed together. He was making fists with his hands.

"Sorry, Staff Sergeant," he said after unclenching his jaw. "What can I do for you?"

"I'm reporting in. Wanted to leave you a copy of my orders. I'll be taking a few days leave to get squared away and then I'll report for duty."

"You're reporting to SWEO?" He pronounced it like a word, swee-o.

"That's what my orders say."

Clark frowned. "Let me see," he said holding out his hand.

Frank handed him a copy of his orders and waited while Clark scanned over them.

"Well, I guess you got the right place. But we weren't expecting any additions to the office. I'd better show these to the Lieutenant."

Clark knocked once on the door frame and entered the office. Frank waited. He didn't really want to meet his CO yet. He just wanted to drop off his orders and get out of there.

"Staff Sergeant Evans, front and center." It was the Lieutenant's imitation of command voice. Frank decided to start off with a good impression. He marched into the office and came to attention two feet from the Lieutenant's desk. He was uncovered so he didn't salute. He stared two inches over the

Lieutenant's head and reported.

"Sir, Staff Sergeant Frank Evans reporting, sir.

"At ease, Staff Sergeant."

Frank went to a rigid parade rest and continued to stare above the officer's head.

"Now what are these orders all about? I didn't request any additional staff."

Frank decided to relax a little and look Cummings in the eye. Except for the uniform, Cummings had a civilian look. He wore his uniform like a business suit. His hair was longer than Frank was used to seeing in the Corps, and Cummings looked like he'd been skipping morning PT.

"I'm just reporting as ordered, sir. Actually, I just wanted to drop off a copy of my orders to let you know I was here and then take a few days of my leave to get squared away."

"Did you request assignment to SWEO?" Again, the Swee-o.

"No, sir. I've never heard of this office. I was due for rotation and assigned here."

Cummings looked him over. Frank saw his eyes stop on the ribbons. Cummings's eyes got a little wider. Frank was getting used to it.

"Is that the Navy Cross?"

"Yes, sir."

"How many cluster on your Purple Heart?"

At least this guy knew awards protocol.

"Four, sir."

"There's no clusters on your Nam service

ribbon. You were wounded five times in one campaign?"

The guy was impressive, he thought.

"Yes, sir."

"Recently?"

"Last year, sir. I spent the last few months in South Carolina after I was released from the hospital."

"I see."

Frank wasn't sure what Cummings saw, but he seemed to be satisfied.

"Maybe that's what this is all about. Are you fully recovered and cleared for full duty?"

"Yes, sir. I spent a lot of time down south getting back in shape."

"You look like it, although you could stand to let your hair grow in some. I'm not a fan of all this gung ho, tough man stuff, Evans. Leave the high and tight grooming to the Recon. You say you want to take some leave?"

"Yes, sir. I have thirty days on my orders, but I figure five will get me squared away with housing and let me explore the area. I plan to report for duty next week."

"What's your specialty?"

"Infantry Weapons Repairman, sir, with a secondary of 0311, Infantry."

The orders Captain Sharp gave him after graduation at Parris Island listed those MOS specialties. He didn't know how he came to get those particular MOSs, but that's what his orders said, so that's what he reported.

"Well, I don't know what I'm supposed to do with you. I haven't got an E6 slot authorized or any work for one for that matter. I'll sort it out while you are on leave."

"Thank you, sir."

"Don't be too quick to thank me. I plan to get you reassigned. You are dismissed, Evans."

Chapter 18

He found a furnished apartment to sublet from a Marine Corps couple in the same complex where he had lived the last time he was at Quantico. It didn't take long to get squared away in the apartment, so he began exploring the area, getting used to traffic patterns, looking for clubs that looked like they might provide some action, and spending the evenings at the NCO club in uniform. The newness of it all hadn't worn off yet. He enjoyed wearing the uniforms, enjoyed the stripes, and enjoyed the respect his ribbons generated. Even after having been a First Class Petty Officer in the Navy, this was different. Going from maggot to SNCO in one day was like ascending to Olympus to join the gods.

He got in with a group of senior NCOs that seemed to accept him at face value. Frank kept his mouth shut and started learning to act and function as a Marine NCO. Every profession has its own language and the Marine Corps is no exception. He learned the jargon, picked up the attitude, and picked up his share of the bar tabs.

He also began noticing the life going on around him, one life in particular. Leaving for work in the mornings he frequently passed a woman on the stairs leading to the parking lot at his apartment complex. She was up early like him every day except weekends. He noticed that she didn't have a ring on her left hand and looked for an opportunity to strike up a conversation. But mornings while they were both in a hurry to get to work wasn't a good time and somehow, he couldn't seem to get home at the right time to catch her on the way in. He said, "Morning" as he passed her each morning and she smiled in return. Nice legs. Very nice legs.

When he reported for duty a week after his first visit to Swee-o, the Lieutenant still hadn't finished checking into Frank's situation or trying to get him reassigned to another unit. He really didn't care. Cummings had a reputation with the enlisted men as being a real prick. He talked down to his Marines and treated them like inferiors. He seemed almost too happy to point out their stupidity. Frank was very careful to avoid giving Cummings any reason to go after him. He requested, and was given permission to work temporarily in the armory that supported the officer's basic course. He knew it was probably a good idea to put distance between him and Cummings while Cummings worked out whatever he was going to do—and until Frank heard from Captain Sharp. He wasn't sure what was going on.

The Armorer remembered him and was glad to get the help. He put Frank right to work. The work was easy, way below his pay grade, but it was something to do and kept him away from Cummings. It wasn't to last.

"Hey, Evans. Phone. A Gunny Garzinski."

"Got it. . . Hey Gunny, haven't heard from you in a while."

"Well, get used to it. The General wants to talk to you. Be here at 1500."

"I'll let my boss know I'll be gone, and I have to change."

"The General is your boss."

The phone went dead before Frank could ask where he was supposed meet the General.

"Gunny Stout, where the hell is General Muldavy's office?"

"He's at Headquarters."

"At the Pentagon?"

"No. Here at Quantico. Headquarters building."

"Oh. Okay. I've got to take off for a couple hours. Cover for me, okay?"

"No problem. Go on."

He got cleaned up, put on a fresh uniform and made it to the General's office at 1450.

"How's it going, Frank?" Garzinski asked. "You're

looking squared away."

"Yeah. It's starting to come together."

"Told you it would. Come on, we need to see Captain Sharp before we see the General.

Garzinski led him to Sharp's office next to the General's office and knocked once on the door frame. Sharp looked like what a Marine officer should look like. No one would ever mistake him for a civilian, not even if he was in civilian clothes. Even at three in the afternoon, his uniform looked like he had just put it on. He wasn't a big man, at least not physically. Maybe five-eleven or six feet tall, probably one-eighty. But the impression of authority and command he gave was immediate. The two sergeants reported properly and Frank let Garzinski do the talking.

"Thanks, Gunny," Sharp said. "Stand at ease. . .I said at ease, not parade rest. Welcome to Wally World, Staff Sergeant Evans. Are you getting settled in over at Swee-o?"

"Well, sir, I'm working at the Basic School armory. Lieutenant Cummings is working on getting me reassigned. He obviously wasn't expecting me. I guess assignment screwed up."

"Really? He actually told you that?"

"Yes. sir."

"I'll handle it. What you do is none of his business. Your office is there, but you don't report to him. I'll straighten it out. Right now, I think the General is ready for us."

Garzinski and Evans followed Sharp to the end

of the hall. Captain Sharp knocked once on the General's door and waited to be acknowledged.

"Come."

The three Marines marched into the General's office and came to attention. The General looked up from his desk and smiled.

"Welcome home, Frank. At ease. Sit. Everybody sit. Everything working out at the Evaluation Office?"

"There's a slight problem with Cummings," Sharp said." I'll handle it."

The General looked at Sharp and frowned.

"If that. . .fine young lieutenant sticks his nose in this project I'll. . ."

"I'll handle it, sir. It's just a mix up in orders."

"Do that. Ready for work, Frank?"

"Yes, sir. I'd like to do something besides cleaning and repairing M-16s for the Basic Course."

"That's what he has you doing? That will end today. See to it, Wally."

"Aye, aye, sir."

"Okay. Here's the plan. First, are you ready to travel?"

"Yes, sir."

"Good. That wasn't a request, by the way. Just a heads-up. Wally has your orders. You'll leave from Travis on a C-141 on Wednesday so you'll catch a MAC flight out of Andrews for Travis Tomorrow. Draw your weapons and gear here. It's hard to tell what you'll get if you draw weapons in-country. Wally, see that he draws his weapons without any trouble. He'll fly over on military transport, so weapons won't be a problem. Make sure Third MAF has authorization to ship the weapons back. It's hard to tell how they'll route him home. Frank, you'll land at Danang on Thursday and report to Third MAF Headquarters at Camp Horn. Use Camp Horn as your base of operations. When you have completed your survey there, find some grunts in the field and get the straight information. Stay as long as you need to do your evaluation and then get back to Danang and have Third MAF book you back home. Your orders will give you the priority to do whatever you need to do and go where ever you want to go. Here's what I want. . .

The General spent a few minutes outlining Frank's duties and the report the General wanted to see when Frank returned to the states. It appeared the General needed a neutral pair of eyes in Vietnam to assess problems the troops were having with the M-16 and the M-60. But the M-16 was the priority. And he wanted the opinions of the men who used the weapons every day and had to depend on them for their lives. He needed an enlisted spy, in other words. Frank was to be the General's enlisted eyes in-country and the General told him to keep a low profile and keep the results of his survey to himself. The issue was a political hot potato with congress already involved. Muldavy finished his instructions with an admonition.

"Staff Sergeant Evans, stay out of the shit. You are there to observe and gather information. Do not go into the hot zones. Talk to the troops while they are standing down. If you come back with another cluster on your Purple Heart, I will have your ass. If you were to be so stupid as to ignore my orders and get yourself killed, I will have you buried at Arlington so I can stop every day and piss on your grave. Do you understand?"

Well that didn't leave a lot of wiggle room. Just one answer was appropriate.

"Aye, aye, sir."

After the meeting with the General, Captain Sharp gave Frank the rest of the details, his orders, and authorizations to draw weapons from the armory. Garzinski gave him the name of a Sergeant Major at Third MAF who could open doors with companies in the field and could be depended on to keep his mouth shut.

"Frank, keep a low profile," Sharp said. "This M-16 thing came up last spring and congress got involved. A lot of people at headquarters don't want it stirred up again, but the General has his heels dug in. Keep quiet and be careful who you talk to."

"Yes, sir."

"I'll meet you at Andrews and make sure you have everything you'll need," Garzinski said. "What kind of rifle are you going to draw?

"M-14 I guess. It's what we trained with on the island and I wasn't too happy with the way the M16s kept jamming on the mountain."

"Good. Don't even think about taking a mickey mouse M-16. Go on, I'll double check your pack in the morning.

"Christ, Gunny, I'm a Staff Sergeant. I don't need a baby sitter."

"You got the stripes but you're still a boot. Especially when it comes to Nam. You spent one day and one night in the grass, Frank. You have a lot to learn, so shut up and listen to what I say. I had three tours in-country. Tell me something. Have you got a P-38?"

"Last time I looked they weren't issuing fighter planes to enlisted men."

"It's a C-rats can opener, smart-ass. You should have learned that on the Island. That's just what I'm talking about. You don't know shit. Get a P-38 the first chance you get and put it on your dog tags so you'll always have one. I better come over to your apartment and check out your pack before you leave. I can at least make a list of what you're missing. You can pick up what you need at Third MAF or the PX at China Beach. Frank, they didn't tell you the truth and nothing but the truth on the Island. You have to have been in the grass to know what you need to take with you.

"Okay, I'll pick up a twelve pack and you can clue me in tonight."

He drew his weapons. He had to sign away his life, career, and paycheck to take the weapons to Vietnam with him, but he chose his own weapons and knew he could rely on them. The Gunny at the armory provided him a rifle shipment case like the ones the rifle team used when they traveled to matches. The weapons would be picked-up by his driver in the morning. He started for his apartment but then thought he should let Lt. Cummings know he would be gone for a while. Captain Sharp had made it clear that he didn't report to Cummings, but Frank didn't like loose ends.

"Hi, Corporal. Is the Lieutenant in?"

"He's in, Staff Sergeant. And he's been looking for you. Careful in there. He's pissed."

Frank nodded and knocked on the door frame.

"Come."

Frank walked in and came to attention in front of Cummings's desk.

"Evans, where the hell have you been? I called over to the armory and was told you had personal business to attend to."

"I had official business, sir. I just came by to. . ."

"Never mind. I want an explanation and I want it now. I was denied access to your service record. Do you have any idea why?"

"Well, sir, that's what I was saying. I had a meeting. . ."

"I don't care who you were meeting with. What's that got to do with your record?"

"Sir, if you will let me finish. . ."

"Stand at attention. Don't get smart with me, Evans. . ."

"It's Staff Sergeant Evans, sir."

"You are at attention and you will shut your mouth. Private or NCO you are an enlisted man and you are speaking to a commissioned officer. . ."

"Captain. You have a call on line one," the Corporal yelled through the door.

"Corporal, I told you not to interrupt. . ."

"Sorry, sir, but you better take this one. It's General Muldavy's Aide, Captain Sharp."

"Line one, you said?"

"Yes, sir."

"Remain at attention, Evans. I'm not through with you."

"Captain Sharp, this is Lieutenant Cummings. How may I help you, sir? . . . Yes, sir, he's in my office now . . . I wasn't aware of that, sir, I . . . No, sir, I have no objection, but . . . sir, there's no need to . . . yes, sir . . . yes, sir . . . aye, aye, sir."

Cummings's face was red as he gently set the receiver on the cradle. "That will be all, Staff Sergeant Evans. You are dismissed."

The corporal was looking down at his desk when Frank shut the door to Cummings's office, but he had a big shit eating grin on his face. Frank noticed that the phone on the corporal's desk was off the hook. The corporal looked up at him, reached for the phone, and gently hung it up.

"Funny how Captain Sharp called just at the right time," Frank said quietly.

"Amazing, wasn't it?" the Corporal said and grinned

"Do you know Captain Sharp, Corporal?"

"I know his number, Staff Sergeant."

"Thanks," he said.

He thought about Cummings on the way to his apartment. He had made an enemy that day. But he didn't have time to worry about it. It was time to pack and drink some beer with the Gunny.

Chapter 19

The smells were foreign and only vaguely familiar when he exited the C-141 at Danang Air Base. The heat and humidity almost took his breath away. Frank checked the date on his watch but remembered they had crossed the international date line somewhere over the Pacific so it was either a day earlier or a day later; he couldn't remember which. He asked the load master and was told the date was the 21st of September, 1967.

He had been told to expect hot, humid weather and probably a lot of rain. Early fall was a transition period between the southwest monsoon season and the northeast monsoon season. The weather would be unpredictable for a few weeks but it would be getting more rainy, humid, and cooler as November approached. He slung his rifle and rucksack and pulled his sea bag to the terminal to arrange transportation to Third MAF.

A World bird had just delivered a load of fresh troops, mostly Navy enlisted, and a couple of drivers were loading the Navy personnel into cattle cars. No kidding. Cattle cars just like you see on Texas highways. Frank was sure that would put the troops in the right frame of mind. He asked a driver if he was going by Third MAF.

"I go by there, but I can't stop on the way. I'm delivering these guys to Camp Tien Sha. You can ride along if you want. It's easier to get to Camp Horn from Tien Sha than it is from here. You can catch a bus at the gate to take you back out toward Marble Mountain."

"Not sure I want to ride in a cattle car," Frank said.

"Beats walking."

He thought about it for a moment. Sweat was dripping into his eyes.

"There it is," he said.

Sand everywhere. Camp Tien Sha was in East Danang on the Tien Sha peninsula at the base of Monkey mountain. With massive forklifts, frontend loaders, and big trucks of every kind in both lanes, the road looked like an access road to an American port facility. And it was. Danang port was the entry point for most of the equipment, munitions, and supplies for I-Corps. And the cargo yards were just down the road from Tien Sha.

He was struck again by the contrasts in Vietnam. Contrasts for a Marine, that is. There were places in the country right that minute where Marines were fighting desperately for their lives, trying to take hills or hold on to the ones they had already taken. Places like the mountain top where he had received five wounds. And then, there were places like Danang and Saigon where the biggest enemies were boredom, apathy, bureaucracy, and bullshit.

He watched the Vietnamese civilians and soldiers go by on foot, scooter, cycle, bus, and contrivances he couldn't put a name to. He didn't get into Saigon city during his last time in-country so he hadn't seen many Vietnamese—except over the sights on his rifle. Now he watched a steady stream of working class Vietnamese passing on the road and had to readjust some of his ideas. Either they didn't tell me the whole story, he thought, or there are an awful lot of Viet Cong in Danang. Whenever the press talked about the Viet Cong, or VC as they called them, it was always VC in black pajamas. Almost all of the Vietnamese passing, men and women, wore black pajamas. Not really pajamas, just loose fitting black tops and bottoms that looked like pajamas. It appeared to be the national dress. Strange, he thought. When they were shooting at me I didn't notice what they were wearing.

In front of the main gate to camp Tien Sha, a young boy stopped on a motor bike and looked Frank up and down. Hard to tell with Vietnamese, but Frank figured he was maybe thirteen or fourteen. That was his person. His eyes were old and shrewd.

"Hey GI. You want fuck-suck?" the kid asked in a

voice that would have done credit to a Times Square porn huckster.

"What did you say?" he asked, not quite believing what he heard coming out of the kid's mouth

"You want boom-boom? Numba one boom-boom girls. Cheap. Long time. I ride you there and bring you back. Fifteen dolla."

"No!" he said. "Get the hell out of here."

"Fucking numba ten honcho. You jerk-off GI."

The kid spit by Frank's feet and then put the bike in gear, looked straight ahead, and took off with his chin in the air. Christ, he thought, teenage pimps. Frank didn't want to admit the kid scared him. The kid wore a camouflage boonie hat, red tank top, skin tight jeans with pointy toe shoes, and probably weighed all of ninety pounds, wet. Probably VC, he thought. He might take me there, but I wouldn't be coming back. After Garzinski's warnings at home and the war stories at the NCO club, Frank was just a little paranoid.

A group of sailors in green utilities came through the gate. The utilities they wore were the same OD green utilities Marines wore, but the sailors were obviously sailors. A civilian might not notice the difference, but a Marine noticed right away. There was a laxness in the sailors, a lack of attention, a casual manner you wouldn't see in a Marine. They wore the uniform casual, like jeans or overalls. Each of their utility shirts had white stains in big circles under the arms, the consequence of taking salt tablets for heat regulation.

Several of them had apples in their hands. They probably just left the mess hall. As they started walking toward the port, a gaggle of Vietnamese children spotted them and ran at them with their hands out. Very quickly the apples were in the kid's hands and they ran off giggling. War or peace, east or west, kids are kids wherever you go.

After waiting ten minutes, he boarded a blue school bus with chicken-wire on the windows and dumped his gear in a seat behind the driver. The bus was empty and Frank was the only passenger that got on at Tien Sha. The driver was a sailor in green utilities with a Marine Corps eight-point cover starched to hold its shape but without the stenciled globe and anchor. The cover looked like it had been starched with glue. The driver told him the mama-sans that did the laundry used rice starch. He said he was afraid to ask what that was.

By the time the bus stopped at the main gate to Camp Horn, III MAF HQ compound, his utilities were soaked and he was irritated in all the wrong places. He figured his body temperature had to be over a hundred, and he was longing for a long cold shower. A cold beer wouldn't hurt either. A Marine sentry boarded the bus and looked up and down the aisle.

"Do you know where I can find Sergeant Major Jullian?" he asked.

"Try the G2 hooch, Staff Sergeant."

He checked in, was assigned a berth with the

intelligence section and sought out the G2 (Intelligence) Hooch. When he asked for Sgt. Maj. Jullian, he was pointed to a long table and five men bending over a large map.

"Sergeant Major Jullian?" he said when he stopped at the table.

"Whataya need?"

Jullian was in starched utilities, had gray hair, was tall, maybe six-three or six-four, skinny as a rail, and had the stump of a cigar in the corner of his mouth. It wasn't lit.

"I'm Frank Evans. I'm here on a special assignment," he said. "Gunny Garzinski told me to look you up."

"Yeah? How's Ski doing?"

"He's good to go and working on General Muldavy's staff at Quantico. He said you might be able to help me."

Jullian looked at his watch and frowned. He looked at the map and frowned again. He took the cigar out of his mouth and spat pieces of tobacco into a cup in his hand.

"Nothing more I can do here for a while," he said. "Come on, let's get a beer."

Jullian led Frank to a hooch behind a long barracks. The barracks were two story buildings. From a distance, they looked substantial, but up close they gave a feeling of something temporary. The siding was sort of like lapstrake planking with plenty of space between the planks and screen behind them for a lot of open ventilation. The SNCO beer hooch was a small, temporary building made with a wood frame with screen tacked to it, a roof, and a wood plank floor. The walls were surrounded with a double row of sandbags piled waist high. Four other senior NCOs were already there and drinking beer. A jury-rigged grill made from concrete blocks and steel grating was red and smoking in one corner. A white fridge sat in the other corner and a roughhewn bar with stools formed a semi-circle around the third corner. The fridge was full of beer and the top freezer section was full of frozen steaks.

"How long you going to be here?" Jullian asked.

"Hard to tell. Probably a month."

"Give me twenty. That will make you a member of the mess and you get to drink all the beer you want. It's only 3.2, but it's all we got. Put a couple bucks in the kitty if you want a steak. That's how we pay for the beer. I got a man in Navy Security that guards the Navy cold storage warehouse. I can get a case of steaks whenever I want."

Frank pulled a twenty-dollar bill out of his wallet and handed it to Jullian.

"That's no good here. You need some MPC (military payment certificates). Get the finance office to convert some bills for you. This your first tour?"

'No," Frank said. "Or maybe yes. Shit, I guess it is."

"You don't know?"

"It's confusing. I was in-country last year, but I got wounded on my first day and medevac'd back to the states. I was in a helicopter crash with Gunny Garzinski and never even got to my unit."

"Damn," Jullian said. "Hope your luck is better this time. Ski took a bad hit that time. How about you?"

Frank held up five fingers.

"She-it, boy. One day in-country and five hits. Don't be standing too close to me. So, what did Ski think I could do for you?"

Frank explained his mission and said he needed some help getting embedded with some grunts.

"Shouldn't be a problem. We have a situation developing at Con Thien in the eastern DMZ sector. NVA are hitting the hill with artillery every day. It's a hot zone, but if you want to see the weapons in action and talk to the people using them, that's the place to go. You want to talk to them?"

"Sounds like what I'm looking for."

"Could get real hot. Intelligence says Ho Chi Minh is up to something."

Frank remembered the General's instructions, but he also liked the little thrill of excitement he got when Jullian said it might get hot.

"No problem," he said. "I plan to be in and out in one day. Can you arrange it?"

"I can do that. You may have to ride a mike boat or LCU up to Cua Viet and bum a ride on a slick or convoy to Con Thien. Plenty of slicks going up there from Dong Ha. Wait a minute, there's a PBR in Danang leaving for Qua Viet tonight. It'll be crowded and it might get hairy on the way, but I can probably get you on it if you're ready to leave tonight."

"I've heard about PBRs. Never saw one though."

"Hulls of glass, balls of brass. You'll love it."

The grin on Jullian's face didn't reassure him. But the grunts at Con Thien sounded like just what he was looking for.

"Sure, I can leave tonight. Where do I have to go to catch the boat?

"I'll fix you up with a ride. You can draw a weapon at the armory."

"I brought my weapons. I just need an ammo issue."

"How'd you manage that?"

"I work for a general."

"Must be nice. What do you need?"

"Just a couple bandoliers of 7.62 and some frags. A couple boxes of .45ACP too."

"No problem. You can draw extra magazines and load them yourself. Get squared away and find me at the HQ Quonset hut in about an hour."

The jeep turned right at a split in the road to take another road with a bridge into west Danang, the downtown area. On the left side of the road about a hundred Vietnamese were butchering a water buffalo that apparently had been struck by a vehicle. It was on its side and covered with Vietnamese like ants on a dead bug. Men, women, and kids, all with knives and hacking away. Every ounce of it would find its way into a pot. Protein in a rice fed country is dear. Nothing would be wasted. Hooves would make glue, bones would turn into utensils, tendons would become everything from fishnet bindings to dog leashes. Even the blood would be collected and allowed to coagulate in a loaf pan to slice and fry later. And if the buffalo was killed by a U.S. military vehicle the owner of the animal would be compensated not only for the loss of the animal, but also for any possible progeny the animal might produce for as many generations as the owner could conceive of, all the labor it might have done, and anything else the Vietnamese could come up with to fatten the take. Crazy damn war.

The driver didn't go into the city. Instead he pulled into a riverfront docking area by the bridge with a wide concrete ramp. The PBR was tied up at the dock.

Crap! he thought. That's just a big center-console like you'd see in Norfolk on the Chesapeake Bay—except for the weapons sticking out all over it. Two Navy guards stopped the Jeep. They were in starched utilities and wore black helmet liners with a white stripe around the circumference and "Security Police" on the front. These guys could be mistaken for Marines. Naval Security Intelligence, the unit he was supposed to join on his last visit to Vietnam. The sight gave him a strange feeling. There but for the grace of God . . . The guards talked to the driver and waved the jeep through the gate.

He put his gear on the dock and thanked the

driver. He was standing next to the boat and wondering how it would do in a fight. It didn't appear to have much armor, and it was mostly an open fiberglass hull. Looked like ceramic plates provided some cover for the machine gunners and a little more around the helm. It looked to be about thirty feet long and maybe ten or eleven feet wide. The bow area was open as was the cockpit. Just like a fishing boat, he thought. There was a canopy over the helm. Twin Fifties in the bow were mounted in a tub. Looked like they rotated. Serious firepower. As he scanned the boat he noted a single Fifty in the cockpit, side-mounted M-60 7.62s on each side of the helm, and M-79 Grenade launchers in a rack next to the helm. Damn! This is a hairy little beast.

"Are you Staff Sergeant Evans?" a voice from the helm asked.

"That's me, Skipper. Permission to come aboard?"

"Make it quick, I've got to get the hell out of here while there's still some light. Drop your ruck down the hatch but keep your personal weapon."

"Expecting trouble?"

"Always. I'm BM1 Hodges, skipper of this little part of the U.S. Navy. We're meeting up with another boat on the river. Lieutenant JG Coan is the flotilla commander. He'll be going up the water with us so we can support each other."

"Good to meet you, Boats." Frank said, calling Hodges by the Navy term for a Boatswains Mate.

"It's going to be crowded," Hodges said. "The

two troops in the cockpit are SEALs. I'll be dropping them off on the way up. I just got word you'd be coming along too. It'll be a little better after I drop off the SEALs."

"I appreciate the ride, Boats. Where do you want me?"

"You can stay here in the helm area. If you want to move around after we get moving, you can. Can you man a Sixty?"

"Sure."

"Good. If it gets hot, man that Sixty on the port side.

"Will do."

Later, with the boat stable, on step, and moving fast up the Han river toward Danang Bay, Frank decided to check out the cockpit Fifty Cal. The two SEALs were stretched out and sitting against the transom. They were dressed in black. Black boonie hat, black utility shirt, and it looked like black jeans. Jeans, not utility trousers. Their faces and hands were covered with green face paint with streaks of black breaking up contours.

"How's it going?" he said.

"Fuck off, Jarhead."

Well, screw you and the horse you rode in on, he thought. He looked the Fifty over, decided it was ready for action, and returned to the helm.

"What's with the SEALs?" he asked quietly.

"They don't talk much before an insertion. Just

stay away from them. We'll be dropping them off along the coast in about two hours. Don't ask."

"Yeah. They made that plain. How do you get up to Cua Viet?"

"We'll run the Han river out to the bay and head north up the coast to the South China Sea. I'll run a couple of miles offshore until we're off the mouth of the Cua Viet River. It's about ninety miles. The Lieutenant will run about a mile further out till we get there. We'll look for anything trying to come down from the north while we're patrolling. Ever been up there?"

"No. First time for me. I've got to hook up with a slick to get over to Con Thien."

"Shouldn't be a problem. You can get some shut eye if you want. We'll be out about six hours unless we run into a Vietnamese craft we need to search. Weather is supposed to be good. You were lucky to catch us tonight. This is the first night we've had in a week that's been clear enough to run outside. It might get snotty when we get further north, but I'm hoping the weather holds off for a few more hours."

"Thanks, Boats. Think I will get some sleep, if I can."

The SEALs inflated a rubber boat and assembled their gear in the cockpit. He watched for a few minutes and then closed his eyes. He felt the change in motion when the boat reached Danang Bay, but it was mostly swells, and the motion was pleasant. Frank drifted off to sleep with his M-14 across his lap.

Chapter 20

The PBR ran without lights two miles off-shore for two hours. The hum of the Diesels was hypnotic and lulled him into a deep sleep. Of course, after a seventeen-hour flight on a C-141 and being up all day in the heat and humidity, it didn't take much humming. The cool air on the water was enough to put him out. When he woke up again the boat was dead in the water and the SEALs were launching their little boat. A few moments later and only a few feet away from the boat, the SEALs disappeared into the dark. As the engines started again, his eyes closed again.

He woke up not knowing how long he had slept, but he felt rested and cool. He sat still for a moment trying to figure out what woke him. The motion of the boat had changed. The boat was running slow, the water was choppy, and the four-man crew was at general quarters (battle stations). Boats was still at the helm and watching the radar closely. But the remainder of the crew, three men, were manning the guns.

"Time to get on the Sixty," Boats said.

"Trouble?" Frank asked.

"You never know up here. Right now, we're crossing the bar at the mouth of the Cua Viet River. Anything can happen between here and Cua Viet Navy depot."

"Got it," Frank said.

The big water jets that propelled the PBR bubbled and the diesels thrumbed an easy vibration through the deck. He double-checked the breech of the Sixty and made sure it was ready to fire. He leaned over, crossed his arms over the machine gun, and watched the dark. It was lighter now with a sliver of moon showing, but heavy, fast moving clouds were moving in. Faint edges of shoreline could be seen slipping by. The smell changed from the clean China Sea ocean smell to rotting vegetation, and something else. Smoke. Not just any smoke, but the smoke from explosives. His hands closed involuntarily. He began looking harder at the shoreline for. . .well, for anything. And after a few minutes he found it

"Boats, what are those lights dancing around?"

Boats turned his head and just had time to say, "Shit!" and slam the throttles forward as he yelled, "Incoming." Two loud flutters passed behind Frank over the cockpit and something slammed into the hull. He heard the distant machine gun almost immediately. He didn't have to be told what the lights were then. He aimed the Sixty at the place the tracers were coming from and started squeezing off bursts. The Fifties in the bow swung around and used Frank's tracers as pointers to their target. As the bow lifted and the big diesels began to growl the Fifties opened-up. In just seconds the PBR was on step and flying up the dark river. He lost sight of his aiming point.

"That's what NVA tracers look like when they're coming straight at you over the water," Boats yelled. "The big stuff looks like dancing lights and then, bam, the round hits. Good eyes, Sarge, but don't wait for an invitation next time."

"Next time?" Frank asked.

"Could be. Lots of shit going on up here, and we're not there yet."

The boat settled back in the water and Hodges made a wide circle back to the Cua Vet Navy supply depot near the mouth of the river.

"Another couple of feet forward and you'd have lost a foot," Hodges said. "At least it wasn't on the water line."

BM1 Hodges was looking at a jagged hole in the fiberglass side of the PBR. Frank was looking at the short distance between where he had been manning the Sixty and where the round went through the side of the boat. He had just shivered with the willies when he felt the first drops of rain. The sight of the tear in the side of the boat made the scar on his head itch. It didn't itch for long. As he began his reply to Hodges, a mortar exploded on the sandbar behind the PBR.

"Go," Boats yelled. "There's a bunker at the end of the dock."

As soon as Hodge's helped him off the boat, Frank was running up the dock toward the sandbag bunker with his rifle and ruck. The PBR's engines fired up, and the boat moved out into the river. Frank made it to the bunker just before a mortar hit the floating barge dock. He curled up in the sand below the sandbags and held his helmet on with his arms wrapped over his head. Two more mortars hit further inland. Memories of his night on the mountain came back and He curled his body tighter.

The mortar attack lasted until first light and Frank estimated the base had been hit by thirteen rounds. The base fired maybe thirty rounds back. One floating dock was destroyed, the one where the PBR had tied up, but he didn't know what other damage had been inflicted. It was raining hard by then and the wind had picked up significantly. He shrugged into his ruck and humped into the base to find someone who could tell him where to hook up with a helicopter to take him to Con Thien.

He saw two mike boats (LSM-8 landing craft) on a small sandy point with their ramps down and men loading pallets of artillery shells into the holds. They probably knew their way around the base. He headed that way.

"Hey, Navy. Where do the helicopters land

around here?"

A bare-chested sailor with a Thompson .45 submachine gun slung over his shoulder looked up from a clipboard and gave Frank an up and down.

"Won't be anything landing or taking off today. We're socked in. Where are you heading?"

"I've got to get over to Con Thien. Any ideas?"

"You can ride with us over to Dong Ha. You can see Con Thien from there. Should be able to hook up with something to get you up to the hill."

"Okay, thanks," Frank said. "Where do you want me?"

"Go on up to the wheel house. Find a place to crash. We're leaving in about an hour."

The Mike boat backed off the sand an hour later and turned up river towards Dong Ha. After the mortars, Frank wasn't happy about having to sit in one spot inside of a big target, but he didn't have any choice. The General's orders about staying out of hot spots came back, but Frank was enjoying the tickle in his gut when he thought about being in action again. It was scary as hell, but he was trained now, and battle was the biggest adventure he had ever known—after it was over. He was a Marine and war is what Marines did. Scared to death, and at the same time excited to be near it again.

The boat was slow and he wasn't sure how long they spent on the river, but finally Dong Ha appeared through the rain and mist. The Mike boat wasn't off-loading at Dong Ha, but the skipper stopped at a dock and let Frank get off. He set out in search of a Marine officer that could hook him up with some transportation. He was directed to the 9th Marines Command Post. He heard distant artillery and the sound continued while he searched for the 9th Marines.

Just in time, he remembered not to salute. Saluting identifies officers and makes them perfect targets for snipers. A boot might get away with it once with an ass chewing, but a Staff Sergeant wouldn't get away with it at all. If he had Lt. Cummings and Corporal Clark with him, he was sure Cummings would insist on a salute—and Clark would be happy to render that sign of respect with a smile. And then duck.

"Sir, I'm trying to get transportation to Con Thien. Can you direct me to the right place?"

First Lieutenant Stephens looked at Frank's rank and paused.

"What do you need on the hill, Staff Sergeant?"

Frank explained his mission and said he needed to be embedded with grunts in action to make a reasonable evaluation.

"Are you sure you want to go up there? I've got troops here you can talk to."

"I need to see what's going on, sir. The men know what's going on, but when a weapon malfunctions a Marine is more interested in getting it back in action than trying to figure out why it failed. If I'm there, I can trade weapons and find out what really happened."

"Look up there," the Lieutenant said while pointing. "See those hills? That's Con Thien. All three of those small hills comprise the strong point at Con Thien. Watch for a moment."

Soon Frank heard the distant rumble of artillery and saw smoke rise on the hill. Two more explosions followed quickly.

"Still want to go up there?" the Lieutenant asked. "Con Thien means hill of angels. There's a reason it got that name."

Frank watched as another round hit the hill and thought about the General's orders, but he had come this far and he'd only be there a few hours. If he was careful, what could go wrong?

"Yes, sir. I think that's where I need to be."

"Well, follow me then. I'll see if I can get you on a slick. When you get there, find Lieutenant Hinks, First Platoon, Charlie Company of the Two-Nine. I'm sure he'll be glad to embed you with his platoon."

He got on a medevac slick an hour later. While in route to the hill, he took two frag grenades out of his pack and put them in each of his utility jacket bottom pockets. He had two bandoliers of six M-14 magazines each, crisscrossed on his chest and a full magazine in his .45. If he ever had a jammed rifle during a close firefight again, he was damn well going to have a back-up available even if it was just a side arm.

The pilot took his time with the landing. Two mortar rounds hit the top of the main hill while he was circling. Big mortars. Frank figured they were the 120 mm mortars he had heard about but had never seen. Nothing but bare, pock marked mud below him with some sandbag fortified bunkers. The pock marks were craters, artillery craters. He could see outlines of bunkers and defensive positions and everything was enclosed in multiple rows of concertina wire. The pilot finally decided to land near a group of Marines waiting with stretchers near the center of the base. Frank hopped out as soon as the skids touched the ground and sprinted for the first hole he saw. It was full of water. He spotted another hole with the tops of two helmets showing. He dropped into the mud next to two Marines.

The Helicopter lifted off, tilted to the south and picked up speed. A moment later a mortar hit fifteen feet from where the chopper had landed.

"Get your head down, man. It ain't over."

Another round landed as he sank into the mud at the bottom of the hole. The Marines with him were pressed against the wall at the bottom of the hole.

"Where can I find Lieutenant Hinks, 1st Platoon?" he yelled.

"Wait one. I'll show you when this shit stops."

While they waited, he counted fifteen more mortar rounds hitting the hill. Then it got quiet. When no mortars hit for two minutes, the Marines in the hole raised their heads cautiously.

"That's it till the next time," one of them said. "Who is it you're looking for, Staff Sergeant?"

"Lieutenant Hinks, First Platoon, Charlie Two-Nine."

"They're on the hill, Staff Sergeant. See that CP bunker right there? I think that's Hinks."

"Thanks."

Frank was covered with red mud from the hole. The ground he was walking on was red mud. The whole damn hill was red mud. Most of the holes were filled or partially filled with muddy water, some with men climbing out after being in them with water up to their necks. No grass, no trees, nothing but pockmarked ripped and torn red dirt that had become slimy red mud. His boots sank in the muck and he had to jerk each step to free his feet from the damn sucking red mud. No more mortars hit while he made his way up the hill to the CP, but occasional sniped small arms kept him looking for the next hole. Half way up the hill he had to drop in the mud when a round passed by his ear. He was very glad to get to the CP bunker. He slid through the opening and looked around.

"What do you need, Marine?"

"Looking for Lieutenant Hinks," Frank said.

"You found him," said a dirty, unshaven, exhausted looking Marine officer. "What do you need?"

"Lieutenant Stephens said to look you up, sir. I'm here to. . ."

Frank told his story.

"Staff Sergeant, you're either a very good Marine or out of your mind," Hinks said. "And right now, I'm not sure they ain't the same thing. You might as well have your turn in the barrel too. Hell, pick a hole. You're here at least for the night. We won't see any more slicks till morning—if then. The gooks shut us down for four days last week. Did you bring a poncho?"

"Yes, sir."

"Good. Most of ours are shredded. Like I said, pick a hole. The troops will be glad to get your poncho to cover the hole."

A Marine slid into the CP.

"Lieutenant, we lost Staff Sergeant Jones. Who do you want to take over as platoon sergeant?"

"Shit! Shit! Shit! KIA?"

"No, sir. Just his leg, but he's out of it. The corpsman took him down to the LZ."

"Hell, I haven't got any NCOs ready. Staff Sergeant Evans, have you been in the shit before?"

"Yes, sir."

"Where?"

"Central Highlands, Dak To."

"Are you infantry?"

Frank hesitated, but then said, "Yes, sir."

"With your orders, I can't order you to, but if you want to do something useful, I need a platoon sergeant for about a day."

"I . . ." Frank realized how little experience he had and hesitated. But hell, he probably knew as much as any of the troops in the mud. That's what he told himself, anyway. "Sure. Show me the layout, sir."

"I'll do better. Skinner's my runner. He can

show you. Skinner, take Staff Sergeant Evans around to the positions and introduce him. Have you got everything you need, Evans?"

"Yes, sir. Can I leave my ruck here?"

"No problem. You better get going. We're due for some evening incoming."

Frank tried to remember that night on the mountain with the General and all the things Gunny Garzinski had done to turn a bunch of Marines into a platoon. These guys were already serving together and knew what they were doing, but they'd lost their platoon sergeant. The platoon sergeant anchored the platoon and gave them the point of focus to act as a unit. Rule of threes. Each squad had three rifle teams, each platoon had three rifle squads. Each team leader looked to the squad leader. Each squad leader looked to the platoon sergeant and the platoon sergeant looked to the platoon commander. Frank had to keep the squad leaders squared away. They would keep their squads squared away. It wouldn't be easy. They'd been getting their asses pounded and knew how to work together. And Staff Sergeant or not, he was new.

The rain had become a steady downpour by then, and the foxholes that had been emptied of water before, now had about a foot of water in them again. Most of the Marines were bailing the water out with entrenching tools and anything else that would hold water, but a few had given up and just let the water build up. Stinking red mud everywhere. He knew the water had to be dealt with. When a mortar-round exploded on impact, the force of the explosion and the shrapnel were reflected up and out on an angle.

Getting below ground level even a little bit improved your chances of surviving a close hit, but water-filled holes made Marines reluctant to get in, and they waited until they were sure the rounds were coming at them. Sometimes there wasn't time to wait. He began thinking up ways to make scoops out of old poncho pieces, scraps of wood, or anything that would hold water. Some of the Marines were way ahead of him. Some weren't even trying. And he knew he would have to make it happen. One more thing to check on and lead.

Skinner took Frank to each defensive position and introduced him and then sprinted back to the CP. Frank chose a position on the platoon's flank with only one Marine in it and made it his base. He might be the acting platoon sergeant, but he also had a job to do for the General and he needed to stay with the grunts. Incoming and sniper fire made it dangerous to be in the open, but he knew he had to move along the line and let the Marines know someone was keeping things together. They had lost one point of focus. It was his job to give them another, and they needed to gain confidence in him. The Lieutenant would make the decisions. Frank just had to keep the platoon functional. He handed his folded poncho to the private and told him to help cover the hole. They didn't get the poncho spread over the hole before the next attack began.

He heard a strange sound from the north side of the Ben Hai river. The river was the line that divided north and south Vietnam and was the center of the DMZ (Demilitarized Zone—five kilometers, north and south of the river) He looked up. Someone yelled "Incoming." The private, known as Fragman because of his fascination with grenades, dropped to the bottom of the hole and held his helmet on with his hands. Frank dropped beside him.

"Rockets," the kid yelled.

Three rockets hit the hill and they were big. The concussion bounced him in the bottom of the hole, blurred his vision, and stunned his hearing. He pressed his body into the mud and his head into the mud wall near the bottom of the hole. The hill got quiet again after the third rocket hit. When the silence had lasted for about a minute, he pushed up out of the mud and looked over the edge of the hole. Rain, steam, mist, and smoke hid most of what he wanted to see. The ringing in his ears covered most of what he wanted to hear.

He climbed over the rim of the hole and scraped mud off the side of his face with the edge of his muddy hand. The rain was falling straight down through a mist of vapor and smoke, and the smell of explosives cut at his nose and throat. Through the ringing in his ears he heard a quiet, almost plaintive call for a corpsman. He made it to the next hole on his belly, assured himself the grunts there were okay, and then sprinted bent over to the next position. The calls for a corpsman continued. The rain was coming down so hard, and he was so intent on finding the wounded Marine, he failed to notice the CP.

When he reached the last defensive position closest to the CP, the calls for a corpsman were clearer. They were coming from the CP, and the CP was a smoking, steaming pile of rubble. Frank was up and sprinting and yelling for the corpsman before he realized what he was doing. The corpsman arrived as Frank cleared an opening into the destroyed bunker. It had taken a nearly direct hit. He saw a boot moving and heard a weak voice calling, "Corpsman, help me." He and the Corpsman pulled rubble off Skinner, and while Doc worked on Skinner, Frank looked for the Lieutenant. He lifted beams and pulled at rubble. Finally, he saw the hand sticking out of a pile of ripped and leaking sandbags.

Two men from the platoon joined him and Doc and helped clear away the rubble. A second corpsman arrived with folded stretchers under each arm. A mortar hit on the side of the hill towards the LZ and south gate.

"Let's get them back to the trench," one of the corpsman said. "The Gooks have got to have this place zeroed in."

Frank assigned two men to help with the stretchers and ordered the rest of the platoon back into their defensive positions. The rain had picked up and it was hard to breathe let alone see. He was soaked and freezing, but he moved from hole to hole and made sure the platoon was coping. He wasn't given the time to learn how to be a combat leader. He just had to do what he could.

The only slicks that were landing were medevac slicks and everything but ammunition was scarce. The grunts on the hill hadn't received a resupply of rations or mail in three days. One of the grunts talked about being hungry and Frank remembered his ruck, now buried under the rubble in the wrecked CP. He made his way back to the bunker in quick sprints from hole to hole.

It was a crazy move. The CP had to be dialed in on the NVA mortars out in the bush, but he needed his pack. For one thing, he had two boxes of Hershey's fruit and nut bars in it he'd brought from the states. The excavation took a few minutes, but he remembered where he had left the pack so he zeroed in on it. With the pack in hand he ran couched over back to the hole at the end of the line.

"Christ," Fragman said. "Is the Lieutenant going to make it, Staff Sergeant?"

"Don't know. He didn't look too good. Skinner might be okay, though."

"Who's in command?"

"Hell, I don't know. I just got here."

"Don't matter. You're senior. I guess you're in command."

Frank thought about that for a moment.

"I guess so," he said. "At least until somebody gets an officer up here. You want a candy bar?"

"Is it dry?"

"Should be. Let's see."

He dug into the pack and pulled out one of the boxes. The box was dry.

"Yeah," he said. They're good to go. Here, take one. Keep your eyes open, I'm going to check on the platoon."

He took the rest of the bars with him and handed them out as he checked in with each position. Twenty-four men. No bars left for him. And not much of a platoon either. More like a reinforced squad.

A minute after he got back to his hole, an officer showed up.

"Who's in-charge here?"

He was passed down the line until he found Frank.

"Staff Sergeant, are you the senior man here?"

"Yes, sir. Staff Sergeant Evans, sir."

"Evans, I'm Captain Loeder. I thought I knew all the Senior NCOs in my company. Are you a replacement?"

"No, sir. I'm here on a special assignment."

He told Captain Loeder the story of being drafted as platoon sergeant.

"Well, this is not your lucky day," Loeder said. "Hinks is out and he won't be coming back. I don't have another platoon leader for you so you are in command. Keep the men sharp tonight. We're expecting probing on the wire and I expect a lot more artillery. I'll try to get a radio over here to you as soon as I can. Looks like you're doing a good job so keep it up. I'll get a replacement for Hinks as soon as I can."

The Captain didn't wait for a reply. He turned quickly and ran in a crouch towards the other side of the hill. Frank moved along the line and made sure the platoon knew about the expected probes and then returned to the misery of his muddy hole.

Chapter 21

Con Thien didn't have a good period or rest period during the last week of September 1967. The misery of wet, cold, and muddy, alternated with the misery of wet, hot and muddy. There were no good or comfortable times to make it better. Not even for a little while. But it often got worse. Sometimes the terror of the attacks made you forget how miserable your life was. But even in the filth and terror, life seemed preferable to the alternative.

    The expected probes didn't happen that night, but the artillery did. The hill took mortars near 0300 and a rocket attack just before light. Frank tried to remember how long he had been on the hill and was amazed when he realized he had only been there one day. He tried to figure out the date and calculated it had to be the twenty-fourth of September. Quantico seem so long ago and so far away.

That day the artillery bombardment picked up considerably. The Company Commander's runner brought Frank a PRC-25 radio and he made Fragman his radioman. That evening, the Skipper told him the hill had taken over three hundred rounds of artillery, mortars, and rockets during the day. He believed it. His head hurt and his hands wouldn't stop shaking. If he could have seen his own face he wouldn't have recognized the unshaven, dirt crusted, slack cheeked visage of a lost soul he had become. And the look in his eyes would have shocked him, the same half focused stare he saw in his Marine's eyes, a bewildered look, as though they had an important question to ask but had forgotten what it was. Two of his Marines were lost to a mortar-round that day, both of them above ground, reluctant to get in a water filled hole, waiting until the last possible moment. They waited too long. He began to think that coming to the hill, maybe, hadn't been one of his best ideas. But he did get to see and experience how the M-16 held up under adverse conditions. Duty helped him hold on to sanity.

During the day, his platoon had plenty of opportunity to use their weapons. The platoon was at less than half strength and without a platoon leader, so the Captain relieved them of patrol duty. Even under constant artillery attack the company continued to send out patrols. Talk about jumping out of the frying pan into the fire. No relief. Staying on the hill was a hazard. Patrolling was a hazard. Coming back was a hazard. The NVA tried to breech the wire with Bangalore Torpedoes in the fog, and a company sized attack took place in the afternoon behind a mortar attack.

Fragman's weapon malfunctioned while Frank was with him so he had a chance to trade weapons and examine the malfunctioned weapon. Fragman was a small Marine and Frank's M-14 rocked Fragman each time he fired it, but he stayed in the fight and gave Frank time to clear the jam in Fragman's M-16 and inspect the weapon. It had the same kind of jam he had experienced with M-16s on the mountain at Dak To. He talked with each man in the platoon and got the same report from all of them. The platoon fought well, but malfunctioning weapons slowed them down and hindered their effectiveness. Most men had cleaning rods fastened to the barrels of their weapons but not all of them. When the rods were pulled off to clear a jammed casing stuck in the breech, it was usually during a firefight. When a Marine is trying to get back in the fight he has his mind on more pressing matters than remembering to refasten the rod to his barrel. The rods ended up on the ground and got damaged or lost.

Three men had to use a rod to clear a casing jammed in the breech that day. Not a lot, but enough to shake the Marine's confidence in the weapon. That's not a good thing when there's nothing between you and the enemy except the wall of lead you can push down range. There were malfunctions from other causes also. At first he figured the malfunctions were due to environmental conditions, but he wondered. The weapons were fouling, but not from the mud and water. The men couldn't follow normal maintenance routines in those conditions but they cleaned their weapons when they could. The fouling appeared to be from excessive powder residue and it seemed to build up quickly after the rifle was cleaned. He'd have to look into that. But right then wasn't the time.

He had two cleaning kits in his ruck he had put together for his own use in the armory. He also had extra brushes, plenty of patches, and gun lube. The lube wouldn't last long. No one else seemed to have any. He issued the cleaning materials to the Marines in his platoon and ordered them to alternate cleaning by fighting hole, one man on duty, one man cleaning his weapon whenever they could.

He learned another lesson about being a platoon sergeant. The "when they could" part often meant only when he told them to. The increased cleaning routine eliminated some of the problems, but the Marines still experienced stuck casings in the breech occasionally. What bothered him was, the stuck casings weren't misfires or duds. The rounds had fired, but the empty casing caught in the breech and failed to extract. In addition, some of the rifles had been in the moisture too long with too little lube available for proper maintenance. Rusty receivers and rusty magazine springs were common. Others just seemed defective and probably had been that way the day they were issued.

When he was busy working with the platoon and during

incoming and firefights, he could forget the mud and misery for a while. But when a lull set in the misery returned. Frank tried to find some comfort by sitting against the dirt wall of the hole with his feet in the water and mud. His utilities were soaked top to bottom anyway. But his feet had been wet for so long, the flesh on his toes felt like it was peeling away. And he had only been there for a day and a half. His hands weren't much better. The skin on his fingers was white and puckered, and it cracked if he squeezed anything too hard. Fragman was worse off than Frank. His feet had been wet for so long they were cracked and bleeding. Dry boots weren't available and changing socks didn't help. Dry socks became soggy socks in minutes. And worse, when you finally had the comfort of dry socks wrapped around your feet, and your feet were warm and comfortable for the first time in God knows how long, the comfort could make you reluctant to jump into a water and mud filled hole again, could make you hesitate for those crucial last few moments before the incoming hit.

On the night of the 24th and morning of the 25th the bombardment was relentless. It was impossible for any of the Marines to sleep or even get any rest. All normal activities were suspended and Marines stayed in their holes. Normal necessities of living were impossible. Eating became a quick bite of something, usually soggy, when you could force it down your throat—and when you had something to put in your mouth. Rations were scarce. Bodily functions normally requiring regular attention all but stopped. The NVA pounded the hill with 152mm howitzers, 120mm mortars, 122mm rockets, 82mm mortars, and 75mm recoilless rifles. Twice during the night, the troops were rocked by huge rockets the Marines called Trashcans. They were 155mm munitions and rare, thank God. Add to the incoming the blasts from friendly artillery and air support, and the Marines lived in a constant environment of mud, water, shock, noise, and destruction. Frank did his best to check on the platoon during the night, but he couldn't move fast in the mud and the men yelled at him to stay in his hole. Leadership sometimes flows upward. He did manage to make two inspection rounds though.

The bombardment increased when morning came on the 25th. The men were scared, cold, mad, and frustrated. The bombardment was causing casualties and there was nothing to do but take it. Every man on the hill lived minute to minute with a fear the next one would fall in their hole. Most of the men were on the edge of hypothermia from soaked clothes and cool temperatures. The NVA stood off on the north side of the Ben Hai, pounded the hill with artillery, and didn't commit troops to the battle.

Frank felt the frustration, and being the lone representative of the authority keeping his Marines on the hill, he became the focus for their anger. Having been relieved of patrol duty hadn't been a relief for the platoon. At least the patrols got to hit back. He was taking the same pounding they were, but they needed a thing to hate, anything that wasn't them. It was sullen, suppressed anger, but it was there.

The reaction he was getting from the Marines hurt and baffled him. What was wrong with the bastards? He was risking his ass to keep them in the game, and they gave him this bullshit? He began to return the resentment. Frank hadn't been a Marine NCO long enough to have shed the natural desire to be liked. But he had some excellent examples of real NCOs to fall back on. He suppressed the resentment and tried to figure out the problem.

His best reference was his experience on the mountain with Garzinski. Why hadn't Ski been resented in that battle? Well, for one thing he probably didn't give a shit if he was resented or not. That just wasn't part of the equation. One doesn't even recognize resentment from one's weapon. Ski used his platoon like it was a living tool, like a multi-capability weapon. He didn't ask. You don't ask your rifle before you pull the trigger. The platoon was Ski's rifle. He didn't wonder. He didn't speculate. He decided and led his platoon.

But there was more to it than Ski's style. The situations were different. Here in Con Thien, the troops were getting the crap pounded out of them and they just had to take it. That's where the frustration came from. On the mountain, every man in the platoon got to hit back. They got pounded, but they pounded back. They got scared, but they didn't get frustrated or resentful. They gave as good as they got.

Frank couldn't magically make the artillery go away or put enemy targets in front of his Marines—but he might be able to relieve some of the frustration. He looked out at the distant and foggy tree line near a flooded rice paddy and then visited each platoon fighting hole and pointed to a spot on the tree line about four hundred meters away. He told them to fire into the trees on his tracers and on his command. When he got back to his hole he had to wait while a couple of mortar rounds hit nearby, but then he raised up and yelled, "Ready on the left. Ready on the right. Ready on the firing line." Someone yelled back, "This ain't the range, Staff Sergeant." He fired a tracer and yelled, "Commence firing," The entire platoon let loose at one time and emptied a magazine each. Two M-79s dropped grenades on the same spot.

"Again!" he yelled, and the platoon cut loose with another ripping blast into the trees. Several men laughed as they ducked back into their holes.

"Check your weapons and let me know if there were any malfunctions." He dropped into his hole and grinned at Fragman. The radio squawked as soon as he hit the bottom of the pit.

"One-Niner, this is Charlie Six. What the hell are you firing at?"

Frank took the hand-set and replied.

"Charlie Six, this is One-Niner. I saw movement on the tree line. Negative contact. I say again, negative contact, over."

"Roger. let's make sure. Give me the grid."

"Charlie Six, I haven't got a map. Can you see the tree line?"

"That's affirmative."

"I'll put a tracer where I saw movement."

"Roger, I'm watching."

Fragman was grinning. "Oh shit," he said. "The Skipper is going to have your ass."

"Shut up and watch."

He checked his magazine and slid a couple of rounds out until the next one was a tracer. He loaded the tracer. He sighted in and fired. The radio sounded again.

"Roger, One-Niner. I have the target. stand-by."

"What do you think he's going to do?" Frank asked.

"What were you thinking?" Fragman asked and then yelled down the line. "Everybody cover."

He and Fragman sat in the bottom of the hole and Fragman laughed. Then he heard Artillery fire from the south. Fragman said, "Outgoing." Then he heard four rushing, whooshing sounds pass overhead followed by four massive explosions moments later. The explosions actually bounced him in the hole.

"One seventy-five mike-mike," Fragman said. "You just spent about four thousand dollars to knock down some trees." Fragman laughed again and Frank heard cheering up and down the line. Didn't kill anything but trees, he thought, but it was worth it. The grunts had been getting pounded and just had to take it. They needed to see something blow up, needed to feel like they were hitting back, needed to feel their power.

The radio sounded again.

"Good eyes, One-Niner. Whatever it was ought to be moving on now if there's anything left of them."

'Roger, Charlie Six. This is One-Niner, out."

"You got to be the luckiest Staff Sergeant in the Marine Corps," Fragman said. "The Skipper isn't a dummy."

"The benefits of a pure heart," Frank said.

"Sergeant fucking lucky," Fragman said.

The artillery incident was the only break they had that day. The NVA resumed their bombardment with a vengeance before the smoke cleared from the tree line. They threw every type of ordnance they had at the Marines. Incoming and outgoing became indistinguishable. The NVA had slipped in close with big mortars, probably 120s, and incoming artillery and rockets from across the river kept up a steady bombardment. Mixed in with the noise of the incoming rounds was the noise of friendly outgoing hitting close to the hill and friendly airstrikes in the DMZ on both sides of the river.

Frank had thought the mountain with Garzinski was the worst he would ever experience—until that day on the hill. The mountain had been bad, but the bombardment Con Thien experienced that day was probably the most devastating any American unit had ever experienced in Vietnam. 1200 rounds of incoming artillery in an area about the size of a sports stadium. Every Marine, soldier, and Seabee on the hill received some kind of trauma. Many were wounded by shrapnel; many killed or wounded by explosive blast; the rest were traumatized by the constant shock and terror of almost constant incoming.

Frank and Fragman had to re-dig their pit after a rocket hit behind them. The explosion splashed an avalanche of mud into the hole, soaked them with slime and buried their legs up to their knees. And the rounds kept coming. It got so nasty he had to restrict his leadership to yelled commands and encouragement. The Marines were shell shocked and sat in the bottom of their pits shaking with wide eyes, staring at the walls with their hands over their ears. He had lost five more men and caught a small piece of shrapnel or stone in his right arm from one blast.

The wound bled and hurt like hell, but he couldn't bring himself to call a corpsman out. The pulsing hole in his arm was small. He dreaded what the General was going to do to him if he found out. He took a skivvy shirt out of his ruck and wrapped the wound.

Fragman said something into the radio handset around 0400.

"Charlie Six," he said handing the handset to Frank.

"Charlie Six this is One-Niner."

"One-Niner, how many effectives are in first platoon?"

"Fifteen, but two are wounded, over."

"Get your gear together. I'm taking you off line. Ten men will arrive shortly to reinforce the platoon and I've got a Gunnery Sergeant to take over for you. My runner will be there in a few minutes with instructions."

"Charlie Six this is One-Niner, roger out."

He handed the handset back to Fragman and said. "Looks like I'm out of here. The Skipper is reinforcing the platoon and sending a Gunny to lead the platoon."

Fragman shook his head and said, "Sergeant Fucking Lucky," and gave Frank a big shit-eating grin. And from that day forward, with what was left of First Platoon of Charlie Company at least, and even after he was gone, Frank Evans would be known as Sergeant Fucking Lucky in 2/9 war lore. The demotion was entirely honorary. Staff Sergeant fucking lucky just didn't have a zing to it.

Frank didn't feel very lucky right then. His arm hurt like hell and had never stopped bleeding. This shit wasn't fun anymore, and the tingle in the tummy was gone, and the General was going to have his ass on a platter.

The Captain's runner showed up ten minutes later with a Gunnery Sergeant and told Frank to report to the CP as soon as he turned the platoon over to the Gunny.

He moved along the line and told the men to make room for replacements. The NVA seemed content to rest for a time and the barrage trickled down to just a few rounds several minutes apart. He found the Company CP on the other side of the big hill near the crest. High stress, lack of sleep, and fatigue were taking their toll and his arm was hot and hurting like a toothache. He slid through the entrance hole using one arm to ease himself into the CP.

"Captain Loeder, Staff Sergeant Evans reporting, sir."

The Captain took his binoculars away from his eyes and turned.

"You did a good job over there, Evans. I just wanted to tell you that before you bugged out. Thanks for hanging in with us."

"Glad to do it, sir. I can hang around if you need me."

"No, we're rotating off the hill in a week anyway. Somebody else's turn in the barrel. What command are you with?"

"I work out of the Special Weapons Evaluation Office at Quantico, sir."

"Who's your commanding officer?"

Frank was getting dizzy and couldn't think well at that point. He felt hot and had spots in his vision. He could only remember one name. "Captain Sharp, General Muldavy's staff," he said. That was as far as he got before his legs gave out and he dropped to a sitting position on the floor.

"Are you okay?" Loeder said.

"I'm just a little tired, sir. Let me rest a minute. I'll be fine."

"What's wrong with your arm?" Are you wounded?"

"Just a scratch, sir."

Frank was feeling lightheaded and he grinned at the Captain.

"Shank, help me with Evans."

The Captain and his runner, Shank, slid Frank to where he could lean back against the wall of the bunker and the Captain untied the undershirt. The wound was red, swelled, and still seeping blood. The sleeve and side of Frank's utility blouse were wet with drying blood.

"Corpsman!" Loeder yelled. "Corpsman up!"

"Just a scratch," Frank said and grinned again.

The corpsman arrived and began examining him.

"I think there's still shrapnel in there, Captain," Doc said after he cleaned the blood from the wound. "It's not very big, but I don't like the looks of his arm. The wound is already infected. Why didn't the idiot call for a corpsman? This wound has to be several hours old."

"Hello, I'm right here," Frank said.

"No you're not," Doc said. "You're in Lala land."

"I suspect he was a bit busy, Doc. He probably didn't want to leave his men."

"Well, he should have. The damn infection could kill him even though the wound isn't that bad. This damn place has bugs we haven't even heard of. . . He's not in shock but the pain could take him there. The morphine should be taking hold soon. Let me get a stretcher. He's got to go out on the next slick."

"Sergeant Fucking Lucky," Frank said and smiled.

"Yeah, the morphine is working. Let's get him down to the LZ."

He woke up with pain shooting up and down his arm. A doctor in utilities was leaning over his arm and digging at the wound.

"Owwl," he moaned. "What the hell are you doing to me?"

"Zap him," the doctor said without looking up.

Frank watched the lights get dim.

The next time he woke up, his arm was bandaged and he was in a slick flying over jungle covered mountains. He stayed awake for the rest of the trip and watched the landing at the Navy medical facility at Marble Mountain near Danang. He looked around, thought, The General's going to have my ass, and then he laughed and drifted back into a morphine induced sleep.

Frank was on the ward for two weeks while they pumped him full of antibiotics. His wound was a minor one and with the shrapnel out, started healing as the infection subsided. The docs said the prognosis was good.

One morning he woke up to find an older nurse with silver oak leaves on her collars looking at his chart.

"Good morning, Sergeant. Just out of curiosity,

is Fucking your first name and Lucky your last or is it the other way around?"

"Ma'am?" he said.

"When you came in you told everyone your name is Sergeant Fucking Lucky. I just wanted to make sure your chart is correct."

"Ma'am, I don't. . ."

"Remember? I guess not. But it would have made my day if that's really your name. No? Oh well. I guess the chart is correct after all. How are you feeling, Sergeant Evans?"

"I'm feeling good. When can I get out of here? I've got to get back to the states."

"Strange you should mention that. Looks like everything is in the green. If you promise the doctor that you will follow his instructions faithfully and check in with the medical facility at Quantico, I think we might get you out of here tomorrow."

"Hey, that's great. I'll do whatever it takes. Is there a phone here I can use to call Third MAF? I need to get my sea bag so I'll have a uniform to put on."

"Already taken care of. A Sergeant Major Jullian delivered it two days ago. He didn't hang around because he said he didn't want another ass-chewing from your General. Have any idea what that's all about?"

"Oh crap. You all didn't tell the General about my wound, did you?"

"Were you planning on keeping it a secret?"

"From him? Yeah."

"Without the infection you might have succeeded. The corpsman that treated you in the field could have returned you to your unit if the wound had been clean. It really isn't much of a wound. But you let it get infected. By the time you got here, the infection was going systemic. Sorry. He knows. General Muldavy, isn't it?"

"Yeah. I guess my ass is grass and he's the lawn mower. It won't be a happy home coming."

"Don't be too sure. I talked to him myself. He was more concerned than angry. How did a Staff Sergeant come to be so close to a Major General?"

"We're not really close," he said. "It's just that he and me, we were. . ."

She seemed interested and Frank didn't have anything else to do so he told his story to the nurse. She was a Navy Commander and probably in her late forties, but she listened well. As he found out later, Commander Bowers was the chief nurse for the whole hospital. Well, Generals have pull. When he finished his story, Commander Bowers, lifted his gown and looked at his chest.

"This is where the round came out?"

"Yes," he said. "And don't ask to see where it went in."

"I don't need to ask. I've seen a lot of wounds in my time. They did a nice job on your head. Well, now you have a new scar. Keep this up and you won't have any room left on your ribbon for any more clusters."

"I was hoping we could just forget about this

one," he said. "But I guess that's out of the question now."

"Yep. It's already in your medical record and the General said to send your file to his office. Sorry."

"Well, it's my own fault. Commander, can you find out what happened to my weapons?"

"I forgot to tell you. The Sergeant Major told me to tell you he took care of them."

"That's a relief. Thanks.

Frank managed to delay his departure by two days and somehow convinced Sergeant Major Jullian to let him visit Echo Company west of Marble Mountain in the sand dunes. Once the antibiotics killed the infection he bounced back quick and he wanted to get one more visit in before he returned to Quantico. Maybe his attention to duty would appease Muldavy. Jullian took some convincing since the dunes were in Indian country. The General had made it clear that Frank was not to be allowed outside of the safe zone in Danang and was to be escorted to the airfield and put on his flight home.

"You're going to get my ass in trouble again," Jullian said while he and Frank sipped a beer in the NCO hooch. "But damn it, we've received the same reports about the M-16 from every unit in the field and nobody in Washington seems to be doing anything about it. If you think another trip will help you get the problems fixed, I'll take the chance. But—daytime only. I'll send you out with an APC (armored personnel carrier). You get six hours and then the APC brings you back. And listen, numb nuts, you will not permit anyone to convince you that you have somehow become attached to Echo Company! Get what you need and get your ass back here before dark."

Echo Company rifleman confirmed his previous opinions about weapon malfunctions and gave him an opportunity to breakdown several weapons that had been turned in due to multiple malfunctions. He talked with grunts and made his notes. By the time he finished with Echo Company, he was beginning to zero in on one problem that seemed to occur with all the rifles. Excessive Fouling. The weapons built up carbon in the chamber faster than other assault rifles. Significantly faster. Sometimes the rifle fouled and malfunctioned after one magazine (19 rounds) was fired. The M-16 is a gas operated rifle and he suspected the fouling and therefore the malfunctions had to do with either the gas system or the powder since it was the hot gasses of the fired round that operated cycling mechanism.

The visit was doubly valuable because he confirmed a second suspicion he had formed on the hill in Con Thien. The troops didn't have adequate cleaning kits. And that was a problem throughout the country. Most of what they had consisted of one cleaning rod fastened to the barrel and jury-rigged collections of cleaning materials that varied from Marine to Marine. Much of what they had, came from friends and family through the mail, not the Marine Corps.

So, he had a weapon that fouls at an excessive rate coupled with an absence of effective cleaning supplies. His report wouldn't be hard to compose.

Chapter 22

The C-141 was going to Travis AFB near San Francisco. It was already on the taxiway and warmed up. Frank had been given orders and an open ticket to hitchhike a ride on a cargo flight out of Danang. The big high wing C-141 was preparing for departure when Frank checked in with the Air Force routers. He was told to wait in sight of the desk and was called when the Load Master on the C-141 determined he could take twelve passengers on the flight. The accommodations weren't first class, but it was going in the right direction.

The pilot invited the troops in the cargo hold to visit the cockpit if they wanted to while the flight was still out over the Pacific Ocean. Frank was the only one who took them up on their invitation so he got to spend a couple of hours watching what they did and talking with the pilots. He guessed the pilots got just as bored as the passengers on a seventeen-hour flight.

He was in service-charlies and his Purple Heart ribbon now had one silver star-cluster instead of five gold individual clusters since the maximum number of clusters on a ribbon is limited to four. The small silver star-cluster represents five individual clusters. Multiple awards of the Purple Heart are made for wounds received in separate incidents, but not if multiple wounds are received in a single incident. A single grenade might wound a man in three places, but that is one incident and one award. Each of his wounds were received in separate incidents so he rated six awards of the Purple Heart, one medal and five clusters. Very few men have the small silver star-cluster on their Purple Heart ribbon—or want one. Most would prefer to forgo that particular ribbon altogether.

He wore his ribbons, but he wasn't as impressed by them as he had been when he got them. The fighting on Con Thien, although just a few days of battle for him, had changed his mind about a lot of things. He almost took the clusters off his Purple Heart. Except for one, the wounds they represented were minor and he no longer felt like they should be recognized. Marines were killed on the hill, and all they got, or all their families got, was a purple heart. That perspective changed his views on a lot of things.

He caught a bus to San Fran International from Travis to board a flight to Washington National. He sat outside of the passenger terminal and just looked around, sniffed the air, and listened to the normal noise of the U.S. of A.

The transition he was going through was confusing and disorienting. He hadn't had time to get the foreign smells out of his nostrils or the memories of incoming, death, and mud out of his mind, and yet, there he was watching Americans zipping in and zipping out in their typical haste without a care in the world, at least not a care rooted in explosives and death. He would be pouring a miniature into a highball glass soon on a clean, dry airplane and no one was shooting at him or wanting to. The thought made him dizzy.

During bull sessions between attacks, the Marines on the hill had talked about the hippies in California and how they could be hostile to military men coming back from Vietnam. The anti-war movement was just getting started in the U.S. and like for most new fads, California was the epicenter, in 1967, maybe the only center. He watched for long-hairs in the terminal but didn't see any particularly hostile ones. Almost every male in America was a long hair of some sort by that time, at least by Marine Corps standards. Most of the folks he ran into were pretty nice. Only a few looked at him with distaste on their faces. The Stews on the flight treated him just like the rest of the passengers.

When the plane pulled into its gate at National, one of the Stews helped him get his AWOL bag down from the overhead compartment. As she stretched to pull his bag down, her skirt rode up her legs exposing a lot of rear thigh.

It's been a long time, he thought. Need to do something about that.

He caught a cab to his apartment. His arm was still sore and he still had a small patch bandage over it, but the infection and swelling were gone. Still, he didn't take any chances and after stacking his bags and pack on the curb, he carried his baggage to his apartment in three trips using only one hand. His weapons had been shipped from Danang direct to the Quantico armory and he had the receipts. He didn't want anything to make the General think his wound was anything but a small scratch. He'd claim that he had been caught in the wrong place by surprise and got out of there as soon as he was able. With any luck he could avoid discussing his role as platoon sergeant. Yeah, that's the ticket, he thought.

He stopped at the bottom of the steps on his third and last trip with his final bag. The wound, the trip, and the emotional exhaustion of the transition were catching up with him. He was feeling a little light headed and sat on the bottom step for a moment with his head on his knees to steady down. He heard the footsteps coming but ignored them.

"Are you okay?" a soft voice asked.

"Yeah," he said through his hands. "Long trip."

"Where are you coming from?"

The voice was feminine and concerned. He lifted his head to see who he was talking to. It was the woman he passed on the steps each morning before he went to Vietnam. She was a nice looking woman. Not especially pretty, but nice looking anyway. Tall too. Maybe five-eight or five-nine. Good body. Windblown brunette. Good legs. Really good legs. He liked her outfit. Most tall women don't have the knees for above the knee skirts, but she did. Her long sleeve filmy blouse with ruffles on the cuffs offered just a touch of prim. It worked well for her.

"West coast," he said.

She cocked her head and smiled.

"Did you fly or walk?"

Frank grinned at her. "Well, there was an ocean back there too."

"Oh," she said. It was a sing-song "Oh" that rose in the middle and tapered off on the end. "You just got back?"

"Yeah. Sorry, am I blocking the steps?"

"No. Are you feeling better now? Need some help?"

"I'm good. Jet lag, I guess."

"Sure," she said and picked up his last bag. "Which apartment?"

"Two B. I can get that."

"No problem. You have to get your key out. Come on, you can't sit there all night."

He led her up the stairs and back to 2B. The rest of his bags were stacked near the door. After he unlocked and opened the door she helped him with the rest of the bags. They dumped them in the living room.

"I'm Frank Evans," he said. "Can I offer you a beer?"

"Carol Lucas," she said. "Okay, I guess I earned it. What's wrong with your arm?"

"I hurt it. Is Bud okay?"

"Sure. Bud is always okay. Can we sit at the counter?"

"Works for me," he said. "Are we neighbors?"

"Right next door. I'm in Two A. I remember seeing you a while back, but then I haven't noticed you around for a couple weeks. I thought you moved out."

"No. I had a special assignment. Should be back for a while now. Do you work at the base?"

"Quantico? No, but I know my way around the Corps though. I was married to a Marine."

"Was?"

"Yes. Young and foolish. Him too. He didn't come back."

He stopped and looked at her more closely. She had spoken that news matter-of-factly.

"From Nam?" he asked.

"Two years ago. Closed coffin. I see you've been working on it too. What's that cluster on your Purple Heart mean? I've never seen one like that."

"Five," he said and turned away quickly. He took two Bud long necks out of the fridge and opened them. Carol tilted hers and took a long pull.

"Ahhh. That hits the spot," she said. "Is one of the five what's wrong with your arm?"

"No. That's the sixth. Just a scratch though.

Look, uh, is it okay if I ask you about your husband?"

"Sure. I guess I don't seem very broken up by it, do I? Let's just say things were in the works before he left. He was living with someone else. A female someone else. Sorry. I shouldn't have dropped it on you like that. And this is getting awfully personal, awfully fast."

She was silent for a moment while she looked at Frank and frowned. She seemed to make up her mind about something and continued.

"It was good for a couple of years," she said. "But it went sour fast. It was probably harder getting over that than getting over him not coming back. He was already history before he left. I was just waiting out the year till the final came through. How about you? Any special relationships in your life. A girlfriend? A wife somewhere?"

Carol wasn't a beauty queen but she was real and was blessed with naturally heavy eyelids and beautiful hazel eyes, and she dipped her sexy eyelids in a slow sensual question mark when she spoke, not exactly flirtatious but with an awareness of assets she had and how to use them. Her eyes were her best feature and drew your attention like a softly whispered exclamation, an appositive necessarily following any attempt to describe her face. It was hard to look away.

"No," he said. "I haven't been in one place long enough to have anything resembling a relationship. Are you hungry? We could fix something or go out. I'll have to go out and pick up something anyway."

She looked at him with a tiny smile on her lips.

"Thanks for the beer," she said. "You're too easy to talk to. I think I'll pass on this one. I'll see you around, Staff Sergeant Evans."

She tilted the bottle up and drank the last of the beer. She smiled at him and then tilted her head down and looked up at him with her eyes. "Take care of yourself, Frank." And then she was gone.

He stared at the door for a while and then turned back to his beer. "What did I do?" he asked his beer bottle. But the bottle was busy making rings on the counter and didn't enlighten him.

When he arrived at the Swee-O office in the morning, he found a name plate over the door next to Lieutenant Cummings's office. *SSgt Frank Evans, USMC*. Below his name were the words, *HQMC Staff-Field Studies*. Well, that makes the chain of command clear enough, he thought.

The office had an OD green desk and chair, two chairs for visitors, and a gray typewriter. The OD green filing cabinet was stocked with office supplies. Since he was the only one in the office and he hadn't been officially summoned by Sharp or the General, he put paper in the typewriter, but then stopped and stared at the paper. Hmmm. Everything in the Marine Corps had a required format, and he didn't know how to draft a report of the kind he needed to submit to the General.

Frank went to Corporal Clark's desk and looked through the book shelf next to Clark's filing cabinet.

One binder was titled *HQADMINMAN*. That was easy enough to figure out. Headquarters Administration Manual. Probably what he needed. He ran his finger down the index and stopped on Chapter 7, Staff Studies. He took the manual with him.

The first draft of his report was done by 1000. Lieutenant Cummings hadn't come in, but Clark was at his desk typing away.

"Corporal Clark, can you give me a hand? I just need you to look over this report and tell me if I did it right."

"Yeah, sure, Staff Sergeant. The Lieutenant is off today, so I have some time. When do you need it back?"

"Pretty quick. The General is waiting for it."

"Okay, I'll take a look soon as I finish this letter. Do you have my admin manual?"

"Yeah, sorry. I'll get it."

Clark brought the report into Frank's office twenty minutes later with red marks and underlines on all three pages.

"You have the format right, but you have to be careful with your spelling and punctuation. Fix what I marked and you'll be okay. Uh, Staff Sergeant Evans, can I give you some advice?"

"Sure. You're the expert."

"I'm not talking about admin. Maybe you should run this by Cummings before you submit it. M-16 ammo studies are his baby."

"Haven't got time. This has to be in General Muldavy's hands before I see him. He's not happy with me right now. Tell you what. Why don't I copy Cummings and leave you a copy for his review?"

"If you say so. He isn't going to be happy about it."

"Can't help it. It's got to go out this morning."

Garzinski called Frank at 1300.

"Hiding in your new office isn't going to do you any good," the Gunny said. "Sharp wants to see you. Are you mobile?"

"Yeah, I'm fine. It was just a scratch, Gunny. Is the General pissed?"

"He ain't happy. Your report may have saved your ass though. Sharp wants to talk to you about it. 1330. Be here." Garzinski hung up before Frank could say anything else.

Two raps on Captain Sharps doorjamb at 1328. Not taking any chances Frank marched into the office, stopped two feet in front of the desk at attention, and sounded off. Sharp sat back in his chair and looked him over. He didn't give the command for at-ease, so he remained at rigid attention. Finally, Sharp looked him in the eyes.

"Show me the wound," Sharp said.

"Sir, the wound is under the tiny little bandage on my right bicep, sir."

"Would you, Staff Sergeant Evans, repeat for me the General's orders to you about staying out of action."

"Sir, the General ordered me to stay out of hot zones and avoid combat, sir."

"And did you follow those orders, Staff Sergeant Evans?"

"Sir, it was necessary for me to observe the weapons under the conditions that were causing the weapons to malfunction. I attempted to avoid direct action with the enemy and spent only the minimum time in the hot zone necessary to carry out my mission, sir."

"Let me get this straight, Staff Sergeant Evans. You needed to observe the M-16 in action so you picked the hottest action in Vietnam to do your observation, is that correct?"

"Sir, not being familiar with the current combat conditions. . ."

Sharp interrupted him and pointed at the chair.

"At ease. Consider yourself chewed out, Frank. Sit. Now tell me about Con Thien and then we can get to your report. Did you really assume command of a platoon in combat?"

"How'd you hear about that, sir?"

"Well, based on the citation I have sitting in front of me submitted by the commanding officer of Charlie Company of the Two-Nine, you will probably get a cluster for your bronze star. He says some pretty impressive words about your performance while you were—let's just say observing the use and effectiveness of the M-16 while avoiding combat as per the General's orders. Tell me about it."

"Captain, I want to make it clear I only intended to stay for a few hours and then get out of there. But the bombardment picked up right after I arrived on the hill . . ."

He told his story as best he could remember. Captain Sharp didn't interrupt except to encourage him when he slowed down or obviously skipped over events. Sharp was shaking his head when Frank finished up.

"Frank," Sharp said, "you do have a way of getting yourself right in the middle of the hottest shit around. Okay, I'll give you the benefit of the doubt and assume you were trying to follow the General's orders. Now tell me about your report. Give me more detail and a recommendation. This is your first evaluation so you get to slide a little. But remember this. When you do a staff study for this office you always conclude with a recommendation, even if it's just a recommendation to do more evaluation.

Frank went over his report and described what he had seen and experienced with the M-16 in the mud and heavy use on the hill. He pressed the point that the complaints seemed to be wide spread and accurate.

"What's your recommendation?"

"Well, sir. We've identified a couple of problems, but I haven't really discovered the root causes. I need to take a few weapons on the range and push them until they malfunction. So I guess I'm recommending that you give me some help and let me complete the study. Knowing what the problems are doesn't help the grunts. They need the problems fixed."

"How much time do you need?"

"I don't know. I've never done anything like this."

"You have to be specific, Frank. I can't take an open ended recommendation to the General."

"Can I have a month?"

"I need a recommendation not a question."

"Then make it a month. I'll try to figure it out."

"You will report a solution within the next thirty days. Frank, your report is going to step on a lot of toes. There's a lot of commanders and procurement people saying the problem is cleaning. They say our Marines aren't cleaning their weapons. You are saying it goes way beyond that. You need to back up your findings with facts from tests and a recommended solution."

"Can I have some help?"

"I can give you Garzinski."

"Okay. That will help."

"Why'd you copy your report to Cummings?" Sharp asked.

Frank looked up and wasn't sure what to say. Cummings was a Lieutenant and he was an NCO. That seemed like answer enough. But Sharp knew that.

"His clerk helped me smooth the report," Frank said. "He said I should run it by Lieutenant Cummings before I submitted it, and he said M-16 ammo is

Cummings's responsibility."

"Okay. But from now on your reports will come to me only. I'll decide who needs to be copied."

"Yes, sir."

Sharp drummed his fingers on the desk in front of him for a moment and let out a big breath.

"I think we'll let the General cool down for a few days before you see him. You're lucky he's got other problems right now. He's been meeting with people at Headquarters every day for a week. Something's up. Keep your head low and work on some solutions. I'll call you when I think the time is right."

"Thanks, sir."

"Go on, get out of here."

That night he left base early and waited in his car in the parking lot near his apartment for Carol to show up. Maybe he could talk her into another beer. He didn't know what she was driving, but he was sure he could recognize those long legs from a block away. A Corvette pulled in and stopped on his end of the lot. The passenger door opened and Carol got out. She leaned over and said something to the driver and laughed. As the Corvette pulled away she waved.

Frank started to get out but hesitated. Maybe he had miscalculated. The farewell at the car had seemed friendly, almost intimate. If she had something going on with someone else, he didn't want to be a nuisance. And he sure wasn't in the Corvette class. She started up the steps and he opened the door to get out of his car. He held back so she would have time to get inside her apartment and then he started up the steps.

When he turned toward his apartment he saw Carol in front of his door with her finger on the doorbell.

"He's not home yet," he said.

She turned and grinned at him. "Do you think he has any beer?"

"If he doesn't, he damn well better go get some," he said. "I was planning to buzz you."

"Buzz me? she said and grinned.

"Doorbell. Can I offer you a beer?"

"You smooth talking fool."

Chapter 23

In the morning Frank and Garzinski drew a dozen brand new M-16s from the armory and cleaned each of them thoroughly. Next they put each rifle on the bench and tore them down, verifying that everything in the weapon was machined and assembled properly. They drew the same ammo the Marines carried in the field and took the rifles to the range. Frank seemed to pause often and grin at nothing for no good reason, in Garzinski's opinion.

At the range they fired 100 rounds through each rifle on semi-auto and then fired five magazines through each rifle on automatic. Or at least that was their goal. Three rifles malfunctioned during the semi-auto single fire test, and two others had malfunction by the second or third magazine on full automatic. But some of the rifles, seven of them, worked well throughout all of the tests. They recorded serial numbers, the number of rounds before each malfunction, and wrote a description of the malfunction and what they found when they field stripped the rifles after each malfunction. They also recorded the time of day, weather, temperature, and humidity during each of the tests. When all twelve rifles had been through the firing regimen, they were taken back to the shop and torn apart. Each step was recorded and what they found was described in detail.

Frank had a Marine Corps photographer take close up shots of the fouling he suspected was the main problem. But the fouling didn't explain the occasional stove piping of a round in the chamber after a round failed to eject from the breech. Some casings just seemed to grab hold of the steel breech and stick there, so much so that the extractor would either slip over the rim of the cartridge or rip right through it. When that happened the only way to remove the round from the breech was to ram a cleaning rod down the bore from the muzzle and push the spent cartridge out. They had too many unanswered questions. They cleaned the weapons and took them back to the range and started over.

Unknown to lowly grunts like Frank and Garzinski, the issue of malfunctioning M-16s in the field was becoming a major controversy for all the services and especially the Marine Corps. Unresolved field reports from company and battalion commanders complaining of vexing and unfixable problems with the weapon were stacking up on staff officers' desks. Having been advised by procurement and weapons board staff with a vested interest in defending their testing and procurement decisions, the Commandant of the Marine Corps had publicly defended the M-16 and in hearings told Congress the only problem with the M-16 was getting enough of them.

Part of the problem was senior officers' reputations were on the line. But the reluctance to take complaints seriously went beyond self-interest. Generals who had been around when the M1 replaced the '03 Springfield remembered how the Corps had balked at giving up their tried and true Springfield rifles. The M1 was clearly a superior weapon in rate of fire, but Marines being men of tradition, refused to accept it. Nothing is more difficult than changing an established system. There were rumors of defects and malfunctions then, just as the M16 was being maligned in current times. The M-14 when it came along faced the same kind of resistance. Now the M-16 was getting the same treatment. Senior officers knew bringing change to the Corps was a difficult task. Many were convinced the M-16 was a lighter, faster, higher capacity and therefor superior weapon for the modern battlefield and were reluctant to accept the same old arguments and complaints they had faced every time a change was implemented. But complaints from the fighting forces in Vietnam kept piling up and were coming from all of the services. Horror stories of weapon failures resulting in deaths had made it into hometown newspapers from correspondents, and congressmen were getting letters from worried moms.

With typical military establishment efficiency, the rear guard closed ranks to protect their asses. And Major General Muldavy was right in the middle of the controversy—and on the wrong side, from the point of view of the establishment. The rear guard dug in their heels and criticism of the M-16 by anyone was considered disloyal. The complaints were turned back on the troops. Instead of taking the complaints seriously, which might mean having to pull millions of dollars' worth of weaponry and ammunition out of the field and reissuing the older M-14 until the problems could be analyzed and fixed, a serious and valid issue in itself, the rear guard chose to believe that all of the problems were caused by the stupidity and laziness of the fighting men and lack of leadership by the fighting officers. The controversy was reaching critical mass while Frank and Garzinski, diligently and unaware, tried to solve the mystery of fouling and jamming M-16s.

Over the next two weeks they tried several different brands of lube and cleaning solvents, tried brushing out the chamber and as much of the mechanisms in the lower receiver as they could reach between each magazine change without tearing down the whole thing, and tried anything else they could think of to reduce the residue build up in the receiver. They even tried oil in the breech to keep the rounds from sticking. But excessive oil collected carbon and increased fouling, and oil in the breech could penetrate primers and cause rounds to turn into duds. The extreme measures they took kept the rifles firing, most of the time, but grunts in the field and under attack couldn't be expected to stop and clean their weapons between each magazine. And having to use the rod to clear a jam could get the rifleman killed in a hot battle, especially if the enemy was right on top of him.

Frank also improved his military education in the evenings. At the NCO club he had developed a reputation as a young NCO who asked good questions, was willing to listen to answers—and of course, was willing to pick up the beer tab. He sat with a group of senior NCOs, including several Gunnery and Master Sergeants, and described the situation at Con Thien. It took a lot of beer to keep the conversation going, Marines don't do anything for free even when they enjoy it, but it was worth the price. The combat experienced Gunny Sergeants, most with two wars behind them, cleared the table and used bottles, nut bowls, and even nuts and smokes to diagram how they would have set up the defenses and deployed the troops.

What many people unfamiliar with the Corps don't know is Gunnery Sergeants are often the most experienced combat commanders in the Corps, some with two and even three wars under their belts. When Platoon Commanders are killed in action, Gunnery

Sergeants often take command of the platoon. Gunnery Sergeants have even assumed command of companies. When a company is short on Lieutenants, Gunnery Sergeants are given command of platoons.

The Gunnies Frank met weren't bashful about explaining in detail why their tactics would work or criticizing the way the hill was actually defended. Then they spent an hour arguing with each other about how to best attack Con Thien the way it was. Frank wasn't bashful either. He took notes and asked lots of questions. One of the Gunny Sergeants who was an instructor at the Officers Basic Course invited Frank to observe a day of field operations with a class of future platoon leaders. He took a rare day off and took the Gunny up on his offer. Experience was coming slow, but his knowledge was growing quickly along with his maturity as a Marine NCO. Frank didn't realize how much he had changed.

He also improved his knowledge of Carol every night. She liked beer and she liked a wild roll in the hay. He was glad to provide both. She was a manager in operator services for C&P Telephone Company of Virginia and made as much money as a Major in the Marine Corps. And she liked a wild roll in the hay. And beer. It was a match made in heaven.

Then he discovered Carol was very comfortable to be around and comfortable to talk with. He was changing, his experiences making him more inward, and he didn't find people as interesting as he used to.

Conversations had to be worked at now unless he was talking about leading Marines with other Marine NCOs. He sensed his loss of interest, but he didn't have time to worry about it. It was different with Carol. She knew how to listen and she enjoyed being listened to. She liked to play with his ear while he talked.

Day by day he began to think about her more and more and anticipation made him cut his meetings short at the NCO club. He'd never had a romance, not a real one. There had been the breathless vows of eternal love in high school that changed from semester to semester, but real romance, the kind that makes you start to think about the future, your future, her future, a place to settle down, that kind of romance, had somehow eluded him through college and his early twenties. He had always been a loner and enjoyed it that way. Now, he wasn't so sure. If Carol had to work late or couldn't see him, his empty apartment seemed gloomy.

Some nights she would be waiting for him and some nights he would be waiting for her. Whichever it turned out to be, they were both happier when they got together. The talk would start as soon as they got into his apartment and opened a beer. The love would start right after the first beer. They laughed a lot and thoroughly enjoyed each other without any pretension or posturing. No one else was needed after their first night together. And after the first night together, he knew almost everything about her past. She knew very little about his. Not because he held anything back, but he just seemed so damn interested in her. He enjoyed hearing about her and about what she did. He didn't try to, but he made her feel important and special.

Back on the base, Frank and Garzinski didn't know it, but their weapons testing at the range was beginning to make some people in procurement uncomfortable. Procurement people asked people on the weapons board if they were responsible for the weapons testing that was taking place. Weapons board people asked the test and evaluation sections if they were conducting the tests. The answers all came back negative. The names, ranks, and reporting organizations of the two sergeants using all the range time were obtained and passed up the line.

    They weren't the only Marines who worked for General Muldavy who were being looked at by people interested in what they were doing. The MMOA (Manpower Management Officer Assignments) had been looking at Captain Sharp's career for several weeks. Company commanders were needed in Vietnam and a command assignment was next in Sharp's career plan. On top of that, General Muldavy, behind the scenes, was pressing the Commandant for a combat assignment. His wounds had cut his Vietnam tour short and he wanted command and out of the Washington scene.

One morning near the end of week two, Garzinski stopped working at his bench and called Frank over.

"Look at this gas tube and key," Ski said. "The damn things are a mess. Now I'd expect a gas operated rifle to need cleaning more often than a recoil operated mechanism or a bolt. The gases pushing down the tube to operate the action carry some power residue, so the action on a gas operated system is always going to get dirty faster than mechanical recoil systems. But damn, Frank, they shouldn't be getting like this as quick as they are. The ammo has to be part of the problem. Have you looked up what kind of powder we're getting in the ammo we buy?"

"Hadn't even considered it, Gunny. They did the full range of acceptance tests before the M-16 was adopted by the services. Powder problems would have been caught then, wouldn't they?"

"The .223 was a new round then. The manufacturers probably supplied the ammo for the tests and they would have optimized the ammo to get the best out of the weapon. I'm wondering if the powder we're using now is different from what they used then. How can we get a look at the data from the acceptance tests?"

"Maybe Cummings can help us. Clark said ammo is his baby."

Garzinski thought about it for a moment, but only a short moment.

"I hate to let that asshole into our business, but I guess we have to. You want to ask him or do we need Sharp involved?"

"Hell, how much of a problem can it be? He's a

Marine, an asshole for sure, but still, he's a Marine officer. He'll want to get to the bottom of this problem."

Ski looked at Frank with one eyebrow raised.

"Your innocence amazes me sometimes," Ski said. "Well, let's give it a try."

Frank took Garzinski back to his office. They put their heads together to figure out how to ask for Cummings's help without letting his nose too far into their tent.

"Crap, Ski," he said. "He's going to figure out what we're doing no matter how we ask. I'll just ask for the data straight out."

Garzinski drummed his fingers on the desk for a few moments and then looked at Frank.

"Okay. We can always go to Sharp if Cummings gets his back up."

"Is the Lieutenant in, Clark?"

"He's got a Major from procurement with him right now. I think they're done with business and just visiting though. Want me to interrupt.?"

"Will it get his panties in a twist?"

Clark grinned. "No, I don't think so. He popped out a few minutes ago and said they were through. I'll check."

Clark lifted the phone and waited for Cummings to answer.

"Lieutenant, Staff Sergeant Evans wants to see you. Do you want me to tell him to come back later? . . . He's right here . . . yes sir." Clark hung the phone up.

"Go on in."

Frank knocked once, opened the door and left it open. He marched to Cummings desk and stood at attention.

"At ease, Evans. Do you know Major Snodgrass?"

Frank relaxed into a loose parade rest. "I don't believe so, sir. Good to meet you, Major."

The major was of a type with Cummings, a high level clerk. He obviously enjoyed eating and from the redness of his cheeks probably enjoyed a nip or two now and then. He was in service-charlies, but managed to make them look like civilian casual. Snodgrass nodded, but he watched Frank with interest—and maybe a little anger.

"What do you need, Staff Sergeant?" Cummings asked.

"Sir, I'm doing an evaluation of field problems with the M-16 and . . ."

"If they'd keep the damn things clean, there wouldn't be any problems," the major said. "And if the platoon leaders and you sergeants exercised some leadership, we wouldn't have all these complaints."

"Yes, sir, I'm sure that's part of the problem, but I think we might have a problem with the ammo. . ."

"There's nothing wrong with the ammo, or the weapon," the major interrupted again. "The ammunition was evaluated thoroughly and the procurement decision was fully justified."

"I'm sure it was, sir. But I've got to complete my

evaluation. Lieutenant Cummings, how can I get access to the acceptance test data for the M-16?"

"What do you need it for?"

"I want to compare the results we're getting now with the test data for when the weapon was first evaluated."

"What's that going to tell you?" the Major asked. "We have quality control processes in place that assure us the weapons meet military specifications."

"Yes, sir. What I want to see is the ammunition data, especially the powder that was used."

"Do you think the ammunition we are issuing is causing malfunctions?"

"I'm not sure, sir. But the weapon is fouling a lot more than it should. I suspect at least part of the problem could be the powder."

"Do you think we would procure and issue ammunition to our Marines that doesn't meet specifications? Is that what you think?"

"Sir, I don't know what the problem is. I need to verify everything. The spec itself could be a problem."

"Why you arrogant. . . who do you think you are? Thousands of hours and years of experience went into the development of those specs. Stand at attention, Marine! Do you think you have the right to question . . . ?"

A knock sounded at the door. "Excuse me, sirs," Garzinski said. "General Muldavy is on the phone for Staff Sergeant Evans."

Major Snodgrass stopped in mid-sentence and

stared at the Gunny."

"What did you say?" Snodgrass asked.

"Sir, excuse me for interrupting, but General Muldavy wants Staff Sergeant Evans on the phone. He said immediately, sir."

Major Snodgrass looked at Frank with his hands made into fists. His face got red, but he knew better than to say anything else.

"You are dismissed, Evans."

Frank did an about-face and marched out of the office. He closed the door to his own office after he and Garzinski entered.

"What line is he on?" he asked.

"He ain't. I made it up to get your ass out of there," Garzinski said. "But you better get on the line to Sharp and tell him what just happened. That pogue chair-warmer is covering something up and he's going to be after our asses."

Major Snodgrass walked to Cumming's door and pulled it shut.

"Can you believe the arrogance of that . . . that knuckle-dragger? What is he doing evaluating the decisions and action of his superiors? Answer me that, Cummings. What does an enlisted man know about weapons?"

"He reports to Captain Sharp, sir. So, in effect, he reports directly to General Muldavy. I tried to get him transferred out of here when he first reported, reported without my knowledge and without my having requested additional billets, I might add. But Sharp shot that down and in so many words told me to keep my nose out of the Sergeant's business."

"General Muldavy just won't let this thing go," Snodgrass said. "He's old infantry and they never change. But that's neither here nor there. Stirring this thing up again will do nothing but cause unnecessary trouble for everyone. Christ, Cummings, the congress is getting involved again. We need to do something to manage the fallout before it starts and I may need your help. Give me a copy of the report the sergeant submitted to Muldavy. I know some people who need to see it. I can't do anything about Muldavy, but staff sergeants should be leading platoons, not doing staff studies an educated officer should be doing. I think a word to the enlisted assignment system people is in order. Perhaps from a General officer with more clout than General Muldavy."

"Major, I'm not happy about Evans playing in my sandbox either, but sir, he's just an enlisted man following orders."

"An enlisted man who would be much happier doing what he was trained to do, Cummings. Staff Sergeants should be leading platoons. I think the quickest way to deal with the current study and testing is to put the sergeants where they belong and transfer the study to your office. It's for the good of the Corps, Cummings."

Chapter 24

Captain Sharp listened as Frank described the scene in Cummings's office. The more he heard the more disgusted he became. His disgust was increased because he had talked to General Muldavy earlier and knew about things going on that Evans and Garzinski didn't know.

"Frank," he said into the phone, "Come over to the office and bring whatever data you have with you. I think we need to give the General a progress report. Bring Garzinski with you."

"Yes, sir." he said. "What should I do about that Major?"

"Nothing. He's our worry. Avoid him and stay away from Cummings too. It was probably a bad idea to co-locate you in the Swee-o office to begin with. Make sure you bring me everything you have so far. Don't leave anything in your office for them to find."

"Do you think Cummings would look through my files while I'm not here?"

"What do you think?"

"Okay. I'll clean out the office."

"Take your time and be thorough. I'll see you and Garzinski at 1400."

"Aye, aye, sir."

Sharp hung up the phone and rubbed the back of his neck. Evans and Garzinski couldn't know about the crap that was going on at headquarters, crap that had been going on long before they got here, but they are in the middle of it now, he thought. The General had been in a lot of meetings with the commandant for the last three days and Sharp had a feeling the General's time in Washington was nearing an end. Muldavy had been campaigning for a combat command ever since he had been sidelined by his wounds. If he was being successful, his staff's future was also in question. Sharp had a lunch appointment with Muldavy and figured he might be getting some news. Maybe good. Maybe not so good.

Now that Snodgrass knew about the project, somebody was going to do something to quash it or get it under their control. Garzinski and Evans were good Marines and just following orders to best of their abilities, but that wouldn't matter to the assholes sitting out the war on their fat asses and protecting their turf.

Sharp closed his eyes, took a deep breath, and let it out slowly. That wasn't fair, he thought. There weren't many fat asses in the Corps. Some of them did spend most of their time covering their own asses and playing the game, but for the most part even here in Washington they were good Marines just trying to do a tough job in a war nobody seemed to want.

Captain Sharp was a grunt at heart. He hated sitting in an office as a General's Aide and he wanted a line company. Assignment as an Aide was a career builder and was given to officers who were seen as having potential for higher command, but he had been assigned to General Muldavy, and right then, being Muldavy's Aide may not have been the best career builder around. Muldavy was a maverick. He had been an outstanding combat commander, but he couldn't seem to fit into the headquarters political scene. Or maybe he just didn't want to. He admired him for that, but knew that Muldavy's time in Washington and maybe his time in the Corps was nearing an end. If you couldn't handle the politics, you weren't going any higher than two stars. He thought it was amazing Muldavy had been selected above bird colonel.

The M-16 thing had gone ballistic in the past three days and he was smart enough to know there were good arguments on both sides of the issue. The Marine Corps Development Board backed by the entire procurement organization, and sadly, the Commandant himself, were circling their wagons and considered anyone not supporting their views to be disloyal to the Corps and a threat. And to add to their fears, Congressman Lowe, encouraged by a ton of mail from his constituents had launched his own investigation. And the media loved the controversy.

The media hated the war. Join the fucking crowd, he thought. We're not too fond of it ourselves. But the lying, self-serving bastards hated the military too and actually made it harder to fix a problem. When the media got involved, people in Washington circled their wagons and nothing got done.

Well, he thought, a good commander takes care of his Marines. It's time for me to get my troops under cover. And it is time for the General to do the same. Problem was, the General already had something going on and it might be too late to do anything to change things for Garzinski and Evans. He told the Sergeant Major to give him thirty minutes on the General's schedule as close to 1500 as he could make it.

Frank picked up the photographs of fouled weapons from the photo shop and put them in the box of files he had in the back seat of his car. Nothing was left in the office that wasn't there when he arrived on his first day. Garzinski cleaned and turned in the test rifles. They went off base for an extended lunch and Frank found a pay phone to give Carol a call at work. He had been doing a lot of that lately.

"Hi, it's me."

"Marine me, Army me, or Navy me?" she said.

"Marine me. I ran the Army and Navy off."

"Oh. Were they mad?"

"Furious."

"Well, a girl likes to feel wanted. Feel like riding over to Annapolis and having a dreamy, romantic dinner on the water tonight?"

"Long drive."

"Only about an hour. Besides, we need a change of scenery."

"Let's make that a maybe. I'm all for it, but some stuff is going on at work. If everything works out, I'll call you later and maybe we can get an early start. If not, maybe tomorrow night."

"Okay," Carol said. "Call by three if you want me to take off early."

"I will. Can't wait to see you."

"Me too. See you, that is."

"Bye."

Frank and Garzinski drove to the base HQ building at 1330 and waited outside of Sharp's office for the Captain.

Sharp returned to his office at 1350 and waved the sergeants in.

"Sit," he said. "I've got some news and it's only partially good news. I had lunch with the General. The General is meeting with the Commandant at this time and I've just finished talking with MMOA. I am being reassigned. I was up for a company anyway, but I expect that General Muldavy is also being reassigned. This is good news for us. I'm getting my company and the General has wanted out of Washington since he got here."

"Jesus, what happened, sir?" Garzinski said.

"The needs of the Marine Corps," Sharp said. "Company Commanders are needed in Vietnam and I guess the Corps figured I was being wasted here in Quantico."

"Not that, sir," Frank said. "Isn't this all kind of quick? We didn't even know you were up for transfer."

"We're in a war, Frank. Things like this happen during a war."

"Does it have anything to do with what happened this morning?"

"I suspect it's been in the works for a lot longer than that. Our Patrick has ruffled a few feathers during his time in Washington. But If Major Snodgrass talked to the right people, he probably forced a few hands and brought things to a head."

"What about us?" Garzinski said.

"I was getting to that. You will be made available for reassignment. Look, I haven't got all the dope yet. But the General will want to see both of you first thing in the morning. Have either of you talked with anyone about your project?"

"No, sir," Garzinski said. "Not since we talked to you."

"No civilians have contacted you?"

"No, sir. Who's looking for us?"

"No one, I hope," Sharp said. "There are a couple Congressional Aides on base and they've been given permission to go anywhere and talk with anyone they desire. Stay away from them. In fact, both of you take the rest of the day off and get off base and stay off base until morning. Be here in my office at 0800. Do I make myself clear?"

"Yes, sir." Frank said. "Will you know something about us in the morning?"

"We should. The General is working on something he won't talk about. By the way, Frank, your Bronze Star was approved. You can put a cluster on your ribbon. The general will take care of the citation in the morning."

"Thanks, Skipper. I don't have to wear Blues again, do I?"

"No. I think this presentation will be low key. Wear your Service Alphas in the morning. I have a feeling things are going to move fast for all of us. Now get out of here and stay away from the base."

Garzinski called his wife and told her he was coming home early. Frank called Carol and told her to take off early. After his call Garzinski was quiet for a couple of minutes and stared across the room.

"Christ, Frank. I'm not looking forward to telling Sharon."

"Think they'll move you to another base?"

"Frank, listen," Garzinski said. "There's only one place either of us is going to get orders to. It's hot, dirty, and full of little guys in black pajamas who like to shoot at us."

"Back to Vietnam?"

"Know of any other place with guys in black

pajamas shooting at us?"

"No, I guess not. What do you think we'll be doing?"

"I'll probably get a company slot and you'll get a platoon. We're infantry, Frank. Not much else they can do with us."

"Shit! I can't say I'm looking forward to more of that excitement. I'm not looking forward to telling Carol either."

"You two have been going out pretty steady lately. Getting serious?"

"Hell, I don't know, Ski. I guess it is. Damn it, we're just getting to know each other."

"A career in the Corps can be tough on families. I'd give it up for Sharon, but I've got sixteen years in, three to go. Hell, maybe we'll get jobs training replacements."

"You really think so?"

"No."

The ride around the Washington beltway that night was quiet. But by the time they took the exit onto Route 50 toward Annapolis, Carol had had enough of the quiet.

"Are you going to tell me what's wrong?" she asked quietly.

"Sorry, I . . . it's not you. Don't think that. I guess I was waiting for the right time."

"For what?"

"Carol, I think I'm going to get orders."

"What kind of orders?"

"Overseas."

"Oh shit! Vietnam?"

"Probably. I'm not sure yet, but I should find out tomorrow."

"You knew about this and didn't say anything?"

"No. I just found out today. I'm sorry. I don't even know why. I've only been here for two months."

"The stinking Marine Corps," she shouted. "Why in the hell did I have to get involved with another Marine?"

"I'm not real happy about it either," he said. "Every time they send me over there somebody puts a new hole in me. Christ, I'm sorry. I didn't want this to happen."

Carol sat quietly for a few moments and then slid across the seat and pulled his arm around her.

"We are not going to talk about this tonight. You are going to wine me and dine me and then you are going to make love to me. And then we will discuss this insanity like two adults. Okay?"

He pulled her tight against his side, but didn't say anything.

"Okay?" she asked again.

"Okay," he said.

They sat in the lounge at the Charthouse on the water in Eastport across the bridge from Annapolis. The harbor was lit up by the lights from shore and by anchor lights on the boats tied up at city moorings. The room was packed with diners waiting for their tables and fifty quiet conversations enclosed them in a buzz of privacy. They tried the stiff upper lip routine and forced gaiety, but no matter how hard they tried to ignore the dark thing sitting between them, their eyes would meet and a hollow sense of loss would steal their words and crush their attempt to ignore it.

They had a quiet dinner, their fingers entwined on top of the table. Conversation was hard and attempts ended mostly in single syllables. They walked back to the parking garage, arms around waists, bumping awkwardly when their steps didn't sync, not wanting to let go. On the ride home she tucked herself up under his arm and didn't talk.

They made love gently, both of them trying to give pleasure and receive comfort. Carol rolled to the side when they were done and cried. He held her and didn't know what to say. When her cry was done she turned over and put her head on his chest.

"Will this be a full year tour," she asked. The tears were gone and her voice was steady.

"I don't know. All I found out today is I'm being reassigned. My friend Garzinski too. He thinks it will be Vietnam because we are both infantry. If it is, the normal tour is thirteen months."

"Are you planning to stay in?"

"It's all I know."

"You have a degree. You told me."

"In Math. What can you do with a math degree?"

"It's a degree. It can open doors. You could get

a management job anywhere."

"Doesn't much matter now. No matter what the future holds, I'm in for three and a half more years. And I'm on my way somewhere in the next few days."

"This is shitty," she said. "We were just getting. . ."

"I hope we are," he said. "I know I am."

"I want to write to you," she said. "Is that okay?"

"Yes. As much as you can."

"Frank, I can't promise you anything. I won't wait for you. I mean I will be waiting but not anything official. I won't promise that. I don't think I can do that again."

"Will you tell me if you meet someone else?" he asked.

"Yes. I'm not looking. I won't be. But we won't even know each other a year from now. We've had three weeks together. That's hardly even an affair. Is that enough to last for a year?"

"I wish I knew," he said. "We can write and hope, can't we?"

"I can write."

After Carol returned to her apartment, he pulled the cleaner's plastic off his service alpha blouse and put his ribbons on it along with his badges and brushed it off. He'd have to stop at the PX and get a cluster for his Bronze Star and find out how to position the cluster with the valor V. He took a shirt out of the cleaner's wrapper and hung it on a hanger. The weather in Virginia was cooler now and the jacket would be welcome. He put his garrison cap on the bed and brushed it off.

Memories of the hill at Con Thien kept popping into his mind. He took his black low-cuts to the kitchen and spit shined them on the kitchen table. He'd been in Vietnam twice, both for extremely short periods, and he'd been wounded both times. He didn't have any good memories to make the Captain's news easier. He hoped he'd get a good platoon leader who could make him into a good platoon sergeant. He knew a lot more about being an NCO than he did when he left for Nam the last time, but he still felt like he didn't know didly damn.

He stared at the ceiling for a long time that night. Carol's eyes—memories—faces—sounds—fears. Finally, he closed his eyes and drifted off.

The ride to the base was a quiet one in the morning. Garzinski's evening hadn't gone too well. Sharon cussed the Marine Corps for most of the night. But she was a Marine Corps wife and knew it had to happen sometime. By bedtime she was ready to comfort her man. Still, Ski felt like hell.

Captain Sharp was in his office and the Sergeant Major was with him.

"There's enough fruit salad on those two chests to outfit a company," Sharp said.

"Hope there's enough ass under them to lead a platoon," the Sergeant Major said.

Frank and Garzinski marched into the office and came to attention two feet from the Captain's desk.

"At ease. You're out of uniform Staff Sergeant Evans. Where's the cluster for your Bronze Star?"

"The award hasn't been presented yet, Captain. Was I supposed to put it on?"

"I'm pulling your chain. Get squared away, you two. We see the General in ten."

"Reporting with detail for awards Ceremony, General."

"At ease. You are out of uniform, Gunny."

"Sir, I . . ." Garzinski started to say.

"I was talking to Evans. Well, we'll get to that later. But you, First Sergeant, are out of uniform also. Gentlemen, it is an honor to read the following citation for the second award of the Bronze Star medal for valor to Gunnery Sergeant Frank Evans. Attention to orders."

Frank was totally confused and thought the stress was getting to the General. How could he forget Frank's rank with his stripes right there on his arms? In any case, he and Gunny Garzinski snapped to attention.

General Muldavy read the citation written by Charlie Company's commander shortly after the company was rotated off the hill of angels (Con Thien). He then reread the part that described Frank's performance as temporary platoon leader for the first platoon. "Staff Sergeant Evans, wounded during the attack, refused medical attention and continued leading his platoon."

"I repeated this part of the citation, Staff Sergeant Evans, because it plays into what comes next. But first, Congratulations. Captain Sharp?"

"Yes, sir. Congratulations, Frank. You did one hell of a fine job on that hill. I hope to have the privilege of serving with you again. Sergeant Major?"

"Yes, sir. Congratulations, Evans. For a boot NCO you did okay. Gunny?"

"Good job, Frank. You earned it."

"And with those endorsements," the General said, "we come to the next order of business. Yesterday afternoon during a meeting with the Commandant, I had an opportunity to share this citation with him and made a recommendation that was endorsed by the Commanding Office of Charlie Company of the 2/9 and by the Division Commanding General. He is an old friend, by the way, and owes me a favor, not that that had anything to do with his endorsement.

"Being that the Commandant was desirous of my cooperation in the matter of my own reassignment, he was inclined to accept my recommendation. As you may or may not know, combat meritorious promotions for Marines in the pay grade of E6 may be made on the recommendation of Commanding Generals by the Commandant of the Marine Corps. Marines at the rank of Staff Sergeant recommended for a combat meritorious promotion to Gunnery Sergeant must have demonstrated outstanding leadership to a degree rarely attained by Marines of equal grade regardless of time in grade or time in service. After a review of Staff Sergeant Evan's file and past awards, and verifying Staff Sergeant Evans has the required time in service, last evening the Commandant approved my recommendations for a combat meritorious promotion to Gunnery Sergeant for Staff Sergeant Frank Evans. Congratulations, Frank."

The General picked up a set of stripes with three chevrons on top, two rockers below and crossed rifles in the middle, and after handing them to Frank, shook his hand.

"Frank, you deserve these stripes. I couldn't keep you out of the assignment section's hands, but I made sure you'll have the rank to do something worthwhile when you get in-country."

"Thank you, sir. I don't know what to say."

"Then don't say it."

The General turned back to his desk and lifted a file folder.

"Gunny Garzinski, you have done an outstanding job for me. I asked Captain Sharp to allow me to be the one to give you the good news. I have here the results of the E8 promotion board selections. Not published, by the way, so the following cannot be repeated until the list is officially published. I am happy to inform you that you have been selected for the grade of E8, First Sergeant. You have a very low promotion sequence number and can expect to sew your new rocker and diamond on in January of the new year. And that makes you eligible to be assigned as a Company First Sergeant immediately. Congratulations, First

Sergeant. Captain Sharp, congratulate your new First Sergeant."

Sharp slapped Garzinski on the back and shook his hand. "Congratulations, First Sergeant. I'm going to be depending on you to keep my company squared away."

Garzinski just stared at sharp with a big grin on his face.

"Wake up, Garzinski," the Sergeant Major said, "your new commanding officer spoke to you."

Garzinski shook his head and grinned some more.

"Thanks, sir. I . . . Christ, this is a total surprise. I knew I had a good shot, but, jeeze, I thought I'd be way down the list."

Sharp handed Garzinski a set of stripes with three chevrons on top, three rockers below, and a diamond in the middle.

"You earned it, First Sergeant. Get used to it. Your world just got a lot bigger than you ever thought possible."

"And that concludes today's business, Muldavy said. "Frank, your date of rank is tomorrow, November 28, 1967. Take the rest of the day off and get your uniforms squared away. I haven't received your orders yet, but I'll have them either tomorrow or the next day. Stop back in the morning and check. I'm sorry about the rush, but it's part of the deal. Avoid the press and any other Washington types who might ask to talk to you about weapons. Is that clear?"

"Yes, sir. General, can I ask where you're going?"

"Yes. It will be public by the end of the day. Saigon. I will be assuming new duties as Marine Corps liaison to General Westmoreland's staff at MACV Headquarters in Saigon. Sorry to rush you, gentlemen, but would you take your celebration to Captain Sharp's office. I've got a lot to do. Wally, see me when you're done with the festivities."

On his way back to his apartment to get his uniforms Frank's thoughts jumped around and he had trouble grasping what had just happened. Gunnery Sergeant, he thought and shook his head back and forth slowly. Chief Gunners Mate in the Navy I could handle, but in the Corps I'm not much more than a boot. Christ, this is a screwy world. At least Ski has some good news for his wife. I wish my promotion would be good news for Carol, but it's probably the last thing she wants to hear."

Chapter 25

Carol had said her goodbye and didn't seem interested in extending it so Frank spent most of his time on base. His orders didn't come in the next morning and they didn't come in the day after that, but his uniforms with his new stripes did. Not having a final assignment for him and wanting Frank out of harm's way, harm for them, the powers behind his transfer issued him orders to report to Camp Pendleton transient barracks in California to await further orders. That was about as far away from Quantico as they could put him until his orders for overseas duty were ready.

He called Carol and told her about his orders. She decided she needed to say goodbye again, took the rest of the day off, and spent the night with him. They woke up together on the morning he had to leave for California. The crying was done and the words ran out. She returned to her apartment and left for work without coming back for one more goodbye. His car was stored. His lease was canceled using the military transfer clause, and his bags were on the sidewalk waiting for the cab. He looked around and shut down his emotions, a thing every military man learns to do. Time to get the hell out of there.

When Frank reported-in at Pendleton, the officer-in-charge of the transient barracks didn't know what to do with a transient Gunny Sergeant. He could have put Frank in charge of some make work detail, but why bother, it's good to be a Gunny, so he told Frank to check-in at morning formation and then get lost.

Not having anything else to do, he wandered over to the Armory and traded sea stories with the Gunny-in-charge. He wore his service-charlies with ribbons in hopes that the ribbons would make it look like he'd been around enough to be a gunnery sergeant, but he felt like a phony. He needn't have worried. Without recognizing the extent, Frank had changed, in demeanor at least. The mountain at Dak To and the hill at Con Thien had begun the process, a gradual process Frank wasn't entirely aware of. His wounds and recovery added some polish and fatalism; recruit training worked its grinding, brain-washing magic; and the bullshit at Quantico added just the right amount of cynicism to make him seem authentic. And the fact was, in knowledge at least, he was authentic. He just needed a chance to accept it.

Gunny Meeks at the armory was an old line Marine nearing retirement. But he was a Gunnery Sergeant wise in the ways of the Marine Corps. And he didn't waste words.

"Going to your first gunny assignment?" he asked.

"Yeah. is it that obvious?"

"You're young for an E7. Fact is, you're young for an E6, but since the shit started in Nam, they keep getting younger. I figured you just got selected. Am I right?"

"Yes," Frank said. "I just put the stripes on three days ago."

"Did you get it below the zone?" (a small percentage of outstanding Marines promoted ahead of their peers.)

"Combat meritorious," he said. "I haven't got time in grade but CM only requires minimum time in service for the grade."

"Thought it had to be something like that," Meeks said. "Well, you got the merit badges. Is that a Navy Cross?"

"Yes."

"Was that the action that got you the recommendation?"

"No," Frank said. "It was my second Bronze Star. The Cross probably didn't hurt though. And I had a General's recommendation."

"That always helps. Which General?"

"Muldavy."

"He was almost killed last year, wasn't he?"

"Yep," Frank said. "I was with him."

"Ah ha. Did you have anything to do with him

getting out alive?"

"He thinks I did."

"Well, there are worse things in the world. Are your new responsibilities making you nervous?"

"Do I look nervous?" he asked.

"You look scared."

"To death," he said.

"How long were you a staff sergeant?"

"Not long enough. I was E6 for two and a half years." He didn't mention that most of that was as a Navy petty officer.

"Want I should clue you in about what to expect when you get to your company?"

"Do I have to cut off any body parts?"

"Na. Go get your utilities on and help me out with these repairs. We can talk while we work."

Gunny Meeks spent the rest of the day telling Frank what his duties as a company Gunnery Sergeant would be and how that would be different from being a platoon sergeant. He explained what a company commander would expect. He told Frank that being a very junior Gunny, he might be put in a platoon as a platoon sergeant if his company was at full strength and had a good company gunny already. He described the Gunny's training responsibilities, his responsibilities for keeping his platoon or company, company facilities, and company weapons squared away, and the likelihood that he would have to fill in for the First Sergeant when the first-shirt was away or when they didn't have one.

"You are responsible for discipline," Meeks said as he and Frank disassembled an M2 fifty Cal. "Evans, you are not hardcore yet and you need to be hardcore. The grunts expect it. They need it. A tough Gunny gives them confidence. You are the expert, the man to go to when the grunts or the company commander have a problem. You can be as fucked up inside as you want to, but you better be the only one that knows it. The company is only as good as their company gunny."

"Gunny, I thought you were going to clue me in and make me feel better. You're scaring me more."

"Christ, Evans, stop whining. You sound like a snot nosed kid. I'll tell you something. I don't have any sympathy for you at all. You got a hell of a good deal and at the expense of some deserving and experienced staff sergeant who's been working towards those stripes for a lot of years. You better grow into those stripes pretty damn quick and stop whining or you're going to get some Marines killed. You had to do something that made somebody think you could do the job. Hell, you know the weapons as well as any Gunny I know."

"Yeah, I know weapons," he said, "but the only time I ever led a platoon was on the hill at Con Thien. I've never even been on patrol."

"You learned what you need to know at ITR."

"I've never been to ITR."

"You're shitting me!" Meeks said. "How'd that happen? Did you switch MOSs or something?"

"I got my staff stripes right out of boot camp. I

guess I better tell you about it."

He told Meeks his story. He was interrupted by a lot of comments similar to, "You're shitting me." When he finished, Meeks just stared at him for a few moments.

"You're shitting me," Meeks said.

"Nope, that's the no-shit truth."

"If I'd heard that story at the NCO club, I'd have called it bullshit. Let me give you some advice. Don't ever tell that story again. There are good Marines out there wearing gunny stripes that took them twenty years to get. They wouldn't take your tale too well. So you don't have any infantry training at all?"

"Nope, other than actually fighting."

"Well, that's something. What's your MOS?"

"Primary is 2111, Infantry Weapons Repair. But they also gave me a secondary MOS of 0311, Infantry. I can function as a 2111 without any help. But I can be assigned to a rifle company as a platoon sergeant or a company gunny.

"Well, that could be a problem. Less than you think though. ITR is here at Pendleton. I've got a friend over there. Want me to hook you up with a class while you're here?"

"Yeah right, I can see that," he said and frowned. "A gunnery sergeant going to ITR with the boots."

Meeks watched Frank and frowned.

"Evans, do you want some help or do you just want to whine?"

Meeks waited while Frank got over his pity party.

"Sorry," he said. "I want some help. How do we work it out?"

"You don't have to be a student. I'll tell Gunny Blain you want to observe the latest training techniques to incorporate in your company training program. He can put you with a class as an observer."

Frank thought about that. It was a good idea. He could ask questions and cover his inexperience with a story about needing details and trying to look at it from the grunt's perspective.

"Yeah, that would work," he said.

Frank was able to call Carol a couple of times, but the conversation was strained. After his second call, he gave up. The calls weren't helping. He tried to put it out of his mind and concentrate on what he could learn from the infantry school.

Military life is a great life for single men and women, men and women who want to stay single. It's not so great for those who get attached to other people in a permanent way. The military, especially the Corps demands absolute loyalty. It always comes first. Your personal problems do not enter into decisions. The needs of the Corps are the first and only consideration. Men who can live with that often have exciting, challenging, and rewarding careers. Often their families, if a Marine chooses to have one, don't find the career as rewarding. Some, those that can take the separations and uncertainty, do find it rewarding and interesting. But they will always come second. The Navy was the same. When the ship leaves, you leave with it, regardless of what is happening in your life or the lives of the people you love. And if leaving right then might destroy something precious before it can really develop, well, that's the price you pay. You *will* be at the appointed place, at the appointed time, in the specified uniform.

Chapter 26

Frank's orders came in on the 20th of December 1967, and since he wasn't moving with an assigned Marine unit, he was sent by bus to the Air Force base in San Bernardino to catch a cargo flight to the 3rd Marine Division on Okinawa for further assignment. 3rd MarDiv kept him one day and shipped him out to III MAF HQ in Danang for assignment to a company. He arrived in Danang on December 22 and reported to Camp Horn, USMC III MAF Headquarters.

The smells, sights, and sounds hadn't changed. Small, funny looking buses, some nothing more than a three-wheel motor scooter with a big passenger cab powered by a two-cycle lawn mower engine, or it seemed like it, ring-ding-ding-ding, zipped by with Vietnamese people stuffed inside and more hanging on to the sides. Luggage, baskets, and animal cages were piled up and strapped down on top. Motor scooters with two, three and even four people onboard wove back and forth through traffic. Skinny old men in coolie hats and black pajamas with huge bundles of what looked like marsh reeds balanced on both ends of a yoke-like shoulder carrier trotted along each side of the road with veins puffed out on their legs and a faraway look on their faces. Vietnamese soldiers walked along the road holding hands. All Vietnamese held hands, men, women, and children. Military busses and vehicles with chicken-wire over their windows to keep grenades out slowly made their way through traffic that had no pattern what so ever. And it was hot. Totally foreign and yet, too familiar. Frank sat back and watched it all go by with a sinking feeling in his gut.

What the hell am I doing in this place again? he thought. Vietnam wants to kill me. It's out there waiting for me to screw up again. I can feel it. Aren't six wounds enough? How many more before they get it right? He slid down in his seat on the bus and pulled his eight-point cover down around his ears. Talk about a merry-go-round, he thought. Shit has been happening so fast since the mountain, I don't even know how I got here. Not just little things either. Big life changing things, one after another, no warnings, no control over them, taking me somewhere. Shouldn't I have a say in this?

The bus stopped at the main gate to Camp Horn and he looked around to see if anything had changed since he was there last. Nothing had changed. A white pagoda like arch formed the main gate. Three Vietnamese words adorned the main arch: TRAI NGO QUYEN. It was kind of exotic, but the sandbag bunkers that lined the fence along the road and the military barracks behind them spoiled the effect. He didn't know what the words meant and had never been interested enough to ask. To the side was a smaller red sign with gold letters and a globe and anchor announcing Camp Horn as the Headquarters of the III Marine Amphibious Force. He looked back over his shoulder to see if the ammo dump was still across the road in the sand. It was.

After an MP sentry checked the inside of the bus, he waved it through the gate. To the right, inside the gate, five old Vietnamese women in black long sleeve shirts, black pajama bottoms, and straw coolie hats were filling sandbags and building a bunker. He assumed they were old, they looked like it, but it was hard to tell in Vietnam. Women aged fast doing hard labor in the war zone. He wondered if any of them were pacing off distances for VC mortars. He'd heard that many of the VC in the Danang Area of operations had day jobs at U.S. military bases. What a screwy-assed war.

The concrete water tower was still in the northeast corner with the mess hall below it. The streets and areas were policed and in good military order. A Marine base is a Marine base no matter where it is. The bus passed a row of barracks on the left and then passed the Armory on the right and stopped next to one of two long Quonset huts on the left. The second Quonset hut towards the Han river was the HQ building. A helipad was next to the river. He could see the White Elephant, headquarters building for Naval Support Activity, directly across the river. Sights, sounds, and smells he remembered and wished he didn't. Frank stacked his gear at the door of the first hut and checked in with the Personnel Office.

Relieved of his orders, he was told to check in with the H&S company office. H&S (commonly known as the Heat and Steam company) was the Headquarters and Services Company. He left his gear at the personnel office with a Lance Corporal keeping his eye on it and found the H&S Company office. The First Sergeant spotted him as he came through the door.

"What do you need, Gunny?"

"Checking in, First Sergeant. I just got in-county."

"You're checking in for H&S?"

"My orders didn't specify where I'd finally land, but H&S is my first stop."

"Let me see your orders."

He gave First Sergeant Roberts a copy of his orders and waited while he scanned the cover page.

"Strange orders," Rogers said. "Come on with me. The Captain will need to see you."

"Is Sergeant Major Jullian still here?" Frank asked.

"Rotated back to the world two weeks ago. You've been here before?"

"I was here back in September for a few days. Jullian helped me out with a project I was doing."

"Well, you just missed him. Come on, I'll let the skipper know you're here."

He followed Roberts to the CO's office and was told to wait outside for a moment. Roberts went into the room and closed the door. A few minutes later the door opened and Roberts leaned out.

Report to the CO, Gunny."

Frank marched in and came to attention.

"Gunnery Sergeant Evans reporting as ordered, sir."

"Stand at ease. Gunny Evans, I'm not sure what to do with you. I need to find out why you're being assigned through Third MAF. Normally Third MarDiv would have slotted you. Do you know anything about why you're here?"

"Captain, I was reassigned when General Muldavy moved to new duties. His whole staff was reassigned. It seems like I've just been shuffled around since then. I think part of it is I wasn't due for reassignment when the staff was disbanded, and I had just made Gunnery Sergeant."

"It still doesn't make any sense. Let me look into it. . . "

The Captain was interrupted with a knock on his door.

"General Phillips on your line, Skipper."

"Stand fast, Gunny."

Powell picked up his phone.

"Captain Powell, General . . .Yes, sir, he just reported in. Yes, sir, no problem, I was just finishing up with him. May I ask what this is about, sir? . . . Yes, sir, I'll send him right over."

"Well, someone seems to know what's going on. It seems General Phillips was expecting you and wants to meet you. Do you want to tell me what this is all about?"

"Sir, I have no idea. I don't even know who General Phillips is."

Powell watched Frank's face for a few moments with a blank look on his own.

"All right, we'll play it by ear," he said. "Report to General Phillips in the HQ Quonset. Report back to the First Sergeant for your duties while you're here. You are dismissed."

Frank did an about face and marched out of the office.

When Frank was gone, Powell turned to First Sergeant Roberts.

"First Sergeant, I'm not sure what's going on with him. If Phillips is interested, we need to handle him carefully. He's a 2111. Can you use him in the armory?"

"I can always use a weapons repairman. He's a gunny though."

"Hell, it's only temporary. As you said, he's a Gunny. He'll want to be useful."

"I'll work it out," Roberts said.

After his meeting with General Phillips Frank left the HQ Quonset hut feeling better than he had since he arrived in-country. General Phillips reminded him of General Muldavy, an old war horse who did things his own way. Phillip's was Commanding General of the Third Marine Division and an old friend and Annapolis class mate of General Muldavy. He was in Danang for a meeting with MACV. Frank's round-about shuffle from Okinawa to Danang began to make some sense. Looks like the ass warmers aren't the only ones writing letters. When he told the General he wanted a platoon and not a headquarters company, the General said he had just the place for him. He needed to talk to the commander of the 26th Marines first, but he was sure one of the companies in First Battalion at Khe Sanh would jump at the chance to get a Gunny of Frank's caliber. If not, Third Battalion would.

He reported back to the H&S First Sergeant and told him, hell yes, he'd work on the company's weapons inventory.

As it turned out, the weapons inventory was in good shape and the armory already had a good armorer, so there wasn't much for Frank to do. Late that afternoon he checked with the First Sergeant to get a jeep to make a trip to the China Beach PX to get some supplies to take to the field. Roberts didn't have a vehicle available, but told him to take the rest of the afternoon off and hitchhike to China Beach. It wasn't that far and most of the military vehicles going by the camp would give him a lift.

Frank walked a couple hundred feet down from the gate and stuck his thumb out. He hadn't hitched a ride like that since he was a boot sailor trying to get home from Norfolk for a weekend liberty. But he was to find out getting anywhere in Vietnam was usually a matter of hitching a ride on something. Jeep, truck, boat, helicopter, plane, all were willing to take you where they were going if they had the room. And there were very few scheduled means of transportation.

An Army jeep stopped and waved him in. The jeep was going into Danang, so a couple miles down the road the driver dropped Frank at a split in the road and drove off toward downtown. He was left standing in a group of Vietnamese, all of them jabbering in the Vietnamese sing-song language. Pretty Vietnamese girls dressed in silk pajamas and holding hands glanced up at him bashfully and looked away quickly. No way to tell if they were teenagers or adults. He felt like the jolly green giant, except he wasn't very jolly right then. Several Vietnamese young men in black pajamas were watching him and they weren't bashful about their disdain for him. The black pajamas didn't mean anything, but the looks did. Frank wasn't armed, and he felt the absence of his weapons acutely.

He walked a few steps back to the main road that runs the length of Tien Sha Peninsula and wondered how long until he would get another ride. As he watched the traffic, looking for a military vehicle, a Vietnamese bus stopped on the other side of the road and an old woman wearing black pajamas and a coolie hat got off and jabbered at the driver. The driver jabbered back for a moment and then they got into an argument. Soon she turned around and spotted Frank standing on the other side of the road. She crossed the road and started jabbering at him.

"I don't know what you're saying," he said.

She pointed at the bus piled high with luggage and boxes and jabbered some more.

"I don't understand you," he kept saying. What the hell does she want? he thought. Is she trying to get me over there so someone can drop a grenade on me? "I can't understand you," he said louder. Louder always improves understanding.

She grabbed his hand and tried to pull him toward the bus. "Oh no you don't," he said and jerked his hand back. "Go on, get the hell out of here."

She jabbered again, but her tone, even in Vietnamese, was pleading. She pointed at the bus. By this time all the Vietnamese in the area were watching and the looks weren't friendly. A Vietnamese policeman walked quickly toward him. He was about five feet six inches tall, his uniform was neat and starched and he moved with authority.

"What is the trouble, Sergeant?"

He spoke good English and Frank was relieved.

"I don't know," he said. "She keeps trying to get me over to that bus."

The policeman turned to the old lady and slapped her on the side of the head and pointed at the bus. She turned with slumped shoulders and walked back to the bus."

"Not a problem," the policeman said and walked away.

Frank watched her stop next to the bus and walk up and down jabbering at the passengers. Finally, two Vietnamese boys got off the bus and climbed on top. They untied a suitcase and threw it down on the ground."

Frank stared at the old lady as she grabbed her suitcase and carried it across the road. As she passed she looked over her shoulder at him. There were tears on her face.

Oh God, he thought. She just wanted some help from a tall round eye. Someone who could reach the top of the little bus. I didn't know, damn it. Stop looking at me like that. He felt lousy for the rest of the day.

Later that evening, another incident increased his melancholy. The First Sergeant asked him if he wanted to ride out to a POL depot behind the airbase and see some of Danang. He was bored and thinking about Carol too much, so he agreed.

Near the airbase they drove along a paved road outside of a tall chain-link fence next to some huge hangers with a large paved storage lot behind them. The road was almost like a country road in Virginia. The area was residential with a lot of bungalow like houses on quiet streets. Tree branches reached out and covered the road with shade. The feeling was pleasant for a while. It was hard to believe they were in Vietnam.

First Sergeant Roberts was talking and Frank was watching the cargo lot go by when he spotted huge stacks of some kind of cargo containers. As they got closer he could see that they were green rectangular containers stacked about ten high and fifty or sixty across, enough to cover a football field ten deep. And there were three of those huge, football field sized stacks of containers. Each container was about seven feet long, three feet wide, and two feet deep. It seemed like they drove past the stacked containers for a long time. There were thousands of them. What the hell were they used for?

Roberts noticed Frank looking and said, "You don't want to go home in one of them."

Coffins! New military shipment coffins, stacked and waiting for the bodies they would carry home. Thousands of them. The sinking feeling in his gut came back along with an almost irresistible feeling of despair. Frank was quiet for the rest of the ride and didn't sleep well that night.

One day later Captain Powell sent for Frank.

"Gunny Evans, get your gear together and get over to the airbase. Looks like the Marine Corps figured out what to do with you. A C-130 is leaving for your new home at Khe Sanh. Report to Third Battalion, Twenty-sixth Marines. You'll have to move it because the flight leaves at 1400. The First Sergeant has a jeep waiting."

Short and sweet, he thought. He lucked out on

weapons. The Armory had a shipment of repaired M-14s and .45 pistols going back to 3rd Battalion at Khe Sanh. Since he was going into a hot zone and Camp Horn had 3rd Battalion weapons, he was authorized to draw weapons, ammo, and field gear at Camp Horn. He drew his 782 gear, an M-14, a .45 and a combat load of ammo and grenades from the armory and carried it all back to the H&S office to catch the jeep that was taking him to the airbase. Fortunately, the Gunny at the armory had warned him to take cold weather gear with him since the northeast monsoon was in full force and the temps in the Khe Sanh area sometimes dropped into the forties at night.

Chapter 27

The pilot of the C130 made one high pass over the combat base before setting up his final approach. From a distance and at altitude the base was just a long dirt gash on a hill with higher and greener hills around it. Looking at the unbroken expanse of jungle canopy that ran all the way to the China Sea, Frank wondered what was so important down there that needed a major Marine base to protect it. As the plane approached the base, wire perimeters, roads, sandbagged structures and the long runway began to take form and give an idea of size. Khe Sanh's wire enclosed a lot of real estate in the middle of nowhere.

The weather and visibility were marginal at best, but Frank got a good look at the layout on the downwind leg as the plane set up for landing. The runway ran along the long axis of the base roughly ESE to WNW beginning outside of the wire on the east perimeter and extending to just past the midpoint on the long axis. In the short time he had to look, he could see an artillery battery, probably 105s, on the southeast side of the base near what looked like an ammo dump and another battery slightly south of the end of the runway near the center of the base. There was armor parked near the west end of the runway also. Tanks or armored carriers. Another artillery emplacement was closer to the west end, but he couldn't identify the weapon system. It looked like another ammo dump was positioned almost dead center on the base. The base was recognizable as a military installation, but it was outpost raw, a fort in the middle of Indian country.

The C-130 touched down and rolled hot until just short of the unloading tarmac then braked hard and reversed his props. The deceleration shoved him forward hard against his straps. When the plane stopped, he shrugged into his pack, slung his M-14, picked up his sea bag, and exited via the cargo ramp. He looked at the date window on his wristwatch. It was the 28th of December 1967.

He asked the first Marine he found and was pointed west to the 3/26, H&S Company CP in the Red Sector. Frank wasn't happy with what he saw as he humped to the CP. Too many structures above ground; crates, pallets, and other trash stacked in various locations; and a whole shit-pot full of munitions stacked outside of the Ammo dump. He passed defensive positions that were only waist deep and wondered what the hell the people in charge were thinking. He was under the impression the things he had learned from experienced NCOs and at Con Thien and on the mountain were common Marine Corps knowledge. But he wasn't seeing any of it here. Listening to sea stories from experienced NCOs can serve a larger purpose than just entertainment if you can sort out the hard earned knowledge nuggets from the bullshit. They often focused on what went wrong and how something should have been done in the past. What Frank was seeing as he humped to 3rd Battalion CP was the what went wrong part. Trash wood and metal containers were piled everywhere ready to become secondary shrapnel if a mortar hit them. He started cataloging items to remember to check on when he got to his platoon. Con Thien had been a hard and fast experience, but it taught lessons not soon forgotten and left images in the mind that served as an encyclopedia of what can go wrong.

He found the CP and checked in with the First Sergeant. He was required to report to the Company Commander, but he was becoming an old salt now, or so he was thinking, and knew it was smart to seek out the First Sergeant's advice and council before he reported to the Commander.

"Checking in, First Sergeant."

First Sergeant Mills didn't look up from the report he was working on.

"Three, Twenty-sixth?" he asked.

"That's what they told me."

Mills held out his hand still not looking up.

"File and orders."

Frank put his file in Mill's hand and waited. Mill's continued running his pencil down a list while holding Frank's file in his outstretched hand. Then he stopped on some line item and said, "There you are, you little bastard. I told Loeder I ordered it."

Finally, Mills looked up to see who he was talking to. Mills was six-two, about 230, built like a weight lifter, and black as coal. Well, not quite that dark, but more black than brown.

"Sorry, Gunny. This place is crazy today. Captain Loeder is going to be glad to see you. We're hurting for company gunnery sergeants. I think he's available but let me give him your file to look over for a few minutes before you report. Find a place to crash. I'll find you."

Frank stepped outside of the CP and leaned against the sandbag wall of a covered bunker next to the underground CP. Loeder? he thought. Na, couldn't be. Captain Loeder had Charlie Company at Con Thien. Probably just sounds the same. Frank slid down the bags and rested on the dirt with his back against the wall. Cooler than Danang and wetter, he thought. A cool wind was blowing in from the east and Frank could feel rain in it. He looked around. Primitive, he thought. A big change from Camp Horn and its barracks, mess halls, rec facilities, and Quonset huts. A lot of bare clay and dirt here. Sandbags everywhere. More like Con Thien, but not as beat up. Good open fields of fire though.

Concertina wire several rolls deep made a formidable perimeter. A lot of green surrounding the base, but still, the base just gave the feeling of dirt, dust, rock, and sand. The base was surrounded by jungle covered mountains of the kind you might see in rural West Virginia. Not big mountains like in Colorado. The tallest of these were maybe three or four thousand feet. But he knew no matter how roughhewn and outpost-raw the camp looked right then, if Ho Chi Minh decided to take offense at the Marine's presence in Khe Sanh, a day would come when it would look like the Hill of Angels (Con Thien).

He had just pulled his steel pot down over his eyes when a siren sounded and troops began running for the bunker he was leaning against. Frank didn't need an invitation. He dove in the entrance. A rocket hit at the far end of the runway with an all too familiar rocking of his senses. He waited for a repeat, but the base remained quiet. First Sergeant Mills came to the entrance of the bunker and said, "All right, back to work."

The H&S CP was mostly underground with only about three feet of the structure sticking up above ground. The roof was covered with big sandbags, bags about three feet long by two feet wide. They were piled three deep on top of what looked like steel mesh on top of thick timbers. The steel mesh was the kind Navy Seabees used to make temporary runways called PSP for perforated steel planking. The sandbag layer sat on two layers of ammunition boxes. The top boxes were filled with rocks to burst time-delay fuses on artillery and the lower layer of boxes were empty to act as a buffer to disperse the blast of a direct hit.

The CP was a long, wide, dimly lit underground room. The center of the room held a large map table and benches for radios with antennae cables hanging down from the overhead. Field tables and makeshift desks, some made from ammo boxes, lined both sides of the room and some of them had makeshift dividers set up to give the occupants a modicum of privacy. A rough plank floor had been laid down in places, but even there, sand and dried clay had worked up through the cracks and covered most of the floorboards. Mills led Frank back to a semi-private office partitioned off with what looked to be scrap lumber salvaged from cargo pallets. The partition provided only two walls in an L shape. Captain Loeder sat behind a field desk "inside" the cubicle.

When he came to attention in front of Loeder's little desk, Loeder said, "At ease, Sergeant Fucking Lucky. Looks like it's Gunny Fucking Lucky now. First Sergeant, did I ever tell you about Con Thien?"

"Only about a thousand times," Mills said, and then after a suitable pause added, "Sir."

Loeder laughed. "Yes, I guess I have. How about Sergeant Fucking Lucky?"

"Yes, sir. I believe you told me that story once or twice."

"Good," Loeder said. "We don't have to screw

around with introductions. Gunny Evans, it's good to see you again. When we served together on the hill I wasn't aware of how impressive your file is. First Sergeant, did you know Gunny Evans has the Navy Cross and five clusters on his Purple Heart?

"No, sir. I wasn't aware of that. As you said, impressive. I hope he picks a bunker well away from mine."

"Two Bronze stars for valor, too."

Mills looked at the overhead and said, "Yes, sir, impressive."

"Yes," Loeder said. "I'm running on again, aren't I?"

"It's an endearing trait, sir," Mills said.

Loeder grinned at his First Sergeant and mouthed a silent, *well, fuck you, first sergeant*. "Okay, nuff said. Gunny, I need some time to think about your assignment. The problem isn't finding a home for you, it's going to be figuring out who I'll have to turn down. Both India and Mike companies need senior NCOs. Hell, I need a Gunny to square away the reaction team and get the defensive positions in the Red Sector squared away. First Sergeant, do you think we can put him with Lima on the wire in Red Sector for a couple of days until I can sort out a permanent home for him?"

"I'll talk with the CO, sir. I'm sure they will welcome the advice and counsel of an esteemed gunnery sergeant. They better. Gunny Evans, I assume that you are prepared and able to apply some mark one, mod zero jungle boot to multiple gluteus maximus."

"Kick some ass? Sure, if I need to. What's the problem?"

"Marines don't like to dig," Mills said. "And new lieutenants are sometimes willing to let things slide, and probably the biggest problem, we haven't had enough incoming to motivate them. Let's get you squared away with berthing and then I'll introduce you to the children."

"Shouldn't we talk to the Platoon Leaders first. Lieutenants can get a little touchy about their commands."

"I was talking about the lieutenants." Mills said.

"Pay no attention, Gunny," Loeder said. "The First Sergeant probably called Chesty Puller a boot."

Mills showed Frank into a bunkered hooch and told him to take the bottom rack on the right.

"We're short on Senior NCOs," he said. "The line companies have priority, so we have this hooch to ourselves. Handle it anyway you want, Gunny, but if you want some advice, meet the troops today, get them started on what you want done, and then get some sleep. You'll be back out there all night. Sleep during the day, because the Colonel put us on full alert for the night hours."

"Expecting trouble?"

"Patrols have been making contact all over the area. Signs of troop movement are all over the AO. G2 says there's NVA in the area and they're up to something. The something is probably us. First Battalion is doing a sweep to the north searching the Rao Quan River Valley, so the camp defenses are light for the next three days. The Captain will probably keep you here till First Battalion gets back. Are you okay on ammo?"

"Yeah. I picked up a full combat load before I left Danang. I'll need to stop at the water point though."

"You got cool aid?"

"About a hundred packs. I stocked up before I left Third MAF."

"You'll need it. The water tastes like crap even without purification tabs. I'm glad to see you still have your M-14. India Company had theirs replaced with the Mickey Mouse gun."

"M-16?"

"Is that what you call it? Looks like a plastic toy to me. Lima Company still has a few 14s, but I'd look inside them if I were you."

"Okay, thanks. Let's get down there so I can see what the line looks like in daylight."

The Lima CO and the Staff Sergeant acting as Company Gunny were glad to get some help even if it was temporary. Captain Franks of Lima briefed Frank on deployment of his platoons and introduced Frank to two of his rifle platoon leaders. Third Platoon was on patrol doing an extended sweep west of the base.

Captain Franks was one tough looking Marine officer. He was big boned and had a lot of muscle over the bone. Probably wore a size forty-eight jacket and a nineteen-inch collar. His hands looked like they could crush rock. He wore a Naval Academy class ring. He looked tough, but he spoke softly. The contrast was disconcerting at first until you realized he didn't need to speak loudly. People tended to listen when he spoke.

Third Battalion having been recently diverted to Khe Sanh while in route to another location because of III MAF concerns with signs of growing enemy strength and activity in the area, was close to full strength. India and Mike Companies were holding Hill 881 South, northwest of the base. Lima was held at the main combat base to reinforce the 1st Battalion defenders. 1st and 2nd Platoons of Lima Company were at strength with forty-seven riflemen each divided into three squads, two corpsmen, platoon leaders, radiomen, and embedded machine gunners from the weapons platoon. But the company was short on experienced NCOs, not an unusual situation in Vietnam. 1st Platoon had a Staff Sergeant in the platoon sergeant slot, but 2nd platoon was using a sergeant E5 in the slot. A few squad leaders were E5 sergeants, but many were corporals and in one case, a lance corporal.

The Marine Corps was a small service and also, generally, the first service to be cut back after a war was over. When the next fight came along, the Corps always found itself having to rebuild. You can rebuild a lot from scratch, but experience takes time. When the Johnson administration expansion of forces in Vietnam took off in 1965, with inexperienced troops and junior officers being rotated yearly, experienced NCOs were at a premium and coveted by every combat commander. Gunnery Sergeants, the backbone of the Corps, were especially at a premium.

Captain Franks turned the Platoon Sergeant and Gunny Evans loose to inspect the defensive positions on the wire in the Red Sector at the northwest side of the perimeter. The first thing Frank noticed was the cold. Fog had settled in and the monsoon rains had given up the short break they had taken that morning. The next thing he noticed was how shallow the trenches were and how unoccupied the grunts were. At a fire base as exposed as Khe Sanh, the Marines should be improving their defensive positions every chance they got. There was always something that could be done to make them safer. Khe Sanh was not a temporary field expedient; the Marines were going to be there for a while. But Lima Company seemed content with waist deep trenches and ponchos for cover. 3rd Battalion had just arrived a few days before Frank got there, but that was not an excuse. Marines were screwing around when they could be digging and improving their chances of surviving a mortar attack.

He might be a boot Gunny, hell, he still considered himself a boot Marine, but he knew weapons and he knew a thing or two about digging a hole that would protect your butt when the crap was dropping on your head. The key word with defensive positions is improve. Improve, improve, improve. When you think it's the perfect hole, improve it some more every chance you got. There was always something you could do to make it better and safer. Remove stones from the walls, dig grenade sumps, widen, deepen, build overhead cover, add timbers, dig spider holes, find ways to drain water off, sandbag the walls, build sandbag partitions in the trench, do something. There is always something that will make it better. These Marines and their leaders obviously did not have a clue. Well, he thought, if you don't know everything, start with what you do know.

Frank let the platoon sergeant introduce him to the troops and then he started at the right flank of the Red Sector defensive line and talked with each of the squad leaders. When he was sure the squad leaders understood what he wanted, he talked to the 2nd Platoon, Platoon Sergeant, and with him talked to the squad leaders in 2nd Platoon.

He wasn't happy with the attitude of the NCOs in Lima company. They were too willing to go with the flow and the flow with grunts is to avoid digging as much as possible. He wished he had a couple of NCOs who had spent some time on Con Thien. But if he had them, he wouldn't have the problems he was looking at. Well, he was the Company Gunny and temporary or not he was responsible for discipline and the condition of company facilities no matter how junior or inexperienced he was. The defensive positions were company facilities. Screw it, boot Gunny or not, it was his job to square it away.

Frank called the platoon sergeants together and

told them what he wanted to see when he returned. He got some resentment, but he stomped on it.

"Square your Marines away or you and me have a problem. You've got one hour to show me some progress. I want to see working parties with entrenching tools cutting dirt when I get back. One man on watch, one man digging. Put a working party filling sandbags. Find some damn picks to break-up the clay. Find some timbers to build overhead cover. Make some progress. One hour."

Frank turned on his heel and walked off. He had to give them a chance to step up. The platoon leaders should have done this a long time ago, he thought. But without squared away sergeants, a boot Lieutenant hasn't got a chance.

He returned to the CP to warm up and swapped sea stories with the acting Gunny for an hour. And what the hell have you been doing while your company sits around with their thumbs up their asses, Frank thought? I hate to say it, but you folks need a few mortars dropped on your heads. You might start acting like an infantry company then. An hour later, Frank returned to the line in his field jacket with a poncho over it. The poncho made a decent tent half, but it made a lousy raincoat. It was going to be a wet, miserable night.

A few men were digging but not nearly enough. Frank tried to find the platoon sergeants but only one was with his troops. What the hell do I have to do to get their attention?

Hmmm, he thought. A couple mortars on their heads. Yeah, that's exactly what they need. Frank went back to the company CP and found the CO.

"Skipper, can I have a minute?"

"Sure, Gunny. The First Sergeant says you're turning the company to. About time. What can I do for you?"

"Can I give you some advice, Skipper?"

"That's what you're here for."

"Put you're acting Gunny back in second platoon. They need a good platoon sergeant more than you need a half assed acting gunny. He isn't doing the job."

"Strange you should mention that. He was on his way, anyway. Loeder talked to the colonel and you've been assigned to Lima. Looks like I got a permanent company gunny. Welcome home, Gunny."

"Damn, that's good news. Thanks, Skipper. It's good to finally have a home. . . Uh, I've got one other little thing on my mind, sir."

"What's that?"

"Can you get me permission to fire a couple sighting mortar rounds off the Red Sector? Like real close to the wire?"

"Don't see why not. But the area off the Red Sector is on the grid and preregistered. The mortar crews have it all dialed in. I doubt they need any further test firing."

"I'd like to double check. And sir, don't warn anyone in the company."

Captain Franks raised his eyebrows and looked at Frank from the corner of his eyes. Then he grinned.

"I'll notify the COC," he said. "Take a radio with you and I'll let you know when."

"Got it. I'll use Lima nine."

"And, Gunny. . .not *too* close."

"Got it."

Frank found the mortar pit he wanted back near the runway and explained what he wanted to the crew leader.

"That close, Gunny?"

"Yeah. Not close enough for shrapnel to be a danger but close enough to rock the trenches."

"Okay with me, all the patrols are in. Let me dial it in."

Frank sat back and waited for the Captain's call.

"Lima Niner this is Lima Six, over."

"Six this is Niner, over."

"Lima Niner, there are no friendlies in the area. You are cleared for two sighting rounds in red zone, over."

"Roger, Lima Six. Stand by."

"Okay, Sergeant, put two in the air and then secure."

The mortar gunner double checked his settings and told the assistant gunner to drop a round. When the round was out of the tube, he made a small adjustment and told the assistant gunner to drop the second round. Frank lifted his binoculars and watched the Lima Company trenches. Some men were in the trench and others were standing around shooting the shit. Suddenly the first 81mm mortar hit in the fire zone in front of them and was followed moments later by the second round fifty feet closer. He could feel the impact in the mortar pit so he knew the men on the trench line got a good taste of concussion.

"Lima Six this is Lima Niner. Sighting exercise complete. The mortar crew has secured their weapon."

"Roger, Niner. This is Lima Six, out."

"Thanks, Sergeant. I think that did the trick."

"Whatever you say, Gunny." the team leader said with a grin.

When he got back to the trenches, Marines were digging, cussing, and bitching, and mud was flying. A bitching Marine is a happy Marine, he thought. Lieutenant Hitchens, Platoon Commander of 1st Platoon, caught up with him as he walked down the line. Hitchens shook the rain off his poncho and looked around.

"Gunny Evans, can I have a word?"

"Yes, sir."

"Gunny, why didn't you inform me you were going to test fire the mortar? We thought we were under attack until Captain Franks informed me it was only a test."

"Sorry, Lieutenant, I should have. But it was good training for the men anyway. I think they're thinking about the depth of the trenches right now."

Hitchens didn't say anything for a moment, but Frank noticed Hitchens's hands were closed into fists.

"Look, Gunny," Hitchens said quietly. "Let's cut the shit, okay? You should have warned me. I've got no problem with a little demonstration for shock value. Hell, it did seem to shake them up. But get something straight. This is my platoon. If you do anything like that again without warning me, I'll come down on you like a ton of bricks."

"Yes, sir," Frank said. "Like a ton of bricks, sir."

Hitchens stared at him for a few moments with an angry look. Then the fire went out of his eyes and he grinned.

"Okay, so you're not scared to death. Gunny, I need your help here. It won't work if I can't depend on you to support me."

He thought about it for a moment. Fact was, he was blustering his way through a situation he thought might end with him being sent packing back to Battalion HQ. It was time to square with the Lieutenant.

"You're right, sir. I was a little out of line and I should have brought you in on it. I will in the future. Now, what can I do to support you?"

Hitchens watched Frank's face for a moment. Frank could see the suspicion in his look and in his posture. He was the same height as Frank and he was staring straight into his eyes. He's wondering if I'm putting him on. Christ, I wish I had more experience. Hitchens relaxed and looked out over the wire.

"For starters," Hitchens said, not looking at him, "You've had time to look over the platoon. What advice do you have for me?"

Probably a good officer, Frank thought. Garzinski said the ones who ask for advice can be depended on.

"Sir, the best thing I can advise you right now is to square away your Platoon Sergeant. If you do that, he'll square away your platoon. If he can't or won't, get rid of him. You're better off with an E5 who can do the job than an E6 who won't. Do you have the perimeter tonight, sir?"

"Yes. Lieutenant Carter is reserve tonight. First Platoon is up."

"Want some company in the CP?"

"You'd be welcome."

"Let me get some chow and a couple of hours sleep and I'll be back after dark."

Chapter 28

Frank decided to get some chow at 1st Battalion mess hall. He looked around as he ate. Big fat target, he thought. This place would have lasted for maybe three seconds at Con Thien. He returned to his hooch and stretched out on his bunk for a couple of hours. Sleep wouldn't come. Memories of his nights with Carol kept intruding and his mind wouldn't settle down. And the tingle of excitement in his stomach was back. Charlie likes the night. Could get exciting.

He thought about his own performance that day. He'd got some things done, things that needed to get done. He was acutely aware of his own shortcomings as a Gunnery Sergeant, but he was pleased with the way the officers and grunts had accepted his leadership. He was pleased with the way he had stepped up without even thinking about it. Hell, he *felt* like a Gunny. For better or worse, Lima belonged to him.

The early part of the night was quiet. Frank spent time with each of the squad leaders and then spent more time with the platoon sergeant. They were good Marines, but he didn't feel any sense of urgency in them. He returned to the platoon CP at 0130.

Near 0300 he heard small arms firing on the other side of the base and an illumination flare was hanging in the air on that side. Hitchens was contacted by 1st Battalion COC (Combat Operations Center). Bravo Company of 1st Battalion on the eastern perimeter reported enemy probing their wire.

"Time to make sure the line is awake," he said. "If they're probing on the east, they'll probably test us on this end. I'll make a round to let the men know."

"I'm notifying Staff Sergeant Pike now. Watch your ass, Gunny. We've had a sniper plinking at us since we got here. He's not very good, but everybody gets lucky sometime."

"Don't worry. I've got enough scars," he said.

He moved down the line slowly and low to the ground. The Platoon Sergeant was doing his job and the Marines were alert. He decided to spend some time near the center of the line to observe how the Marines were dealing with the potential for action.

"Gunny Evans. You getting some grunt time in?"

"Yeah," he said. "Slumming in the trenches. See any movement out there?"

It was a stupid question. If they had seen anything everyone on the line would know about it. But sometimes you just said stupid stuff to have something to say.

"Nothing yet. Those First Battalion pukes are seeing ghosts."

"Don't be too sure," he said. "That's how it started at Con Thien. The NVA would probe the line looking for weaknesses and trying to draw fire to locate the Marine's positions for their mortars. Other times they'd slip a Bangalore Torpedo under the wire and blow the hell out of the concertina. Anybody got an entrenching tool?"

"Yeah, here you go, Gunny. You gonna do some digging?"

"No, I want something to scratch my ass with. What the hell do you think I'm going to do with a shovel?"

"Sorry. What are you going to dig?"

"Well, I'll tell you. Your trench is a little better than it was yesterday, but it's still too damn shallow and way too narrow. Maybe you don't care if a mortar blows your head off, but I like mine. I'm going to dig a hole I can feel comfortable in. If we had defensive positions like this in Con Thien, we'd all be dead. But you men go ahead and use the hole you have. I want to make sure I'll still be around to call a corpsman for you when the shit starts. I'll tell him to make sure he has plenty of body bags ready."

He shoved the folding shovel into the dirt and began deepening and enlarging his position. The dirt was mostly mud by that time, but that just made it easier to dig. No one said anything.

"I really hate to think about all the damn work I'm going to have getting the replacements up to speed," he said quietly, as to himself. He continued to work at the hole. "It's putting the body parts back together after a mortar attack that's the bitch," he said quietly.

Later, he heard another shovel at work. Then another on the other side of his position. Soon he could hear digging in several places along the line. He should have just busted their asses and made them dig until he was satisfied, most gunnies would have, but he was new and feeling his way. And every leader has his own style.

"Lima Niner this is Lima One-One."

Frank squeezed the handset transmit button and said, "Lima Niner, over.

"Niner, I have a report of suspected movement on the wire west of your position. Check it out."

"One-One, are you going to illuminate?"

"Negative, over."

"This is Lima Niner, Roger, out."

"Well, boys," he said in a quiet voice. "Duty calls."

He moved quickly and quietly to the west side of the Red Sector perimeter. Red Sector was on the northwest end of the base and the perimeter wire formed a rough horseshoe with the open end facing east and the interior of the base. He bellied and sprinted across the area enclosed by Red Sector and then along the trench asking for the Marine who saw the movement. When Frank found him, he slid into the trench alongside of the Marine. Staff Sergeant Pike was already there.

"What have you got?" Frank asked.

"Moss said he saw something move right there," Pike said leaning across the edge of the trench and pointing."

Frank put his binoculars to his eyes and focused on the spot Pike was pointing at. The binoculars were 7X50s and not much good at night, but the 50mm lenses could gather more light than his eyes could. He could vaguely see the outlines of the wire but not much else.

"All right," he said. "I can't see anything. Pass the word to watch the wire closely."

The command wasn't necessary. The squad was hyper-alert. But being new, he felt the need to say something, to give direction.

"Staff Sergeant Pike," someone said from about ten feet away. "I think we have company on the wire."

"Where?"

"Right in front of my position. I think they're dicking with the wire."

Frank moved his binoculars slowly down the

wire, watching for movement and several feet to the left he saw it.

"Don't anyone fire," he said. "Pike, I need some elevation. Make sure the squad stays down. Don't mark your positions—or mine."

"You got it, Gunny."

He slid over the back side of the trench and bellied over the dirt pile behind the trench. It would give him three or four feet above the trench. He managed to get a halfway decent prone position. He put his sights on the spot where he saw the movement and waited. The front sights were hard to see, but by focusing slightly to the side he managed to get a half-assed sight picture.

He waited, trying to hold on to the dim image of his sights. He tightened his finger on the trigger and took up the slack. And suddenly, there it was. A phantom of movement in the wire. He pulled the rifle tight into his shoulder and squeezed the trigger. The shot punched at his ear drums and the muzzle blast took his night vision away.

"Sergeant Pike, call for illumination. Every other man sit in the bottom of the trench and close your eyes and keep them closed until I tell you to open them."

Frank waited with his rifle pointed at the spot he was interested in. He heard the mortar tube behind him, heard the pop overhead, and then the weird twilight spread over the landscape as the flare burst into light. He continued to wait with his rifle ready. As the light got brighter he began to see the wire and then he could see a shape under the wire.

"Staff Sergeant Pike, notify the Lieutenant we had a probe on the wire. Everybody stay down and hold your fire."

Frank waited for the illumination to fade and scanned the fire zone for other movement. Nothing. When it was fully dark again, he slid over the dirt pile and back into the trench.

"Everybody back on watch," he said.

A few men had actually followed Frank's orders and sat in the trench with their eyes closed. But most hadn't. But that was okay for now. His own fault. He should have told Pike to have every other man sit and close their eyes. Pike could have made it happen with specific instructions to individuals. At least he had a few pairs of eyes fully adjusted to the dark. The rest would get their night vision back over the next ten minutes.

"Staff Sergeant Pike, keep a close watch. They might try again. I'm going back to the CP."

Another unnecessary and useless order, but he was learning.

Frank made his way carefully back to the CP and explained what he had seen. When he was done, he had a question for the Lieutenant.

"Lieutenant, why didn't you illuminate on the first report?"

"You observed the platoon yesterday," Hitchens said. "If I had put light up, I'd probably have caught half the platoon sitting on the side of the trench instead of in their holes. I figured waiting until you got there was a better decision."

Frank thought it over. It felt right.

"You're probably right. We better check the wire on the whole perimeter as soon as we have light."

"I'm way ahead of you. Pike is taking a patrol out to sweep the area and give us some cover. Gunny, I need you on the line so he can put the patrol together and get them ready."

"On my way," he said.

The rest of the night was cold, wet, and quiet except for several reports of hearing something or seeing movement. Light was popped each time, but nothing was seen. After the first probe, grunts sitting above ground had ceased to be a problem. Pike took his patrol through the fog and out through the wire just before first light and the Lieutenant made the Red Sector a controlled fire zone until the patrol returned. No one was allowed to fire unless directed to by the CP.

When they had enough light, Frank and the Lieutenant went to the wire to look for the body. The body was gone, but they did find a blood pool and drag marks on the other side of the wire. Frank looked around for signs of tampering on the wire and suddenly froze.

"Oh shit, sir. Get back to the trench right now."

Hitchens didn't waste time or words. He spun and ran with Frank back to the trench and rolled into the hole.

"What?" Hitchens yelled.

"Wait," he said. He stood up and yelled. "Everybody stand away from the claymore clackers. Do not touch the claymore triggers."

He climbed out of the trench and ran behind the platoon repeating his instructions. "Do not, I say again, do not touch the claymore triggers."

When he was sure everyone was clear about his instruction, he returned to the Lieutenant.

"Gunny, the clackers aren't connected, Hitchens said. "I gave specific instructions to run the wire but not to connect the triggers."

"Make sure, sir. Some of our claymores have been turned around toward us."

The M18A1 claymore mine is a directional, above ground, anti-personnel mine filled with C4 explosive and metal segments about the size of a .22 caliber bullet. It is slightly curved to provide wide coverage of its target area. Claymores were placed at the edge of the wire with the curved firing face facing outward and used as anti-intrusion devices. Triggering wire was run back to the defensive positions and connected to a plastic trigger device called a clacker. The NVA knew all about claymores and used the dark and fog to creep in and turn the mines around so that they faced the Marines. If the Marines of First Platoon had triggered their claymores, thousands of metal balls would have shot across their positions ripping anything above ground to shreds.

"Squad Leaders," the Lieutenant yelled. "Verify

that your claymore clackers are disconnected and report. I say again. . ."

The squad leaders reported, but 3rd squad took a little longer than the others. Finally, 3rd squad leader reported his clacker was disconnected.

Frank moved along behind the platoon and said, "Show me." When he was sure it was safe, he took the Lieutenant back to the wire and showed him the claymores.

"Good eyes, Gunny. I think a valuable lesson would be taught by bringing one squad at a time out here and letting them see what the enemy was doing last night."

"Yes, sir. And right now too. They can eat later and think about it."

The lesson was given and the Marines were properly impressed. Frank noticed a lot of digging going on when he walked back to his hooch to get some sleep. And he wondered how the Marine Corps had come up with this fascination for holding muddy hills instead of hunting enemy. Marines were supposed to take hills, not sit in holes waiting to be taken.

Chapter 29

During the day while Frank slept, the trenches were deepened and widened. Sandbags were filled and used to fortify the fighting positions. The platoon sergeants and squad leaders did their jobs and ignored the bitching at the additional workload. Both platoons were turned out and worked on the defensive line. Then they began working on their hooches.

That evening he invited Staff Sergeants Pike and Walmsley, Platoon Sergeants for 1st and 2nd platoons, back to his hooch for a Betty Crocker luau. Khe Sanh had a small PX still operating and most of the troops had a stash of gedunk and pogey bait (junk food) from the PX set aside to add a little variety to their diets. Often their stash was augmented with bake-goods received in the mail from moms and girlfriends (hence the name, Betty Crocker Luau).

To hold a Betty Crocker Luau, a few troops got together and brought selected items from their stash. Everything was put into a common pot, so to speak, and everyone chowed down on whatever they wanted. Vienna sausages, pork and beans, Slim-Jims, ravioli in a can, sardines, crackers, cookies, homemade banana bread, the luau generally boasted an impressive and eclectic spread. Most of the time it was washed down with cool aid flavored water from canteens or pop when the troops had it. The water tasted like crap unless you put some Cool Aid powder in it. Even then it was just barely drinkable. But he had a pleasant surprise for the sergeants. He had a stash of beer. The Luau served its purpose and eased the tension that was building up between the platoon sergeants and the company gunny.

After shaving, and then washing his armpits and crotch with the soapy water that remained after his shave, he put his two days worn utilities back on. The caked mud on the trousers and shirt had hardened, but when he flexed his knees and arms, most of it popped off. He shook out his field jacket and swatted the caked mud off it. Water was tightly controlled on the base. They had a water point north of the base off Blue Sector, but it was only a spring and had to support two battalions. And if the shit started, the enemy would probably cut their water supply. The water point was outside of the wire in Indian country. Washing bodies and clothes was severely restricted and men hoarded water for drinking and shaving.

The command had in the past authorized water to be heated in fifty gallon drums over a fire made from trash and diesel fuel once a week to do platoon laundry, but that practice was curtailed, supposedly temporarily. Partly the restriction was due to water conservation and partly it was due to the great marker and wind direction indicator the smoke made for enemy mortars. Remembering Con Thien, Frank suspected temporarily was going to last for a while.

Men were still working on their positions when he got to the perimeter. 1st Platoon had the perimeter again, with 2nd Platoon in reserve. That day was the second day of a three-day duty stretch. The Marines in 1st Platoon were edgy about the coming dark, but all in all, the previous night had been a God-send for Frank. The troops didn't need any encouragement to keep improving their positions now. They had the knowledge from ITR when they got here, he thought. They just needed a little motivation. It looked like Ho Chi Minh was willing to provide the motivation.

The previous night had ended without casualties. Always a good way to end the night. The one coming up looked like it might be a little better, at least as far as the weather was concerned. The rain had let up and the fog had lifted. He could see the wire clearly. The Lieutenant was communicating on the radio when he got to the CP.

"Gunny, Pike is leading a small patrol to set up a night ambush about three hundred meters northwest of the wire. Red Sector is a controlled fire zone tonight while they're out there. There's something you probably don't know about, too. During the day, Second Platoon inspected the wire around Red Sector and found two places where the wire had been cut and put back together to look like it was okay. Also First Battalion is due back tomorrow. They didn't find a lot of enemy but they did find several hardened bunkers and supply caches. The NVA has something going on in our Area of operations (AO). How about staying with the platoon tonight until I bring Pike back?

"Yes, sir."

Frank figured he had about a half hour of light left and decided to put it to good use. Starting at the near end of the perimeter defense line he began inspecting Marine's rifles. The M-14 was a little more tolerant of dirt and moisture than the M-16 was, but they all had to be cleaned regularly. Each time he found a rifle that didn't meet his standards he told the Marine who owned it, "Your rifle is dirty. It could fail tonight if you have to use it. When the Skipper writes the letter to your parents, I'll make sure he doesn't tell them how stupid you were. See that it is clean tomorrow—if you are still here tomorrow." That usually got their attention. As he moved down the line and looked back, he saw a lot of weapon cleaning going on. Frank was getting a reputation.

Battalion HQ had issued two starlight scopes (night vision optics) to Lima Company to help watch the perimeter. He made sure they were about a fourth of the way in on both ends of the line so between them they could watch the top curve of the horseshoe perimeter and both of the legs. Night comes quickly in the mountains, but that night had enough light leaking through the clouds to make the starlight scopes effective.

The starlight scope couldn't "see" in the dark. It magnified available light up to 30,000 times but had to have at least a little light to work. Starlight, as the name implied, was usually enough. Dim Moonlight was perfect. Too much light washed out the screen. It was a scope without magnification and shaped like a large spotting telescope. The effective range was about the same as regular sights.

The operator pressed his eyes into a rubber gasket at the rear of the scope to look at the green lit screen. The gasket was necessary to keep the screen light from lighting up the operator's face and making him a perfect glowing target for a sniper. The Marines using the scopes that night hadn't quite grasped the concept. Frank gave them some SOJT. (Supervised on the job training) The supervision was Gunny gentle. He was learning quickly.

Around 0300 Hitchens called him back to the CP. Hitchens had a map unfolded.

"We have a situation, Gunny. Look here. This is

where Pike is dug in. He spotted several unknowns moving toward his position, but they stopped right about here. He's not sure what they're doing and wants some help before he challenges them. I'm sending a squad out. Send Second Squad back here and fill in the line. Then stand by to support them."

"Why challenge them, sir? It's a free fire zone for the patrol. If something moves, kill it."

"COC wants to make sure it isn't friendlies from the SOG compound. (Studies and Observation Group, a secretive base just outside the wire off the Gray Sector on the south side of the combat base operated by Army Special Forces and CIA)

"Got it, sir."

Frank ran back to the line and sent Second Squad back to the CP. After he had them on their way, he pulled a couple of men out of each squad along the line and filled the gap in the line made by the absent squad. With that task done, he told the rest of the platoon what was going on and put them on full alert.

He sat next to the Marine with the starlight scope and took the scope. He watched the squad leave the wire and tracked them for as long as he could and then tried to find the unknowns the patrol had reported. No luck. He couldn't see enough detail to distinguish people from bushes.

They ought to be to Pike's position by now, he thought. Come on, challenge the bastards. And then he heard it. He couldn't understand the words but he understood the attitude in the sound. Identify yourself now or die! Not those words, but the sound said it all. And then he had a target. It was the light from a muzzle blast as the unknowns opened-up on the reinforced squad. A moment later Hitchens called on the radio.

"Lima Niner, open fire. The squad is with Pike below ground level. Fire over their position."

Frank clicked the transmit button twice and yelled, "Open fire on my tracer."

The entire perimeter poured fire into the area showing the muzzle flashes. Rifle teams opened-up first following Frank's initial round, and tracers crashed into the area marked by his first tracer round. Then the sixties opened-up using the outgoing tracers as a guide. Targets couldn't be seen, but Marines saturated the area that had sprouted muzzle blasts just a few moments before. Then the sound of tubing came from near the runway. Three 81mm mortars lit up the night as they exploded on the unknown's position.

The muzzle blasts disappeared and soon the call for "Cease fire" came over the radio. The Radioman yelled at Frank to cease fire. He yelled down the line to cease fire and the call was taken up and passed along. In just a few moments the line was silent.

The Marine acting as his Radio operator handed him the handset and said. "Lieutenant."

Frank took the handset. "Lima Niner."

"Keep a lid on the line, Gunny. The patrol is searching the area to see what was out there."

"Roger, this is Lima Niner, out."

He ran along the line and made sure everyone held their fire. When he returned, his radioman handed him the handset.

"Lima Niner, over."

"Niner this is One-One. Hold fire. I'm bringing the patrol back. It's too dark to find anything."

"Roger, Holding fire. Lima Niner, out."

He passed the word the patrol was coming back in. And that was tricky for the patrol. The defensive line had hostiles in the grass and friendlies on the way in. Hitchens brought them in right. Pike gave Hitchens a warning on the radio and then popped a finger flare. Hitchens reported the color and Pike confirmed. As they got closer, Pike picked another color and popped another flare. Finally spotted with the starlight scopes, they were brought through the wire on the run. Frank had the Marines he was with cover behind the incoming squad. The troops were back. He could begin to relax, but not too much. There was still a lot of night to go.

The rest of the night was stressful but uneventful. In the morning, Hitchens sent a patrol out to search the area. An hour later the patrol leader reported they had found five dead enemy. With all of 1st platoon safely inside the compound, and Platoon Sergeant Pike leading his platoon, Frank checked out of the area with Hitchens and left Red Sector to find some chow and get some sleep. The *crachin* was setting in and the rain had started, so the runway would probably be closed until the fog lifted and minimum visibility and ceiling were available again. Good news for sleeping, but not good news for resupply. (crachin: a name the French had given to the thick, white fog mixed with drizzle that was common in the area, loosely translated from old French as wet spit.)

National Route 9, the only road back to Dong Ha, sixty-three kilometers to the north and the main resupply point just south of Con Thien, was effectively closed. The old Vietnamese National Route had served as an MSR for supply convoys during the early days of Khe Sanh occupation by the Marines. But even then, the thirty or so crumbling bridges along the route and the ever present potential for ambushes by the NVA made resupply by convoy extremely dangerous and undependable at best. By the time Frank arrived at the combat base, use of Route 9 had been abandoned. The base was totally dependent on resupply by air.

The runway at Khe Sanh had been upgraded by Navy Seabees in the fall when a large rock outcropping was discovered near the base. The outcropping provided a source of crushed rock for a new runway bed. On days that met at least the minimum conditions, Medium load C-123 and heavy load C-130 aircraft touched down all day long and most of the night. They brought mostly munitions and explosives to build up an extended supply of ammunition on hand, but the massive air supply operation brought its own problems for the combat base. Growing stores of supplies, especially munitions, overwhelmed storage facilities resulting in poorly stored munitions and unsafe conditions at primary ammo dumps and ammo supply points.

Frank had seen it on his first day in the camp. No problem lives in isolation. Problems always propagate and are the source and cause of other problems. Building a base is subject to the same requirements as building anything else. If you start out with a small error and don't correct it, the error grows progressively bigger as you progress with the construction. Overstocked ammunition storage facilities were a big and growing problem.

With the focus and priority on combat and munitions supply, other needed supplies such as fortification materials had to wait. Building materials of any kind were hard to come by and forced the Marines to jury-rig and improvise with whatever they could find or devise. Bunkers and defensive positions, sleeping hooches and command posts, all were constructed and reinforced with whatever the Marines could salvage from any source available. Discarded ammunition boxes, spent artillery casings, old runway metal grating torn up by the Seabees when they upgraded the runway, tree trunks from nearby rain forests, rocks and stone, sandbags filled with the local laterite clay, metal pallets, anything that could provide stiffness or hardness and stop a bullet or shrapnel disappeared quickly into bunkers and defensive positions.

Besides lack of fortification material, two things contributed to inferior fortifications at Khe Sanh. The northeast monsoon season hit the Khe Sanh area particularly hard in the early fall of 1967 dropping close to three feet of rain in a single week at one point. Many underground bunkers, trenches, and fighting positions were washed out and had to be rebuilt. But digging in clay was very hard work and many, too many bunkers and facilities were rebuilt above ground making them particularly vulnerable to heavy artillery. Marines don't like to dig.

Since the Hill fights of the previous year (the maneuvers and battles in which the Marines captured the important hill tops surrounding Khe Sanh) the Khe Sanh combat base had not been seriously challenged by the enemy, most of the activities against the Americans taking place in the hills to regain the high ground. Occasional mortars, rockets, and sniper fire were more harassment than challenges to Khe Sanh's perimeter up until early January of 1968. Calm tends to breed complacency.

The Khe Sanh location was a good location for a combat base in many ways. Compared to the surrounding terrain, it was relatively flat and level and could support a long runway. It had good fields of fire in all directions. The soil was stable, except in the worst of the monsoon when nothing was stable, and the topology provided good drainage.

With Marine companies holding most of the high ground on the important hills that surrounded the base, the location was defensible. Its weak points were remoteness causing difficulty in resupply, and the weather. The combat base could be cut off from the outside world by the enemy or the weather. The enemy closed Route 9 and the weather closed the runway.

Chapter 30

When Frank visited the Company CP that evening he was told about the five bodies recovered that morning. They were apparently North Vietnamese Army officers. The base was definitely being observed, probed, and assessed by the enemy. G2 had identified a major NVA unit of regimental strength near Khe Sanh and Ca Lu to the northeast. A full division was believed to be in the general area. None of that news was good news for Frank. Big time misery was brewing.

Probing continued, and Marine patrols made occasional contact with NVA platoon and squad sized forces over the next two weeks. He grew comfortable with his responsibilities, but not with the situation. He wanted to take a patrol out and hunt NVA, but he had to remain inside the wire while others led patrols. Con Thien was too fresh in his memory to allow him to get comfortable sitting in one place and trying to defend a patch of mud, but he did his job.

Thoughts of being a boot Gunny retreated as men, both officers and enlisted, began depending on his judgment, and he discovered his judgment was pretty good. All those hours with experienced NCOs hadn't been wasted. There was nothing left of his earlier tentative manner. He began to think like a leader and of his Marines as weapons. Responsibility, for those with the potential, tends to grow leaders. Frank had the potential and the motivation.

On January 6th, Operation Niagara was launched to locate and identify enemy units around Khe Sanh and identify targets for saturation bombing by B52 Stratofortresses. Signs of enemy movement and supply were being discovered almost daily. On the 7th, S2 (Battalion Intelligence) received reports from III MAF Intelligence indicating that traffic coming down from North Vietnam on the Ho Chi Minh trail in Laos had increased significantly and the Khe Sanh area seemed to be the terminus for the supplies. Sniper fire increased around the hill outposts, especially around Hill 881 south where 3rd Battalion companies India and Mike guarded fire support bases providing covering fire for Khe Sanh with 105mm howitzers and 106mm recoilless rifles.

While on patrol, a company from 1st Battalion ambushed an enemy reconnaissance patrol and killed several NVA soldiers not far from the combat base. Captured documents were sent back to G2 (Division Intelligence) for analysis. Frank began to hear talk of sieges and getting cut off from the world. Dien Bien Phu where the Viet Minh defeated the French forces with a long and deadly siege was brought up repeatedly.

The situation maps in Battalion HQ began to show a disturbing picture as plots marking sightings and suspected enemy positions from spy technology brought in for operation Niagara began to send back indications of enemy movements, and patrols reported possible enemy sightings. It was beginning to look like enemy forces were building up and the Marines at Khe Sanh might be heavily outnumbered.

On January 10th, the base commander announced that he expected a major enemy attack on the main Khe Sanh combat base within days. Frank and Third Battalion continued to improve their fighting positions and began the almost impossible task of providing fighting positions with overhead protection. The task was almost impossible because of the shortage of fortification materials.

Patrols took working parties of engineers to the forests surrounding Khe Sanh on a daily basis to select and cut raw timber to be used on the base. Grunts roamed the base and trash dumps looking for anything that could be salvaged for use as reinforcing material. Seabees used front end loaders and bulldozers to fortify bunkers and fighting positions with banks of dirt and rock. The combat base began to take on the character a city landfill.

Patrols continued to make contact with small, sometimes just squad sized, enemy units. The NVA continued to probe the perimeter at night, and on morning inspections, the Marines often found cut wire that had been carefully replaced in its original position to hide the cuts. They began adding additional razor sharp strips of metal to the wire and booby traps with C4 explosives that could be detonated from the trenches. Frag grenades were rigged to trip wires as additional protections for the perimeter. The claymores had been turned around by the enemy so many times the Marines built a special booby-trap line outside the wire to protect the claymores.

On the 13th, Khe Sanh was warned by Third Marine Division G2 to expect major enemy activity beginning sometime around the 18th of January. The pace of fortifying fighting positions picked up. Captain Franks told Gunny Evans to expect a lot of noise and concussion at night. The area around Khe Sanh had been given priority for Operation Arc Light B52 strikes beginning on the 16th. Captain Franks ordered his Marines to wear helmets and flak jackets and carry weapons twenty-four hours a day. Frank made sure every Marine in Lima Company carried a full combat load of ammunition with them at all times, and moved as much ammo to the trenches as could be stored with at least a minimal degree of safety, but the priority was on having enough ammo on hand, not on safety.

Something big was brewing.

Over the next two days a Marine patrol was ambushed on the slopes of Hill 881 North one kilometer from their home base on hill 881 South, and a slick was downed by enemy fire. Sniper fire increased on Red Sector and the number of probes increased on the eastern perimeter. Incoming rocket and mortar fire increased and began doing enough damage to the runway to test the Seabees ability to keep up. Lima company on the Red Sector perimeter took a 122mm rocket inside of the wire close to the line and suffered two wounded. Frank also lost a man who fell into a trench and broke his leg during a mortar attack. Things were heating up.

By the 15th of January, the indicators couldn't be ignored any longer. Although the NVA were avoiding contact in force, Ho Chi Minh was moving large numbers of infantry into the area. 2nd Battalion, 26th Marines (2/26) was ordered to Khe Sanh to reinforce the First and Third Battalions and when they arrived on the 16th, the entire regiment was together at Khe Sanh. One Company of 2/26 was dispatched to a hill three kilometers north of the base overlooking the Song Rao Quan river. Later that day the rest of Second Battalion moved to the hill to establish a battalion sized strong point to support the combat base.

By the middle of January, what had been a one battalion camp became a regimental base supporting three infantry battalions and all of their support units and elements of the 13th artillery battalion. The

Marines were stronger, but blessings can disguise curses. Camp facilities were stretched to their limits and beyond. Water was a special problem. The Hill outposts had to be supplied water by helicopter in fifty gallon drums, taxing not only the water supply at Khe Sanh, but the 26th Marine's air assets as well. Third Marine Division began resupplying the Hill outposts out of Dong Ha using large formations of medium and heavy-lift helicopters.

Munitions supply was the second curse in blessing's clothes. The remoteness of the base and difficulty of supply by air made Khe Sanh a classic target for siege. The strategy was simple: cut off supplies, blow the hell out of the base, starve them out, or over-run them when their ammunition ran out. Building up the ammo supplies to supply the regiment for a minimum of thirty days, and possibly a little longer, became a high priority. Three battalions of infantry can go through a lot of ammunition in battle. And with an artillery battalion supporting the infantry, massive stores of munitions built up at the combat base. Munitions storage areas were increased to three—but their designs weren't improved.

The main ammunition dump was located on the east side of the camp near the runway. One ASP (ammunition supply or storage point) was located at a strategic point near the center of the base and another was located on the western end of the camp near the artillery emplacements. The main dump was below ground with protective revetments. But the growing supplies filled it to capacity, and crates and pallets of munitions began to pile up outside of the revetments. The ASPs were in the same condition, a very scary situation in light of increasing incoming artillery, rockets, and mortars and one that had worsened since Frank's first day on the base.

On the eighteenth of January Frank got a letter. Carol said she missed him and thought about him a lot. Sharon Garzinski had stopped by one evening and introduced herself and gave Carol Frank's address. Sharon said Ski had written and asked her to stop by and say hello. She explained that Frank had just been assigned to a command and finally had an address to write to. Carol wondered why he hadn't written. He felt ashamed. He'd been so busy only flashes of Carol popped into his mind occasionally. He wrote back immediately. It wasn't a long letter, but he asked her to write again soon. He put her letter in his top pocket and read it again several times.

While the combat base was dealing with its supply and fortification problems, the hill outposts were dealing with enemy up close and personal. India company based on Hill 881 South was taking casualties when patrols attempted to get close to Hill 881 North, another peak about a mile north of their position and not held by the Marines. Needing a better understanding of what he was facing on 881 North, India Company Commander requested permission to conduct a company sweep of the area around Hill 881 North. Permission was granted.

Near 0900 on the morning of the sweep, India Company came under fire and was pinned down. The situation developed quickly, and it soon became apparent India Company was in contact with a strong enemy force. The Battalion Commander decided he needed his command group closer to the action and called for a helicopter to take him to 881 South. Frank was drafted to run the Battalion Operations Center when the command group departed. Most of the Battalion operational functions were transferred to the 1st battalion COC so he was left with only relay and monitor responsibilities.

Later, after a day of heavy fighting and having taken casualties, India commander was directed to break off contact with the enemy and return to Hill 881 south. He wasn't happy about the order. What India Commander didn't know and 1st Battalion COC giving the order to retreat did know was incidents were happening all over the Khe Sanh Operations Area indicating widespread and significant enemy aggression against American outposts. Fear that India Company could be cut off from their fire base by superior forces, leaving the firebase only lightly defended, influenced Battalion's decision to have them return to Hill 881 South as quickly as possible. The hilltop was too important to risk.

Incidents taking place near Khe Sanh's perimeter while India was fighting on Hill 881 North provided 1st Battalion S2 with intelligence that caused them to put the outposts and the main combat base on high alert. During the middle of the day while India Company was trying to take the summit of Hill 881 North, a patrol conducting a sweep near the eastern perimeter of the main base reported capturing an NVA soldier near the base. The NVA was holding a Chieu Hoi pamphlet (Chieu Hoi or open arms was a program by the South Vietnamese Government to encourage NVA and Viet Cong to defect). The NVA soldier provided a load of intelligence, but the shocker was the NVA, in force, would attack an important outpost that night, and big doings were planned all over Vietnam for the Tet holiday just two weeks away.

The Chieu Hoi's intelligence seemed to support other intelligence indicating the NVA was preparing for immediate action against Khe Sanh and its outposts. The Commander of the 26th Marines ordered his Marines, main base and outposts, to stay inside their wire and prepare for a major assault. Frank worked with Company Commanders from the COC to prepare 3rd Battalion for the alert.

Chapter 31

Frank's night in the Battalion COC wasn't boring. Shortly after India Company returned to their hill top, Kilo Company on Hill 861 (situated between 881 South and Khe Sanh combat base) was attacked. Frank listened on the radio as a very nasty and nearly successful attack on the Marine outpost took place. The battle lasted through the night and the outcome was in doubt several times. The intelligence indicating a well-planned attack on an outpost had proven to be correct.

Finally, near first light, the Marines on 861 pushed the NVA off their hill top and secured their perimeter. Kilo company lost their Company Commander, Company Gunny, First Sergeant and four other Marines that night. After listening to the action all night, he had to peel his fingers loose from the radio handset.

The Battalion Commander's chopper landed at 0510 and Frank was released to return to Lima Company. He checked in at the company CP. The CP was full of busy people. All of the platoon leaders were conferring with Captain Franks. Franks spotted Frank and waved to him.

"Are you back with us for a while?"

"Yes, sir."

"Good. First and Second Platoons are both manning Red Sector. Three is doing a recon toward Khe Sanh Village. A CAP (Combined Action Platoon) reported a lot of activity in the area around their location at the village. Gunny, I want you in the CP today. I've got a feeling it's going to get a might busy."

As Captain Franks finished his prophetic remark the clock on his desk registered 0530 and the first round of enemy artillery incoming hit in the area near the 105mm C Battery at the other end of the base. All of the probing and observing had served the NVA well. They apparently knew exactly where the most valuable targets were.

Within seconds, artillery and mortars were falling all over the combat base catching many Marines in the open and unprepared. Mortars fell on bunkers and more fell on the trenches guarding the Perimeter. The barrage didn't build up. It started as a coordinated time on target attack that seemed to hit every part of the base at the same time. Death and destruction rained down, stunned senses, and left no time to prepare or adjust.

Moments after the beginning of the attack, the first disaster occurred. The main ammunition dump took direct hits from more than one artillery round, and over a thousand tons of stored munitions and explosives, much of it outside of the revetments, began burning and exploding. The exploding ammo dump blew shrapnel and unexploded munitions into the air and they began falling all over the base, into fighting positions, on bunkers, and all along the runway.

Three unexploded 81mm mortar rounds landed near the Lima company CP, one actually hitting the roof and bouncing off to land against the sandbags of the exposed northern wall. A round lying near the entrance to the CP was smoldering. Everyone in the CP was still dazed from the shock of the opening rounds of the attack.

Frank stared at the smoldering mortar round through the entrance for a moment not fully comprehending what he was looking at. Then comprehension came and he felt his skin get cold. If it exploded, the mortar round would blast shrapnel and superheated gases through the entrance and devastate everything and everyone in the CP.

"Get down," Captain Franks yelled.

Frank hardly heard the command. He started walking slowly toward the smoldering round. Taking his flak jacket off as he walked, he held it out in front him, as if that would offer protection against an exploding 81mm mortar round. If it blew, they wouldn't find enough of him to bury. When he got to the mortar, he put his flak jacket gently over the projectile and folded it into the jacket. He took a deep breath and shuddered as he let it out slowly. His hands slowly tightened around the jacketed projectile and he lifted it like a baby until he could cradle it in his arms. He carried the projectile to a nearby hole, stepping softly, climbed in and set the round gently in the sand at the bottom of the hole. Even more gently, he eased his flak jacket from around the projectile and then sat on the edge of the hole. He lifted his legs slowly, not wanting to cause any vibrations at all, and scooted backwards away from the lip of the hole with his hands. When he had a few feet between him and the hole, he rolled onto his stomach and started crawling toward the CP. That was when he saw the projectile lying against the north wall.

"Aw shit!" he said out loud, but the sound was lost in the cacophony of exploding munitions and incoming rocket, mortar, and artillery. He had to duck and cover his head when an artillery round hit in the Tank Company area behind him. Incoming continued to hit all over the base. Each time he began to get his brain working again a new concussion would rock his head and scatter his thoughts. He began bellying toward the north wall of the CP dragging his flak jacket with him. At least this one wasn't smoldering. Incoming artillery began hitting in the Red Sector and he didn't have time to play around with the second round. He scooped it up in his flak jacket and found another hole to put it in. He set that one down quickly and recovered his flak jacket.

Almost to the CP entrance, he heard and felt a massive explosion behind him and looked over his shoulder. First Battalion's mess hall had taken a direct hit. He dove through the CP entrance and rolled to the side of the opening.

"Gunny, you are out of your mind," Captain Franks said and grinned. "As soon as the ASP stops cooking off, we need to get a look at Red Sector. First and Second platoons are taking a pounding. Our own ammo is doing more damage than the enemy. What the hell else is going to screw up?"

As if in answer to the Skipper's question, Frank lifted his nose and sniffed. "Skipper, do you smell that?"

Captain Franks sniffed the air and his eyes opened wide. "Gas masks!" he yelled. "That's CS." (tear gas).

Fortunately for Frank he was the company Gunny and was required to set a good example. He had his gas mask with him, as an example if nothing else. Most troops kept their mask with them for the first few days in-country, but after a while began leaving them behind in their hooch or discarding them completely in the field as useless pieces of equipment and extra weight. He strapped the mask on, put his hand over the filter, and sucked to create a vacuum seal on his face.

He and the Captain went to the CP entrance to see what was happening. A misty cloud of CS was moving slowly toward them from the second exploding ASP near the center of the camp. That ASP contained fifty gallon drums of powdered CS. The cloud's thin outer edges swirling on turbulent air had given the CP just enough warning.

"Skipper, there's a crate of masks in the supply hooch. I better grab some and take them down to the platoons. I know damn well half the grunts in the trenches ditched their masks. They are about to learn a nasty, snot nosed lesson." His voice sounded nasal and dim through his mask. He had to press his mask against the captain's to be heard.

"Careful, Gunny. There's unexploded munitions all over the place. Fact is, I'm tempted to let them suffer and learn their lesson."

"Me too," he said. "But we need at least a few people with clear enough vision to watch the wire."

What he didn't mention, and what the CO was probably aware of anyway, as Company Gunny it was his responsibility to see that his Marines were prepared to fight. Sure it was the Platoon Commanders' and Platoon Sergeants' job, but Captain Franks depended on his Company Gunny. If they didn't have required and mandated equipment with them, it was his responsibility. He was feeling his lack of experience acutely right then.

Frank wove as many gas mask case straps as he could hold into his fingers and took off for the trenches. Every step was treacherous with unexploded and unstable munitions littering the ground and more falling, although at a slower rate now. He only had ten masks and quickly distributed them to men with running eyes and snotty noses. About half of the Marines had brought their masks with them so the line still had a large number of men able to watch for enemy and fight effectively. The platoon NCOs had at least shown some leadership after the problem arose. The Marines without masks had been directed to pour water on t-shirts and cover their faces until the CS dispersed. No permanent harm done, and probably a valuable lesson taught.

Frank checked in with the platoon CPs and then decided to stay with the Marines in the trenches. The trenches he entered that day were a far cry from the waist deep minimal cover he had seen on his first day with the company. Many places along the line had good overhead cover built from logs harvested from the nearby forests. On top of the logs were a couple layers of sand bags. It wouldn't protect them from a direct hit from something big, but it would stop bullets, shrapnel, and grenades. In addition, sandbag partitions had been built inside of the trench about every thirty or forty feet. Somebody was thinking and providing some leadership. The partitions would limit casualties to a small location if a round landed in the trench. And that was a distinct possibility that day as the burning and exploding ammo dumps threw unstable munitions all over the camp.

He moved along the trench, talking with Marines, checking weapons and ammo supplies, and even stopping to repair a rifle that had jammed with the bolt locked back and unable to move forward.

Near 1000 he decided to get back to the Company CP. The ASPs were still cooking off ammo but seemed to be burning themselves out and the ordnance techs were getting the fires under control with fire extinguishers and sand. The incoming artillery still pounded the base, but not with the intensity of the opening attack.

Frank climbed out of the trench on his belly and waited for an opportune moment to break for the CP. One moment seemed as good as the next so he stood in a crouch and took a step—and then the lights went out. The shockwave from a massive explosion knocked him off his feet, threw him through the air, and dropped him in the trench on his back. A large store of C4 plastic explosives exploded when construction explosives around it in the ASP detonated. The resulting shock wave, equal to a 2000-pound blockbuster bomb rocked the base and destroyed everything above ground for three hundred feet in all directions. Further away, sandbags were blown off roofs of bunkers and thick timbers were cracked. Frank was lucky he wasn't closer to the source of the explosion. He didn't hear the call for a corpsman and wouldn't hear anything for several minutes.

He woke up with a corpsman waving an ammonia capsule under his nose. His eyes fluttered open and he felt the pain seep into his brain. And with the pain came the knowledge he had been knocked down again. Knocked down without a chance to hit back, again. And with the knowledge came frustration and rage. The corpsman's voice seemed to be coming from a deep place with echoes, but he was understandable. He flipped a light across Frank's eyes a couple of times and put it away.

"Don't move until I check you out," Doc said. "I'm going to lift your head just a little. Tell me if it hurts."

Doc lifted his head slightly off the ground. "Anything?"

"No," he said. "Feels normal."

"Okay, turn your head side to side. Do it slowly."

He turned his head and everything seemed to be okay.

Doc checked all of Frank's limbs and then told him to try to sit up. He was sore all over, but sitting up wasn't a problem except for slight dizziness.

"You're lucky," Doc said. "I was sure you would have a spine injury."

Yeah, Frank thought, Sergeant Fucking Lucky. Getting the shit pounded out of me and I'm doing what? Living in holes, that's what. I want one of those bastards in my hands. I want to choke the living. . .

A round hit near the southwest end of the trench and a call went up for a corpsman.

"You're okay," Doc said. "Find me if you have any problems."

The corpsman didn't wait for an answer. He moved down the trench and squeezed around the sandbag partitions.

Enemy incoming and exploding ordnance continued for the rest of the day and evening. Captain Franks called the platoon CP and told them to keep Frank with them. He didn't want Frank to risk the dangerous trip back to the company CP. Frank worked the soreness out of his bruised muscles with some stretches and short bent over walks up and down a section of trench. By evening chow time, he was feeling almost normal again. Squad leaders sent runners to the CP for C-rats at 1800. The grind of incoming was becoming routine by then and the men ate their rations cold in the bottom of the trench.

By 1900 the fog was beginning to set in and a light drizzle had started and was turning the trenches into a slimy sewer. With the slime and mud another misery made itself known. The human body's waste function continues to work even when conditions such as exploding ordnance keeps men from leaving the trenches to find remote sites for their waste. Frank had learned from the Marines at Con Thien the importance of providing for waste disposal or at least storage for later disposal during a long siege, and he had tried to impress upon 1st and 2nd platoons the necessity of maintaining piss points under cover and solid waste alternatives in the trenches. When you are stuck in a hole and have to live with what you bring there, field sanitation is king.

But Marines are assault troops and not well

suited for manning trenches. And when nothing happens for a long period of time allowing habitual use of remote waste sites, grunts tend to get complacent, and little things like artillery shell casings sunk in the clay to use as piss points and solid waste storage expedients such as cut-off thirty and fifty gallon drums are ignored and when they get in the way, are sometimes removed and not replaced. Add to that the reluctance to move at all while exploding ordnance is hitting all around you, and the presence of an entrenching tool is close at hand, Marines sometimes do the obvious thing: bury it. Not a big problem when the ground is dry, but when the rain sinks in, waste rises. Having contained Marines for thirty-six hours for the first time without relief, the trenches were becoming odious and odiferous.

At 1930, 2nd platoon on the southwest perimeter sounded an alert. They had movement on their wire. A squad of 1st Platoon moved their sights to cover that section of wire. Frank saw a tracer from 2nd platoon and followed it with his eyes. He had to blink to verify what his eyes were seeing. A large force of NVA, at least platoon size, was attacking the wire.

      2nd Platoon opened-up with rifles and M79 grenade launchers and then a M-72 LAAW (66mm shoulder fired light anti-armor weapon) was launched at the attackers. The M-72 was a crazy move by someone, but grunts do strange things sometimes with enemy in front of them.

The attacking force was probably the lead element of something bigger or it was just a probe. A single platoon wouldn't be assaulting a combat base. A squad of 1st platoon Marines on the end closest to 2nd platoon added their fire to the fight. Then, with Marine positions located, an enemy automatic weapon opened-up on 2nd platoon and continued sweeping up the line to 1st platoon.

He saw movement directly in front of 1st platoon's section of the perimeter. A satchel charge exploded on the perimeter and blew a gaping hole in the wire. The platoon opened-up, firing into the dark. The Sixty filled the wire gap with tracers. A Bangalore Torpedo blew another hole in the wire near the western end of the platoon's perimeter. That end of the line opened fire on the new threat. But there weren't any targets. The NVA were staying down.

Frank ran along the trench yelling at the Marines.

"Single fire only. Find a target. Single fire only. The ammo dumps blew up. What you have may be the only ammo we get."

Automatic firing slowed and then stopped. Marines began looking for targets, but the NVA seemed reluctant to press the attack. Shooting in 1st Platoon slowed to a stop. Frank moved between the squads telling the grenadiers to load Willie Peter rounds (white phosphorus) but wait for a target. Firing slowed from 2nd platoon and a lull set in. Both platoons watched the wire and tried to distinguish NVA movement from fog that was beginning to swirl in the fire zone.

Frank removed his magazine and topped it off with loose rounds from an ammo can nearby. He told every other man to do the same thing and then had the others top off their magazines. Full magazines were available in every squad, but he knew some Marines would be waiting with only one or two rounds in their magazines when the shit started again and would have to change magazines with enemy in front of them. Not the best way to start a fight.

He was just pulling his rifle into his shoulder and sighting at the dark when tracers from an automatic weapon raked the line. The man next to him had just stood up to sight his rifle, a very stupid thing, and was knocked back against the trench wall and slid down to a sitting position in the bottom of the trench. His neck was a jellied mass of ripped red meat. His eyes were stretched wide open as he hit bottom. As his body settled in the trench his eyes remained open, staring at nothing.

Frank screamed for a corpsman. Every man in the trench pushed their selectors to full automatic and opened-up on the source of the incoming tracers. M-79s popped in every squad and frag rounds exploded all over the fire zone. He had to scream for single fire again. Marines weren't listening. He ran squad to squad jerking men away from the wall and screaming in their faces to regain control. The firing changed to single aimed fire slowly.

The fight lasted for an hour and probably

involved at least a company of NVA. The southeast perimeter also took incoming. When it was over, a dozen enemy dead were found in the Red Sector fire zone. Some were in the wire and had unexploded satchel charges with them. Several troops in 2nd platoon reported they saw NVA dragging other wounded and dead away as they retreated. 1st platoon had one Marine KIA and two others with slight wounds. 2nd platoon had two Marines KIA in the initial attack and three wounded during the sustained action.

All told, in the day long action including the bombardment, the combat base had suffered fourteen dead and forty-three wounded, some from their own exploding ammo dumps. Two ammunition dumps were destroyed severely limiting the base's ammunition supplies, especially for the artillery battalion. A helicopter was destroyed along with most of the base infrastructure and a large section of the runway was no longer usable. Only 1800 feet of runway remained undamaged, and the night lighting system was gone. Resupply was going to be a bitch.

But bitch or not the logistics support command was already moving before the ammo dumps had cooled. Late that night six light cargo aircraft with short field capability landed after dark and delivered several tons of ammunition. Later, after the fog had set in, one of the big twin rotor choppers called a *Phrog* got in and delivered critical medical supplies and lifted out the most seriously wounded. Frank's Marines, except for the KIA, had only minor wounds and could be returned to the fight.

While Frank and his Marines were crouching in trenches under artillery attack earlier that day, the NVA were showing their strength against the outposts also. He had listened to the attack on Hill 861 prior to the main base being attacked, but he didn't know that India and Mike companies on Hill 881 South came under fire with enemy mortars during the day too. Several Marines were wounded and one of the big choppers was destroyed while trying to evacuate casualties.

The NVA seemed reluctant to commit large numbers of infantry against the main combat base, but they weren't bashful about the outlying units. That made a lot of sense. If Charlie could take the high ground around the combat base away from the Marines, Khe Sanh was in for a lot of hurt.

Around the time the initial rounds were falling on the combat base, NVA infantry struck against the South Vietnamese Regional Force and the Combined Action Platoons in Khe Sanh Village about two miles south of the base. An unknown number of NVA (probably greater than battalion size) attacked the small force of less than 200 mixed Vietnamese RF, Bru Tribesmen, Marine Corps and Army advisors.

Two attempts were made to rescue the embattled defenders. In the first, a platoon from 1st Battalion at Khe Sanh attempted to reach the village but couldn't break through the NVA surrounding the village. In the second attempt, the Army tried to bring in a

South Vietnamese RF Company with helicopters. The attempt ended in disaster. The NVA killed over 25 of the American pilots and crew and over 70 of the RF troops.

The 21st of January, 1968 had not been a good day for Frank or for Khe Sanh. Ho Chi Minh was launching an offensive in force against the northern districts in South Vietnam.

Chapter 32

On the 22nd of January with fears that NVA forces around Khe Sanh were in greater numbers than first believed, the 26th Marines were reinforced by the 1st Battalion, 9th Marines. 1/9 landed under fire and quickly dispersed into existing positions with the 1/26. On the 23rd, 1/9 moved out and occupied a small hill about a mile southwest of the main base and began clearing and recon operations in that area. Khe Sanh was getting stronger but G2 said they were facing possibly two divisions of NVA.

Also on the 23rd, the Red Sector on the western perimeter began receiving accurate sniper fire in addition to the continuous bombardment of artillery. It looked like the enemy had replaced their inept sniper of the previous few weeks with a much better shooter.

The platoons tried to locate the sniper, but he was in cover and shooting from 600 or 700 hundred yards away. Frank couldn't even find an indicator with the best binoculars in the CP. Lima company was pinned down during daylight. Men watched the tree line with periscope binoculars from below the top edge of the sandbags along the trench. (Special binoculars in the shape of a long Z that allowed the Marines to remain below the sandbags with only the lenses of the binoculars showing.)

After the CP lost two runners to sniper fire, one of them a young Marine 1st Platoon had been training to take over as a rifle team leader, Frank decided to do something about the invisible sniper. He tried saturating the area the sniper had to be operating from with mortar rounds, but an hour later another Marine was wounded. Patrols were sent out after dark to set up ambushes, but they came back without contact. Daylight patrols were becoming suicide missions for at least one of the patrol. Even small 3rd Force Recon patrols were taking casualties and they were the sneakiest bastards in the Corps

The artillery incoming was bad enough, but the sniper with his accurate and personal shooting was causing a special kind of terror within the company. Artillery was impersonal and the risk was random. But the sniper was a very personal danger zeroing in on specific individuals. The troops all felt like they had a bulls eye on their chests. And the Marines had to stay in one place. The sniper could move to any location he wanted. That torqued Frank's jaws more than anything.

Frank waited until dark and then made his way carefully to the company CP.

"Skipper, I'd like to try something to get this sniper off our asses."

Captain Franks looked up from his maps and nodded.

"I'm open to just about anything right now," he said.

"I want to go out in the dark and hunt the son of a bitch. I'll take enough provisions for three days and stay out there in hiding until I get him."

Captain Franks considered the request and looked at the map.

"It's a pretty big area, Gunny. What makes you think you can find him if a full platoon can't?"

"A platoon is too easy to track," Frank said. "He knows when they leave the wire even at night. Hell, sir, he just goes to ground and waits them out. But one person alone can get through the wire undetected and can move around and wait him out. Each time he fires I'll be in the general area and I'll get a little closer. I can be very patient."

"You might run into a company of NVA too. I won't be able to support you and the area will have to remain a hot fire zone."

"I'll make sure I have cover and I'll take a radio to monitor artillery strikes."

"You sure you want to do this?"

"No," he said, thought, Hell, yes. "But we have

to do something. Platoon and even squad sized patrols aren't going to cut it. Skipper, we have one man out there pinning down a whole company."

Captain Franks watched his Gunny's face for several moments. He drummed his fingers on the map table for a few moments longer. Finally, he decided.

"Go ahead and get your gear together. I'll talk with the COC. If they haven't got any problems with it, I'm willing to give you a shot at it."

Frank went to his hooch and repacked his ruck for a three day stay in the grass. Three days without artillery pounding in his ears. He had his K-Bar (bayonet like knife), M-14 rifle, .45 pistol, and four frag grenades. He put eight 7.62 magazines, two .45 magazines, and two claymores in the ruck and kept one mag in the rifle and one in the pistol. Five freeze-dried LRRP (long range recon patrol meals), six candy bars, two canteens of water mixed with cool aid for taste and sugar for energy, Halazone tabs to purify water, and one red and one green pop flare completed his pack. He picked up a PRC-25 radio with a fresh battery from the company CP and made his way back to the 1st Platoon CP. The Captain called at 0100.

"Lima Niner this is Lima Six."
"One this is Niner, over."
"Niner, Operation is approved."
"Roger, Lima Six. I'm moving out now."
"Lima Six, out."

Frank had his face and hands blackened. His dog

tags were taped and anything else that could rattle or make noise was taped, wrapped, or otherwise silenced. He nodded at the Lieutenant and started out the door.

"Careful out there, Gunny," Hitchens said. "I hate breaking in new Gunnies."

Frank gave him a thumbs up and a grin. Now that it was time to start his plan it didn't seem as foolproof as it did when he explained it to the Skipper. It felt downright stupid. He was going to be in the grass alone for three days with NVA all over the area. What the hell was I thinking? he thought. But he couldn't deny the little tickle in his gut. What he was about to do scared him silly—but it also excited the hell out of him. Instead of sitting in trenches ducking artillery, he could hit back and cause a little hate and discontent.

He dropped into the trench and made it to the western end under cover. The end of the trench was close to the opening in the wire he had to get through undetected. A mortar hit in the middle of the base and when that light died down, he went through the wire on the run with heavy fog for cover. He had a long and careful stalk across open ground spotted with scrub and mangled trees and tufts of elephant grass to get to the tree line and he had to be there before light. He had time and he took it moving slowly and carefully in short spurts and going to ground often.

The fog made the landscape eerie and dangerous. Fog swirled in the light breeze and tufts of elephant grass made shadows in the fog that looked like people. Stare at them long enough and they seemed to move, just small movements like a man standing in the dark and looking around. NVA could be anywhere and he could walk right into them if he wasn't extremely careful. He estimated his progress by counting his paces. He stopped, checked his course, and listened carefully before each forward movement.

One hundred yards outside of the wire Frank heard something that made him freeze in place. Sliding footsteps, several of them. Several people were moving right towards him. The fog was thick and he couldn't see anything. He took his pack off and stretched out prone on the ground, just a lump, an indistinct shape in the dark and fog. His pulse pounded in his ears as the sounds of shuffling feet got close. His ears clogged. He opened his mouth wide to clear his ears and felt the pop in his inner ear. He waited.

The sounds got closer. At first the NVA were just dim impressions in the white fog. Then several ghostly shadows began passing his position on both sides, silent except for the shuffle of their feet. They were bent over and he could make out dim outlines of rifles. He pressed his face into the dirt and didn't look at them.

The sound of shuffling moved beyond his position. He remained still and let the shaking in his hands and legs settle down. Hugging the ground felt very good, but he had to move. He thought they had all passed and was about to get up to move away toward the tree line, but he heard another shuffle just in time.

He stretched out again. Another shuffler was coming right at him.

Frank slipped his K-Bar out of his belt sheath and waited. The shuffles got closer, coming right at him. Shit! He remained still, watching for the shadow. The fog in front of him darkened and then the shadow appeared. The intruder was bent over and taking careful steps, shuffling each step forward and feeling for obstacles. Son of a bitch, he's going to step right on me.

Fear can cause you to freeze up or it can make you eerily fast and strong. Fortunately for Frank the eerie part took hold. As the leg moved forward, his hand shot out and grabbed the ankle as he raised up to his knees lifting the leg over his head and dumping the intruder onto his back. The Vietnamese screamed a short terrified gurgling sound before he hit the ground. But then his back hit hard and Frank was over him in an instant.

He didn't think about what he was doing. Fear drove him and instinct blocked out all conscious will; survive, survive. He brought the point of his K-Bar down with a swing starting over his head. As it came down he clasped his other hand around his first and stabbed the big blade right through the Vietnamese's breast bone and fell on his hands holding the knife. The blade sank in to the hilt and must have hit dirt on the other side stopping the knife and driving the butt end into Frank's breastbone causing him to grunt.

Frank's face was inches from the Vietnamese soldier's face, both hands around the hilt of the knife,

Frank's chest and his full weight on the knife. The Vietnamese went rigid, twitched for a moment, and sighed a long airy, "Ahhhh." He stared into Frank's eyes. Even in the dark Frank could see the soldier's eyes, wide open, two dark empty caves, no one home. For a moment as he felt the soldier twitch and felt warm life pulsing silently out of the wound across his fingers, he felt a total, terrible emptiness. Bile rose in his throat and he had to swallow hard to keep it out of his mouth. He paused and stared at his grisly work, up close, in the fog, alone, no one to tell him it was okay.

He didn't know how long he waited like that, but survival instinct is much stronger than remorse, and training is stronger than regret. He had to move. He couldn't pull the knife out of the Vietnamese's chest with his slippery hands. He put his foot on the chest and yanked, but the bone it had pierced held tight. He heard small animal sounds coming from his own mouth and clamped down on his emotions. It had to be done. He sawed the knife back and forth and felt the bones crack, but he kept sawing and jerking until he felt the knife come free. His hands and arms were covered with blood and the warmth and coppery smell was sickening. He grabbed his rifle and pack and moved away toward the tree line as fast as he could without making too much noise.

When he had covered a couple hundred feet, he turned on the PRC-25 and called Lima One-One.

"Lima One-One this is Niner. Seven Victor

Charlie one hundred meters from western perimeter. I am clear. I say again. I am clear. Out." He turned the radio off. That would have to do. He didn't have time to wait around for a reply or the shooting. Nor did he want to be in the general area. Frank was well away from the action and under cover when the first illumination round popped. No shooting followed. He waited it out and started moving again when the dark returned.

Shortly after 0300 he reached the trees and thick elephant grass. Tipping it slightly to catch enough light to see the needle, he checked his compass again and set a course through the grass. In his mind he could picture the view from the perimeter of the point he thought he had entered the trees, but he couldn't be sure he had actually arrived at that point in the fog. It didn't matter. He was in the trees and moving in the right direction. He continued moving into the jungle for an hour and then began looking for a hide-hole to wait for light. The sniper was out there somewhere and Frank figured he'd have to move several times before he would be in place to take a shot on the sniper.

He was amazed at how calm he felt. He ought to be scared to death, but he wasn't. Being out there in the grass all alone in the fog was a lot less scary than sitting in a trench or bunker waiting for a mortar round or rocket to fall on your head. He was getting to like the feeling of freedom and security the dark and fog gave him. No one knew where he was and no one could give him orders. He could fight any way he liked.

He was soaked to the skin and shivering. The

nights got cold around Khe Sanh, especially during the northeast monsoon, and the constant wetness magnified the cold. In the morning that would all change when the day heated up. He would end up just as wet from sweat. He needed to stay hydrated, but he also had to conserve water. Without water, the mission would end quickly. That was a strange thought with so much of it coming down and soaking everything around him. But the water in the jungle wasn't the kind you wanted to drink even with purification tabs. Things lived in it, things that wiggled and grew, things that would end up living in you.

As he continued moving forward he saw a large dark shape in the fog ahead of him. He paused and waited for the shape to decode itself in his brain. A hut? He moved forward slowly and listened. Not a sound. He closed on the hulking shadow and listened some more.

Frank approached whatever it was slowly and carefully, no sound, even his breathing as quiet as he could make it. He couldn't detect any sound or movement. The jungle around him was as silent as it ever gets, but a jungle is never completely silent. Water dripping off leaves, animals large and small, bugs, people, hopefully not people, create a constant buzz of sound. He had to get close and see what was there. He didn't need any surprises when the light came. He eased up to the dark, silent shape on his stomach. He reached out and touched it. Rock. He stood up and ran his hands across the surface and felt the crevices and sharp jutting edges of the basalt rock outcropping he had thought was a hut and let out a silent sigh of relief.

If he could find an opening or a deep crevice, the outcropping would make a good place to hole-up and wait for daylight, and the rock would provide good cover. Basalt outcroppings were common all around Khe Sanh. A large one near the base had provided the rock and stone to upgrade the runway to support heavy aircraft like the C-130. He circled the rock feeling with his hands. It wasn't a large outcropping, but it was big enough to make him lose track of where he started. He stuck a sharp piece of rock in a crevice about shoulder high as a marker and started again. By the time he reached the marker again he hadn't found anything big enough to get into.

But Frank did find a separation in the outcropping. He could only see the shapes vaguely but he could tell the outcropping had two peaks separated by a large crevice in the shape of a V. He started moving up the crevice with his hands outstretched and touching both walls of crumbling rock until his hands couldn't reach across the crevice. Each time he touched the rock he got a case of the willies. He couldn't see what he was touching and there were plenty of things in the jungle you didn't want to put your hand down on. Things that crawled and things that bite. The bottom of the crevice was solid and felt clear of rubble. Probably washed by rain runoff every day. Near the top, about ten paces up the crevice, he saw a place on the left rock that was darker than its surrounding rock. He reached out to touch it but there wasn't any rock there. It was an opening, maybe just a depression, but it was worth exploring.

The opening turned out to be a miniature cavern almost high enough to stand in. It wasn't deep, hardly enough to get him and his ruck into, but it was the best cover he had so far. The floor of the mini-cavern sloped downward and was formed by jagged fingers of sharp rock. No problem. Frank shrugged out of his ruck and sat on it. Okay, I don't know what's around me, he thought, but at least I have cover.

Now that he had a little security, his mind was able to deal with more than simple survival. He could hide from the enemy there, but he knew he couldn't hide from the sounds and pictures in his mind. Close up, face-to-face death, the kind you can smell and feel, is a lot different than taking a shot at a distance. He told himself it was war and it was him or them. In the dark, in the silence, all alone with his thoughts, it didn't help. He leaned back against the wall of the mini-cavern and waited for light.

For three hours, he slept fitfully. Things buzzed near his ears. Things bit his face and hands. Things crawled in his hair. Light and the sounds of massive explosions off in the distance woke him up. At first he felt relieved and rested. And then he remembered what his mind wanted to forget. He pushed it back somewhere in his memory bank, a place for parking an inconvenient conscience. He had a job to do. He sat very still and listened to his surroundings. Dead silence. The fog was still thick but sunlight was getting through the canopy giving the fog a diffused glow. It wasn't much, but better than night time. He scratched at his face.

He took two drinks of water, poured a little water into the freeze dried eggs from a LRRP packet and put the mixing bag under his armpit to warm up. He waited and listened. No sense in getting in a hurry. He'd have to leave the rock sometime, but it was as good a place to wait for the sound of the sniper rifle as any.

Twenty minutes later he opened his LRRP pack and ate the egg mush with a squirt of hot sauce. It wasn't eggs benedict, but it was high quality protein. He had a candy bar for dessert to load some carbs. Two more drinks of cool aid flavored water washed down the dry instant coffee he put on his tongue. Not as good as a hot cup, but it got caffeine in his system. The empty packets went back into his ruck. Waste discipline. One of the holy three: Light discipline, sound discipline, and waste discipline. Be a ghost. Don't leave even a footprint.

The Vietnamese were supposed to be able to smell Americans fifty feet away by their body odor. Not a flattering thought, but one to keep in mind, if it was true. Some of the infantry troops who had done a lot of patrolling and ambushes said you could definitely smell the VC. Every one of them had a strong odor of Nuoc Mam fish sauce (Nuke mom, to the Marines). He tended to believe that one. Every Ville and every Vietnamese town smelled of fish sauce and you could usually smell it before you could see the Ville. Frank wished he had eaten some Nuoc Mam sauce with rice before he left camp. Then he'd smell like a Vietnamese and they wouldn't notice. The silence lets you think too much, he thought.

The morning got brighter and the fog lifted. The heat started early when the rain stopped. Good day for sniping, he thought. Maybe today will be the day. The bombardment of the base had been sporadic during the night, but it picked up with the coming of light. He decided to move closer to the edge of the tree line so he could figure out exactly where he was in relation to the area where the sniper seemed to operate, or at least the area where 1st Platoon thought the sniper always set up. No one was really sure. He moved back toward the edge of the jungle using the noise from the incoming at Khe Sanh to guide him and cover his movements.

The jungle he was in was one of the reclaimed areas around the Khe Sanh base. Reclaimed by the jungle, that is. It was probably cleared for coffee by the French at some time in the past and abandoned. It was a single canopy jungle that let a lot of light in. Many of the jungles in the region were ancient growths with two canopies. The taller trees could reach ninety feet tall and blocked a lot of light. A secondary growth rising to sixty feet formed a second canopy and shut out almost all sky light. Those jungles were sparse on ground growth and easy to move through. No such luck for Frank. The single canopy growth he was moving through allowed plenty of light to nurture elephant grass, bamboo, and climbing vines. The elephant grass provided a lot of concealment, but it was difficult to get through and held a lot of water. And lord knows what else. The bamboo stands were so thick they simply had to be avoided. He was soaked through again with both water from the grass and sweat by the time he reached the edge of the tree line.

He had a good view of the northwest perimeter from his position so he decided to make it his stand and wait there to see if his adversary would take a shot. He checked his rifle and wished he had brought some lube. Everything on him and with him was soaked. Mold would start quickly. Rust wouldn't take long. He settled in and waited.

A rocket hit the base near the runway. He saw the flash then heard the boom. A plume of smoke rose and was caught in the wind. A C-130 made a pass over the runway and parachutes blossomed behind it. More supplies even when they can't land.

Frank had good concealment at the base of a tree so he relaxed back against the trunk and waited some more. Bored to death, he thought. Two artillery rounds hit the base near the now defunct ammo dump. Endless boredom punctuated by moments of sudden terror, He quoted in his head. He opened his binocular case and focused on the western perimeter.

Men were working on the positions. The trenches now had a triple wall of sandbags on the outer edge stacked three high and a dirt embankment behind the inner edge. He spotted two flashes of reflected light on top of the sandbags at one point on the perimeter. Periscope binoculars, he thought. No one wants to stick his head up. They're learning. Men darted in and out of the positions, but they didn't stay out for long.

And then he heard it. The sharp crack of a high powered rifle to his left. It would just be a soft report to the men in the trenches, if they heard it at all. He turned in the direction of the sound and waited for another shot. Fifteen minutes went by in silence.

He moved slowly and quietly toward where he believed the sniper was hiding. He wouldn't get there this time, but he would get closer. He had picked up several leeches while moving through the jungle. You can't really feel them until they get heavy with blood. He tried to pull a leech off his arm. He got one end of it loose but the other end was attached also. His arm started bleeding from the bite. Then the damn thing reattached on both ends again.

Screw it. He knew he had other leeches under his clothes, hard to avoid them in the tall elephant grass, but he couldn't take time to rid himself of his passengers. He also began to notice the bug bites. He hoped they were from mosquitoes, but he hadn't been alone in the rocks. Crawley things lived there. Malaria was always a threat in Vietnam, so maybe he ought to hope it was something else besides mosquitoes. He should have brought some repellant. If pigs could fly. . .get focused dumb ass.

He kept moving through the grass, stopping frequently to let the grass behind him lift back up. It was nearly up to his shoulders and so thick it couldn't be parted. He just had to push through. That kind of stalking was scary as hell. If the sniper saw him first there wouldn't be much left for Frank, just a flash of light in the brain and then nothing.

During a resting period, he heard a sound in front of him. It was quiet, still a hundred yards ahead of him, but it was human. A laugh. He moved closer to the edge of the trees to find an easier path toward the sound. He heard another sound. Something hitting metal. He started up a small knoll gaining a few feet of elevation. The knoll continued upward toward the sound. Then the rifle again. Another shot. Someone at Khe Sanh had given the sniper a target. Hope he missed. He could feel the skin on his arms tingling and he needed to pee. He shrugged out of his ruck and picked a landmark to guide him back to it.

Frank started stalking. Free of the ruck he could move faster and quieter. He could hear quiet talking now. Someone hawked and spat. Loudly. Someone was in a tree and someone was on the ground. They weren't talking loudly, but they weren't whispering either. It was obvious to him they felt safe in their hide. The knoll continued upward. It must be the small rise near the point in the trees he had picked as his target area from the base. It would be perfect for a sniper. The shooter had a little elevation and a clear field of fire. Khe Sanh base had clear fields of fire in all directions for several hundred meters. But the problem with clear fields of fire is the clear part works both ways. He moved forward on his stomach. He pulled at another leech but had no better luck than he had with the first one. Keep your mind in the game, Evans. The voices sounded louder. He was getting closer. He was getting anxious, wanted to take the shot and get the hell out of there.

Frank squatted in the thick-bladed grass. He took a deep breath and let it out slowly, reminded himself he was stalking soldiers, men trained to fight, to kill, men who could and would kill him if he gave them the slightest chance. He reminded himself they might be small, but they were professionals just like him. It's the attitude that keeps you from getting anxious, careless, and dead. Slow down. One inch at a time. Wait for the right shot, only the perfect shot, nothing less. It doesn't have to be today. It just has to be.

He rose to his knees and searched the tree tops ahead of him. Stomach acid rose up the back of his throat. He swallowed twice, tasted sour fear. Belched quietly. Nothing in the tree tops. The shooter must be lower in the trees. He stood in a crouch so his head didn't protrude above the grass and searched lower in the branches through the tips of the grass.

And he saw a shadow in a tree. A big shadow. Way bigger than a man. Frank watched silently. Slowly his eyes decoded the shadows. The shooter had a platform in a tree that was three trees back from the edge of the tree line. No wonder they couldn't see him or hear a clear shot from the base. The foliage dissipated the sound and the shooter was hidden from even the strongest binoculars. But inside of the trees the sound was sharp and clear.

Frank checked his rifle by the numbers. A round is in the chamber, selector on semi, sights set, sling attached properly. He didn't need to make any sight adjustments. He estimated the shot to be about 100 yards. His rifle was zeroed at 100 yards. The shooter was in a prone shooting position on the platform so Frank would need more than one shot to be sure. He thanked the Marine Corps for his 7.62mm M-14. A rinky-dink 5.56 M-16 would be useless for this shot. He decided to wait for the shooter to shoot again so his attention would be on Khe Sanh and not on his surroundings. Frank needed a first shot hit and a quick follow-up. But a hundred yards was nothing. Marines qualified at 500 yards.

He watched and listened, anticipation making him restless. Settle down, settle down. No need to rush. It doesn't have to be this time. It doesn't have to be today. Wait for the perfect shot. But his gut wanted it to be then, right then. And then he heard noises deeper in the jungle behind the sniper. Several people moving and they weren't worried about noise. He squatted down and squeezed his eyes shut. Damn, damn, damn. If he took the shot, he was going to have NVA troops on him in seconds. This is not the right situation. Frank eased up to a crouch again.

He studied the platform. It appeared to be made from bamboo poles or branches. It wouldn't stop a 7.62mm military round. He'd aim for the estimated armpit, and bamboo be damned. A fast second shot would make sure. Then he could move out of range quickly, maybe set an ambush. He felt the thrill in his gut again. Frank wrapped his sling on his arm and prepared for an offhand standing shot.

This is stupid, he thought. I don't need to do this now. The smart thing is to wait, wait for the right shot, wait until I can get clear.

The expected shot from the sniper came and Frank stood quickly and drew his rifle tight against his shoulder knowing the sniper would be looking through his scope, looking at his kill. Frank's sling gave him a tight and solid brace to steady his aim. He found his sight picture and carefully squeezed off the round. He saw the bamboo shatter when the bullet hit and he quickly found his sight picture again. A man's head raised up. Frank squeezed off a second round. A rifle fell out of the tree. Frank took a step toward the sniper's tree with his rifle still pulled tight for another shot. And then he dropped straight to the ground.

The hard sound of an AK47 on full automatic filled the air and screaming rounds filled the grass. A second rifle opened-up, and then a third. Then two more from further away. Sounds of men crashing through grass and bamboo followed immediately. He hugged the ground and tried to dig through the grass to get lower. The sound of the Kalashnikovs seemed to go on and on. Frank turned his head sideways to get it lower. He should have waited. Rounds tore up the grass around him.

Finally, the closest shooter must have emptied his magazine and he didn't wait around. He only had seconds to get further away. He jumped up and ran through the grass bent over towards his pack. Now the other shooters were a blessing. Their firing covered the noise of his escape. The closest AK47 started in again and Frank hit the ground. This time the shooters only fired bursts and waited. They were listening for his sounds. He crawled as quietly as he could, trying to reach his ruck so he could change course and get out of the line of fire. But he needed his ruck. Everything he needed to survive was in it.

The nearest shooter fired another burst, but none of the rounds came close. He picked up his pace, found his ruck, and worked his way back to his rock outcropping.

When he sat down in his hole he let out a big breath and laughed. Damn, he thought. Damn, Damn, Damn. And he laughed again. This is the way to fight. Sitting in a hole and getting your ass pounded with artillery isn't. And he still had two days to go. He decided to stay in his hole for the rest of the day and rest up. He made a quick call to the base and let them know the sniper was history, or at least, one of them was. He ate another meal with some water and started working on the leeches.

He had six leeches on his arms by that time. He was afraid to drop his drawers. He could feel them in his trousers. He tried to remember his training about how to get them off. Something about using your finger nails. He did remember clearly the warning not to try to burn them off or use aftershave or any of the bullshit methods Marines commonly swear by. If you did those things the leeches regurgitated and you'd end up with an infection that was much worse than the leech bite.

He remembered that they didn't present a real danger of blood loss. Even though the ones on his arms were getting pretty fat, about four or five times as big as they were that morning, the amount of blood they could suck wasn't normally dangerous. He remembered you could just let them get their fill and they would drop off without any prodding. That was the safest way. But he couldn't stand the thought of carrying the things around with him while they sucked his blood.

The leeches attached on both ends. He picked a leech and pressed his finger nail into his skin and slid it toward the small end of the leech. He used his nail to push the suckers out of his skin. Okay, cool. Now the other end. He shouldn't have thought about it. The damn thing reattached before he could get the other end out.

After trying a couple of different approaches he finally managed to get one leech dislodged on both ends and flicked it off his arm. Then it was just repeat the same thing six times. That took care of his arms. Now for the legs—and anywhere the sun doesn't shine where they might have attached also. It took some persistence, and a lot of willies and shudders, but he got it done. He felt pretty good then.

But feeling good wasn't going to last. He had stirred up a mess.

Chapter 33

That day was spent running, hiding, and running some more. The NVA moved into the jungle in force and drove Frank out of his hide and away from the tree line deeper into the jungle. He tried doubling back and sneaking by their patrols but there was always another patrol behind the first and one behind that. He tried going to ground and waiting for them to pass, but there were only a few areas that were passable in the thick grass, vines, and bamboo, for him and them.

He didn't have a machete to cut his way through and couldn't afford the noise anyway. And they knew the area better than he did. Finally, in the late afternoon, exhausted, frustrated, and lost, he took a chance, snaked off into vines and grass on his belly, found a hide, and waited for dark. He wasn't sure where he was, but he felt reasonably confident he knew the general direction of the tree line.

That night Frank didn't do any better than he had during the day. He did much worse. While moving cautiously through a depression between two small hills, more like a gulley full of elephant grass, he discovered a path of crushed and chopped vegetation that seemed to run in a direction toward the tree line. By then he was tired and scared and willing to take chances just to get it over. He was able to move faster on the trail, and he let his fear overcome his sense of caution. His inexperience was catching up with him.

Right then he just wanted to get the hell out of the jungle, get somewhere he could identify and call for help. Moving along the semi-trail too quickly, he blundered into a wire that had been strung on stakes across the trail and up both sides of the gully. Fortunately, it was only an intrusion alarm, a noise maker made of cans and scrap metal, anything that would rattle when shaken. Moving too quickly along the trail, he didn't even feel the wire until he heard the racket.

Fate in the form of his own panic intervened. As soon as he heard the racket, he turned ninety degrees and crashed through the grass moving up the left side of the gully. Headlong panic may have been the best thing he could have done after stupidly following a trail in Indian country, and terror may have been his best companion.

With Terror came that eerie strength and speed. Moments after tripping the alarm a rifle fired a single round and then the night was lit up with tracers and muzzle flashes. Frank fell forward in the grass but continued crawling upward. Two Grenades exploded fifty feet behind him but he wasn't touched by the shrapnel. As he neared the crest with firing from the NVA covering the sound of his movements, he slowed and took inventory. He still had his rifle in one hand and his radio was still on his ruck. He had a grenade in each of the lower pockets of his utility shirt. The firing slowed and then stopped. He stayed very still in the grass ten feet from the crest.

He heard movement to his right, more than one person moving cautiously down the slope toward the bottom of the gully. He eased his body toward the crest. At least he would have high ground if he had to fight. He slid forward an inch at a time, quietly, pushing the blades of tall grass apart and moving between them. The dark was thick and oppressive. As he neared the top of the gully, he heard a sound. Very close.

A voice called out in Vietnamese from directly in front of him. Another voice answered from the bottom of the gully. Then another voice called from the top of the gully to Frank's right but maybe thirty or forty feet away. He eased his head up, couldn't see anything, eased up further.

An NVA soldier was standing five feet in front of Frank with his rifle to his shoulder pointed at the bottom of the gully. Frank eased back down in the grass. The Vietnamese called out again and he was answered with a shout. He started side-stepping down the side of the gully. Frank waited. He let go of his rifle and slipped his K-Bar out of its sheath. He could see the top half of the soldier above the grass now. The Vietnamese took a sideways step—and slipped. Frank didn't wait any longer.

As the Vietnamese lifted his hands and raised his rifle over his head to catch his balance, Frank rose up like a silent demon out of the earth and lunged. The Vietnamese couldn't even defend his life. The sudden appearance of the dark specter in front of him froze his muscles and paralyzed his vocal cords. Frank drove his knife through the soldier's throat, clamped his hand over the soldier's mouth, and pulled him to the ground.

But he didn't anticipate the thrashing of legs and arms. And when he let go of the soldier's mouth to still the arms, loud gurgling sounds started. Frank let him go and pulled a frag grenade out of his utility pocket. He felt around for his own rifle and after he found it, pulled the pin on the grenade and tossed it to the bottom of the gully. He didn't wait for the detonation. He retrieved his knife and crawled quickly over the crest of the gully as the grenade exploded. He kept on crawling into the grass on the other side. The shouts started moments after he reached flat ground. He kept moving as quickly as he could.

The NVA called in help and hunted him and pushed him back into the jungle. He couldn't get any distance between him and them, and he couldn't shoot and give away his position. More NVA troops joined the hunt and pushed him harder. They seemed to be herding him but they didn't give him time to think about it. Each time he tried to change direction, a new unit would make itself known with shouts and beating on the grass and vines.

Near morning, exhausted, dehydrated, hungry, and terrified, he had had enough of being hunted like an animal. He didn't know where he was or what direction he was moving in, but he knew they were moving him somewhere he probably didn't want to go. He didn't know where he was, but he knew where they were. Terror spawned killing rage like it had on the mountain at Dak To. The dark thing that lived deep inside of him came back. The rage came and he stopped running. Running wasn't doing him any good. It was time to start killing. It was time to get it over with.

Frank's decision to turn on his hunters was a good one. Running had allowed the NVA to control the game. Hunting them changed the game. Besides making the enemy more cautious and slowing them down, Frank began to identify land marks and slowly figured out how to navigate his patch of jungle. As he became familiar with his surroundings and began seeing the same landmarks where they were supposed to be when he expected them, the jungle became less terrifying and he felt more in control. Without panic driving him and keeping him from thinking and planning, he was able to find hides and avoid the NVA patrols. He started thinking and anticipating. He started making kills and causing a little terror of his own. The soldiers on patrol began looking over their shoulders and sometimes shooting at shadows, shadows made by their own troops. Survival is a good teacher, and Frank was learning quickly.

He stayed out three days hunting the NVA, totally alone except for plenty of enemy soldiers, and he liked it and hated it. He couldn't get back to the tree line without taking risks he was no longer willing to take. So he hunted, he hid, he stalked, he ambushed. The bastards weren't the only ones doing the killing now. The killing stopped bothering him except when he returned to his hide and the silence crowded in, when the terror was gone, when the rage subsided. Then the blood on his hands and his shirt brought back the visions and sounds of sudden death in the night, what it must have been like for them, their terror, the sudden knowledge they couldn't do anything about it, searing pain, then nothing. But then he remembered his own terror and his conscience gained a new callous.

Fresh blood has a metallic smell, fresh and clean, but only at first, then it turns to something sickening. When your clothes are soaked in it you can't get away from the smell and your brain has lots of time to file away memories that will never go away. But after a while you become insensitive to even that smell.

Fighting on the mountain was different, and at Con Thien, and with the sniper. That was impersonal and at a distance. But the soldier on the way out in the fog, killed with the knife, that was close up and personal. Most of his kills in the jungle were very personal, very close up, one on one.

Frank's options were limited. He couldn't make a noise. The first kill was hard to shake loose from his brain, the sounds, the feel of squirming dying terror. But he went on. He had too. He had to get through them. He had to get them off guard, find a way to get past them. He had to make them stop hunting him, find a way to get back to Khe Sanh. The second kill was easier, but more terrifying. The third was almost mechanical.

It got easier to not think about it. They weren't interesting people or people at all. They were enemy. They were hunting him. They were killing his men. Easier to think of them that way. Not someone's child. They came to this place to kill him and his men. He came to this place to kill them. He wasn't fighting for freedom, or the U.S. of A., or South Vietnam. He was fighting to stay alive and to keep his Marines alive. Everything else was bullshit. He killed them first. It could have been the other way around.

By the third day his hunt became more than an attempt to get back to Khe Sanh. Little by little, as his conscience quieted, the hunt became the most exciting game he had ever played, terrifying, yes, but exciting. He started liking it, fearing it, detesting it. And liking it a lot. And he started dreading having to go back to the mud, filth, and noise of the combat base.

Maybe it was in him all the time. Maybe it was in him before the Marine Corps and just needed the opportunity for Frank to discover it. But it bloomed and matured in that jungle. It was primitive and it was exhilarating and it was something wholly natural. He discovered he could live with the terror and the dark. Frank discovered he could hunt with deadly intensity, and fear, and detest what he was doing all at the same time.

Frank made many approaches to camps and groups of NVA, but he backed quietly away on most of them. He learned quickly. Wait for the perfect situation. It would come if he was patient, careful. Hunting them was more difficult than he thought it would be once the rage wore off. Killing to keep from being killed or to stop them from killing his men was one thing. Slipping up in the dark and killing silently, killing someone who was just trying to stay alive, was another thing altogether. But each approach and each time he slipped away from them undetected taught him about the night and the jungle. It taught him about fear and how to control it. It taught him how much the Vietnamese feared the night. He gave them a reason for their fear.

By the time his three days were up, he had scored ten kills and knew he could get around them and get home. He took inventory: the soldier on the way in, the sniper, the man at the gully, six at night on careful stalks, and two of them had been at one time with claymores set on a trail in ambush. He didn't like the claymores though. There was something obscene about killing with mines. It's strange how selective your conscience can become.

Night hunting was more difficult because people didn't move around at night unless they were maneuvering or hunting him. And maneuvering troops traveled in numbers. Too dangerous for one man. But every camp had smells. Smoke sometimes, spicy food smells sometimes, and the unmistakable smell of dirty people. Even after only a single day in the jungle with no odors but jungle smells and your own, your nostrils cleared out and your sense of smell developed a new acuity.

You had to be quiet and you had to get close and you had to pick the right target and you had to be willing to pass on the ones that weren't perfect. You had to have a way to retreat, to get away fast. But that was the skill. Get close, make the kill, and get away. Wait for him quietly, one man coming away from his camp to empty his bladder or take a crap. A sleepy sentry, feeling safe, nodding off. A quiet, careful approach, one swift move, and then move away fast and silent. Getting away was the dangerous part, after the job was done, after you began to let down. He hated it. He liked it so much he hadn't turned his radio on since the first day.

But it was time to go back. No excuses now. He knew where he was and he knew how to get home. The NVA troops were nervous, knew he was still there, hunting them. Silent and deadly. They would be setting their own traps. It was getting too dangerous for one man now. Really dangerous and as much because of what Frank was feeling as anything the NVA was doing. He knew that instinctively.

After a few successes it began to feel easy, like you couldn't fail, like you had some kind of divine guidance going for you. Fate was on your side and you began to depend on it and you started taking chances. But fate was fickle and soon Frank would get anxious, take a chance, and make a mistake. He sensed his luck was running out.

He sat back in his hole and looked at the radio. The skipper is going to be pissed, he thought. He stared at the handset. He felt like he was holding a snake. When he was putting off calling in so he could keep hunting, his excuses seemed plausible. Now the very real possibility of Marine Corps disciplinary action tickled at his conscience. But he had to call. He couldn't stay in the grass forever. Hell, I'll come up with something, he thought. He shrugged into his ruck and slung his rifle. He carried the radio in his hand.

Maneuvering through the jungle to get back was exhausting and scary, but he knew what to avoid now, and he knew he would make it if he was very careful and took his time. He did just that. He went to ground and hid when he needed to, and he waited as long as it took to move safely when he had to. It was dark when he reached the edge of the jungle and saw the dark outline of Khe Sanh in the distance.

When he got to the tree line he sat down and

extended the antenna on the radio. He put the handset to his ear and squeezed the transmit button.

"Lima One-One this is Lima Niner, over."

Nothing for a moment, then,

"Lima Niner this is One-One. What is your position?"

"One-One, Niner, I'd rather not say. I've got movement around me. I'm coming in. Please inform the line to keep their damn fingers off the trigger, over."

"Roger, Niner. Call in fifteen."

Frank double clicked the transmit button.

Hitchens talked Frank in close to the wire and Frank popped a green flare to identify himself. Hitchens told him to come in. Frank ran toward the wire gate with his rifle slung and the handset to his ear.

"I'm approaching the gate. I'm at the gate. I'm in the compound."

"Lima Niner, report to the CP.

"Roger."

When Frank walked into the 1st Platoon CP he looked like the grim reaper with chicken pox. He hadn't shaved or washed in three days. He was dehydrated with cracked lips after licking rain off grass for water when his canteens were empty. He'd pay for that later. Things, tiny microscopic things, things that thought of Frank as a wonderful host, lived in that water. And now they lived in him. His utilities were torn and covered with mud and large patches of dried blood. But his face was his worst feature. Mosquito bites covered his exposed skin and his lips and cheeks were swollen with them. His eyes were sunk inside of dark circles and looked wild after three days of staring into the dark and searching for danger. Captain Franks was waiting in the 1st Platoon CP.

"Where in the fuck have you been?"

"I said I'd be back in three days, Skipper" Frank said. "Here I am."

"That isn't what I asked you. One fucking radio report on the first day when you got the sniper and then nothing. You are fucking missing in action."

Captain Frank's was so angry spit sprayed out of his mouth when he yelled, "fucking." Both times. His neck muscles bulged and his face was red. Frank knew it was time to seek forgiveness.

"Christ, Captain, I'm sorry as hell. But I had NVA and VC all around me twenty-four hours a day. Sometimes they were within feet of me. After I got the sniper, they went crazy. I didn't think I'd get out of the damn jungle alive."

"Bullshit, Gunny. You couldn't make contact one time and let us know you were still alive?"

"Sir, I was afraid they'd triangulate on my signal. I had a good hide and didn't want to give it away?"

"Really? And all that changed in one night and you walked right through them? And stopped to use your radio anyway?"

Uh oh. The CO was pissed and he wasn't going

to be bullshitted.

"Sorry, sir. I screwed up. Can we talk about this back at your CP?"

Captain Franks looked around and noticed the Radioman listening. Two other Marines picking up rations were trying to act like they were busy, but they were listening.

"Maybe we should," Captain Franks said. "The platoon probably shouldn't hear their Company Gunny get the worst ass chewing of his career. Tell me this. What was the body count?"

"Ten, sir. Including the sniper," he said trying to put a little meekness in his voice and hoping the body count would give the captain an excuse to suspend his disbelief. Just a little.

Captain Franks stared at Frank for a moment and then raised his eyebrows.

"No shit, sir," he said. "Ten."

"Get the corpsman to look at your face and then see me in the CP. There's a leech on your damn earlobe, too."

The Radioman coughed into his hand to cover a snicker.

The corpsman gave Frank some salve to put on his face and washed the leech bites and other scratches he could find with alcohol. A few men watched the corpsman work on Frank, but they were more interested in the blood on his face, hands, and utility shirt. The word about Frank's ten kills had beaten him to the trench.

The camp was having a rare lull in incoming so he made it back to his hooch without having to jump in a hole. The respite didn't last long. As he was shaving, two rockets hit the base and the 105s opened-up in counterbattery.

The CP had changed, on the outside at least. Big mounds of packed dirt with sand bags holding it down were now piled up against the walls on three sides and sand bags three thick covered the forth side. The roof looked different. Instead of the boxes of rock on top, something shiny was there instead. Frank checked it out. Spent artillery casings, closed end up. That was new and different. A brass roof. He found the Skipper and was told to sit.

"Gunny, that was the most irresponsible behavior I have ever seen from a senior NCO. I ought to write you up. What the hell were you thinking? And let's cut the bullshit. It's just you and me."

"Skipper, all I can do is apologize and promise it won't happen again."

"But why? Answer me that."

"Sir, I . . . hell, I don't know. I just got caught up in the hunt. I was out there all alone and I was finding targets. I liked it. I felt like a Marine, sir, not some mud soaked, shell shocked target. Those fuckers have something to think about now. They're not the only ones doing the pounding. All I could think about was getting back in the game. I hardly slept the whole time I was out there. I was wishing I had a few more days."

Captain Franks watched Frank for a moment. His eyebrows pulled down in the middle and he took a breath and let it out slowly.

"Have you done this before?' he asked. "I mean, hunted alone like that."

"No, sir. But it felt good."

"I've known men who got to like that kind of thing too much, Gunny."

"Hell, Captain. It's what they pay us for. It's not anything weird or anything like that. I just found out I'm good at it, fighting alone I mean. And I took the damn war to them. All the training started to pay off and it all came together. And I did more for my Marines with one shot than I could have done if I'd have been in camp for those days. They've pulled back away from the base now."

"Okay, okay. Hell, I can't criticize a Marine for being a Marine. But that still doesn't excuse not even checking in. You're a Gunnery Sergeant. Christ, Frank, I had you listed as missing in action. And I covered your ass just in case. The colonel thinks you were doing recon for me. You better have some intelligence to give S2. They want to talk to you and that bullshit story of triangulating on your radio won't get you a cup of coffee."

"Well, I saw a lot of NVA out there, sir. I can show them where and describe what I saw."

"Make it good. They're waiting for you."

When he got to base S2 they were indeed waiting for him. So was the Battalion commander. The interior of the CP was full of dark shadows and smelled of damp dirt. Frank marched to the map table and came to attention.

"Gunnery Sergeant Evans, sir."

"Ahh. The illusive Gunny Evans back from the dead, as it were," Colonel Harth said. "Stand at ease, Gunny. Tell us about your little adventure."

"Yes, sir. Anything in particular?"

"Let's start with how a one man recon patrol, recon as in stealth and quiet and staying unobserved, managed to score ten body count."

"Part of that was on the way in, sir. The rest was on ambush when opportunities came up. During the day I found a good observation point and watched what was going on."

Colonel Harth watched Frank for a few moments silently and then he grinned.

"Show us where you were operating," he said.

He pointed out his movements on the map and indicated where he had seen NVA. Major Stride put pins in the map at each point where Frank indicated concentrations of enemy troops of squad size or larger. The base received two incoming mortar rounds while they talked, one close enough to shake dirt through the ceiling boards onto the maps and raising dust in the air making the gloomy interior of the CP even more gloomy.

"Did you see any munitions or artillery? Major

Stride asked.

"No, sir. Mostly it was just small units of infantry. They didn't seem to be in a hurry or have any particular objective. I did notice there seemed to be more of them each day like they were gathering from other places and waiting for something. Once a small unit was in place they set up camp and settled in."

"Gunny, get a cup of coffee and relax for a minute. I need to talk with Major Stride," Colonel Harth said. "But hang around. We need to talk some more."

Frank found the coffee, just a pot of hot water for C-rat's instant coffee. It tasted like crap, especially in the diesel tasting water, but it was loaded with caffeine and killed the headache he was nursing. While he was sipping his coffee, a call came across one of the PRC-25s sitting on the radio bench in the back of the CP. "Rockets, rockets, rockets."

Everyone in the CP hit the deck and held onto their helmets. The interval between the warning and the explosions was only about ten or fifteen seconds, but at least someone was giving a warning. When the noise of the attack settled down, Colonel Harth waved Frank back to the map table.

"Gunny, how do you feel about going back out and doing some more looking around?"

"Fine with me, sir." He tried to sound offhanded, but he had trouble covering the thrill he felt.

"Good," the Colonel said. "Different area this time. I've got recon teams out, but they're working the hills further north trying to identify artillery emplacements and troop concentrations. I need someone on the ground West of the base. These damn rocket attacks are driving the artillery crazy. We can't get counterbattery on them. The NVA shoot them off ten or fifteen at a time and they can set up anywhere they please. They shoot and get away before we can get rounds on target. They're not all that accurate, but they put so many in the air some of them have to hit the base every time. 881 South usually can see the launch, but that only gives us ten or fifteen seconds warning. We'll insert you right about here," he said putting his finger on the map. "You'll have to maneuver on foot into their operating area. For some reason the NVA rocketeers like to use the same launch points over and over. Probably because they don't have to recalculate aiming. Do what you can to screw with their minds. Make it dangerous for them to set up. Locate units and munitions stores if you can and call in artillery. Take direct action if you can do it safely. Want a shot at it?"

"What about bombing runs, sir? Aren't the B52's hitting that area?"

"I'll keep them away while you're in there."

"How long can I hunt, sir?

"Three days and then you find an LZ and we extract you."

"Works for me," Frank said. "Can you insert me tonight?"

"Get your gear together."

The slick didn't even touch down. The LZ was small and

the elephant grass was high. Frank only had a few minutes of twilight left when the Huey rose straight up, tilted its nose and accelerated away. He'd learned a few things on his last mission. No steel pot this time and no flak jacket. If he got himself into a situation where he needed them while alone in the jungle, his time was up anyway. He knew he was going to be wet and cold at night no matter what he wore and he was going to sweat during the day, so he only had a boonie hat on his head and utilities on his body. Green and black face and hands and a camo sheath around his rifle. He had a new K-bar too and this one was ground down to a narrow point sharpened on both sides to penetrate bone and tendon. And to allow it to release more easily. One side of the blade was razor sharp.

Frank only brought three LRRP meals this time. He wanted more room in his ruck for Claymores. He didn't like the mines, but his claymore ambush on his last mission had worked well. It had been tricky though. He had set a claymore on both side of the trail facing each other and ran both detonation wires along the trail for fifty feet. The position he picked to wait was perpendicular to the claymore fields of fire and back blast, so he didn't have to worry about getting caught in his own trap.

The NVA rifle team came down the trail right at him. That was good up to a point. When he detonated the mines the fire team was turned into hamburger—all but one, the point man who had passed through the kill zone. And he was facing Frank when Frank decided to bug out before reinforcements came. The little guy was fast too. He got two shots off before he spun and ran the other way. Fortunately, he wasn't accurate.

He had to think on claymore setup before he did it again. It was a nasty way to kill, but it was also very effective. His job was to disrupt the enemy, make them nervous, ruin their sleep, encourage desertions, anything that would be an advantage for his Marines. When they knew they weren't alone in the grass, that a phantom was stalking them in the night, they would make more mistakes, get in a hurry on night missions, and hopefully screw up. And each one he took out was one that couldn't attack his Marines. That's what he told himself.

His pack consisted of a strobe to mark the pickup LZ, binoculars, maps, insect repellant, energy bars, water purification tabs, LRRP rations, an extra canteen, grenades, and claymores. He also had a PRC-25 with an extra battery strapped to the top of his ruck. His cartridge belt held two spare pistol magazines, his K-bar, a first aid kit, two canteens and an extra 7.62 magazine. It was going to get cold without his field jacket, but he was more interested in being light, fast, and quiet than in being warm. He compromised on the field jacket by wrapping his ruck with his poncho, but no liner. If he needed to warm up, the rubberized fabric of the poncho would warm him quickly.

Frank squatted in the grass and listened closely to his surroundings. The fear came and made his stomach churn. He looked back at the LZ. He had to get out of the area. But the fear held him right there, the fear of what was out there and the fear of what he was going to do, the fear of the sounds he would hear and the spasms. . . he squeezed his eyes shut and waited for the thrill to start. His stomach didn't disappoint him.

He used his compass to set a course and began the long slow hump into the valley. He had chosen a small hill near the area of reported rocket activity for his observation point. From there it was watch, adapt, and improvise. He counted a hundred paces and tied a knot in the string hanging from his belt. The string would record his progress in distance traveled.

Crachin settled in and Frank moved slowly through a silent, misty tunnel with undulating walls of Elephant grass and ghostly wisps of fog for company. A good night for stalking, and not only for Frank. He might not be the only predator in the grass.

While he paced off distance and tied knots he remembered stories of tigers from his time on Con Thien. The constant shelling and foliage clearing had deprived them of their natural habitat and food. Dead NVA and Marines provided a convenient alternative source of protein. The tigers were said to like the alternative since it didn't run away. So the tigers in the area had tasted human flesh, and Frank was human flesh. Maybe true, maybe bullshit, but the memories made his night stalk a little more interesting. Things in the night. Childhood dreams. Dark things coming at you. The dark things never leave you, not when it's dark and you are alone. They follow you a step behind, their warm breath on the back of your neck, tempting you to look over your shoulder.

Later that night he started up a small rise. He counted the knots on his string and the distance came out right. The rain started. Out in the valley the first of a multiple rocket launch lit a small patch of ground and rose with a trail of sparks. He grimaced. The game was exciting, but it wasn't fun.

Frank played the game for four days.

Chapter 34

"Colonel, it's time for Evans to check in. Do you want to bring him in?"

"Yes. Tell him to get back to the LZ. I'm calling in an Arc Light strike on that valley. Don't take any shit from him this time, Major. No more extensions. If he isn't out of that valley in two hours he's going to be dodging 500 pound bombs."

"Lima Niner, Lima Niner, this is Two Six, over."

Only static came over the speaker.

"Lima Niner, Lima Niner, this is Two Six' over."

"Two Six this is Lima Niner, wait one, out," came a scratchy and weak reply.

Colonel Harth stood up and looked at the speaker.

"Wait one? Who the hell does he think he is?"

"He might be busy, sir. He's out there alone."

"I said no shit this time, Charlie. Get his ass back to the LZ."

"Two Six this is Lima Niner, over."

"Lima Niner, Two six. Proceed to the LZ for extraction immediately. Arc Light begins in two hours, over."

"Two six this is Niner. Can you hold off on that for a while? I'm setting up a situation here. Need a couple of hours."

"Lima Niner this is Two Six. That is negative. I say again, that is negative. Proceed to the LZ. Arc Light is laid on."

"Shit!" The single word scratched out of the speaker. Then, "Two Six this is Lima Niner. Roger, LZ in one hour thirty minutes. I say again, LZ in one hour thirty minutes, Over."

"Lima Niner this is Two Six. Roger, One hour thirty minutes, out."

Frank scouted the area around the LZ carefully when he arrived and then talked to the slick on his radio when it was three minutes out. He put the strobe in the middle of the LZ and took cover.

The trip back to the LZ from the valley had been a lot lighter than the trip out. The claymores, food, and most of his water were gone, but he still had all of his ammunition. And he was sure the tigers were happy. He'd left them plenty of alternative protein. He hadn't been able to stop any rocket launches, but he had called in artillery on two camps and witnessed secondary explosions both times. So, some number of rockets never got to the launch sites.

And then he hunted. He couldn't use his rifle or pistol, but he found getting close to the NVA was a skill he was good at. The NVA were alert for large troop movements, but they weren't expecting a single Marine to move in amongst them. It was almost like attacking boy scouts. Or like hunting on a game refuge. The prey wasn't spooked. Each time he approached a camp, he used his K-bar on only one sleepy sentry and then he slipped away to let the camp find a comrade soldier dead in his hole in the morning.

That game had its particular risks though. They were little guys for the most part, but they could make the most ungodly sounds. His first infiltration had almost been his last. The Vietnamese he picked had flopped around and loud gurgling and hissing sounds came out of his opened throat. Frank had to crawl out with bullets zinging over his head. He learned an important lesson though. You have to shove their heads down hard to stop the sounds and you had to fall on them and keep them from flopping and kicking.

He was getting better at it and he felt like he was accomplishing something. His four days in the grass hadn't been enough, but there would be a next time. He'd make sure of that.

Frank wasn't looking forward to all the bullshit coming up at the combat base. He'd have to endure the questions, but he'd rather skip the talk. Lately it seemed like people talked too damn much.

Waiting those last few seconds after he heard the wump-wump of the rotors was the most difficult. NVA were out there somewhere, maybe close by, and they could hear the slick too. The slick came in low over the tree tops and that helped. The sound of the rotors sounded like it came from all directions. You couldn't tell where it was coming from or where the slick was going. The door gunner would be keyed up, ready for anything, his finger on the trigger, Frank in his sights until he was sure. The damn thing seemed like it took forever to settle below the trees. Frank waited, kneeling in the grass at the edge of the clearing, selector on full automatic, ready to sprint, to get the hell out of there, heart beating faster moment by moment.

The slick finally settled into a hover and lowered until the skids were just a couple of inches off the ground. He threw his ruck and rifle behind the door gunner and pulled himself in. The slick immediately rose, dipped its nose and accelerated away from the LZ. The trip back to Khe Sanh was uneventful, but the landing was a bitch.

By that time, the night of February 5th, 1968, the combat base was under almost constant bombardment. Ho Chi Minh was getting serious about pounding the Americans into the ground. The rest of Vietnam was still reeling from the NVA and Viet Cong offensive that took place during the cease fire called for the Tet holiday from January 27 through February 3. The Viet Cong and NVA attacked every major and most minor cities and towns in the south during the cease fire. The offensive took the South Vietnamese and Americans by surprise, but was a dismal military failure. The Viet Cong in the south was almost wiped out, but U.S. Army and Marines were still fighting to clear VC and NVA out of many of the South Vietnamese cities. In the north of I-Corps, especially around Dong Ha and Khe Sanh, the cease fire had been canceled by the Americans because of the suspected buildup of NVA forces, so they weren't surprised by the offensive. Daily battles and bombardment were the norm.

The slick hovered just long enough for Frank to throw his ruck out and follow it as fast as he could, and then the helicopter rose and flew off into the night. He ran to the nearest bunker and dove in. A mortar round hit the sand a hundred feet away.

"Hey, man, are you wounded?" one of the grunts huddled in the bunker asked.

"No," Frank said, "Shut the fuck up."

He listened for a lull and ran to a bunker closer to 3rd Battalion CP. No one spoke to him there. They just watched him and gave him room. He waited, steeling his nerve for a dash to the CP. This crap was ten times worse than the nights in the grass. Finally, after his heart settled down, he sprinted to the CP and down into the COC. Major Stride turned as Frank came through the opening.

"Are you wounded?" Stride asked.

"No, sir." Frank looked down to see what the Major was looking at. The entire front of his utility blouse was soaked in blood, some of it caked, some of it not yet dried. What he couldn't see was the dried blood on his face and neck. He looked at his hands and turned them over.

"The blood isn't mine," he said.

"Oh." the Major said. "How many?"

"I stopped counting, sir."

"Take a guess."

The question irritated him. It felt like being asked about your sex life or something else very intimate. And the Major sounded like some boot-assed pogue just in-country.

"Maybe eight," He said quietly.

The Major watched Frank quietly for a moment. His eyes stopped on his web gear. He stared for a moment.

"Can I see your K-Bar?" he said.

What is wrong with this guy? Frank thought. But he handed the Major his K-Bar.

Major Stride looked at the blood encrusted blade and the gore around the hilt and handed it back. He wiped his hand on his utilities.

"The Colonel will want to debrief you in the morning. I think we can authorize an extra ration of water for you to wash up with. How are you for usable utilities?'

"I'm good, sir."

"Okay. Get some rest and get cleaned up. Report back here at 0700."

"Aye, aye, sir."

Frank returned to his hooch and stripped. He used a clean T-shirt as a wash rag to clean his body. He didn't get the blood from under his nails and missed a few other spots too. But he didn't have a date that night and wasn't too particular. Then in a fit of extravagance he heated a pan of fresh water to shave with.

He ought to check in with the Captain, but he didn't feel like talking. Later, after a quick meal from a C-ration box he crawled into his sleeping bag. He rolled up his Field Jacket for a pillow and put his K-bar under it. He closed his eyes as he wrapped his fingers around the comforting feel of the K-bar handle.

Frank slept deeply without dreaming. He didn't hear the incoming that night. He awoke with the feel of someone's hand on his shoulder. He didn't even think about it—he snap rolled with the K-bar in his hand and struck with the point moving at the end of a full arm swing. His hand went numb as the knife was knocked from his fingers and he heard his name being yelled at him.

"Frank, God damn it, wake up." First Sergeant Mills screamed.

Frank froze and looked around. No grass, no trees, no gooks. He came to his senses slowly and recognized Mills.

"Sorry," he said.

"You damn near stabbed me. What the hell are you doing sleeping with your K-Bar?"

"Just used to it. What time is it?"

"0730. The COC called for you."

"Shit. Hand me my trousers."

"Relax. They said to come in at 1000. But you better see the Captain. He's pissed you didn't report last night."

"Yeah."

Mills stopped talking and stared at Frank for a few moments.

"Are you okay?" he asked.

"Yeah."

"Your hands are shaking."

Frank looked at his hands and closed them into fists. When he opened them they still had a tremor. The fact that he couldn't stop the shaking bothered him, but he didn't want to talk about it.

"Just tired," he said.

"How'd your mission go?"

"I got back."

"I can see that. I asked how it went."

"Are we going to talk all fucking day?" Frank said. "It was a fucking mission. That's all. All right?"

Mills stepped back and frowned. "See the Captain," he said and left.

He pulled a can of something out of a C-rats box, opened it with his P-38, and put it on a heat tab stove to heat without looking to see what it was. He nibbled on a hardtack cracker until the can was hot and then ate its contents without thinking about it. His mind was back in the grass rerunning his operations against the NVA. Sometimes you just have to rely on instinct, he thought. There are some things training can't enhance. He took some chances, mostly out of ignorance, and he had to get that under control. When you're alone in the night with no one to ask, ignorance can kill you.

He thought about taking the bodies with him the next time, wondering if the disappearance would create more fear than finding the body. He decided that leaving the body in the hole was better. Seeing what the night phantoms did had to cause more terror than wondering what happened to the men. And terror would make some of them defect. Less NVA to shoot Americans. If he killed one and that caused two or three to defect, or made many reluctant to attack, his effectiveness was multiplied by two or three or by many. Next time, he thought. He was determined there would be a next time.

Captain Franks was waiting for him when Frank arrived at the CP.

"Sit down, Gunny. You look like hell. Any good reason you didn't report in last night?"

"Just beat," Frank said. "It was a long mission, sir."

"Yeah, it was. How are you doing? You've been out in the grass almost nonstop for the last two weeks."

"I'm good."

Captain Franks didn't say anything for a while and let the silence get uncomfortable. But Frank didn't seem to mind the silence and didn't seem to have any desire to elaborate on his condition or his mission so Franks leaned back and tried again.

"Gunny, you did a good job getting the platoons squared away. The NCOs have stepped up and are showing some leadership, but there's still a lot to do. You don't have to go back out. I still need you here."

"I'm good, sir. It needs doing and I know how to do it."

"Frank, you're turning out to be a pretty damn good Gunny. You're a natural leader. Look, we're going to need platoon leaders. You might get your own platoon. Forget this lone wolf shit. I can square it with the Colonel."

"I'm good at this too, sir."

Captain Franks watched Frank for a few moments. They were both right. Frank was a natural leader, but he was good at what he was doing also. And the COC needed eyes in the grass. He gave up. "Before you report to the COC, check on your Marines," he said. "They've been asking about you."

"Yes, sir. I planned to."

"Okay, Frank. Get some rest before you go out again."

When Frank was gone, First Sergeant Mills entered the CP.

"Captain Franks," Mills said.

"Come on in, First Sergeant. Not enough to do at Heat and Steam?"

"Plenty to do, sir. How'd the Gunny seem to you?"

"A little frayed around the edges, but solid. Why do you ask?"

"Did he seem awful quiet?"

"Well, yes. He isn't wasting any words. But I guess that's to be expected from a man who just spent a lot of time in the grass alone. No conversation out there."

"Big difference from the shaky Gunny that reported here for his first gunny assignment."

"Yeah," Franks said. "Something bothering you?"

"Yes, sir. I've had a chance to look over his file. Gunny Evans is a very unusual Gunnery Sergeant. He wasn't a staff sergeant very long and was promoted to Gunny on a combat meritorious promotion."

"That's a bad thing?"

"No, sir. That's not what I'm getting at. Did you know he was never a corporal or a sergeant?"

"I've heard some of the story. He also holds the Navy Cross and two Bronze Stars. What are you getting at?"

"Captain, when we saw our first combat, what did we have that Evans doesn't?"

"Get to the point, First Sergeant. I don't have time for twenty questions."

"We had buddies, sir. We took care of each other. We gave each other a reference for what's normal, what's right. We had corporals, sergeants, and gunnies to teach us. Evans came out of boot camp a Staff Sergeant. He went to war as a senior NCO. No buddies. No background as a Marine. No reference. He's his own reference and I worry about the decisions he's making."

"He's done a good job with Lima. Do you think he has a problem?"

"He needs to be with a company, not running around alone in the grass."

"Maybe, but that's not a problem. He's doing what needs to be done.

"He just seems awful quiet, sir. He's changing."

"He just spent a lot of time alone in the grass."

"Maybe too much time in the grass," Mills said. "He wasn't trained for recon."

"Some people are naturals. Frank seems to like it."

"Maybe too much," Mills said.

Frank ran in short spurts between holes and bunkers. Finding holes wasn't a problem. The base was becoming a burnt out gash in the earth pockmarked with artillery and rocket craters. The nearest Frank could come to a comparison was the thought he had before. It looked like a landfill. A bulldozed over trash dump. Almost every structure was embanked with bulldozed dirt now. The only way you could tell the bunkers from the surrounding jagged and torn terrain was by the sandbags—they didn't have artillery craters in them, at least not the ones still in use.

He dropped into the northwest end of the trench line and stopped to talk with the men manning that end of the trench. They had changed. The trench was their home now and the effect of the constant bombardment could be seen on their faces. No one slept for more than a couple of hours at a time. Even when they weren't needed to watch the perimeter, incoming rockets and artillery shook them awake. The trenches had changed too. The Marines continued to fortify, deepen, widen, and branch out with spider holes. Very few people were moving anywhere on the base, and when they had to, it was in short sprints from hole to hole. The bunkers and trenches had become their world.

"Hey, Gunny. You still humping in the Grass? Man, take me with you. I've got to get out of this hole."

"You'll get your chance. There's a lot of gooks out there."

"Shit, I hope so. Sitting here and taking this shit without being able to shoot something is crap. This shit's for the Army pukes. We're Marines, damn it."

Frank didn't have a good answer for that. He agreed completely. He continued along the trench and noticed the eyes. Shellshock was setting in. Christ, they looked like the Marines at Con Thien already. At least they hadn't started letting things go yet. And someone was showing some leadership.

The fighting positions were wet and slick, but the Marines had devised a lot of ways to drain off the worst of the water. Even so, he could see a siege mentality setting in. Or maybe it was siege necessity. There wasn't a single set of fresh utilities, or even close to fresh, anywhere along the line. Marines were living in their clothes and the clothes stayed wet. They worked, ate, and slept in flak jackets and helmets.

As Frank slid around a partition, one of the Marines filling sandbags behind him nodded his chin toward him and said quietly to his buddy, "That's one scary muthafucker. Man, did you see his eyes?"

"Yeah," his buddy said. "He don't say much anymore, does he?"

"The Gunny's hard-core, man."

"I hear he killed a hundred gooks with his bare hands."

"I was there when he came back from getting that sniper. Man, he was covered in blood. Somebody told me he cuts off their ears and has them on a string around his neck."

"That's hard-core, man. A guy in second platoon told me. . ."

Frank made his way back to the northwest end of the trench and started working his way back to the COC. He didn't hear the bullshit stories that were turning him into a local legend, but he heard the whispers and felt the new separation between him and his Marines. Didn't matter now. The platoon NCOs were doing their jobs. For just a moment he felt a sense of loss, but he pushed it down and starting planning a new argument for getting back to the grass.

Chapter 35

Frank was told to rest the day of February 6th, but he didn't need rest. What he needed was knowledge. 1st Battalion, 9th Marines were now in place on a small hill about a half mile west of the base. The 1/9 Commander was working with the Special Forces troops in SOG FOB-3 (Studies and Observation Group, Forward Operations Base 3) near the combat base to coordinate patrols and intelligence gathering. He wanted to talk with some Special Forces (SF) guys. Spending a lot of time in the grass alone or near alone was what they did for a living.

While his command thought he was catching up on sleep, Frank contacted the 1/9 CP and asked for help getting in touch with the SF. It didn't take long. The SF and their partners (the partners being described as Civil In Attitude by one and Charity In Action by another) being the curious folks they are invited Frank for a meet. When he returned to Khe Sanh base late that afternoon, he had several new ideas and a new frequency and call sign for his radio. The SF and CIA had a new asset. He also had a letter waiting for him.

Carol had received his letter and said she was relieved. Khe Sanh had been on the news and she wondered if he was safe. She was afraid for him. She wished he was home. Sharon Garzinski had visited again and assured her Frank was okay. If anything had happened, Ski would have heard. That made Carol feel better. She chatted about her work and things that were happening in D.C. She asked him to write back soon.

He didn't want to write. His feelings right then weren't the kind of feeling you can write about. But he needed to touch her, even if it was just with words. He wrote a quick letter and told her he had a mission and would write more when he got back. He closed by telling her he missed the softness in her eyes.

Earlier that morning after Major Stride and Captain Franks described Frank's behavior on his return from his mission, Colonel Harth agreed to have Frank rest that day and to return him to regular duties with Lima Company on the 7th. But it didn't work out that way.

About mid-morning the Army Special Forces fortified camp at Lang Vei, nine kilometers south of Khe Sanh, reported hearing armor maneuvering in the surrounding area. No one in the COC wanted to take the report seriously even though a Laotian outpost just across the border had been overrun by NVA armor recently. Everyone knew the NVA had learned a hard lesson about what happened when they attempted to bring armor into South Vietnam; they lost their tanks quickly to air strikes. At least that was the official line.

But the Marine base at Khe Sanh was responsible for reinforcing the Army SF at Lang Vei if it was attacked. And since Lang Vei was only two klicks from the Laotian border and the Ho Chi Minh trail, Major Stride shared the report with Colonel Harth.

"Christ, Charlie, we need to look into this. But that nine-klicks is a bitch down route nine to Lang Vei. Ambush country. Remember the platoon we sent down there last month to find a quick response route away from route nine. It took them almost a full day and night in the jungle to get there."

"Yes, sir. route nine would be difficult," Stride said. "It would be suicide for a platoon."

"But one man good in the grass might get in the area and look around," Harth said. "If the SF can hear tanks from those massive bunkers they're in, someone out in the grass ought to be able to hear them better. And we need to know what's waiting for us if we have to send reinforcements down there."

"Evans?"

"He's good at it."

"You heard what Captain Frank's said."

"Yes. But this is necessary, Charlie. I'd rather risk one Gunny than a whole platoon, and I can't spare a company. But we ought to discuss it with Evans. Let him decide if he can do it."

"I'd hate to burn him out, sir. We haven't got many men who can operate alone like he does."

"Hell, Charlie, every Marine on the base is burnt out, and this crap doesn't look like it's going to let up anytime soon."

"I'll get him up here. Tonight?"

"Yes. If there's anything to the report, we have tanks nine klicks from our wire. We need to know. After you send for Evans, get me the latest report on the casualties from the action on Hill 861A. And when you've got that I need the results from the Arc Light and artillery attack on the suspected regiment northwest of 881."

"I'm on it, sir."

Frank agreed he could do the mission. First Sergeant Mills wasn't happy about the decision. He was more concerned than ever with the recent changes he was seeing in Frank. Mills had seen a lot of Marines in battle. With three years in the Korean conflict and now on his second tour in Vietnam, Mills knew Marines, and he knew the signs. Evans was a good man and he was quickly becoming a good Gunny. Mills didn't want to lose him to what Mills called war lust. You had to be good at it, but you shouldn't like it. But some men did, though. It came natural to them.

Frank went through the wire on the southeast

perimeter as soon as it got dark. He had to cover about six miles through thick jungle at no more than a mile an hour. If that. He decided to stay on Route nine for the first two miles and move fast as silence and caution would let him. Once he was near Khe Sanh Village he would move into the jungle. He could do two miles in twenty minutes on the road, leaving four miles to go in the bush. He decided to take only his K-Bar, his .45 pistol, his poncho, radio, and plenty of water. The mission was to stay undetected and observe. The rifle would be useless and the thing was heavy. The only weight he carried was in his canteens and his radio. He wore a boonie hat and utilities and moved fast and quiet.

The trip down route nine took a lot longer than he expected. He made it to just north of Khe Sanh village on the road without encountering any hostiles but he wasn't doing ten minute miles. His time in the grass had taught him caution and route nine provided plenty of reason to exercise it. Getting past the village went quickly in the surrounding jungle. But he encountered his first NVA concentrations just south of the village. He was moving cautiously a hundred feet off the road when he smelled cigarette smoke and heard quiet talking. He bellied closer.

A group of Vietnamese soldiers in helmets and flak jackets were squatting together and smoking near the road. Lousy discipline, Frank thought. One soldier was addressing the rest in a low voice. They didn't seem to be concerned with defense so they must not be expecting any action for a while. He watched for a few minutes from just a few feet away. Then he thought he saw glowing light from the other side of the road and about fifty yards south. The pin points of light would suddenly glow brighter and then dim. More troops sucking on cigarettes.

He wondered if they were ARVN. But the helmets didn't look right. ARVN used mostly American military gear. These guys wore helmets that looked like the old world war one flying saucer helmets or maybe safari helmets. He backed away quietly and moved deeper into the jungle. When he was far enough away from the troops he called base and reported two platoons of suspected NVA straddling route nine in ambush mode.

The first encounter made him extra cautious. He moved back toward the road, but moved slower, stopping frequently and listening. If the NVA had tanks in the area, they would probably be using roads, or at least open areas. Even tanks would have problems moving through the thick jungle he was in. His caution paid off.

Frank encountered two more ambush locations. The second group was large. He estimated company strength. He reported the troops and locations and began his approach to Lang Vei village. He hadn't seen or heard any tanks yet, but close to a battalion of NVA were setting up ambush points on route nine. They were preparing for something.

The SF camp would be south of the village. It was time to find some high ground for observation. This was SF territory and the SF were tricky night fighters. Being trained by the SF, the indigenous troops led by the SF would be tricky bastards too. Operating in this area could be hazardous to one's longevity. Friendlies could be as dangerous as NVA to an unknown intruder.

After his conversation with the SOG FOB-3 SF, Frank had no doubt the area he was approaching would be full of nasty surprises for any kind of intruder. He didn't mind sneaking up on troops. They could be found, fooled, and avoided if necessary. People made noises and did stupid things. Always. They couldn't help it, because people are creatures of habit. Give them enough time on a dark night and they will do something to give away their location. Cough, sneeze, burp, fart, scratch, light a cigarette, something.

But booby traps scared the hell out of Frank. The damn things were absolutely silent and didn't care who or what set them off. And once set they just waited, waited, and waited. Well placed booby traps can be better than a Battalion of watchers. And the SF were experts at placing them well. Hell, even without booby traps, SF troops were spooky as hell anyway. Frank climbed a small hill overlooking Lang Vei Village.

"Two Six this is Lima Niner, over.
    Static.
    "Two Six this is Lima Niner, over."
    Static.

Two Six, Two Six, this is Lima Niner, Lima Niner, over."

"Lima Niner this is India One, hear you weak but readable, over."

Frank wasn't reaching Khe Sanh COC, but India company high on top of Hill 881 South was getting his signal.

"India one, this is Lima Niner, are you in contact with Two Six? Over."

"That's affirmative Lima Niner."

"This is Lima Niner. Roger. Relay the following message. Stand by to copy. Time twenty-three forty-five. Strong enemy force maneuvering near Lang Vei Village. Estimate Battalion strength. Lima Niner confirms armor in the area. Over."

"Lima Niner this is India One. Roger. November Victor Alpha Battalion strength near Lang Vei Village. Armor confirmed. Is that correct? Over."

"This is Lima Niner. That is correct, over."

"Stand by Lima Niner."

"Two Six, Two Six, this is India One, over."

Frank couldn't hear Two Six reply but India One passed the message.

"Lima Niner this is India One. Two Six rogers your message, over."

"This is Lima Niner. Roger, out.

Frank pulled his poncho over him and used his penlight to change frequencies on his radio and made his second transmission. If Khe Sanh couldn't hear him then the SF

FOB3 near the camp probably wouldn't hear him either. But he had to try. The SF officer that briefed him had been specific about radio procedure when using commo with the SF. Keep it short and sweet.

"Foxtrot this is Mike."

The reply was immediate.

This is foxtrot. Authenticate Romeo Juliette."

Now how in the hell did they receive. . .that's some spooky people.

Frank clicked the light on his code sheet, found the date, and crossed the letter R in the left column with the letter J on the top row.

"Mike authenticates Alpha."

"Roger, over."

"Twenty-three Forty-five. Lang Vei Village. NVA battalion strength with armor, over."

"Roger, out."

He checked his watch. 0020 (12:20 A.M.). He folded his poncho and continued observing. Ten minutes later Frank heard explosions and saw tracers south of the Village. It looked like the SF camp was under attack. He pulled his poncho over him again and called India One to relay first and then gave the report to Foxtrot. His report apparently reached Foxtrot before the SF in Lang Vei notified them. They asked him to monitor their frequency.

Three minutes later Foxtrot released him to return to the Marine's frequency. The ferocity of the fighting increased at the SF camp and NVA troops were maneuvering around the Village. Big guns were firing into the SF compound and big guns were firing out from the compound. The big guns firing in were moving around. Tanks. Twenty minutes later India One relayed a message from Khe Sanh.

"Lima Niner this is India One, over."

"One this is Niner, over."

"Niner, Two Six wants to know if you can get closer to Sierra Foxtrot (SF) and provide a situation report."

"India One, this is Niner. That is a negative. I have enemy maneuvering between me and Sierra Foxtrot. It would take most of the night to get there."

"Roger, Lima Niner. Stand By."

New flashes and bigger explosions joined the continuing sounds of battle at the SF camp. Frank could hear the sound of big diesel engines maneuvering. Then the sound of artillery outgoing from the SF camp and hitting locally. Then incoming Artillery from Khe Sanh. Frank could hear it go over his position. The Khe Sanh 105mm batteries were supporting the SF base. The radio sounded again.

"Lima Niner this is India One. Do you have targets for artillery in sight? Over."

"One this is Niner. Roger. Stand by for Grid coordinates. Wait one."

He lifted his poncho and scanned the lower ground around the village and noted troop and vehicle concentrations. He ducked under his poncho, put dots on his map, and keyed his handset.

"India One stand by to copy. Target one. . .coordinates follow. . ."

Frank read out coordinates for three targets and then poked his head up to confirm the enemy positions.

"Roger, Lima Niner. Stand by."

He heard the whoosh of the 105 as it passed overhead just before it hit about a hundred meters behind his first target.

"India One, First round one hundred meters south of target."

Frank wasn't a trained artillery observer, but his report was clear enough for the battery to convert his report to an artillery adjustment of drop 100.

"Stand by."

The next round erased three trucks and an unknown number of NVA. It was a big target with a concentration of trucks and troops, but still, that was great shooting.

"India One, that one was on target. Put a few more right there."

Three more whooshed over his head and made a mess of trucks and men. Frank keyed his radio.

"Target two is moving south. Move coordinates fifty meters south."

"Stand by."

The first round was close enough. More trucks destroyed. Frank keyed his set.

"India One. Target two destroyed. Target three is dug in. Fire."

The first round was again south of the target and Frank called in a correction. The next round was on target or close enough. The 105mm gunners were on their game.

Frank raised up to assess the damage and dropped back to the ground quickly. A platoon of NVA were moving up his hill in a long line.

"India One this is Lima Niner. I've got a platoon moving right at my position. I'd like some covering fire while I get the hell out of here."

"Roger, Niner. Give me coordinates.

He quickly looked at his map. Christ, he hoped none of the rounds would be short. He read off the coordinates for the middle of the slope.

"Roger, Lima Niner. Stand by."

"Stand by, hell," he said into the mouthpiece. "Lima Niner is moving. Out!"

Frank shut the radio down, gathered his poncho and maps, and started running on a northwest oblique to get away from the NVA and artillery. He wanted to put the crest between him and the artillery. The 105s hit as he started down the opposite side of the hill. The grass and vines slowed him down, but caution didn't. After the shock of the first round made him trip and fall headlong in the grass, he gathered up his equipment and moved faster. Two more rounds hit, but the crest of the hill blocked most of the shock from the explosions. When he had covered another three hundred yards, he slowed down and started moving more cautiously.

How the hell did they find him? Not hard to

figure out. Three accurate hits, two after corrections. Their own artillery people had to know an observer was in position to call in the shots. They probably hadn't been sure he was on the hill, but they would have picked the best place for observation in the area. Hell, he did and he wasn't artillery trained. Three more rounds fell on the other side of the hill as he worked his way to the small valley on the north side.

He stopped long enough to let India One know he was off the hill and moving into the jungle. The Artillery strikes moved away from the hill and then stopped altogether in the area of Lang Vei village. 105s were still coming over, but it sounded like they were hitting in the SF camp area south of the Village.

Later, Frank found a good hide and turned the radio on. He heard his call sign as soon as he put the handset to his ear.

"Lima Niner, Lima Niner, this is India One, over.

"India One this is Niner, over.

"Niner, what is your position? over."

"I'm east of the village, over."

"Lima Niner, can you get to an LZ, over."

"One this is Niner. I've got jungle and no way to clear an LZ."

"Roger Niner. Two Six directs you to seek a safe LZ and report in."

"Lima Niner. Roger, out."

Frank looked around and put his hand on the hilt of his K-Bar. Time to hunt.

Chapter 36

"Have we heard from Gunny Evans?" Colonel Harth asked as he reached for the morning report from Major Stride.

"Nothing yet, sir. He's probably lying low waiting for a chance to move and find an LZ."

"It's been light for six hours now, Charlie. We should have heard from him."

"He knows what he's doing, Colonel. I expect we'll be hearing from him shortly."

"Let me know."

"Yes, sir."

As the Colonel and Major Stride were talking, Frank was dragging one leg cautiously and painfully toward Lang Vei Village. He was bleeding from his left thigh and was bare chested having cut up his utility blouse for bandages and a tourniquet. During the night he had slipped in close to an NVA squad outside of the Village and screwed up big time. He made his kill without trouble and avoided the NVA as he slipped away from the NVA position looking for another target. He kept his eye on the NVA and maneuvered carefully to avoid being caught or seen by the enemy. What he forgot is—friendly fire isn't.

A 60mm mortar from Laotian troops guarding refugees in the village proved that no matter how random something is, and no matter what the odds are against it, if it happens to you, it happens to you. He was being careful. He knew he couldn't be seen by the NVA or the village. But a random round hit twenty feet from him as he crept through tall elephant grass. The tall grass absorbed most of the blast, but a piece of shrapnel caught him high on the thigh. It was a hard hit.

After he was wounded, he knew he wouldn't be able to avoid capture if he was spotted, so he ditched his radio, code sheets, and maps in a small mortar crater. Taking time to cover them with dirt hadn't helped his condition. He knew something was seriously wrong with his leg and he figured the village was his only chance, but he had to get there through the remnants of NVA left from the previous night's battles.

He watched as refugees entered the village in small groups and waited for the right time. Given his condition, he could be forgiven for his next blunder. But forgiveness wouldn't help. He hobbled right into the middle of a very quiet squad of NVA. He saw the movement of the soldier rising up in the grass but he didn't have time to do anything about it. A rifle butt hit him in the back of the head and he dropped to the ground unconscious.

"Charlie, have India CP try to reach him," Colonel Harth said "They relayed for him when he called in artillery."

"They have been, sir. We had a helicopter in the area try also. Nothing. He's either in trouble and lying low, or. . ."

"Yeah, or. Keep trying. I've got to see the boss. Refugees from the Lang Vei area are piling up at the southeast gate. Christ, what a mess. If we let them in, we'll probably be letting in a load of VC hideouts with them. If we don't let them in, the NVA can use them as a human shield to storm the gate. Give Captain Franks a call and let him know his Gunny is missing."

"Yes, sir. Colonel, he did this the first time out. Remember? Captain Franks even listed him as MIA."

"Well, it's something to hold onto I guess, but this is a very different situation. There may have been a regiment in the area. It happens, Charlie. I haven't got time to worry about one Gunny Sergeant. Keep trying."

Frank came to while he was being dragged along a trail. His hands were bound behind him and someone had him by each arm. He let his head hang limply and tried to figure out his situation. He was obviously a prisoner.

His leg and head hurt like hell. And he was being taken somewhere away from a battle. He could hear artillery in the distance behind him.

The people who had him were moving fast and being very quiet. They weren't concerned about their prisoner's comfort. The pain was almost overwhelming as his boots bounced on the ground behind him. His head cleared a little and a thought came into his mind. *Prisoner of war*. He remembered moving toward the village. Then. . .Then nothing. He must have fought. The back of his head felt like it was going to explode. Then a soft sickly feeling came again and he didn't know anything.

He came to again and he was lying on the ground. He opened his eyes and shut them again quickly. He heard someone speaking excitedly in sing-song. Must be Vietnamese. Then someone kicked him in his wounded leg and kept on kicking. After the first searing pain, the soft, sickly feeling came again.

He was wet and cold. Throbs of pain shot up his leg and into his groin with each heartbeat. His head kept time with his leg. No one was holding him. He was on the ground. Sing-song whispering around him. Excited fear. He didn't want to open his eyes. They might kick him again. Very weak.

Frank chanced opening one eye just a crack. It was dark. He couldn't see. Tensing for the kicks that were sure to come, he opened his eye all the way and moved his head to find the Vietnamese. Six of them crouched on the trail ahead of him. They were whispering and pointing ahead at the trail. They reached an agreement and started to turn back toward him. He closed his eye.

Fingers touched his throat over his juggler. More sing-song. Two men picked him up by the arms again and started dragging him up the trail. They were little, but they were tough little sons of bitches. They moved slowly, not talking. He resigned himself to being a prisoner of war. Maybe they would get him medical treatment.

As he finished that thought the world around him exploded with light and noise. The men holding him dropped him face down on the trail. The pain when he hit the ground was so intense he passed out again.

He woke up on his back. More sing-song talking. But different this time. Someone was very close to him. Screw it, he thought, and opened his eyes wide. A small Vietnamese jumped back and started jabbering to others. Frank moved his head and looked around. He counted eight. They looked Vietnamese but they had camo boonie hats on and camo utilities. Three of them approached him slowly and one poked frank's chest with his rifle butt.

"Stop that," he wheezed out.

The soldiers gathered around him and squatted down.

"American?" the soldier said.

"Yes. Help me."

The soldiers jabbered some more and one pointed at Frank.

"Russian," he said.

"American," Frank said.

"You Russian with Vietnamese soldier."

Well, he was sure they weren't more of his captors. Who the hell were they? Whoever they were they didn't listen very well and his leg was killing him. Literally. He started getting mad.

"I am a fucking American you gook son of a bitch. Now help me sit up, god damn it."

The soldier smiled a big shit eating grin. He nodded sharply, looked at his friends, and said, "American."

One soldier lifted Frank to a sitting position and cut the ropes binding his arms and hands. Then he put his canteen to Frank's mouth.

"Drink," he said. "Talk later."

He let a little water dribble into his mouth. It felt so good he grabbed the canteen and tilted it up. That was a mistake. As soon as the water hit his stomach it came back up and set off a series of cramps that doubled him over. The soldiers laughed.

"Yes, American," a soldier said pointing at Frank and laughing with his friends."

He got his gut under control and looked around. Six dead Vietnamese, his captors, were close by.

"Who are you?" he said.

"You know Green Hats?" the soldier asked.

Frank was at a loss for a moment but then remembered the green berets the special forces wore.

"You mean special forces, American?" he asked.

The soldier shook his head yes with a big smile.

"Yes," he said. "You know Cee eye dee gee?"

He thought about it. Cee eye dee gee. CIDG. Civilian Irregular Defense Group. They were Bru from the SF camp.

"Bru," he said. "Bru number one."

They all smiled. The leader said, "Bru numba fucking one John Wayne."

"Can you get me back to Lang Vei?"

"Lang Vei numba ten, Honcho. Gooks kill Lang Vei."

If I had any doubt before, he thought. I know they've been with Americans now. Gooks calling gooks, gooks."

"Do you have a radio?" he asked.

"Radio numba ten, Honcho."

Number one was anything good. Number ten was anything bad or broken.

"I've got to get back to Khe Sanh. Can you help me?"

"Khe Sanh numba one. Honcho get us in?"

"Get me there and I'll get you in."

"Numba one, Honcho."

While the Bru were carrying him through the jungle on a stretcher made from bamboo, he wasn't aware of the drama that had been taking place at the southeast gate of the combat base during the day. Hundreds of refugees had congregated outside the gate during the day. Some were Royal Laotian troops with their families who had come across the border after NVA tanks had overrun their camp. They had sought refuge at Lang Vei village. Others were Bru CIDG who managed to escape the slaughter at the SF camp south of Lang Vei Village. Still others were simple Bru tribesman from the countryside surrounding Lang Vei.

The combat base didn't have the resources to care for them—the Marines were already on short rations—and on top of that the base was under bombardment and expecting a ground attack. The base commander refused to let the refugees in. To make matters worse, the Marines fearing NVA and VC infiltrators and not being familiar with the Bru or the CIDG, disarmed the Bru before they turned them away. A few Bru CIDG managed to get to FOB3 and told their story. The SF wanted to turn their guns on the Marines.

By the time the eight Bru CIDG transporting Frank reached Khe Sanh, he was barely coherent. One of the Bru had some medic training and stopped the bleeding on frank's thigh, but he had already lost a lot of blood before the Bru found him and the NVA hadn't cared if he bled to death or not.

Fog had set in and the approach was extremely dangerous. He had the Bru stop and put him down a half mile from the base. The night was almost pitch black and the thick fog made it impossible to see anything more than a few feet away. Some flashes lit the night when an incoming struck, but there was no way to approach the base safely in the dark. The Marines on the perimeter would open-up before he could identify himself. He told the Bru to find a hole for them to get in and wait out the night and fog. At the bottom of the hole and by the dim light of a Bru cigarette, he checked the time. 0410. Two more hours until light. He hoped he could make it.

Five minutes later he was glad he had decided to wait. Fighting broke out at the southwest side of the base. It was at least a mile away, but the artillery barrage lit up the fog. The battle went on for an hour and then subsided. He could hear grenades going off, but the big stuff and most of the small arms had stopped. Then just after light the battle started again. If he had approached the wire while the whole base was on full alert, as they most certainly were after the battle in the southwest started, the Marines would have poured fire into anything that moved no questions asked. It was still going to be dangerous in the light with nervous Marines locked and loaded and fingers on triggers. Frank waited some more. His leg was hot and swollen. Even the slightest move shot agony through his groin. He couldn't wait much longer.

At 0700 he had the Bru move him closer. They found an artillery crater. He had them wait some more. Finally, at 0800 with full light and the fog thinning he had them move him to within hailing distance. He waited for the fog to thin some more, but it had to be soon. He was having trouble staying conscious.

At 0830 he hailed the gate.

"Marines at the base, I'm an American," he yelled as loud as he could, but it came out as a croak. Loud but a croak.

"Give me some water," he said to one of the Bru.

He took three large gulps and grimaced. Their water tasted like crap. He tried again.

"Marines. I'm an American. I'm coming in with eight Brus."

It was loud and clear that time, but he didn't have much left.

"Identify yourself," came the reply

"Gunny Sergeant Evans, Lima Company." Frank yelled as loud as he could.

"Wait one, Gunny" a Marine yelled back.

A few minutes later a new voice called back.

"Gunny Evans, tell the Bru to stay there and you approach the gate unarmed." It sounded like Major Stride.

"Can't," Frank said, weaker this time. "I'm wounded. Can't walk."

Silence for a moment.

"Gunny, have two Bru help you, but the rest have to stay there."

The Bru started mumbling to each other. Frank had had enough. He was weak, sick and hurting more than he ever thought possible. And now he was pissed. He had one good yell left in him.

"Fuck you, Stride. They come with me or I stay here."

Silence from the gate. Then,

"Bring your Bru in, Frank. Tell them to leave their weapons there. We can recover them later."

The Bru smiled and put their rifles down. Two put Frank on the stretcher, then all eight found a place on the stretcher, four to a side. They trotted to the gate and set Frank down in the nearest bunker. A Marine leveled his M-14 at the Bru and started pushing them away from Frank.

"If you point your weapon at my Bru again," he said, "I'll take it away from you and kick your ass. At ease, Marine!"

The grunt looked sheepish and lowered his weapon. The threat was obviously empty, but the Marine heard Stride call him Gunny, and Gunny meant something in the Corps. Frank looked at Stride.

"My Bru stay with me until I can take care of them."

"I'll take care of it," Major Stride said. "Christ, Gunny, what the hell happened?"

"Can I get a corpsman, sir?"

"Take him to the COC," Stride ordered. Two Marines started to move to Frank's stretcher but the Bru beat them to it. Eight Brus lifted him and looked at Stride.

"Oh hell," Stride said. "Follow me."

He woke up in the COC with a corpsman working on his

leg. His head was already bandaged and an IV was stuck in a vein in the crook of his arm. A bag of blood expander was at the other end of the tube. A second bag was connected to his other arm with clear stuff dripping in the tube

"Where are my Bru?" he asked.

"They're in a bunker next to the COC eating C-rats," Colonel Harth said.

"Thank you, sir. I've got to take care of them. They carried me all the way from Lang Vei."

"Do you have any ideas what to do with them?"

"Can you get me a radio?"

"Major?"

"Yes, sir. Corporal King. Do you have enough antenna cord on the 25 to reach here?"

"Yes, sir. It should."

King brought Frank the PRC-25 hooked up to an external antenna. Frank set the frequency and made his call.

"Foxtrot this is Mike, over."

"Mike, Foxtrot. Authenticate Lima Hotel."

"Foxtrot, Mike. Authentication table is destroyed. I am in the Khe Sanh COC. I have eight Bru CIDG with me. Can you take care of my Bru? Over.

"Wait one."

A new voice come on the radio.

"Mike this is Foxtrot. What unit are your Bru attached to? Over."

"This is Mike. Lang Vei CIDG, over."

"This is Foxtrot. I hear you got lost."

"Your Bru found me, over."

"Mike this is Foxtrot. Roger. Tell your commander to expect company."

"This is Mike. Roger out."

The Radioman took the radio and Harth said,

"Who the hell was that?"

"SF at FOB-3, sir. I think they're coming to get the Bru."

"How in the hell did you. . ."

"Colonel, excuse me," the corpsman said. "I'm giving him morphine. He has to medevac on the next slick out."

Chapter 37

Frank woke up to a familiar sight. The landing pad at Danang medical facility was blurry through his morphine induced calm. He felt the bump as they lifted him out of the slick and even the morphine couldn't stop the pain that shot up through his hip. He closed his eyes.

Later he woke up again as they were taking him up the ramp of a C-130. The shaking and vibrations kept him half awake all the way to Saigon. The next time he woke up, the surroundings were familiar. The room was all white and the nurse was in utilities. She had green eyes. The pain hadn't started yet, but he knew that was only temporary. His leg was heavy and hard and hanging in a sling. The cast enclosed his hip. He had a bandage on his head again.

"How are you feeling, Sergeant Evans?"

He guessed they had to ask that. People talked too damn much.

"I'm good," he said.

"Any pain in the leg?"

"No, Ma'am. It'll start later."

"I don't have to tell you, do I? You've done this before."

"Yeah. Where am I?"

"You're in Saigon. You almost lost your leg."

"Didn't seem that bad." he said

"May not have been if you had received treatment right away. I think you beat gangrene by just a few hours. And I'm afraid you have a serious fracture. It was only a hair line fracture to start with, but the punishment you gave it pushed it across most of your femur at the top. We had to put pins in. Want to tell me about it?"

Frank was getting irritated. He rested his head against the pillow and looked at the ceiling. His Marines were getting pounded at Khe Sanh.

The Nurse smiled.

"Well, tell me about it sometime. You'll be here for a while."

He spent his days trying to keep Lang Vei out of his mind. By all rights he should be in a North Vietnamese prison camp sitting out the war. Probably not sitting. He'd heard stories about how the NVA treated Marines. Couldn't blame them much though. When he pushed

Lang Vei out of his mind, Khe Sanh took its place. And when he pushed Khe Sanh out of his mind, the hunt took its place. And Con Thien was always waiting if he got bored with the others. Quantico and clean uniforms seemed so far away. And so long ago.

He squeezed his eyes shut. It had been exciting at first. Scared, yeah, but an adventure too. And a freedom unlike any he had ever felt before. Nothing to hold you back. Frank had found something dark inside he didn't want to think about. The stalk with fear growing so strong you almost turned back, stomach churning, a sour metallic taste in your mouth, every time, it never got easier, fearing your next sound, your next mistake, knowing it would happen eventually, had to, but maybe not that time, and you couldn't resist it, and then all your terror, hate, and rage focused into one gamble, one fast, silent, deadly move in the dark. . .

Frank opened his eyes. He knew he would go back. He needed a next time.

Two weeks into his recovery, he woke up from his nap to find a Special Forces Captain in Camo utilities and green beanie sitting in the chair next to his bed. A civilian stood behind him.

"Sergeant, how are you feeling?"

It's Gunnery Sergeant, Captain, he thought. But he forgave him. He was Army.

"I'm good. I'm Marine Corps, sir. Did you get the right room?"

"I know who you are, Mike. Some folks at FOB-3

asked me to check on you and let you know your Bru were taken care of."

Frank's Lang Vei radio call sign, Mike, got his attention. He nodded and gave the Captain a thumbs up. "Thanks. I owed them." he said.

"A man you knew as Foxtrot said you did a good job taking care of them."

"They rated it."

"It's a shame more Marines at Khe Sanh didn't feel that way. Not a whole lot of love left for the Marine Corps after Lang Vei."

Frank wondered what that was all about. And he wondered why he should give a shit.

"Shit happens," he said.

The Captain watched Frank's face for a moment and leaned back in the chair. He looked over his shoulder at the civilian.

"He doesn't know."

"I know they got hit hard," Frank said. "I called in artillery around the village. Couldn't get close to the SF camp."

"And you were wounded and captured during the fight. You couldn't know. Lang Vei was wiped out, Sergeant. A fucking slaughter. And no Marine reinforcements to stop it. Let your command tell you about it. Can we get anything for you?"

"I'm good. I didn't get your name, sir."

"Just think of me as another Foxtrot. Can I ask you a question?"

"Sure."

"What happened to your radio and code sheets?"

"Buried. I had to ditch them. It's all I could handle at the time."

"Would have been better if you burned the sheets."

"Not for me," Frank said.

"Well, not important now. They were only good for three days anyway. But it's good to know the NVA didn't get them. What frequency did you leave on the radio?"

"Hard to tell," he said. "I always spin the wheels when I move. Whatever it was, it won't help anyone."

"Smart procedure. Are they sending you back to the siege when you're released?"

"Siege, sir?"

"It's getting crazy up there, Sergeant. The NVA are digging trenches toward the base every night. Just like a medieval siege. Can't seem to stop the damn things either. B52s overhead dropping the latest munitions and the NVA are laying siege to the base just like the British did in the Napoleonic wars. Crazy shit. Well, if you're good, I've things to do. You did a good job up there, Sergeant Evans. I'd be glad to work with you again. I'm afraid I can't say the same for the Corps in general. Take care of yourself."

"Yeah." Frank said. "You too."

Later, Frank realized the civilian standing behind the Captain hadn't said a word. He hadn't been disagreeable, just quiet. Civil In Attitude, Frank thought with a grin.

That afternoon he had another visitor, this time a welcome one.

"Christ," Ski said as he came through the door, "You ought to have figured it out by now. When they're shooting at you, you're supposed to get behind something."

"Yeah, well, sometimes they don't let you know. How's it going, Ski?"

"Better'n you. Captain Sharp got a call from the General. Said you screwed up again and to check on you. What happened this time?"

"Shrapnel. A totally random shot. I wasn't even near the action."

It was easy to talk with Ski again. He'd been there too. They'd been there together. But it was different now. Frank had to work at being interested.

"Where are you and Sharp at?" he asked.

"We're south of Danang in Chu Lai. Me and Sharp have the Heat and Steam for Three-Seven. Good duty. Nice and quiet. I hear you guys were getting your asses pounded."

"Yeah. It's a meat grinder. How'd you guys do during Tet?"

"We took some shit," Ski said. "A lot of rockets. They hit the ammo dump with one."

"Lot of that going around," Frank said. "Do you figure the VC shot their wad on this one?"

"They lost a lot. But Marines are still trying to

clear Hue city. Another meat grinder."

"Yeah. Do you need a convalescing Gunny up there?"

"Shit, Frank. They'll probably ship you back to the states. What's this, your seventh purple heart?"

"Eighth," Frank said. "The nurse said I got one for the laceration on the back of my head too. It was caused by enemy action. If I had a nice quiet place to heal I could probably talk them into letting me stay. Think Sharp will help me out?"

"Frank, what the hell is the matter with you? Take the ticket home."

"The Corps is my home. Come on Ski, can you help me out? Six, maybe eight weeks, and I'll be good to go. I've only been here a couple of months. I'm not ready to go back to the world yet."

"Why, Frank? Go home. Get drunk. This war isn't going to end anytime soon. Have you heard from Carol lately?"

"I'm not done yet, Ski!" he shouted. "Help me out, damn it."

Garzinski sat back and watched Frank for a few moments. Ski's eyebrows slowly dipped in the middle and the skin on his forehead creased. He cocked his head to the side.

"Are you okay, buddy?" he asked.

"Hell, yes, I'm okay. Stop looking at me like that. What the hell would I do back there? Clean weapons in some armory all day? Bullshit a bunch of boots? Go to the NCO club every night and tell war stories with the other NCOs, wishing I was back here? Bullshit! There's a lot I can do right here."

Garzinski didn't say anything for a few moments. Then,

"You're sure?"

"Yeah. Get me a slot. I just need to heal for a while. I'm good to go."

"Okay. I'll talk to Sharp. I don't know what we'll do with a gimp Gunny, but I'll see what I can do. Talk to your Docs and see if they'll even consider it."

"Thanks. Before you leave Saigon, do think you can sneak me a couple beers in here?"

Chapter 38

By the end of the third week of his recovery, he was getting desperate. He hadn't heard anything from Ski or Sharp and the Docs weren't being cooperative. They needed his bed and the easiest way to get it was to put him on a medevac flight back to the states. Lying in bed gave him too much time to think—and to remember things he had been pushing out of his mind. Forgetting was easy when you went back out every day, when you were in the grass and facing the next thing you would have to forget tomorrow. Yesterday didn't exist. What you did yesterday didn't happen. You can hide it all in that place behind you that doesn't exist.

Now with clean white sheets, people trying to be nice, pain, and too much time, duty and survival were far away and the memories came back and it was harder to rationalize. Dirt was dirt and blood was blood and people were people and he was what he was with nothing to soften it or make it right.

Frank had learned a lot about what was inside of him, and the knowledge didn't leave him any illusions. Every man has a dark, violent spirit inside of him. It's better when you don't know about it, when it hasn't laughed its awful joy and twisted your lips into a snarl. It's better when you don't know how much you want to let it lose. But it's there waiting for the circumstances that will bring you to the place it inhabits. It's a place you can visit, but not a place you can stay, hopefully. Staying is insanity.

The thought of going back to the world scared him. Here he knew what he was and it was at least acceptable. Back there? What would he be back there? Too damn much time to think.

Later that day a young and pretty Vietnamese woman pushed all of the carts and chairs to one side of Frank's room and an old Vietnamese mama-san mopped the floor. They never said a word or even looked at him. He watched them work and wondered what their lives were like. What did they think about the war? And he realized he didn't know anything about the people the war was supposed to be about. He knew what the Corps told him, what the newspapers said, but he didn't know any Vietnamese. He was killing them and didn't know anything about them.

American troops weren't encouraged to get to

know their allies. Unless you were Special Forces or a CAP adviser embedded with the Vietnamese, contact with the Vietnamese people was discouraged, often forbidden. You arrived in-country, reported to your unit, and then you went to war.

Maybe it was easier that way. There wasn't much difference between north and south Vietnamese and no difference at all between Viet Cong and south Vietnamese except political differences. Harder to kill them if you know them as mama-sans and papa-sans with children and neighbors and a home and dreams. That thought didn't bring him any comfort.

They removed the cast to inspect his wound and get some X-rays on Saturday of the third week. The Docs were pleased with the progress but they wouldn't even consider a convalescence in-country. On Sunday morning the orthopedic surgeon pulled up a chair to discuss Frank's leg.

"Sergeant Evans, we need to talk. The nurse tells me you are bugging the hell out of them to let you stay in-country."

Apparently, to the Air Force Doctors and nurses, all sergeants were addressed as Sergeant. E5 to E9 they were all sergeants. He had gotten used to it.

"Yes, sir. Why can't I just get light duty somewhere till I heal and then send me back to my company? The wound is healing. What's a broken leg take to heal, six weeks?"

"I'm afraid it's a little more than just a broken

leg. Sergeant, I think you need to get prepared for some things. And I guess now is a good time to start."

"Like what?"

"First, your fracture is going to take a long time to heal. It started as a hair-line fracture, but whatever happened to you stressed it until it became a major fracture. The crack worked its way right across the bone. Even that wouldn't have been a problem if it had been further down the femur. As it is, the fracture is just below the joint, a very difficult place to get bone to mend. Are you understanding what I'm telling you?"

"Yes, sir. I think so. So I have a fracture high up on my thigh bone and it will take longer to heal. How long?"

The doctor watched him for a moment and then he put his hand on Frank's arm. "It could take months. If it were to be stressed during that time, well, you could end up worse than you were when you came in here. I installed five pins, large screws, if you will, to stabilize the break, but they can fail. You have to be very careful and you have to be checked regularly. Sergeant, I just have to tell you straight up. You may be medically discharged from the Marine Corps."

"Discharged?" he said and blinked.

"That will be up to the evaluation board at Walter Reed. They have a world class orthopedic unit there. I have requested a bed for you."

"Jesus, Doc. I'm a gunnery sergeant."

"And a damn good one from what I've been told. I spoke with a General Muldavy. He wanted a report on your condition. Sergeant Evans, I know it's a hard thing for you to accept, but you have to be prepared. The break is so high on the femur, we may not be able to fix it if the mend fails. Regular daily Marine Corps routine could cost you your leg."

He stared at the doctor for a few moments.

"Christ, Doc. It's all I know."

"You're young and from everything I've heard, you're smart. You will be successful at whatever you try. Try to see it that way."

"You're talking like it's already been decided."

"No. But I'm good at what I do too. And I won't try to give you false hope. You deserve more respect than that."

Frank looked away and tried to comprehend what he was being told. A discharge. How the hell had it come to this without even knowing about it? Christ, what was he going do if they kicked him out?

"When will I be shipped back to the states?" he asked quietly.

"I think we'll keep you another week to make sure the pins are doing their job. As soon as I have confirmation on your bed at Walter Reed, we'll book you home."

He received two letters the next day. H&S in Khe Sanh had forwarded them. Carol hadn't heard from him for a few days and the news on TV was making a big deal out of what was going on at Khe Sanh. News stories with film from all over Vietnam told the story of the Tet offensive. She was worried. In the second letter she had received his short letter written just before he left for Lang Vei. She felt better but told him she was waiting for the bigger letter he promised. That was three weeks ago. He hadn't written since. Had Ski told Sharon about his wound? Has she said anything to Carol? Shit! I've got enough on my mind. I can't think about this right now.

Frank spent the next five days in a deep depression. He didn't want to talk to anyone and he didn't want sympathy. A nice young Navy Chaplain left his room in a huff. Frank probably shouldn't have used that language with a man of the cloth. But hearing that God worked in mysterious ways was just too much cop-out bullshit for him to take right then. Which God? The one in the grass taking care of me or the one in the grass taking care of the NVA whose throats I slit? They aren't all godless communists. Lots of Catholics in Vietnam. If I slit a Catholic gook's throat, did he just forget to pray? Or was God out to lunch right then? Maybe God just likes jarheads. Didn't seem that way in the trenches. The SF at Lang Vei must not have been as good at praying as the gook commander was at preying. Maybe there aren't any atheists in foxholes, but there sure are a bunch of agnostics. God seemed just a little bit fickle when choosing which prayers to answer. The only answer the Chaplain had was, "God works in mysterious ways." Frank could agree with the mysterious part.

He thought about Carol everyday but couldn't bring himself to write. What would he say? Tell her about his adventures in the grass? Tell her how to open a throat without noise? Tell her about how he couldn't get the smell of blood out of his nose or his mind? How it got worse instead of better? How he no longer liked what he was? How they were going to take away the only thing that made it all acceptable? Her letters remained unanswered.

The day before he was to ship out, Ski visited again.

"Hey, buddy. I heard the news."

"All of it?" Frank said.

"As far as I know. They won't let you stay here. Sharp said to come see you. Anything you need?"

"They're kicking me out, Ski."

Ski stopped half way across the floor and stared.

"You're shitting me. For what? A leg wound?"

"It's the bone. It could break again and they might not be able to fix it if it does."

"Jesus, Frank. A discharge?"

"The doctor thinks so," he said. "They'll decide at Bethesda."

"Oh man. That bullshit." Ski looked at the floor and was silent for a moment. "What are you going to do?" he asked.

Frank shook his head back and forth slowly.

"I don't know yet. Hell, maybe they'll find a way to keep me in."

"Yeah. They know a lot of shit in Bethesda. But what if they don't?"

"I guess I'll have to find a job. Got to be something out there for a gimp ex-gunny."

Ski didn't say anything for a few moments. They both looked away avoiding eye contact.

"Have you heard from your girl lately?" Ski asked.

"Got a couple of letters a few days ago. Did you tell Sharon about me getting wounded?"

"Yeah. Of course. I told her you're okay though."

The pauses were getting uncomfortable.

"She probably told Carol," Frank said. "They've been visiting."

"Yeah. She told me about seeing Carol," Ski said. "You'll be close in Bethesda. That's one good thing to come out of this. Have you written her about it?"

"No. I've tried, but I just don't know what to say."

"Hell, have the Red Cross send her a telegram to let her know you're okay."

"That might scare her more than not hearing anything."

They were quiet again for a few moments.

"Well, you should do something," Ski said. "I don't know if Sharon said anything or not."

"Yeah. I'll figure something out. I'm leaving in the morning. Look me up when you get back. I'll look in on Sharon and make sure she has everything she needs."

"Thanks. Let her know I'm in a good place. Chu

Lai is quiet. I doubt I'll even see any action this tour. But she worries. You know how it is."

The hospital put Frank on his medevac flight in the morning. He hadn't sent a telegram. He told himself he could take care of it when he got to the states. Memories of Carol haunted him. He wanted so bad to talk to her, to hear her voice, but he was afraid, afraid he would say the wrong thing, something that would reveal what he was feeling, what was in his mind. Too much time to think and remember and no distractions to take his mind off it.

The Corps held him at the hospital at Camp Pendleton for a week for evaluation and then shipped him to Andrews AFB in Maryland for pickup by an ambulance from Walter Reed. He still hadn't written or called Carol. It was too easy to put it off for another day. Maybe put it off and forget it.

Chapter 39

When he got to Bethesda, knowing he was just a few miles from Virginia, from Carol, his days got worse and his nights impossible. The debate in his head wouldn't stop. The memories wouldn't be suppressed. If he called, she could be there in an hour. The ache for someone to talk to grew inside of him, the ache for Carol made his hands shake. But he couldn't talk to anyone about what he needed to talk about the most. And he couldn't bring himself to call Carol.

His doctors suspected he was suffering from trauma his leg wound didn't account for. His nurses, being with him and trying to talk to him every day and night, knew what the doctors didn't. His case nurse talked with the clinical psychologist. The next day he had a visitor.

"Sergeant Evans, I'm Claude Masters. May we talk for a bit?"

He wasn't in uniform. Frank wondered what and who he was.

"Are you a doctor?" Frank asked.

"I'm a clinical psychologist. I'm not in the military, but I work with military men like yourself. Your nurse is concerned about you. May I call you Frank?"

"Sure. May I call you Claude?"

"Seems fair," Masters said. "Is something going on you want to talk about?"

"Like what, Claude?" Frank said.

Masters grinned. "Let's not overdo it, Frank. I'm on your side. When a man gets back to the states and away from what you've been through, well, he is usually happy to be home and just a little more communicative than you've been. May we talk about that?"

"Do you think I'm a wack-job, Claude?"

"The clinical term I prefer is pyscho-nut. Baby killer and hired assassin have gained some popularity lately, but if you like it, we can use wack-job. Is there any reason for me to consider you a wack-job?"

Frank grinned. This might be more fun than he expected.

"How about, your worst fucking nightmare?" Frank asked.

"We can use that as a working premise—if you really feel that way."

"Na," Frank said, "psycho-nut will do for now.

They're kicking me out, Claude."

"That hasn't been decided yet. But I'll be honest. That's probably the most likely result of your wound. You're a Gunnery Sergeant. And a young one too. A decorated hero. I guess that's a hard pill to swallow."

"You could say that," Frank said with a little less hostility.

"I know it may not seem like it right now, but starting a new career at your age can be an exciting thing. . ."

The talk got easier. Masters was easy to talk to. He didn't offer any judgments, just alternatives for Frank to think about. He didn't try to tell Frank anything. He just asked questions and seemed very interested in the answers, much like Frank had been in the past with others. Frank began to relax and felt some relief having someone to talk to. He decided to take a chance.

"Claude, it's more than just losing my career. Look, if I'm a Marine, what I did over there was just doing my job. Doing what I was trained to do. But if I'm not a Marine, what does that make me? What I did, what does that make me?"

"That was then. This is now. Why should a discharge change anything? It seems to me that Frank Evans has been a lot of things. There was the Frank Evans in college. Then there was the Frank Evans in the Navy. Then Frank Evan the Gunny Sergeant in Vietnam. He seemed to do pretty good with all those changes. He used each experience to build on. Now there is going to be Frank Evans the civilian. Is there something about Vietnam that makes you think Frank Evans the civilian is a special case?"

He was quiet for a few moments. Yeah, he thought. I liked it too much. But he wasn't ready to talk about things with a civilian he hadn't even shared with Marines.

"Maybe we can talk some more later," he said quietly.

"We can do that. Tomorrow?"

"Yeah. Okay."

"Frank, can I ask you one more question?"

"Okay."

"Have you talked to any of your family? It can help."

"Just a sister. It wouldn't help. She's married to a hippie."

"Girlfriend?"

"I . . . She doesn't know I'm here."

"Do you want to call her?"

"When I'm ready."

"All right. Let's talk tomorrow."

"Sure."

Masters walked to the door and opened it. Frank felt the fear rising inside of him.

"Claude."

Masters stopped and turned. "Yes?"

"If you're around. . .you know. . .later. . .I haven't got anything to do this evening."

"All right. If I'm around I might stop and say hello."

"Thanks."

Masters did stop back and talk with him that evening. And then he spent an hour with him every day for the next week. The nurses began sitting with Frank for a few minutes, sometimes a half hour during the day, and got him talking whenever they found him awake at night. The talks helped, but just having normal life around him without mud, explosions, and death helped more. The dark place lessened its hold on him and he began to respond to normal routine and life without violence. Over the next few days he began to believe he could accept his memories and begin to deal with the reality of what was inside of him.

Masters convinced Frank to begin counseling and helped him face his need to see Carol. The changes took place subtly, but they happened quickly once he accepted he wasn't a monster or even very different from other combat troops.

Frank put it off and suffered, but finally, in his bed in Bethesda, he couldn't put it off any longer. She was just around the beltway. He waited until 9 P.M. and called her apartment through the switchboard.

No one answered. That disappointment sank him into a deep depression.

He tried again the next night with the same result. He had screwed up. He waited too long. She may have moved and since he hadn't even written she had no way to let him know. Or she met someone and was out—or too busy at home to answer the phone. He was losing everything. The nurse had to give him sleeping pills. Now that he was ready, he couldn't reach her. He waited too long. The nurse sat and talked with him until he couldn't keep his eyes open.

The following day four doctors examined him and took x-rays. They told him he was doing well and they would have him up sitting in his chair the next day. They also told him he had a tape worm and they would have to give him some nasty medicine that would make him sick to his stomach. But that wasn't all the bad news. He also had a fungus in his scalp they couldn't kill off and they would have to shave his head. And the final news. A board of specialists were to meet the next day to consider his case. When the doctors left, he wondered if he should try calling Carol again. It was then he remembered he had Carol's work number in his wallet. He dug it out and placed the call.

"Directory Assistance. This is Miss Taylor; may I help you?"

"Miss Taylor, I'm trying to reach Carol Lucas."

"Miss Lucas isn't here at this time. Is there anything I can do for you?"

"Do you know where I can reach her?"

"I'm sorry, sir. We can't give out that information. Is this personal or business?"

"It's personal. My name is Frank Evans. Can you

get her a message to contact me?"

"I can leave her a message. Is this urgent, Mr. Evans?"

"Well, I guess it isn't an emergency. I just got back from Vietnam and I'm. . ."

"Oh!" Miss Taylor said. "Mr. Evans. She's been crazy with worry. Where are you? I'll call her right now."

Frank squeezed the phone until his hand hurt. He had to squeeze his eyes shut to stop the tears.

"Mr. Evans, are you there?"

"Yes, sorry. I'm in the Bethesda Naval Hospital," he said. "Or maybe it's called Walter Reed Military Hospital. Anyway I'm in Bethesda, Maryland. She can reach me through the switchboard. Here's the number." He read the number and the room from the card on his side table. "Do you think she can call today?"

"Honey, you just keep everyone away from your phone. I've got a feeling she'll be calling just as soon as I reach her. She's in a three-day class in Richmond and today is her last day. Bye."

Frank waited and fretted. He twisted his hands and watched the phone. A nurse came in and told him she had to take him to down for x-rays.

"No. I can't." he said.

"And may I ask why?" she asked with just a bit of tiff in her voice.

"You don't understand. My girl is going to call any minute. I haven't talked to her since I got back. I can't leave the phone right now."

The nurse looked at her watch and tapped her foot on the floor. Then her look softened.

"You haven't even told her you're here?"

"No. She might not even know I was wounded."

"Well. . .I guess we can wait a few minutes."

She turned and walked out and the phone rang. He snatched it up.

"Carol?"

"Frank, where are you? Linda said something about Bethesda." He heard a little catch in her voice.

"I'm in the hospital in Bethesda. God, it's good to hear your voice."

"I've been so worried. Sharon told me you were wounded in Khe Sanh and they had you in a hospital in Vietnam. I was frantic. I couldn't find out anything. I was waiting for Sharon's husband to find out something for us. It's been weeks. Are you okay?"

Frank relaxed back onto his pillow. A sweet calm eased through him and he closed his eyes.

"Yeah. I am now. I got hit in my leg and it broke the bone. Can you come see me?"

"Try and keep me away. I'm in Richmond now. The class isn't over until four. When's visiting hours?"

"Any time after six. Will you come as soon as you can?"

"Screw it, I'm on my way. I'll be there as soon as they'll let me in."

He stared at the ceiling and smiled. His first in a long, long time. He tried to think back to Khe Sanh and his hunts in the grass. He had wanted to get back there so bad. The memories wouldn't come now. He knew they would come back later, but right then, memories of Carol filled his mind.

The next hours ticked by one minute at a time. One slow minute at a time. His nurse took him down for x-rays and then an orderly shaved his head. He couldn't dissuade them. He asked if someone could get him a hat. At least it helped to pass the time. They tried to give him his tape worm medicine but he absolutely refused. He could do it after Carol left. He was not going to be puking his guts out while she was there. The nurse relented, but told him he was going to have an awful night.

Finally, the door pushed open slowly and there she was. She stood still and looked at him for a moment. And then she smiled and ran across the floor and put her arms around him gently. They spent a lot of time holding, kissing, and holding some more. When the holding was enough, they talked.

"Why are you wearing a hat in bed?" she asked after another kiss.

"They shaved my head. It's embarrassing."

"For a Marine? You guys shave your heads all the time."

"Well, there's a little matter of fungus too."

"Oh. Let's not talk about that."

"Probably shouldn't mention the tape worm then."

"The what!"

"Forget I said it. The jungle over there is nasty."

"Tape worm? You have something living inside you?"

"Yeah. Sick, isn't it? They're going to give me medicine to get rid of it tonight."

"That's encouraging news. Wish you had told me that first. You're skinny. How'd that happen?"

"Rough time. I'll tell you about it sometime if you stick around."

"Oh, don't worry. I'll be around. I guess I'm stuck with another Marine. Crap, Frank, I don't want to be a camp follower again."

"How about if I promise to camp in Virginia?"

"You can't. For a while maybe, but then the Crotch will decide they need you somewhere else."

"Maybe. Carol, were you serious about my degree being able to get me in a good job. Like in management?"

She sat up on the side of the bed and looked at Frank with her eyebrows raised.

"Sure. We hire people into management with your kind of degree all the time. You could go into engineering or plant or, hell, just about anything. But you've still got three years left on your enlistment. Are you thinking about getting out?"

Her voice was just a little wishful.

"Yes. Do you know anyone I can talk to in the phone company? It seems like a good place to start a career."

"You're starting to make me happy. Are you

serious? I'd only have to be a camp follower for three years?"

"Yeah. I'm serious. Let's talk about it again tomorrow. Can you come see me tomorrow night too?"

"Of course. I don't want to leave. Think they could roll another bed in here?"

"Probably not. But I should be able to take some leave soon as I can walk on crutches. Got room for me?"

"If you haven't figured that out I've been wasting my time with all the camp follower talk. Of course I have room. How many beds do you think we need? Uh, that brings up a delicate point. Are you. . .you know. . .able?"

"Well, the wound is pretty high up, but not that high. Able and willing and about to go crazy with all of you sitting right there. God, I missed you."

"Now you're talking. Try this and tell me how it helps."

The kiss lasted for a long time and got quite involved. Finally, she released him and sat back with her eyes closed. "You haven't lost anything in that department," she said.

"I'm going to need a sleeping pill tonight," he said.

They were quiet for a while, just holding hands. Carol looked at his eyes and searched his face. She touched the scar on his head and ran her finger up it to his hair line. She started to say something a couple of times but stopped. Then she looked right in his eyes and took a breath.

"Frank, all this talk about getting out. . .I wasn't expecting it. . .is something going on I don't know about? You aren't in trouble, are you?"

"No. Nothing like that. In fact, I might be getting another medal. Bronze probably or maybe a commendation medal. Let's talk some more about it tomorrow. Could you get me a name to contact in your employment office?"

"Sure. I can do that. I can have them flag your application too when you're ready. But that's a long time away, isn't it?"

"We'll talk about it tomorrow. But go ahead and get me a name."

"Okay. . ." She cocked her head and pulled her eyebrows down in the middle. "Something's going on. How bad were you wounded? Let me see it."

"It was bad enough, but it's healing." Frank lifted the sheet and showed her his leg. "They took the cast off yesterday."

Carol looked where he was pointing and grinned. "Well, it's obvious you didn't hurt *that*. You better cover it back up. If the nurse comes in, she'll wonder what I've been doing to you. Try to make it not tent up like that."

He looked down and grinned. He knew what he was doing.

Chapter 40

The board took longer than he expected. He attended counseling with a group of Marine and Army enlisted. He discovered his fears, memories, and nightmares weren't unique. Probably the fact that he was only in the bad part of his tour for a couple months helped too. Some of the guys he met with had been in the crap for as much as eighteen months.

The board members made their decision but it had to be reviewed and approved by Marine Corps Headquarters. By the end of the week his doctors told him they could not certify him for duty and he would be given a medical discharge. He would be given thirty days' convalescent leave, a final examination, and discharged from Quantico. Carol was early on Friday evening, but the nurses knew her by then and knew of

Frank's news. They let her come up to his room early.

"Hi, sugar. Everybody is being so nice. I didn't have to wait downstairs till six."

"They just can't resist those beautiful eyes. Ready to talk?"

"Sure. Did you find out about your leave?"

"Yep. Two weeks from today, if everything goes okay, I'll be starting thirty days' convalescent leave. Can you take some vacation? You're going to need plenty of rest."

"Honey, I've got so much stored up inside me it'll take you a month just to empty out the excess. You're looking awfully cocky. What's up?"

"Well, I've got some news. I couldn't say anything until they made a decision. They might not have..."

"Frank! What? Stop fooling around."

"I'm being retired. When my leave is over they're going to put me on the TDRL for five years. I'll be a civilian."

"Oh god! I thought you were going to tell me they were transferring you again. Frank don't tease me. Are you serious? What's TDRL?"

"Serious as a broken leg. They won't certify my leg for duty. I'm out. Gone. The Marine Corps doesn't want me. TDRL is the Temporary Disability Retired List. If my leg doesn't improve after five years, and they don't think it will, they'll put me on the permanently disabled retired list."

Carol sat back and watched his face. She

frowned slightly.

"Is this what you want?" she said. "I think I hear a little bitterness there."

"Not about getting out. I'm kind of excited about starting a new career. But yeah, I'm a little pissed at the Corps. Use 'em up and spit 'em out. Did you get me a name to call at the phone company? Do you think I might have a chance?"

Carol smiled. "Sure. After I have it flagged, it's almost a sure thing. Not sure what they will offer you, but with a veteran's preference, a company management flag, a math degree, it's got to be something good. Frank, I still can't believe it. You're really getting out? I don't have to give up my job or transfer to some God forsaken little office down south? I don't have to be a camp follower?"

"Would you have done that for me?" Frank said. "That's pretty special."

"You're pretty special. Didn't you hear me before? I was ready to follow you around camp to camp like a proper little camp follower. And now you're telling me I won't have to?"

"That's the news," Frank said. "It's hard to believe a gorgeous woman like you would just pick up and follow me."

"Honey, I hope I am gorgeous for you, but let's be honest. I don't need an escort to keep my lust crazed fans away. I'm thankful that one handsome man finds me attractive."

"I haven't told you I love you, have I?" Frank

asked.

"Marines seem to have a problem with that."

"I love you," he said.

Carol watched his face for a moment and then took his hand.

"The ball's in my court, isn't it?" she asked with a smile.

"Yep."

"I guess I better make it official then. I love you too."

"Why don't you climb in here with me?"

"Why don't we hold off on that. We don't want any disciplinary actions holding up your leave. Oh, Frank. I'm so damn happy right now. Can't they let you go sooner?"

"Two more weeks and then I'm home. I've got to get my car out of storage at Quantico. I need a suit for job hunting. There's so much to do."

"We've got time. So get your rest now. You won't be getting much sleep when you get home."

The next day Frank began physical therapy. He continued with counseling and began reading the employment pamphlets Carol brought him from the phone company. The first week went by quickly. The following week, his last at the hospital, he filled out the employment application Carol brought him. She took it to the employment office for him. The military draft was still in place in 1968 and Frank found out he was a prime candidate because he already had his military obligation behind him. Good things were beginning to happen.

At the end of the next week he was released for leave. He and Carol didn't leave the apartment for three days. On the fourth day he retrieved his car and made an appointment for an interview at the phone company.

The company recruiter had a carved wooden name plate on his desk. It had captain's bars on one side and a globe and anchor on the other. His interviewer got out in 1963. After the two Marine Corps veterans traded stories about the Corps, the interview went very well. Everything was going so well, he was getting nervous.

Frank took some tests, interviewed with two engineering managers and a district manager and was given a tour of the engineering department. After the recruiter received evaluations from the managers he offered him a network engineering position with months of company schooling to follow. His starting salary was three times his Gunnery Sergeant pay. He was having a hard time adjusting to his good fortune. Vietnam didn't offer many happy endings and he was waiting for the other shoe to fall.

Frank was retired the following month and given a lump sum settlement, a thirty percent disability, and full VA benefits for healthcare. Frank and Carol were married that June when Frank completed the first of his company training courses at the Silver Spring, Maryland training center. He couldn't imagine life getting any better. Vietnam began to fade in his memory. Well, the memories softened, at least.

When they got back from their honeymoon a note was taped to their apartment door. It was from Sharon Garzinski. It said "Call me." he did.

"Hello." Her voice was flat and hoarse.
"Sharon, this is Frank. How are you?"
"Not good Frank. It's Ski. he's. . ."
"What, hon?"
"An officer and his lady were here. They. . ." Sharon broke down and cried.
"Can you tell me?" Frank said.
"It was a rocket, Frank. Ski was killed in action last week."

The other shoe fell. Vietnam didn't offer many happy endings.

End

ABOUT THE AUTHOR

Raymond Hunter Pyle is a two tour Vietnam veteran. He served both tours in I-Corps. Today he spends his time in Florida, enjoying life with his wife of 50 years, and writing tales of war and adventure.

Made in the USA
San Bernardino, CA
08 July 2019